Acclaim for Christina Courtenay's

Echoes of the Runes & *The Runes of Destiny*

'Seals Christina Courtenay's crown as the Queen of Viking Romance. This sweeping tale . . . will leave you wanting more'
Catherine Miller

'An absorbing story, fast-paced and vividly imagined, which really brought the Viking world to life'
Pamela Hartshorne

'A love story and an adventure, all rolled up inside a huge amount of intricately-detailed, well-researched history. Thoroughly enjoyable'
Kathleen McGurl

'Prepare to be swept along in this treasure of an adventure! With a smart, courageous heroine and hunky, honourable hero at the helm, what's not to like?'
Kate Ryder

'An amazing page-turner filled with superb historical detail, it had me gripped from the first page to the last – I absolutely loved it!'
Clare Marchant

'Every story Christina Courtenay spins is better than the last and every world she creates is more real'
Sue Moorcroft

'Brought the 9th century world alive to me and made me desperate to read more about it'
Gill Stewart

Christina Courtenay is an award-winning author of historical romance and time slip (dual time) stories. She started writing so that she could be a stay-at-home mum to her two daughters, but didn't get published until daughter number one left home aged twenty-one, so that didn't quite go to plan! Since then, however, she's made up for it by having twelve novels published and winning the RNA's Romantic Novel of the Year Award for Best Historical Romantic Novel twice with *Highland Storms* (2012) and *The Gilded Fan* (2014), and once for Best Fantasy Romantic Novel with *Echoes of the Runes* (2021).

Christina is half Swedish and grew up in that country. She has also lived in Japan and Switzerland, but is now based in Herefordshire, close to the Welsh border. She's a keen amateur genealogist and loves history and archaeology (the armchair variety).

To find out more, visit **christinacourtenay.com**, find her on Facebook **/Christinacourtenayauthor** or follow her on Twitter **@PiaCCourtenay**.

By Christina Courtenay

Trade Winds
Highland Storms
Monsoon Mists
The Scarlet Kimono
The Gilded Fan
The Jade Lioness
The Silent Touch of Shadows
The Secret Kiss of Darkness
The Soft Whisper of Dreams
The Velvet Cloak of Moonlight
Echoes of the Runes
The Runes of Destiny
Whispers of the Runes

Whispers *of the* Runes

CHRISTINA COURTENAY

First published in 2021
by HEADLINE REVIEW
An imprint of HEADLINE PUBLISHING GROUP

1

Cataloguing in Publication Data is available from the British Library

ISBN 978 1 4722 8267 5

Typeset in Minion Pro by Avon DataSet Ltd, Arden Court, Alcester, Warwickshire

Printed and bound in Great Britain by Clays Ltd, Elcograf S.p.A.

Headline's policy is to use papers that are natural, renewable and recyclable products and made from wood grown in well-managed forests and other controlled sources. The logging and manufacturing processes are expected to conform to the environmental regulations of the country of origin.

HEADLINE PUBLISHING GROUP
An Hachette UK Company
Carmelite House
50 Victoria Embankment
London EC4Y 0DZ

www.headline.co.uk
www.hachette.co.uk

To Carol Dahlén Fräjdin
– honorary daughter and amazing friend –
with love and thanks for everything!

Prologue

Stockholm, Sweden, August 2019

'Oh, come on, don't be a chicken! It's not like anyone believes in fortune-telling anyway. It's just a bit of fun, right?'

Sara Mattsson sighed and sat down next to her best friend's little sister, Maddie, who was shaking a small leather pouch full of stones. The teenager had learned to read the runes as a way of passing the time when her parents took her to Viking re-enactment weekends, and jokingly claimed to be psychic now. She often pounced on anyone who came to the family's home for dinner, offering her services as seeress.

'And anyway, I need the practice to keep my skills up, you know. Please?' Maddie wheedled.

'Fine, but I don't want to hear anything about tall, dark strangers, OK?' That would just remind her of her ex.

Maddie grinned, but then grew serious as she went through the ritual of closing her eyes, selecting three stones from the pouch and dropping them on to a tablecloth with three circles drawn on to it. Each stone had a different rune painted on its surface, and the girl leaned forward to study them. 'Look, they've all ended up in the circle for your future. Excellent!' She picked one up. 'This is Raidho. Means you're going to travel.'

'Well, yes, I know. I'm going back to the UK tomorrow.' Sara had been visiting family and friends in Sweden, but it was time to return to her fledgling business in England. She'd been renting a flat in York for the past year, as well as a small workshop where she created Viking- and Anglo-Saxon-inspired jewellery to sell. It was the perfect place for it, as the whole town seemed steeped in history.

'Hmm, it should be more exciting than that, but whatever. This next one is Berkana, the rune of birth and growth. It promises new beginnings and, um, possibly desire and love?'

Sara snorted. 'Not very likely. I told you, none of that rubbish, please.'

Maddie sent her a stern look. 'I'm not making this up, I'm just interpreting your runes. They whisper to me, you know? Well, inside my head, anyway.' She pointed at the final stone. 'So that one basically says you've got to be strong. There's going to be some delays or restrictions, and you have to rely on your inner strength.'

'What? My plane will be late?'

Maddie leaned forward and gave her a playful shove. 'No! It can mean that you have to face your fears, endure, survive. Be determined and patient. Stuff like that.'

Sara shook her head. Wasn't that what she'd been doing already, this past year or more? And it wasn't getting her anywhere. 'Well, thanks for the reading. Can't say I believe a word of it, but I wish you luck as a fortune-teller.'

'Hey! The runes never lie.' Maddie pretended to look offended, but her sparkling eyes gave her away.

'Hmm, well, hopefully your next customer will be less sceptical.'

For herself, she'd just carry on working hard until the painful memories faded.

Chapter One

North Sea, Haustmánuður/late September AD *873*

'Are you sure we shouldn't go back? That old fisherman said there's a storm brewing.'

'Don't be ridiculous! Anyone can see the weather is perfect for a sea crossing. Besides, that was two days ago – it's a bit late to turn around now.'

Rurik Eskilsson listened as the two men at the stern of the ship bickered. One was its owner, Sigvardr, the other a passenger just like himself, although much older than Rurik's twenty-two winters. Well past his prime, in fact, the worry-guts was clearly not comfortable with being on board, and had been violently sick for most of the journey so far. His face held a grey tinge, and if he'd had anything left inside him, he'd probably still have been hanging over the gunwale.

A quick glance at the sky showed only an expanse of blue, but towards the horizon, clouds were undoubtedly gathering. Sigvardr was right, though – there was no point in turning around, as they were already more than halfway across the North Sea, having left Ribe in the land of the Danes the day before yesterday. Rurik touched the large Thor's hammer amulet hanging around his neck and hoped the gods would keep them safe. His future plans did not include drowning in the salty depths of the ocean. Rather, he was on his way to a new life, an adventure, far from his family and friends, and he didn't want anything to stand in his way.

He'd had to get away from *her* before he went insane, her golden loveliness as far out of his reach as it could possibly be . . . but he refused to think about that now.

'Tie the sail tighter! Not like that, you *fifl*, properly!' Sigvardr shouted out his orders, and Rurik hoped the man knew what he was doing and it wasn't all bravado. He'd been in charge of a ship himself a few times, and as far as he could tell, Sigvardr was an experienced sailor. For a brief moment, though, he wished he was travelling with his older brother, Hrafn, instead. He had his own ship and had offered to take Rurik to his destination, but it was past time to cut the ties between them and strike out alone.

The swell of the waves increased, their tops foaming like horses that had been worked too hard. At first, the large ship cut through them smoothly without any problems, but when the wind picked up, the clinker-built vessel began to buck and creak as it rode the hills and troughs of water. It was superbly constructed, however, and Rurik didn't doubt it could withstand much worse treatment. Norse vessels were made to be flexible yet strong, and it would take a lot to break it.

'We should be sighting land towards dusk,' Sigvardr commented. His voice was loud and carried over the wind so that everyone heard him, but the only one who replied was the worry-guts.

'If we make it that far . . .' he muttered ominously.

Rurik sent him a death glare, hoping to shut him up. No one wanted to listen to his fears, and he was the only one there who was scared. If they were meant to die this day, they would. You couldn't change your fate – the Norns, ancient goddesses of destiny, had decided that ages ago – so what was the point of fretting?

For several hours the ship continued to plough through the waves, which were growing at the same time as a mass of grey clouds rolled over them. It was as if they were about to be smothered from above by an enormous feather bolster. Soon the light faded, even though it wasn't evening yet. Rurik had been forced to cast up his morning meal, the churning motion too much even for him, but he'd not said a word. Neither had anyone else, and even the old man was quiet now, although that might have been because he was paralysed with fear. Certainly he was staring at the water with unblinking eyes, his knuckles white as he gripped the side of the ship.

The sail flapped furiously, ropes taut to the point of breaking. It was a good thing they were made from seal hide, a flexible and durable material, slightly greasy to the touch. The ship's planks were groaning in protest, but the bottom didn't fill up with water, despite the best efforts of the waves trying to break over the sides from all directions. The gunwales stayed above the waterline somehow, but that didn't mean the passengers remained dry. The salty spray had by now drenched them anyway, and although it was only early autumn, Rurik was chilled to the bone. It was a miserable way to spend a day, that was for certain, and he scanned the horizon for a glimpse of land. It couldn't be far off now.

It was darker still when a coastline finally rose up ahead of them, and Rurik could tell immediately that they were approaching it too fast and at an odd angle. Sigvardr started shouting more orders. 'Man the oars! We have to row, away from those cliffs! Hurry now!'

There was a scramble to put the oars into the water. They'd been stowed along the inside of the gunwale on either side of the ship, and had to be passed to each man in turn, starting with the one furthest back. A simple loop of rope was fastened to the ship, then quickly slotted around specially carved notches on the oars, holding them in place. After that, it was just a question of developing some sort of synchronised rhythm, not easy when the ship was continuously tossed about, this way and that. Rurik was strong and used to rowing, and had no trouble following Sigvardr's shouts of 'One, two, one, two!' but not everyone managed it and the ship didn't make as much progress as it needed to. The cliffs came inexorably closer.

Through narrowed eyes, Rurik alternated between watching them and the water around the ship. It swirled like a cauldron about to boil over, and it was clear there were strong currents at work underneath the surface, pulling them along. There was absolutely nothing they could do; their rowing was to no avail. Their only hope now was to get as close to the coast as possible, and then perhaps they could steer the ship towards a beach or jump out and swim for it.

Sigvardr must have had the same thought. 'Put your backs into it! If we can just head further that way . . .' he pointed, 'we should be able to—'

His words were cut off by an almighty crash. Rurik saw the bow of the ship rise almost vertically, its open-mouthed dragon carving tilting backwards. The men who'd been sitting at the front tumbled downwards, knocking each other over like gaming pieces. In the next instant, the planks of the ship were splintering, its hull breaking cleanly into two, and the water rushed in at tremendous speed. He realised they must have hit some underwater rocks, and there was no salvation from that. Men, planks, oars and loose objects scattered amid screams and the ominous noise of wood twisting and cracking. Acting on instinct, Rurik caught hold of a loose piece of the ship's hull, just as the remainder of the ship collided with an even larger obstacle. He knew he'd need something to help keep him afloat, and that was the only thing to hand.

Flying through the air, he vaguely registered the screams of the worry-guts and acknowledged that the old man had had cause for his fear. There were other desperate shouts and swear words coming thick and fast, but all became muffled by the shock of icy water that closed over his head and filled his ears. He wanted to scream too, but remembered in time not to open his mouth. Instead he blinked and tried to see which way was up, not an easy thing to do in the murky water, and with only a glimmer of light above.

He was a strong swimmer, but the water fought for supremacy. He had to kick with all his might to reach the surface. In this he was helped by the piece of planking in his arms, which proved to be buoyant as he'd hoped. He held on to it for all he was worth and looked to see if he could help anyone. The worry-guts briefly appeared next to him, flailing and coughing. Rurik tried to catch hold of the old one's tunic, but the material slipped through his hands and the man disappeared. More screams and shouts echoed around him, but his eyes stung with the salt water and he couldn't see the others among the waves. Foam-topped hills of water washed over him, impeding his sight further. The currents propelled him away from the ship and he kicked with his legs and paddled with one arm as much as he could whenever he spotted land. He didn't want to get sucked out to sea, and battled to go in the other direction. Although he was submerged over and over again, he was determined not to give in. Whatever the Norns thought, he didn't believe it was his turn to die quite yet.

They must have agreed, because eventually, when he was sure he couldn't go on much longer, he looked up to find a beach not too far away. That gave him the strength to carry on fighting until at last he was lying at the water's edge among large boulders covered in bright green seaweed. Waves sloshed over him intermittently, but he barely felt them now. He dug his fingers into the rough sand as if to anchor himself, and managed to raise his body on to all fours.

'Thank the gods!' he exclaimed hoarsely, coughing and spluttering. The back of his throat felt as though it was on fire – he must have swallowed a goodly amount of salt water – but he didn't care. He was alive.

A shiver went through him and he knew he couldn't stay here. He needed to find shelter and get dry. But first he should look for the others, try to save any that he could. Where were they? Had anyone else survived? There was water in his ears still, but even when he shook that out, he couldn't hear any shouts, only the howling of the wind and the crashing of waves against the shore. Gathering the very last shreds of his energy, he struggled to his feet and spotted some items bobbing up and down near the shore. One he recognised – the chest containing all his belongings, everything he needed for his new life, and it appeared to be intact. *Thank Odin for that – what an incredible piece of luck!* He and the other gods and goddesses had definitely been on his side today. He waded into the surf and grabbed the kist just before another huge wave tried to drag it back out to sea.

'Oh no you don't!' he snarled at the swirling currents, which were trying to wrench the chest away from him. He wasn't going to lose that if he could help it.

Back on dry land, he deposited the kist a safe distance from the water, then stumbled along the shoreline on legs that were none too steady, but he couldn't see anyone. 'Hello? *Hello?*' He tried to call out, but his voice was croaky and what little noise he made the wind carried away, so he gave up and forced himself into action, jogging along the edge of the sea while scanning his surroundings for any sign of life. Nothing moved other than the waves and a lot of flotsam and debris. A couple of other sea chests drifted in the water, and he brought them ashore. One was broken and empty, the second undamaged but containing mostly soggy clothing.

After searching for some time, he was about to acknowledge defeat. He'd spied a cave set into the cliffs – the perfect place to build a fire and dry out, provided he could make his wet fire iron work and find some driftwood – but just as he turned his steps towards it, he finally saw pale shapes being tossed about in the foamy water a bit further along. He recognised the brightly coloured tunic of one of them.

'Sigvardr? Sigvardr!'

He ran into the water, grabbing the man's arms to haul him out, but as he laid him on the sand, he could see that it was too late. There was a huge gash on his head and no one could have survived a blow like that. A quick check revealed the truth of this – Sigvardr's heart had stopped beating. He must have been thrown on to the underwater rocks or been hit by parts of the ship as it broke into pieces.

There was nothing Rurik could do for the man now other than drag him further up the beach. Later, when he was warm and dry, he'd bury him. It was what any brave man deserved, and he was sure Sigvardr would have done the same for him.

Two other people being washed ashore nearby had suffered more or less the same fate, and Rurik couldn't do anything for them either, except to pull them out of the water. One was the worry-guts, and he felt a moment's sadness thinking how the poor man had spent his last days so afraid. But he was with his ancestors now, or perhaps with Ægir the sea *jótun* and his wife Rán, not a bad fate.

'Or maybe not . . .' Rurik muttered.

He'd spotted the glimmer of metal at the man's throat and

pulled out a silver amulet in the shape of a cross. That would indicate a follower of the White Christ, one of those who attended meetings in the small wooden building in Ribe, whose bell he'd heard ringing several times while he waited for passage across the sea. A man in long white robes, who introduced himself as Bishop Ansgar – whatever that meant – had tried to entice Rurik in at one point, but he'd refused. His own gods were good enough; he had no need of any more, as had been proved this day.

Darkness was falling and Rurik needed to look after himself now or else he'd perish as well. Perhaps tomorrow he would find some of the others, although there seemed little hope of anyone else being alive. Desolation and a huge sense of loss swept over him. This was a wretched start to his new life, and he sincerely hoped it wasn't a bad omen.

Chapter Two

Marsden Bay, Northumberland, late September 2019

'This is absolutely stunning! Thank you so much for letting me see it.'

Sara reverently held a tiny pin between forefinger and thumb, twisting it round in order to study the workmanship. Norse, probably ninth century, it was an object most people might find insignificant, but as a jewellery maker herself, Sara knew exactly how much work had gone into creating it. And someone had done it over a thousand years ago, with nothing like the sophisticated tools at her disposal.

Amazing!

'It was found in the grave, did you say?' She looked at the man in charge of the dig, Robert McPherson. She'd been given special permission to visit because her grandfather was a renowned Swedish archaeologist and a friend of Robert's from way back.

'Aye, just over there, although the wee pin was more or less on the surface. Erosion most probably pushed it up.' His Scottish accent wasn't as strong as some, but he nonetheless rolled his r's in a way Sara loved. 'Why don't you come over and watch? We're getting down to the actual skeletons now and there are some fantastic finds coming to light.' He looked around and whispered, 'An *Ulfberht* sword!'

'Seriously? Wow!' Sara knew those were the best Viking swords ever made, and they were unmistakable as the smith had marked them all with his name.

'Come on, they should have it out by now.'

'Brilliant! May I just take a photo of this first, please? It's giving me all sorts of ideas for designs and I don't want to forget what it looks like. Something like this would be fabulous for my next collection.'

'Sure, as long as you don't publish the pictures anywhere yet, especially not on the internet. We like to drip-feed news of our finds to the journalists. Keeps them on their toes.' Robert grinned and Sara nodded her agreement. The right kind of publicity, through the proper channels, might mean more funding, and projects like this always needed money.

She snapped images from every angle. Made of pure gold, the little pin was simple, but sharp enough to pierce any material, and topped by a beautifully shaped bird no larger than her thumbnail. It had a graceful curved neck, tiny wings that stuck up on either side of its body, and a narrow downward-curving beak. A raven, perhaps, or a bird of prey? The eyes were some sort of semi-precious stone – garnet probably – and the wings and neck were inlaid with niello, a dark effect produced by adding phosphate into engraved lines. You could clearly see a pattern of feathers. It was quite simply exquisite and she wished she could take it with her, but she'd have to try and make one for herself.

'OK, I'm done. Here you go.' She handed it back to Robert, who stowed it away in a special box lined with cotton wool, and then in a small safe.

'Great, let's go and see how they're getting on outside then.'

He led the way out of the Winnebago he used as his office and over to the dig site, a blustery clifftop on the North Sea coast south-east of Newcastle. The cairn had been found recently after a violent storm had exposed the mound of stones and a human bone. Before that, it had apparently looked like just another grassy part of the terrain, and no one had given it much thought. 'We had to excavate quickly, before anyone got the idea to dig for treasure,' Robert told Sara as they walked. 'And thank goodness we did!'

'Indeed.'

A chilly September wind buffeted them during the short walk over to the trench, and Sara glanced at the sky, registering the dark clouds. 'Lucky you've rigged up a tent,' she commented, not envious of the archaeologists beavering away. This close to the sea they must get pretty cold after a couple of hours of trowelling. The tent was open on two sides, which meant the wind had free access even if it kept out any rain.

'Yes, we can't afford to lose time because of the weather. Hey, Adrian, anything new?' Robert crouched near the edge of the trench and Sara followed suit. 'Oh, you've got the second pelvis and skull now, excellent!'

'Yep, and it's definitely another male.' The guy called Adrian smiled. 'You never know these days, after that find in Birka.'

Sara must have looked blank, as Robert said, 'Didn't your grandfather tell you? A grave there contained a female warrior, complete with all her kit.'

'Oh yes, I remember now.' Her grandpa was always going on about this or that find, but she vaguely recalled hearing about that one. 'So is this a warrior?'

'Definitely. Most likely a chieftain, judging by the grave goods we've found so far. Not sure who the other two are. Perhaps his servants, as most of the items seem to belong to this guy. Hop down and have a look at this.' Adrian, a lanky man who looked to be in his early thirties, held out his hand to help her into the trench while Robert jumped in by himself.

In a long box lined with what appeared to be slightly greasy wool lay the *Ulfberht* sword. The blade didn't look like much at the moment – a rusted, pitted mess – but Sara knew that when examined under a microscope, it would be amazing. Probably pattern-welded steel that would have been sharp and deadly, as well as incredibly strong. The hilt was something else, though – bronze decorated with silver, it was a work of art and the silversmith in her was immediately impressed. 'May I?'

Adrian held out the box to allow her a closer look. 'We reckon ninth century, probably mid to late-ish,' he said.

'Mm-hmm.' She always carried a loupe, and now she pulled it out of her pocket to better study the pattern properly magnified. Typical animalistic motifs with swirls and snarling beasts. 'Lovely!'

Robert had hunkered down to study the skeleton that was emerging. 'Any ideas yet as to what caused his death?'

'Well, it appears he died from a vicious blow to the head. Look there.' Adrian pointed to the skull he'd partially unearthed, where a hollow with splintered bone was clearly visible.

'Ouch! Maybe he was part of the Great Heathen Army and the locals got the better of him,' Robert mused.

Sara had heard of that – a huge army of Vikings that had roamed the British Isles in the late ninth century during the time of King Alfred the Great. 'Did they come this far up?' She'd thought they'd stuck mostly to the central and southern kingdoms of East Anglia, Mercia and Wessex.

'Oh yes. Conquered all of Northumbria and toppled the kingdom of Alt Clud as well. You know, up in Strathclyde.'

'Really? I had no idea.'

Robert and Adrian continued to examine the skeleton, and while Sara admired the sword hilt and pommel, they started discussing bone structure. She tuned out, as that sort of thing didn't interest her at all. Eventually they stood up.

'Coming, Sara? Tea break.'

'Huh? Oh, yes please.'

She followed the two men and a couple of the other diggers towards a more substantial tent set up on a piece of common in between the coast and the nearest houses – presumably their makeshift canteen – but halfway there, she realised she'd dropped her phone when clambering in or out of the trench. 'Sorry, Robert, but I'm going to have to go back. I think my mobile must have slipped out of my pocket – I forgot to button it up.'

'Of course, go! We'll have your tea waiting for you.'

The trench was deserted when she got there, and Sara glanced at the bones that were emerging from the dark soil. She couldn't help but wonder how the warrior and his servants had ended up here on a lonely clifftop with no other graves around. 'Hope you don't mind them digging you up,' she murmured to the biggest skeleton. 'Don't suppose that's what your comrades had in mind when they buried you here.'

She looked for the mobile, which unfortunately was black. That made it more difficult to spot, and she'd walked almost the entire perimeter of the trench before she saw it. 'Aha!'

When she picked it up, there was a text message. She read the sender's name: Anders. *Shit.* How had he got hold of her new number? She'd have to block him. Again. Because here was probably yet another *It didn't mean anything, babe! Please get in touch – I still love you!* message. Like hell it hadn't meant anything. Cheating scumbag . . . And honestly, it had been over two years now. When was he going to get it through his thick skull that she would never take him back? He was only being this persistent because he saw her as his route to the top of the jewellery design industry. She'd won awards and her business was doing well, while he was working for a boring mail-order company creating generic old-lady-type jewellery. Once upon a time, they'd had grand ideas about working together, but he'd ruined all that and he had only himself to blame. She deleted the message unread. He could get stuffed.

'Have the balls to start your own company,' she muttered. 'Not that anyone would buy your mediocre designs.' She took a deep breath. 'I'm through letting you affect me.'

Just as she reached out a hand to climb out of the trench, she noticed a metallic flash nearby and hesitated. At the very edge of the trench, about halfway along, something was starting to protrude and had caught the light. Sara put the phone in her pocket, then touched the item with one fingertip, carefully stroking off some soil. Yes, definitely metal, and not iron, since it was shiny. She ought to go and fetch Robert, but first she wanted a quick peek to see what it was. It could just be junk, an old tin can or something, then they'd laugh at her for jumping to conclusions. Scraping at the dirt with her fingers, she bent down as a small rectangular shape began to emerge. She was mesmerised. What could it be?

A bit more digging, loosening the earth, and she suddenly had the inside part of the handle of a knife in front of her as some of the soil avalanched downwards. 'Oh!' She tugged at it experimentally and the entire knife came sliding out, its single-edged blade over a foot long and quite vicious-looking, with a pointed tip. 'Whoa!' The handle must have been made of bone or wood originally, she assumed, but this had rotted away and only the metal centre and end piece of it was left. The blade, however, was still largely intact, which was weird. If it was steel, like the *Ulfberht* sword, it ought to have been corroded and rusty. It wasn't, though, and along the upper half there was a runic inscription picked out in gold.

With a grandfather who was an archaeologist specialising in the Viking period, Sara had learned to read runes at the same time as the ordinary alphabet. He'd also taught her some Old Norse, and recently she'd been taking lessons because her best friend Linnea had married a man who spoke nothing else. That was a strange story in itself, but she didn't want to think about that now. First things first – what did this knife inscription say?

'*Með blōð skaltu ferðast.*' Absently she ran her finger along the blade as she read the words out loud, then swore as she felt the metal slicing into her finger. How could it be so sharp after being buried all this time? And those words, they rang a bell. Wasn't that something similar to what Linnea had said she'd found on a Viking brooch? 'With blood you shall travel'? Yes, that sounded about right.

Oh shit! That meant . . .

The realisation of what she might have done hit her just as she got an attack of the spin monsters so bad she nearly toppled over. 'No, no, *no*!' This could not be happening.

She had to stop it, but she couldn't move and was having trouble staying upright. Her eyes opened wide as the earth seemed to come rushing up towards her, while nausea roiled inside her. There was a loud noise, like being in a room full of people all talking at once, with the wind whooshing in the background. Faster and faster her head spun, and she had to put out a hand to stop herself from falling head first into the skeleton.

She stumbled onto her knees, barely aware of her surroundings now. They were flashing past in a dizzying frenzy, like being on a merry-go-round that was totally out of control. She swallowed down the nausea and closed her eyes, then everything went black.

Chapter Three

'How did you extract that *seax* from the mound? Give it back this instant!'

Sara opened her eyelids a fraction and blinked against the light from a pale sun. She felt someone tugging at an object in her hands and instinctively held on, even though she didn't know what it was.

'Let go, I say! It does not belong to you.'

Forcing her eyes to focus, she discovered that there was an angry face very close to hers. A seriously attractive male face, but with bloodshot turquoise eyes flashing sparks of fury at her. 'What?' she mumbled, looking down at the tug of war she was apparently engaged in. The long knife was still in her hand, except it couldn't be the same one because this one had a smooth bone handle with a nice pattern where before there had only been metal. She frowned as she noticed that the blade was identical, the golden inscription even clearer than before, just shinier. The man who was trying to take it from her was gripping it carefully so as not to cut his fingers. That meant he couldn't pull very hard, though.

'Give it to me,' he hissed. 'Would you steal from the dead, woman?'

Sara blinked as she registered the fact that he wasn't speaking English, but Old Norse. It couldn't be anything else. Although she wasn't fluent, she recognised the words and grammar, having had quite a few lessons recently, and she had no trouble understanding him. The memory of what had just happened came rushing back, and she moaned. 'Oh, *no*! You have *got* to be kidding me!'

She straightened up slowly, swallowing down the nausea that still lingered at the back of her throat, and looked around her. The trench was gone, as was the awning above it, and the rest of the site had disappeared as well, including the food tent and the archaeologists. The small common, bordered by a row of two-storey semi-detached houses and a road, was no longer there, and she couldn't see the coastal path, nor the lighthouse she'd spotted in the distance earlier. Instead she was kneeling on scraggly grass on an open clifftop near the sea, with a newly built cairn next to her.

A cairn! It couldn't be.

She could tell that the stones had only just been put there, as they didn't have any moss on them like the ones Robert's team had tossed aside. And there was fresh soil spilling out between the cracks. It was definitely the same place, though – Marsden Bay. She recognised the half-moon sweep of the beach some thirty metres below, and the view of two particular rock formations that she'd been admiring earlier. The Lot's Wife sea stack and Marsden Rock, Robert had called them. She shook her head. No, this just wasn't possible . . .

'Give me the *seax*!' The man's voice was angrier now, even though he wasn't shouting.

Sara hadn't really been listening to him. Slowly she turned to reply in his language. '*Hvat?*'

'I said—'

She interrupted him. 'Are you speaking the *Danskr tungu*?'

For some reason Vikings had referred to their own language as 'the Danish tongue' and not 'Old Norse'. That was a later name for it, she knew.

'*Já*. And?' He let go of the blade and took a step back. Perhaps he'd realised she wasn't about to run off with it.

'Oh my God . . .' She closed her eyes and leaned forward, almost felled by the implications of his reply. He really was speaking Old Norse, not some obscure Northumberland dialect, and therefore he had to be a Viking. A real live Norseman. No one went around talking like that these days, which could only mean one thing, and it confirmed what she already feared – that she had travelled back in time.

About a thousand years back in time. *Please, no!*

It sounded unbelievable, and when her friend Linnea had told her that was what had happened to her the previous year, Sara had been very sceptical. It seemed more likely to be a figment of Linnea's imagination. She had disappeared and been feared dead for nearly a year, and people who were kidnapped were often brainwashed by their captors into giving some lame excuse on their behalf. But Linnea appeared sane and rational, telling her story convincingly, and in the end, Sara had kept her doubts to herself. When Linnea's Viking husband had turned up as well, to fetch her back to his own time, there was no option but to believe her friend wholeheartedly.

Though now she didn't want to, because that meant her current predicament was all too real as well.

Trying not to hyperventilate, she hung her head between her knees so she wouldn't faint. She'd never had a panic attack but imagined this might be what it felt like. Where was a paper bag when you needed one? Or a Xanax? Taking some long, slow breaths, she managed to calm her pounding pulse a fraction. *Relax. You can do this.* You've coped with worse, she told herself.

Much worse. But had she? Although she'd survived a near-death experience, followed by months in hospital, this was way out there, unlike anything she'd ever faced before. *Time travel, for goodness' sake!* How was that even possible? At least the buzzing in her head was gone, and although her heart was still beating triple time, she wasn't dizzy any longer. Carefully she sat up straight again.

The man crossed his arms over his chest, drawing Sara's eyes back to him. She belatedly realised he was half naked, wearing only a pair of trousers that looked a bit like pyjama bottoms, tied at the waist with a drawstring. They were extremely creased and looked as though he'd slept in them when they were still wet from washing. *What on earth . . . ?*

She stared at him. It was late September and pretty chilly – that sea breeze wasn't letting up; why was he walking around without a shirt and in thin trousers of linen or cotton? Tough Viking or not, that was just nuts. She took in the physique on display, her gaze roaming over a muscular chest, sculpted abs and arms that looked like he spent a lot of time working out. Impressive. But there was no one to show off his muscles to up here on the clifftop, and she could see that he was cold. There were goose bumps on his tanned forearms and he was shivering visibly. So what the heck was he doing?

'Have you quite finished looking at me?' One eyebrow quirked in annoyance and he put his head to one side, pursing his mouth.

It was a very nice mouth, and Sara couldn't help but stare some more. One of the most beautiful she'd ever seen on a man actually – full lips, but not too full, corners tilted up to make him look like he was amused, and a pronounced Cupid's bow. The artist in her had a sudden urge to draw him. The rest of his features weren't bad either – a cute nose that tilted slightly upwards at the end, those big turquoise eyes under straight brows, and a pair of cheekbones to die for. If he had dimples too, he'd be catwalk material for sure.

But that was in her world. The twenty-first century. And she was almost a hundred per cent sure that this was nowhere near the year 2019. He wouldn't understand what a catwalk was even if she'd known the Norse word for it, which of course she didn't.

And she was in serious trouble.

Rurik waited while the strange woman tried to answer him. He wasn't usually averse to females looking at him with admiration – what man would be? – but lately he had sworn off all women, and right now he was in a hurry to leave this place. He was feeling cold, tired and grumpy, and his eyes stung from yesterday's near-drowning experience in the salty sea, making his vision slightly blurry. He wanted the matter of the *seax* sorted out before he went. How in the name of all the gods had she managed to extract it from the cairn so quickly? He'd heard of grave robbers, but it was only a matter of moments since he'd buried the thing, and he was sure he'd covered both Sigvardr and his possessions with plenty of soil and heavy stones. The other two and their few items as well.

And where had she come from? One minute he was alone up here, the next she was sitting there behind him. It was like magic, *trolldomr*. He shivered. Right now, he didn't care if she was the goddess Freya herself. All he wanted was to go back to the cave and put on his other garments. Hopefully they'd be dry enough by now. He had had to rinse them in a beck he'd found pouring down the hillside in order to get the salt water out of them. Clothes that had been in the sea would have been too stiff and uncomfortable to wear for any length of time. He knew from past experience that they would itch and chafe unbearably, and it was better to be cold for a while than miserable for days. And he might be freezing, but at least he was alive – the sea was a dangerous beast, and he was extremely grateful to have survived the events of yesterday.

A shame no one else had.

He'd looked all along the beach again this morning, but no other survivors had washed up as yet, unless they'd walked off during the night, leaving the seashore behind. No more corpses either – only some of their belongings and various parts of the broken ship. There was always the hope that someone could have landed further along the coast and was still alive, but he'd never know for sure because he didn't intend to waste any more time searching. As for Sigvardr and the other two, he had done his best. The shipowner had been wearing his weapons – sword slung across his chest in a baldric, the *seax* hanging off his belt – and in a leather pouch there had been other items of value. Rurik had buried them all.

The other two – the worry-guts and one of Sigvardr's crew members – hadn't had any possessions apart from that silver cross, in the case of the old man, and an eating knife each. In order to help them in the afterlife, Rurik had added a couple of other items – a cloak pin in the shape of a bird for the worry-guts, and a smaller Thor's hammer for the crewman. Both were objects he'd made himself, and he could always make new ones. As he had no idea how the Christians buried their dead, he'd put the old man with the other two. Hopefully his god would find him there somehow.

He glanced at the *seax* still in the woman's hand. Probably a spoil of war from Sigvardr's earlier excursions to the lands of the Saxons, as it wasn't a Norse weapon. The man had been bragging of past visits to this place when they'd first met. What was Rurik to do with it? He was too cold to start moving the stones again, and maybe she had need of it. She'd looked desperate just now, eyes wide as though she feared someone was about to attack her at any moment. Perhaps he should let her keep the knife, as long as she didn't try to use it on him. Sigvardr had enough weapons for the afterlife without it.

No, he shouldn't encourage thievery. If he waited a moment, she might lose concentration and then he could grab it and fling it out to sea. An appropriate offering to the sea god for sparing his life.

'I was not looking at you!' she muttered now, though the pink that suffused her cheeks told him she was lying. She had definitely been staring at him.

But Rurik didn't care. His teeth were chattering, and if he didn't get back to the cave very soon, he'd freeze to death. The only thing keeping him warm had been the physical work of constructing the burial mound, but now he was standing still in the icy wind, wearing next to nothing. He needed to leave, and quickly.

The woman stood up, swaying slightly, and innate courtesy made him reach out a hand to steady her. 'Do you feel unwell?'

'A little, but it will pass.' She took a few steadying breaths and Rurik saw some colour return to her pale cheeks. Her speech was halting, as if she wasn't used to talking in his language, but at least she was trying, which was something. And she seemed to understand him.

'Good, now give me that.' He swiftly pulled the *seax* out of her hand, and because she was distracted, it wasn't difficult to disarm her this time. She surged forward, protesting loudly, but when she tried to grab it back, he held it up high so that she couldn't reach. She was of average height, but he was fairly tall and there was no way she'd be able to take it from him. 'No! It belonged to a dead man. You can't have it.'

'But I need it!' She continued to struggle, dancing around him and going so far as to hang off his arm at one point. It made no difference, as he was much the stronger of the two, but this was becoming ridiculous.

He raised his voice. 'Leave it, woman! Neither of us can keep it and there's an end to the matter. I can find you another knife if you need one so badly.' And with that, he swung around, catching her off guard, and sent the *seax* soaring out over the cliff edge, and hopefully far into the sea.

'*Nooooo!*'

She stilled, all colour draining from her face, and her eyes opened wide with shock. She was looking at him as though he was the criminal here. Irritation swamped him – at her, at the gods for playing games with him, at the whole situation. Was there no end to the things he had to put up with? All he'd wanted was to start afresh. Not be half drowned and saddled with more problems. He closed his eyes for a moment, trying to rid himself of the soreness and the blurred vision, then opened them again.

'Go back to where you came from,' he hissed. 'I'll be watching to make certain you do not steal anything else.' He crossed his arms over his chest again and glared at her. He hoped to all the gods she'd hurry up and leave. *The trolls take her!*

Instead of answering, she scrambled over towards the cliff edge and leaned forward as if she intended to follow the knife by launching herself into the air. Rurik rushed after her and grabbed her arm. 'No! What are you doing?'

'Let go! Not going to jump.' She sent him an angry glare and struggled out of his grip, scanning the beach far below them. Her shoulders slumped and he thought he heard a muffled sob. 'It is gone,' she whispered, her words almost swallowed completely by the wind.

'It is for the best. The sea god will be appeased now.'

'You do not understand.' She hesitated, then blurted out, 'I need it to go . . . h-home.'

'What? The *seax*?' Rurik stared at her, then frowned as he belatedly took in her strange appearance. He blinked to try and focus properly. Long chestnut-coloured hair, shiny and slightly wavy, was being tossed around by the wind. She had eyes the colour of amber, framed by thick lashes that were dusky brown. Her skin was like a thrall's, tanned from the sun, a smattering of freckles covered the bridge of a delicate nose, and she had lips like pale pink flower petals. Comely enough, but what really bothered him was that she was dressed strangely, almost like a man, in blue trousers, big shoes that were as clumsy as small tree stumps, and a padded tunic of some sort that fastened down the front with round toggles, the likes of which he'd never come across before. How had he not noticed that earlier?

And wait a moment! This reminded him of something, and combined with her sudden appearance – yes, *trolldomr* indeed – a thought took root. He had seen weird clothing once before, and although he'd struggled to comprehend the reason for it, he knew there were a lot of unexplained phenomena in the world. Could this woman also be . . . a time traveller?

Odin's ravens!

No, surely not? That would be the second time his family had been chosen by the gods to receive such a visitor. Why should they be singled out in this way? Rurik saw it as a curse – the gods making mischief for reasons only they knew – although his older brother's opinion was the complete opposite these days, of course. It had certainly created discord, even if ultimately Rurik was the only one who'd suffered as a consequence.

On the other hand, he could be jumping to conclusions; this woman might just be from a foreign country, although how she'd ended up here in that case was a mystery.

'What is your name?' He hadn't meant to bark out the question, but his tone must have been harsh, because she jumped, her gaze flying up to his.

'Huh? Oh, Sara Mattsson.'

'*Sah*-ra?' Not a name he was familiar with, but not everyone had the same ones as the people from his homeland. 'And don't you mean Mattsdottír?' he added with a shake of the head. 'Matts is your father's name?'

'No, it's Jonas?' She didn't sound as though she was sure, but Rurik knew he'd probably confused her.

'Then you are Sara Jonasdottír, are you not?'

'I . . . I suppose, but—'

'You are,' Rurik said, his tone brooking no argument. If what he suspected was true, it was imperative that she learned a few things straight away, or she wouldn't survive long. And she definitely wasn't anyone's son, no matter where she was from.

His heart sank. If she *was* a time traveller, that could only mean one thing – the knife was some sort of magical item, and without it, she was stuck in his time. And it was all his fault. *Aaarrgh!* He'd never asked for specific details about how the other time traveller managed the journeys, and realised he should have done. Still, too late now. 'Can you go somewhere else?' he tried, grasping at straws.

'No.' She shook her head, looking confused. 'Where?'

'I don't know.' Rurik closed his eyes again and bowed to the inevitable. He had, after all, brought it upon himself, although he had a suspicion the gods were toying with him and he hadn't had much choice in the matter. 'Very well. You will have to come with me. For now.'

He could get her back to her own time if he took her home. Hrafn would know what to do. But he'd only just left and didn't particularly relish having to retrace his journey so soon. Better to keep her with him for a while, even though she was a complication he could well do without.

He tamped down another wave of frustration that washed over him at the vagaries of the Norns. After picking up the shovel he'd been using to dig with, he set off along the clifftop muttering curses. He should have just left her when he first saw her, then she wouldn't be his responsibility. And he shouldn't have thrown the *seax* into the sea . . .

'Wh-where do we go?'

He glanced over his shoulder and saw her hurrying after him. 'Down to the beach. There is a cave where I left my possessions. And if I don't return there soon, I will die of cold.' He was shivering uncontrollably now, and tried to jump up and down on the spot as he waited for her to catch up. He pointed in a vaguely downward direction, but she had stopped and was shaking her head.

'I . . . No! No, I cannot go with you. Don't know you.'

Rurik grabbed her arm. 'For the love of Odin, woman! I will not harm you.' She was still digging her heels in and he decided to scare her a little. 'You cannot stay here, alone and unprotected. It would be dangerous for you. Do you wish to be captured? Become someone's thrall?' He didn't add 'my thrall', because unlike his older brother, he had no reason to own anyone, and that was a subject he didn't want to think about right now in any case, as it brought back painful memories.

'*Thrall?*' She blinked at him with dawning horror. 'No! There are no thralls.'

'Oh yes there are. Now come, before I freeze to death.' He tugged her with him towards the steep path that led down to the beach. He'd found it by chance and assumed it had been made by local people, although he'd not come across any *Engilskir* so far. 'Have a care or you'll fall,' he warned. 'I'll go first.'

Sara stopped struggling and followed as though in a daze.

When he looked at her again, he could almost see her mind trying to work out what to do for the best. If she really was from another time, she'd be in a completely foreign environment, with no way of even feeding herself. Utterly dependent on him, a complete stranger. And she was clearly still in shock since he'd apparently robbed her of her only chance of returning to her own time.

He swallowed a sigh. Finding a time traveller had seemed like something that only happened once in a lifetime. Who would have thought he'd come across another one so soon?

Chapter Four

When Sara saw the knife hurtling through the air, she went completely numb, her insides turning to ice as the implication of its loss hit her. That was her passport back to the present, and suddenly it was gone before she'd even had a chance to process what had happened prior to that. Her first instinct was to follow its trajectory to see if it could be retrieved, but as she gazed down towards the beach, she saw only water. It was high tide and that knife would be washed out to sea almost instantly by waves and strong currents.

She was trapped. What was she to do?

The man told her to follow him, and she did, but then she remembered that she didn't know anything about him. Why should she trust him? He could be a rapist or a murderer, or some kind of madman or . . . She stopped and tried to voice her fears without offending or provoking him, but he was clearly becoming impatient.

'For the love of Odin, woman! I will not harm you,' he'd said and it sounded as if he truly meant it.

What choice did she have other than to believe him? She had nowhere else to go. And his added comment about slaves clinched the matter, but she'd be on her guard.

They had reached a path, the thick grass worn away by the passage of many feet through the centuries. It snaked its way downwards, past the layers of limestone that made up the steep cliffs. She slithered behind him, glad he was in front of her as she struggled to keep her balance. The beach seemed quite far below them and she wasn't good with heights. A couple of times she slipped on loose pebbles and had to grab his arm or steady herself against his shoulder. It was disconcerting to touch his skin, which felt warm despite the chilly breeze. Probably because her own fingers were so cold, borne out by the fact that he flinched at her icy touch. She wished he was at least wearing a shirt. It had been a while since she'd been this close to a half-naked male, and the sudden pull of attraction she felt took her by surprise. She hadn't expected or wanted to even like any man ever again. Not after Anders' perfidy . . .

'What is your name? And why no clothes?' she finally asked, curious about him now.

'I am Rurik. And they were all wet. I was in a shipwreck yesterday. Had to swim. Everything was soaked. We were on our way to Jorvik, but the storm blew us off course.'

'I see.' That explained his bloodshot eyes too. 'The men up there?' She nodded towards the clifftop and the grave she'd been sitting next to. A cairn, not a trench with skeletons in it. *Jesus!* This was all totally unreal. Was she dreaming? No, she couldn't have made up Rurik and the *seax*, as he'd called it. She hadn't even known what one of those looked like.

'Sigvardr and two more whose names I do not know,' Rurik said. 'Yes, they died and were washed up on the beach. I can't find any of the others.' His words were clipped, the tone showing clearly that he was not in a good mood, and he was biting his teeth together to stop them from chattering. Sara couldn't blame him for being grumpy. He must be freezing, and now he'd been saddled with her, a woman he probably thought of as a thief.

What would he say if she told him she'd found that knife in the twenty-first century? He'd probably think she was completely mad, if he didn't already.

Once down on the sand, he led the way towards a cave at a brisk pace. She had to half run to keep up with his long strides. The sliver of beach left by the high tide was enough to keep their feet dry. It was proper fine sand they were walking on, although near the base of the cliffs lay a border of larger stones and rubble that looked as if it had just been dislodged. Sara felt rather small there under the brooding cliffs. They had to be at least thirty metres tall, soaring above her, and on her other side was nothing but sea and sky. It was a desolate place, but at the same time achingly beautiful.

In one direction, the cliffs swept towards the two rock formations she'd noticed earlier. Seabirds swooped and dived nearby, their nests obviously built on this sanctuary. Looking the other way, the curve of the beach ended in a headland with outcrops of rock continuing into the sea. She guessed this must be where Rurik's ship had foundered, as it looked treacherous, the spray of the waves showing the force of the currents out there.

'Here we are.' Rurik's voice recalled her to the present. He'd stopped by the cave, which was wedged into a corner where the cliff protruded slightly. It had two entrances, with a large stack of limestone in between. Inside was soft sand at first, but further in, more of the large stones were heaped against the back wall, which was only a couple of metres from the opening. Sara saw the remains of a fire and some clothes draped over stones around it, while other garments hung on bits of the cave walls that stuck out slightly, like improvised hooks. She followed him cautiously and perched on a rock near the cave's entrance, where she'd be able to make a run for it if he showed any psychopathic tendencies. Looking out, she saw the sea framed in a crude doorway, an unexpectedly beautiful view. If she'd had a pencil and paper to hand, she would have loved to sketch it.

Rurik ignored her and picked up a shirt, shaking it out. 'Dry enough,' he muttered, and pulled it over his head. Sara couldn't help but stare at the play of muscles on his chest and toned stomach as he did so – an equally intriguing view. Her cheeks heated up and she turned away, instead looking around the cave.

It wasn't exactly cosy, but at least it afforded some protection from the elements. In here you couldn't feel the wind, and with a fire going, it would be warm enough this time of year. She should have felt afraid, being alone in this desolate spot with a strange man – *a Viking, for goodness' sake!* – but she wasn't, not any more. It was as if all her senses were numb, still reeling from what had happened. And surely if he'd wanted to harm her, he would have done so already? Or was he waiting to do it here in private?

Damn, she shouldn't have allowed him to take that knife away from her.

She swallowed hard and turned back to watch him again as he continued to dress himself. The shirt looked to be made of linen and was of a simple construction. Over it he pulled on a dark green woollen tunic that reached to just below mid thigh, and cinched a belt round his waist. It was probably still damp and crusty from the sea water, as the leather was dark. He'd already been wearing those narrow trousers, but he put a woollen pair on top now. To the belt was added all manner of things – a leather pouch, a whetstone, a knife almost as long as the one she'd been holding, hanging horizontally across his abdomen, and an axe. The rest of the clothing he folded and crammed into a rectangular wooden box.

'My travelling kist,' he said, by way of explanation, as if he'd read the question in her eyes.

Sara nodded. She didn't have any luggage, obviously. Didn't have anything other than the clothes she was wearing and her phone, which she could still feel in the back pocket of her jeans. The loupe seemed to have disappeared – maybe she had dropped it. She couldn't remember. Should she show him the mobile and explain what she thought had happened? No, he might kill her on the spot, branding her a witch or something.

Focus, Sara. Make a plan. There had to be something she could do. Perhaps it would be possible to find the *seax* when the tide went out? It was quite heavy, so there was a minute chance that it had stayed near the beach and could be spotted as the water receded. She'd have to try and look for it. All hope was not lost until she'd done that.

And if she couldn't find it? Time enough to panic then, she told herself sternly, and tried to ignore the butterflies dancing in her stomach.

'Here. This might make you feel safer.'

Sara looked up and found Rurik standing in front of her, holding out a long knife in a leather sheath. It was about the same size as the one she'd had earlier, but the handle was different. She blinked in confusion. 'From what?'

'Me?' He gave her a lopsided smile, which for some reason sent the butterflies into a frenzy, although not in a bad way. She realised it was the first time she'd seen him smile.

And yes, he had dimples. *Typical!*

But that was neither here nor there. 'Um, thank you.' She took the knife and pulled it halfway out of the sheath.

'It is sharp, well honed. The leather is still damp, though. I found it in a chest that had floated ashore yesterday.'

The dampness wasn't the problem, but Sara couldn't tell him

that. One knife was probably as good as another to him. But as she studied the blade of this new one, there was no writing on either side. No runes, and therefore not a time-travelling device. Useless. Perhaps it was worth a try, though? Just to make sure? '*Með blōð skaltu ferðast*,' she whispered, so quietly he couldn't possibly hear the words, then made a cut in her finger with the blade, pretending she'd done it by mistake. 'Ouch!'

'Have a care! I told you, it is exceedingly sharp.' He bent to look at her finger, but she covered it from view with her other hand and he straightened up again.

'It is fine.' She waited a moment to see if anything would happen, but of course it didn't. She'd been grasping at straws. Even so, she couldn't help but feel disappointment surge through her.

Rurik crossed his arms over that muscular chest again and seemed to be waiting for her to say something else. Or was he expecting her to leave now? She couldn't. There was only one thing for it – she had to play for time.

'I . . . I do not feel good.' She pretended to shiver and saw his brows come down into a deep frown.

Summoning her best acting skills – which were pretty much non-existent usually – she dropped the new knife and buried her face in her hands, faking a sob. Actually, when she thought about it, there was no need for acting. The situation she was in was truly terrifying. She couldn't be sure that she had travelled through time, not until she saw more of the countryside and people hereabouts, but deep down, she just knew.

And her only way back had disappeared.

'Sara?' Rurik hunkered down in front of her and removed her hands, staring into her eyes. The look she gave him was as desolate as the sea had been the day before, making him feel ungracious for not wanting to help her more.

'I . . . am in the wrong place,' she finally whispered. 'And I feel weak, not well . . .'

The wrong place or the wrong time? The question was on the tip of his tongue, but what if he was imagining things? She would think him a halfwit if he started asking her about the future and it turned out she was merely a Balt or a Slav.

'Can you find your way to the right place?' That was an ambiguous way of putting it and didn't give away his suspicions.

She closed her eyes and pulled in a long breath. 'I don't know.'

Rurik could see that she was overwhelmed and he'd need to give her time to allow the situation to sink in. Fear was stopping her from accepting what had happened, and he couldn't blame her, if his hunch proved correct. It must be truly terrifying to be stuck in a different time to the one you were used to. For now, he would have to let her be until she had recovered enough to think rationally.

He went to fetch a cloak that was more or less dry and spread it on the sand by her feet. 'Here, lie down for a while and rest.'

She didn't protest, but did as he suggested, curling herself into a ball of misery. Rurik bit his lip. It could be an act to catch him unawares so that she could steal something else, but all his valuables were well hidden. If it was a ruse, it would be to no avail. And perhaps she hadn't stolen the *seax* at all – she might have found it in another time. He shook his head. That thought was just too strange for words.

'I must go and try to find us something to eat. You should be safe here, but keep this with you at all times.' He picked up the knife she'd dropped and placed it next to her.

She nodded. '*OK* . . . I mean, yes.'

'Good. I may be some time. Wish me luck. I'm not sure the *Engilskir* will be willing to sell me anything.'

Provided he could even find any of them – he might be far

from any habitation. There was only one way to find out. And with a bit of luck, perhaps Sara would have gone back to her own time when he returned. Mayhap the gods could transport her in some way without the use of a magical item? He'd make sure to give them all the time they needed.

Sara waited a while in case Rurik came back for some reason, but when she judged that enough time had passed, she got to her feet. She had readily agreed to his suggestion that she stay behind while he went in search of food, but had no intention of remaining in the cave. The tide was ebbing now and she needed to look for that *seax*. If only she could find it, she'd be gone by the time he returned. That would be the best possible outcome for both of them.

She picked up her new knife, took a deep breath and set off towards the path that led to the top of the cliff as fast as she could. The first thing she had to do was try to judge where on the beach to look, and that could only be done from the top.

It was a lot harder going up than down, at least when you were on your own. Several times she slithered on the loose stones, which rustled off in mini avalanches, bouncing on the cliff face. Once, she made the mistake of looking back towards the beach, which already seemed a long way below her. Dizziness assailed her and she sank to her knees in order not to fall. 'Come on, you can do this!' she whispered to herself. And she had to hurry, before Rurik came back.

With a lot of determination and no further peeking downwards, at last she made it to the top. By this time, her thigh muscles were burning, even though she knew herself to be reasonably fit. Quickly she headed over to the newly created grave mound, and from there to the edge of the cliff. This time she approached it more cautiously, having seen from below how the grass overhung the limestone in some places. She didn't want to risk tumbling head first on to the sand and rocks below.

The waves were receding, leaving behind large whitish boulders covered in seaweed. Sara held up a hand to protect her eyes from the light and scanned the beach. She tried to calculate how far from the path she was, noting particular stone combinations at the water's edge.

'Right, let's do this.'

Hurrying again, she made her way back down on to the sand. The descent was even scarier this time, without Rurik to brace herself against, but she held her breath and kept her eyes resolutely averted from the drop next to her. A few times she had to almost scoot down on her bottom, but at last she made it. On shaking legs, she approached the lapping waves, trying to spot the boulders she'd seen from above.

Everything looked different down here, though, and she couldn't be sure she had the right place. She paced back and forth, staring into the water as she went, while at the same time admiring the intense neon green of the seaweed covering the boulders. It looked spongy and inviting, but this was not the time to be noticing such things.

'Come on, come *on*!' she muttered. 'Where are you?' The knife had to be here somewhere. Surely it was too heavy to be dragged out to sea so soon?

But even though she widened her search area, the *seax* was nowhere to be seen, and in the end, she had to admit defeat. Swallowing down tears of frustration, she dragged herself back to the cave and sank down on to the cloak. A scream was building in her throat, but she bit her teeth together hard and tried to stem the tide of panic rushing through her. It threatened to drown her, like the North Sea had obviously done to the knife, but she refused to let it.

'Damn it all!' she shouted, the words echoing around the cave walls. 'This is so unfair!'

Her thoughts turned to Linnea. Was this how she had felt when she travelled back in time? From what her friend had told her, it had taken her a while to realise that was what had happened, and she'd been very confused. Sara wasn't – even though Rurik was the only person she'd met so far, she just knew she wasn't in her own time. The question was, what could she do about it?

The *seax* was gone, but Linnea had also travelled through time using a magical item – a brooch in her case. If Sara had ended up in roughly the same era – and that was a big if, since the Viking age had lasted hundreds of years – she could try to find her way to Sweden and her friend. Linnea would be able to help her, if she was there. If not, at least if Sara went to the place where her friend had lived, or was going to live – depending on which year this was – all she'd have to do was look for a brooch with an inscription. Then she'd have her passport home. It had to be possible.

Well, it was a plan. The only one she had right now. It would require courage and determination, but it could be done. As long as she managed to stay safe and alive until she found a way of leaving England. She'd have to persuade Rurik to let her tag along with him to Jorvik. At the moment, he seemed the least threatening of her options, and looked like he'd be able to defend her if need be. What was called York in her time had been a hub of activity in the Viking era, and a trading port with connections to the Continent. From there she should be able to find a ship going to Denmark or even Sweden itself without any problems. Perfect.

Her breathing calmed and her heart rate slowed down a couple of notches. All was not lost. Yet. 'You've just got to learn to survive here for a while,' she muttered. Easier said than done, perhaps, but Linnea had done it. Why not Sara?

Something her Grandpa Lars had said flashed through her

mind. 'Look on the bright side. There's always a silver lining.' He'd been talking about her break-up from Anders, claiming that she was better off finding out what a bastard the guy was before it was too late. But perhaps it was a motto that applied here too, if you thought about it. This really was a unique experience. After all, how many people got to travel through time? It had sounded quite exciting when Linnea told them of her adventures – and of falling in love with a hunky Viking – and if Sara was honest, she'd been just a teensy bit jealous. Well, OK, a lot jealous. Her own life had been far from a bed of roses lately, and getting away from it all was extremely tempting.

She snorted. 'I hadn't counted on going quite *this* far.' And she wouldn't exactly call it an adventure right now – she was still too scared for that – but would it be so bad to be here for a while? Say, a couple of weeks? Months, even? She was a jewellery designer who specialised in Viking and Anglo-Saxon motifs – where better to study them than in their original environment? If she could stay with Rurik, she might be OK. She'd understood from Linnea that the Viking age wasn't always ideal when you were a woman and alone, but with a strong man as protection, she wouldn't have to worry about that.

Yes, when you looked at it like that, this was quite possibly the opportunity of a lifetime. Her grandfather would definitely have thought so, seeing as how he was obsessed with the Vikings. He would have loved every minute, despite the dangers. It was ironic that she should have been the one to end up here and not him. What would he think when he heard she'd gone missing? He'd probably assume the worst, and her heart ached for the agony he'd be going through. He was her closest living relative since her parents had died in the car crash that had almost killed her too, and he must be worried sick about her by now. There was an outside chance that he would put two and two together and realise her disappearance was very similar to Linnea's. He was a clever man, after all, but it might seem too fantastical. If only she could send him a message, but of course that was impossible. She swallowed down the lump of misery that was forming in her throat. Would she ever see him again? Have a chance to tell him about this? She certainly hoped so, but for now, she was on her own.

'I can do this,' she whispered, trying to be positive. 'My turn to have an adventure.'

But in truth, right now it felt more like a nightmare.

Chapter Five

Outside the cave, it was starting to get dark, which made Sara jumpy and nervous. What if Rurik didn't come back? Someone could have killed him, or he might have decided that his belongings – and Sara – weren't worth returning for. She had no idea how much time had passed since he'd left. It seemed like for ever. She tried checking her mobile phone, but realised how stupid that was. Although it still had some battery life left, the time was stuck and all the other functions frozen. Obviously it couldn't tell the time or update itself without access to some satellite or other. *Duh!*

When she heard footsteps scuffing the sand on the beach nearby, she tensed and gripped the handle of her knife until she heard Rurik's voice.

'Sara?'

She relaxed. 'Yes, here.'

He came into view carrying a pile of wood and with a small cauldron hanging off one arm. On the other dangled a dead hare – at least, she hoped it was dead or else she felt very sorry for it having its front legs tied together like that. It might have been her imagination, but was that a fleeting expression of disappointment she'd seen before he masked it? Had he expected her to be gone? Too bad. Unfortunately for him, she was staying whether he liked it or not.

'Is all well?' he asked, dumping the wood on the ground and setting his other burdens down on to a flattish boulder. 'You'll never guess what I—'

She cut him off, her rumbling stomach reminding her of just how long it had been since she ate. 'You have food?' She couldn't look at the hare. Somehow she'd expected him to come back with bread and cheese or something.

'Mm-hmm. The family in the only dwelling nearby were very poor. They sold me this pot, the hare and some barley, but that was all.' He shook his head. 'They were exceedingly wary of me. Apparently there have been Danes roaming these parts who just take what they want without paying or asking first. But listen . . .'

'*The Heathen Army*,' she muttered in English, not really registering the rest of his tale. She could understand the locals not wanting anything to do with the Vikings. From what she remembered of British history, this was a time of marauders and berserkers who struck fear into the local population and looted wherever they went.

'What was that?'

'The *micel hæðen here*?' For some reason she remembered what the Anglo-Saxons had called it. She'd read that somewhere.

'Ah, I see. I doubt it is that large a group, although now you come to mention it, I did hear Sigvardr talk about an army. You speak *Enska*, the *Engilskr tungu*?'

'No.' In a way, she did, but he wouldn't consider her English the same thing, as it had changed out of all recognition down the years. She also spoke Swedish – it was her first language – but that didn't bear much resemblance to Old Norse either, having evolved just as much.

Before he could ask any more questions, she jumped in with

the one uppermost in her own mind. 'Rurik, please can I stay with you? Go to Jorvik?'

His eyebrows shot up and he stared at her. 'You want to stay here?'

She nodded. 'Yes, for a . . . time.' She couldn't remember the Old Norse words for 'a little while'.

'But I f—'

Determined to persuade him at all costs, she blurted out, 'I want to see Jorvik! Very much.' She stared at him beseechingly. He was her only hope.

'Are you sure? You no longer wish to go home?' He was looking extremely dubious now, his gaze intense. Sara got the feeling he wasn't at all happy about this, and as if to confirm it, he shook his head, scowling.

He was going to say no, she just knew it, and the thought of being stranded here alone and defenceless made her panic. Her mouth went dry and her heart started racing, making her breathless. It wasn't that she didn't want to go home – of course she did – but that was impossible from here. And if he didn't let her stay with him, she'd be lost. As good as dead, really. She needed him to guide her through this terrifying place and protect her. She'd never make it to Sweden on her own. In fact, she probably wouldn't make it to the nearest village in one piece, being way out of her depth here. 'Yes, I'm very sure. Please, Rurik? Please! I . . . I will try not to be a, um . . . in your way.' She didn't know the word for 'nuisance' but hoped he understood that was what she meant.

'I don't know.' He hesitated. 'I had not reckoned on having a travelling companion. I was heading for Jorvik alone.' He emphasised the word 'alone', as if solitude had been one of his main goals. Sara wondered why, but that was not her biggest concern right now.

'I hear it is a . . . a wonderful town. Interesting. Lots of people and . . . and goods. Please will you take me there? Then, after, I will leave, I promise.' As long as she could find the wherewithal to pay for passage to Sweden, but that was a problem for later. She couldn't reimburse him for his assistance either, but he hadn't mentioned it so she kept that thought to herself.

He was quiet for so long she thought the suspense would kill her, but finally he gave a curt nod.

'Very well. But you stay at your own risk,' he warned. He glanced at her clothes, frowning. 'And you can't wear that, whatever it is. You will attract too much attention. Best to blend in.' He opened his kist and took out the pile of clothes he'd put in there earlier. 'You'll have to wear some of mine.'

'Men's clothes?' Sara looked at him. Did women wear male clothing in this era? Wouldn't that draw even more attention? But it wasn't as if she had a choice; she couldn't possibly go around in twenty-first-century gear. He was right about that.

Rurik shrugged. 'It is not ideal and I know it is forbidden in some places for women to don men's garments, but it is all I have for now. Here. We will need to burn yours.' He handed over some of the clothes.

'Thank you.'

'You are absolutely sure you would not rather return to your . . . home?' He gave her a hard stare, as if he was willing her to say yes.

Sara wished she could, but . . . 'No.' She shook her head. 'Not yet.'

'Then so be it, but if at any time you change your mind, tell me.'

'I will.' *When we get to Jorvik*. But she didn't say that out loud.

She looked for a secluded place to change, but there were only two small alcoves filled with rocks at the back of the cave. Nothing to hide behind. 'Er . . . can you turn?' She frowned at Rurik, although he appeared to be busy lighting a fire with the wood he'd brought. For a moment, she became distracted, watching him strike a fire iron against a piece of flint and raining sparks down on to a bundle of dry grass, which quickly started burning, but then he looked up.

'What? Oh, yes, yes.' He flapped a hand at her as if he had no intention of watching.

Sara hesitated, then turned her back on him. Perhaps he had no interest in her as a woman. She would just have to hurry, but she'd be on her guard in case he intended to jump her. The knife was still in her hand, and it gave her a sense of safety when she placed it against the cave wall in front of her, within easy reach.

She shrugged out of her warm jacket and immediately regretted its absence. It might be warmer inside the cave than on the beach, but it was still chilly. She shivered and pulled off her sweater and T-shirt as well, then looked through the pile of new clothes. There was a linen shirt like the one he'd put on earlier. It looked clean, thank goodness, and a cautious sniff confirmed that it didn't stink of someone else's BO. Instead, it had a faint scent of the ocean; perhaps he hadn't quite managed to get all the salt water out when he'd rinsed it. She pulled it over her head and tugged it down over her hips, then rolled up the sleeves a bit so that they wouldn't cover her hands. It was much too big for her.

'Ahem. You have to remove the . . . er, tiny undergarment too,' Rurik commented from behind her.

Sara swung around and glared at him. 'You should not look!' she said accusingly.

'Well, it's a good thing I did or you would have forgotten.' He didn't seem contrite and instead flashed her a mischievous grin that sent a spark shooting through her. It made a nice change from his usual scowl, but she couldn't let it distract her.

He was right, though. If anyone here saw her wearing a bra – and it did show through the linen of the shirt, no question about that – they'd find it very strange, and it would give rise to all sorts of questions. It had to go. She undid the clasp at the back and managed to disentangle herself from it without removing the shirt completely. As she dropped the bra on to the ground, she heard a quiet chuckle, but ignored it. Being without it felt strange but oddly liberating. She kind of wished she was a smaller size, as that would probably have been easier, but she'd get used to the sensation of freedom, she was sure.

A woollen tunic came next, and that too was pulled over her head. Presumably it had three-quarter-length sleeves when Rurik wore it and was thigh length, but on her the sleeves reached all the way down past her wrists and the hem was below her knees. She heard another muffled chuckle but again ignored it. Unless he had a needle and thread, there was nothing she could do to alter these garments. She wriggled out of her jeans and Timberland boots – she'd definitely miss those – and started to pull on a pair of trousers made of linen.

Rurik cleared his throat behind her again. 'Um, the other tiny undergarment too, Sara.'

'Huh?' She swivelled round to stare at him, and he pointed vaguely in the direction of her behind. 'Oh!' She felt her cheeks heat up. How did he know she was still wearing her underwear? Was he psychic? And surely she wasn't meant to be completely naked underneath the trousers?

But he nodded as if confirming this. 'All your own clothes.'

'Oh, very well.' She tugged them off and threw them on to the ground next to her before dressing in the linen trousers again, followed by a pair of woollen ones on top, both tied with a drawstring. This would take some getting used to, as she felt half naked without her underwear. For her feet there were strange crocheted socks and a pair of leather shoes fastened with a toggle. They were sort of like 1980s pixie boots, a bit pointy and with a flat sole without any heel. She thought they'd seen better days, as they were quite worn. And unfortunately a size too big, as well as a bit damp and crusty.

She glanced at Rurik's feet, which looked a lot bigger. 'These are yours?' she asked, pointing at the shoes.

'No, someone else's. I am sorry they're still wet – they should dry if you put your feet by the fire.'

Just brilliant – damp feet. Maybe staying here wasn't going to be so great after all. And she felt ridiculous in this outfit.

'Happy?' She turned to show him that she was dressed and spread her hands out as if to say *ta-dah!*

He shook his head. 'Not quite.'

Coming over to stand before her, he unhooked a belt that had been hanging off his own. Sara hadn't noticed it, but saw now that it was a bit shorter and obviously made for someone with a smaller waist. 'Where did you find this?'

'Some of the other people's belongings floated to shore and this was in a sea chest.'

So now she'd be wearing a dead person's belt as well as their shoes. Fantastic.

Rurik reached around her and fastened the belt for her. She held her breath, as it seemed like an intimate thing to do; he was so close she could smell the tang of the sea in his hair. Although it was quite gloomy inside the cave now, she noticed that he'd pulled it into a tail at the back of his head, tying it with a string of some sort, and the golden waves hung down past his neck, glinting in the light from the fire. Again she had the urge to draw him, as the shadows played across the planes of his face. His hands nudged her waist as he gauged how tight the belt should be, and a tremor shot through her at this slight touch. She ignored it, telling herself she was just cold and on edge.

'There. Now all you need is the cloak.' He stepped back and pointed at the final garment, which was still lying on the sand. 'I think I have a pin you could use in my kist. Let me have a look.'

'Thank you.' Sara picked up the cloak and shook off the sand. It was made of heavy-duty wool with some sort of woven band around the edges. It appeared to have been fashioned out of three or four panels of material, sewn together to make a bell shape. As she draped it across her shoulders, it enveloped her like a cocoon, fitting perfectly, and felt quite weighty, swirling round her ankles in a rather satisfying way. It was lovely and warm but smelled a bit like wet dog. She wrinkled her nose, even though she knew she ought to be grateful.

As Rurik rummaged in his chest, she gathered up her pile of modern clothes and felt the mobile in the pocket of her jeans, as well as her car key. She'd left her wallet in the car earlier – well, back in her own time – but she couldn't keep these things. Swiftly she scuffed a hole in the sand near the cave wall and buried both items. She'd have to come back for them one day, or else live without them. Finally she fastened the leather sheath containing the new knife to her belt.

'What shall I do with these?' she asked, indicating her clothes.

Rurik glanced over his shoulder. 'Burn them.'

'But . . .' That jacket was almost brand new, and she hadn't had the Timberlands for long either. Both were expensive items.

'Sara . . .' His voice held a note of warning, and she gave in. He was probably right.

'Fine.' She crouched by the fire and began to feed the voracious flames. It wasn't long before her clothes were all gone. All that was left was a lingering smell from the burning of the feathers that had filled her padded Burberry jacket, and the metal buttons from that and her jeans. Rurik told her to leave those, as he'd bury them when the fire had gone out. The Timberlands proved more of a challenge – the leather burned eventually, but as the flames reached the soles, the cave began to fill with a foul smoke.

'*Pah!* No!' Rurik used a stick to push the boots out of the fire, throwing some sand over them. 'What *is* that?' He flapped a hand in front of his nose as the stench of burning rubber surrounded them.

Sara shrugged. There was no way of explaining it to him.

'We'll bury those too,' he decided. 'That is a horrible smell!'

As she watched him cover them with sand, Sara felt as though her former life was being buried with them. The modern Sara was gone, at least for now.

Rurik hadn't been surprised to find Sara still in the cave, but he'd brought the solution to the problem. Earlier, as he'd set off in search of food, almost the first thing he saw on his way to the path was the *seax* he'd thrown off the cliff. The tide was on its way out and the knife was sticking up, its blade buried deep in the sand. That was probably why it was still there. Either that, or the sea god was trying to tell him something – that he should send Sara back to her own time.

'Very well,' he'd said out loud. If Ægir and Rán didn't want his offering, so be it. He picked it up and hung it off the back of his belt for now. He could give it to Sara later.

When he'd returned, she seemed recovered, sitting up and with more colour in her cheeks. He hoped that meant she was over the shock and ready to travel back – or forward in this case – to where she'd come from. He'd tried to tell her the good news immediately, but she'd cut him off and then distracted him with her mention of a great army. Then, before he could return to the subject, she'd surprised him with her question.

She wanted to stay here? In his time? Why?

His first, instinctive reaction was to refuse absolutely. He didn't need the added burden of looking after someone else, and he had no doubt he'd be acting the nursemaid if he let Sara come along on the journey to Jorvik. She seemed not to know the first thing about anything. And why should he take care of her? She was nothing to him. No, the gods had probably sent her to test him in some way, but had changed their minds and given him the means to send her back. He ought to do that at once.

Her desperate expression gave him pause, though. There had to be some reason why she wanted to see Jorvik so badly, but he couldn't fathom it out. He tried looking at it from her point of view – if he'd suddenly been transported to another time, would he not be curious about it? Want to learn more while he could? That made sense. There was nothing wrong with having an adventure now and again; it made life more exciting. Was there really any harm in letting her stay for a time?

He took a moment to consider and realised that it could be interesting to find out more about her too before she left. He had lots of questions he'd never dared ask his brother about the future, and here was his chance. The only downside was that he'd have to watch her like a hawk. She was as helpless as a newborn, and completely out of her element. He had to assume she knew nothing about his time and couldn't leave her to fend for herself at any point. It would be a bind, but he could put up with it for a short while.

Earlier, while walking, he'd had time to think. He had surmised that the gods might have sent Sara to this particular place – and to him – for a reason. He was the only person here who would believe her if she got round to confessing where she was from. All this indicated strongly that she was meant to be here, and the purpose of her presence would become known to both of them in due course. Although if she was meant to stay, why they'd given him back the *seax* was a mystery. As a precaution, perhaps? A safeguard? The gods in their wisdom would no doubt reveal all.

When they felt like it.

Rurik gave in. She could remain, as long as she was absolutely certain that was her wish.

It would be on his terms, though, and first of all he needed to make her blend in. That meant starting with the way she was dressed. The other time traveller he knew, his sister-in-law Linnea, had arrived in his time wearing summer garments – thin and unbelievably stretchy. Sara's clothes were different in that they were probably meant for colder weather, as they looked thick and sturdy, but once she'd started to take them off, he had glimpsed what was underneath. He and his brothers had been especially intrigued by Linnea's underclothes, and he was now totally convinced that Sara was a time traveller – that breast-holder she'd been wearing was almost identical to the one he'd seen before, and he was sure no women in his time wore such a thing, no matter where they were from. But when would she admit it?

Linnea had tried to tell his brother she was from the future as soon as she'd realised it herself, although Hrafn hadn't believed her then. Sara, on the other hand, apparently wasn't planning on telling Rurik. Should he confront her and ask outright, or wait until she was ready to confess? It was probably better to wait. One thing at a time.

There was something else he needed to know, though. He'd noticed that Sara's back and legs were criss-crossed with scars. Fairly recent, though well healed judging by their pale colour, but visible nonetheless and quite extensive. 'Did someone hurt you?' he asked casually, trying to make his tone gentle in case it was something she'd rather not think about. She must have been in horrendous pain, whatever had happened to her. An attack on her home settlement, perhaps?

'What? Oh, you mean . . . my wounds?' Her face became suffused with colour. 'Very ugly, I know.'

'Scars.' She obviously didn't know the word. 'And no, they are not ugly.' He could tell she was self-conscious about them, but there was no need. Scars were not uncommon. He had quite a few himself.

'I was in a . . . misfortune?' She frowned, as if trying to find the right way to explain.

'An accident? A fight?' He would have guessed someone had cut her with a sword or an axe. How she was still walking normally was a mystery. Some of the biggest scars had been all the way down one thigh. He'd bet all his silver that leg had been broken and she ought to be limping badly.

She shook her head. 'No, not a fight. A wagon going fast. It hit another wagon and broke. My leg broke too and my . . . inside.' She gestured towards her lower back and stomach.

Odin's ravens, that must have been quite a collision. And if she'd been in between two wagons, her injuries would have been severe. Rurik found it hard to believe anyone could survive that, but she looked fit and healthy now. 'You must have had a very good healer.'

She smiled, as if his comment amused her. 'Yes, very good.'

At least now he knew she hadn't been molested or deliberately hurt by someone – that sort of thing left terrible scars in a person's mind as well and would be difficult to deal with. Another thing intrigued him – the fact that she appeared to be sunburned all over, which would indicate that she'd been walking around almost naked during the summer. Apart from wearing the breast-holder and tiny undergarment, as there had been white marks on her skin matching those. Fascinating.

Thralls always had tanned arms and faces from working outdoors all year round, but they never shed their clothing. Could Sara have been someone's thrall in the future, without clothes? But she'd been adamant that they did not exist. He'd have to find out more, but decided now was not the time to ask about that. If only he'd been able to talk to Linnea about these things, he would have been more knowledgeable, but truth to tell, he'd spent most of his time avoiding her so he wouldn't stare at her like a lovelorn *fifl*.

Now he was tired and hungry, and dealing with both those matters was more urgent.

Chapter Six

'Right. Food.' Rurik took out a sharp knife from his leather pouch and picked up the hare. It was lucky the people at the farmstead he'd found had been willing to let him buy it, as the food Sigvardr had brought was at the bottom of the sea.

'I come in peace,' was the first thing he'd told them. Although they spoke *Enska*, he knew they'd understand him, as their languages weren't that different. Basic words were similar and you could indicate your meaning with gestures too, of course.

When he'd showed the farmer a handful of silver, the man had nodded and allowed him into the house. A newly killed hare and a small bag of barley was all they'd been able to spare, but that was enough for now.

'What are you doing?'

Rurik looked up to find Sara watching him with a horrified expression.

'Er, preparing our evening meal.' Honestly, what did she think he was doing?

'*Eeeuuuww.*' She made a face as he carried on skinning the creature.

'What? You do not like hare?' Rurik had never met anyone who'd objected to this meat. He'd had it before; it was very tasty and made for a good stew.

'Don't know. I have never tried. But . . . the little animal, it's pretty!'

'Huh?' He stared at her, at a loss as to what the hare's looks had to do with anything.

'How can you kill a . . . thing so sweet?'

Rurik took a deep breath, thoroughly confused. 'You only eat ugly animals?' What madness was this?

'No, but . . .' Suddenly she laughed and shook her head. 'You think I am stupid. I am, yes. It is all food.'

'Mm-hmm.' He watched her for a moment more, then finished skinning the hare and was about to cut its extremities off. 'Um, you'd best look away now.' If she had strange notions about what to eat, perhaps she'd never seen an animal butchered before. He didn't want her being sick or fainting at the sight.

When she turned away, he quickly finished the job and cut the meat into smaller pieces, which he added to the pot. 'I'm just going to fetch some water,' he said, and went out to fill the cauldron. He decided to partly use sea water in order to add a bit of salt to the taste, as he didn't have any herbs. Just hare and barley would be boring.

Sara didn't appear to object to eating the finished stew. In fact, she wolfed it down, only making a face a couple of times when she encountered bones. 'Thank you,' she said after she was done.

'You are welcome. Now we had better sleep. You should be warm enough wrapped in the cloak, but I'll give you something to rest your head on.' He took out another tunic from his kist and folded it for her. He had a lot of extra clothing now, as he'd salvaged everything from the spare sea chest that had floated to shore last night. As no one else seemed to have survived, they wouldn't have need of their garments, but Sara did. 'There. Sleep now. In the morning, we walk south.'

'Why are you going to Jorvik?'

'I am a silversmith and I aim to establish a workshop there and sell my wares.'

'You are?' She surprised him with a big smile that made him suck in a hasty breath. It made her look quite radiant. 'I also.'

'You also what?' Rurik regarded her with his head to one side. She was a strange woman, no doubt about it, and there was much he didn't understand. He still wasn't sure he ought to let her stay, but she intrigued him.

'I am a smith. Silver. Gold. I make beautiful things in my . . . work house.' She gesticulated with her hands as if to illustrate various types of jewellery.

'Workshop,' he corrected automatically. '*You* have your own?' He had heard of wives and children helping their menfolk with their work, especially decorating the pieces of jewellery they made, but he'd never come across a female who was a silversmith in her own right. 'Are you a widow then? You inherited your husband's premises, you mean?'

'No, it is only mine. No husband. I start it myself. I make everything. I can show you, yes?' She was still smiling and he found himself grinning back.

Why not? He'd be interested to see what she could do. Then his smile faded. No, what was he thinking? Hopefully she'd be gone long before they reached his destination, but there was no point mentioning that now. Instead he muttered noncommittally, 'Perhaps, but first we have to reach Jorvik. You are absolutely certain you wish to travel with me?' He knew he sounded grudging, but she didn't seem to notice.

'Yes. Please. I want to come. Learn about your work.'

'Very well.' He was too exhausted to debate the issue further, either with her or himself. 'Get some sleep then. I bid you goodnight.'

And tomorrow he'd confront her about her origins, come what may.

The following morning, they set off, and Sara was almost sad to leave the cave. It felt safe somehow, whereas God only knew what she'd find outside in the strange world she'd ended up in. Or what if she was wrong and Rurik was a weird twenty-first-century man who was just messing with her head?

No, she couldn't be mistaken – she was in his time.

She'd thought she would find it difficult to sleep, but had drifted off almost immediately the night before, reasonably comfortable on the sandy ground despite the fact that it was a lot harder than her springy mattress at home. Perhaps it was all the nervous energy she'd expended that had exhausted her, but either way, she was surprised. She should have been on edge, wary of Rurik and listening out for every little sound, but her body had obviously had enough. Amazingly, she felt very awake now and ready to face the day, whatever it might bring.

She'd slept in her clothes, and it felt odd and a bit decadent not to have a shower or brush her teeth, but she went down to the edge of the sea and at least rinsed her mouth with salt water and washed her hands using sand. It wasn't ideal, but it would have to do for now.

Apart from a terse 'good morning', Rurik was silent as he packed up his things and made sure the fire was properly out. He disappeared for a short while and came back with his hair all wet but neatly combed, and she guessed he must have been to a spring nearby. His clothes were still rather crumpled, but apart from that, his appearance was neat and tidy.

'Time to go.' He picked up the chest with his belongings and nodded towards the now scoured pot and a small sack with a few extra items. 'Please carry those.'

That seemed only fair, so she didn't argue. She followed him along the beach and up the steep incline to the top of the cliffs, then tried to keep up with his long strides as he set off in a southerly direction. His expression was inscrutable – possibly a tad grumpy – and she decided it was probably best not to antagonise him by talking. Perhaps he wasn't a morning person. Or maybe he regretted letting her tag along. She couldn't afford for him to change his mind, so she would tread carefully until she knew him better.

They had walked in silence for quite a while when he suddenly turned to her and asked, 'Where are you from, Sara? Garðariki?'

The question took her by surprise, even though she should have expected it. No, she wasn't from Garðariki, which was what the Vikings called Russia. It was obviously the most foreign place he could think of so she must have looked very exotic to him the day before. But how to explain? Rurik had slowed down and was walking next to her, his kist hoisted on to one shoulder. She'd wondered why he didn't put his belongings into a bundle or pouch of some sort instead. It would have been much easier to carry and not half as heavy, but it wasn't any of her business.

'No, I . . .' Crunch time. Should she tell him or not? She remembered Grandpa Lars saying that the truth was always best. But was it in this case? 'Um, you will not believe me,' she muttered.

'Try.' Although his eyes were narrowed and the look he sent her was fierce, his turquoise gaze seemed direct and Sara had the feeling she could trust him with any secret. Which was ridiculous really, as she hardly knew him.

'I am from another time,' she blurted out, then felt her cheeks heat up. He was going to either laugh at her or tell her she was crazy, or both.

He did neither, just said matter-of-factly, 'I thought so. You are from the future, yes?'

Sara's mouth fell open and she had to force herself to close it. She stopped dead and stared at him. 'You . . . you believe me?' Linnea had told her it had taken her ages to convince any of the people in the past that she'd time-travelled, and no wonder. It was pretty incredible really. She didn't want to believe it herself.

'Yes. I've met . . . others.' Rurik looked serious and not in the slightest bit incredulous. If anything, he seemed more annoyed than before, his mouth set in an uncompromising line.

'Others? There are more?' She knew it. These damned magical items were obviously a lot more common than she'd thought. 'Where?'

'Not here. They are far away.' He shrugged. 'I have travelled a lot.'

'Oh.' That was a shame. She could have asked them for help to go back, or at the very least been given some tips on survival in the Viking age.

'You said you wanted to stay here,' he pointed out. 'Have you changed your mind? You can always—'

She interrupted him quickly. 'No! I mean, yes, I . . . I will stay for a time.' She didn't know whether to mention that she didn't have much choice right now and it was his fault she was stuck here. Perhaps it would be best not to at this point. She didn't want to antagonise him or he might tell her to get lost and fend for herself.

Rurik was scowling again, but he nodded. 'Very well. It may be your destiny.'

'You think?' He could be right. It did seem like too much of a coincidence that she had ended up here only a year or two after the same thing had happened to her best friend.

He muttered something she didn't catch and heaved a sigh. When she looked at him again, he was wearing a long-suffering expression. He was clearly unhappy at being lumbered with her, and it made her feel guilty, but she reasoned that he'd only have to put up with her for a short while. She wasn't intending to stay for ever, and maybe she could make it up to him by teaching him some new jewellery techniques or something?

'You do understand that it is dangerous for you to be here? The other . . . er, time travellers found it difficult to live in my time. It took them a long while to adapt and they were almost killed several times.' He put the kist down on to the ground and crossed his arms, once again drawing her attention to his powerful physique. He was strong and could easily have hurt her, but he hadn't, so he must mean the threat was elsewhere. 'You must promise to listen to me.'

'Yes, I promise. I will try not to be . . .'

'A nuisance?' He raised one eyebrow, as if he was already assuming she would be, which was annoying although possibly accurate.

'Nuisance.' She repeated the Norse word and committed it to memory, understanding from the context what it meant without him having to explain. 'No, I will not be a nuisance.' At least, she sincerely hoped not.

'You give me your oath?'

'I do. I swear I will listen to you.'

He regarded her with what she interpreted as scepticism, and asked again, 'There is nowhere else you can go?'

'No.' What a stupid question – where did he think she could go? It wasn't as if she knew anyone in this century. Well, apart from possibly Linnea. But she didn't say that out loud, as it wouldn't help. She'd have to hope he was gentleman enough not to want to leave a woman to her fate. Not that Vikings had much of a reputation for being gentlemen – far from it. The thought of that almost made her smile, but she also realised she'd been extremely lucky not to come across a veritable brute.

He bit his lip while he contemplated her words, drawing her attention to the perfect shape of his mouth yet again. Honestly, there had to be some part of him that was flawed, surely? 'Very well.' He sighed again. 'But if you wish to stay with me, you will follow my lead if we meet anyone. Do you agree?'

'Yes, I agree.' She'd do whatever it took, and she wasn't stupid. Anyone could see she'd need him to keep her safe.

'Good, then let us continue.'

Rurik hefted the kist on to his shoulder again and stalked off, not bothering to check whether Sara was following. If she was going to survive here, she'd have to learn to keep up. He wasn't a nursemaid and had no intention of altering his plans because of her. In fact, he should have just given her the *seax* and told her to go back to her own time. So why hadn't he? He must be turning into a halfwit, but apart from his hunch that the gods had brought this about and were toying with them, he still found himself unable to refuse her request to stay.

Perhaps it was the earnest look in her amber eyes, which sparkled in the early-morning light, and the fear he saw lurking in their depths. Or the fact that a small part of him was pleased to have his own time traveller, even if she didn't actually belong to him the way Linnea did to his brother. He'd always been curious about the future, but hadn't wanted to spend too much time talking to his sister-in-law. That way lay danger and intense heartache, because he wanted her more than he'd ever wanted any woman before. But Linnea had never had eyes for anyone except Hrafn. The two of them were so in love it was ludicrous. Joined at the hip, completely in tune with each other, and even now they were married and had a child – and possibly another on the way – there was no sign of their love abating.

Rurik knew that to keep his sanity, he had to stay well away from her. He'd had to leave. Now all he had to do was forget her and forge a new life for himself . . .

But here was another time traveller, one he wasn't head over heels in love with, who could presumably answer all his questions. With his heart unaffected, he'd be able to listen to her without being distracted – perfect. As this was all new to her, however, he'd let her become accustomed to his time before badgering her. And he would need to help her learn to speak his language better too, so that she'd be able to explain things to him. She wasn't doing too badly, but there were obvious gaps in her knowledge and she was lacking words. No matter, she'd soon acquire them.

They followed the wild and windswept coastline in a southerly direction, walking for hours without coming across any habitation. Rurik was getting hungry. The last of the stew had been shared before they left that morning, and he knew he'd have to find something else for them to eat soon. 'Let us head inland,' he suggested. There might be a greater chance of coming across either people or a forest, both of which could provide sustenance.

Sara trudged after him without commenting. He could tell she was having a bit of trouble walking in shoes that were too big for her, but she didn't complain. Good. He didn't want to listen to endless moaning. If she was staying for any length of time, however, he'd have to buy her new ones as soon as they found a market of any kind, or her feet would become raw from chafing. But apart from that, she did not appear to be tired. She must be used to walking.

The landscape changed and became a mixture of farmland and wooded areas, hilly but not unduly so. To Rurik's relief, they came to a small river teeming with fish – trout if he wasn't mistaken – and he fashioned fishing rods for them both out of strong hazel branches and some hooks he'd brought.

'Have you fished before?' Linnea had, he remembered, but he wasn't sure if everyone in the future would be taught this skill.

'Yes.' Sara proved it by baiting her own hook with a squirming worm without flinching, something not everyone relished.

It wasn't long before they'd landed a respectable catch, enough for a midday meal.

'Can you collect some wood for a fire, please? I'll gut the fish,' he said.

She nodded and, without him asking, built a small stone circle to contain the fire.

'Good. So you learn that in your time as well?'

'Not all people, but some.' She watched with interest as he struck sparks with his fire iron, blowing on them when they landed on the dry moss he'd picked up to use as tinder. 'Is it difficult?'

Rurik shrugged. 'Not if you practise. I will teach you, but not today.' He glanced about, alert to all the sounds around them. 'I want to continue as far as possible.' The Saxon farmer's obvious wariness and talk of roaming groups of men had made him uneasy. He wasn't afraid, but he'd rather stay out of their way in order to reach his destination faster.

The fish tasted good and was soon eaten. For the rest of the day, they followed various tracks, trying to stick to a southerly route. They didn't always go in a straight line, but as long as they were going in roughly the right direction, that was fine. Towards dusk, Rurik spotted a farmstead in the distance.

'Let us go and see if we can be allowed to sleep in their barn,' he said. Although he'd slept outdoors many a time, a barn full of sweet-smelling hay was definitely preferable.

As they approached the buildings, however, it soon became clear that something was amiss. Rurik stopped, sniffing the air, and held out a hand to prevent Sara from continuing onwards. 'I can smell burning.'

'What?' She glanced at him, anxiety flashing in her gaze. 'Not from a hearth?'

'No, something much bigger. Look at that plume of smoke.' A thick cloud of it spiralled into the air in a sudden puff beyond the nearest building. Rurik decided extreme caution was needed. 'Wait here.'

Using trees and clumps of bushes as cover, he made his way over to the farm buildings, scanning the area for signs of life or danger. All seemed quiet, almost eerily so. Dashing across an open patch as quickly as possible, holding his axe in readiness for a fight, he peered round the corner of a building that was seemingly not on fire and saw a yard devoid of movement. There were no sounds of any kind; even the birds seemed to have stopped singing. Whoever had lived here was obviously gone, as were their attackers, else he would have heard them in the process of raiding the place. He beckoned to Sara, who came sprinting over to him.

'All good?'

'Not exactly.' Rurik walked slowly into the farmyard and stopped again, listening intently.

'Oh no!' Sara exclaimed, staring at the smouldering remains of what must have been a fairly large dwelling directly in front of them. 'What happened?'

Rurik bit his teeth together. 'Marauders.' He called out, 'Hello? Is anyone here?' His voice echoed among what was left of the buildings, but there was no reply. A small noise of distress from Sara made him turn to see the body of a man slumped against a wall just around a corner. If it hadn't been for the open eyes staring sightlessly at the sky, and the copious amounts of blood on his shirt and tunic, he could have been resting. Rurik couldn't detect the smell of decay and guessed this place had been attacked fairly recently.

At first he was inclined to leave immediately, but then he reasoned that whoever had done this must have taken what they wanted and gone. If they'd intended to stay, they wouldn't have torched the main house. He made a quick search of the other buildings, telling Sara to stay outside, which was just as well, since he found the rest of the man's family and other inhabitants all slaughtered in the most gruesome fashion. Women, children and a couple of old people, not one of them left alive. And the food stores were completely empty. The only thing left was a chicken clucking forlornly to itself inside one of the outbuildings. *Aumingi!* Why had it been necessary to kill these ordinary people? They'd probably have gladly given up their possessions in return for their lives. He went back outside with a sigh.

'We stay?' Sara was looking around with big eyes and kept glancing at the dead man. Rurik guessed she'd never seen a deceased person before, or at least not one who'd been murdered.

'Yes. And there is our evening meal.' He pointed to the chicken, then teased, 'Or is it too pretty for you to eat?'

Sara punched him on the arm and said '*Fifl!*', then alarm flared in her eyes as if she wasn't sure whether he'd retaliate or become angry with her.

Rurik just moved out of her reach. Not because she'd hurt him, but as a joke to ease the tension he sensed in her. Even though he was still annoyed about her presence, there was no need for her to fear him. 'Let us choose somewhere to sleep tonight.'

There wasn't much choice, but fortunately whoever had raided the farm hadn't bothered to take all the hay, and he told Sara to spread her cloak on the softest part. 'You'd better stay here while I see about that chicken.'

'*OK*.'

'Is that a yes in your language? Oh-kay?'

'Yes.'

'Hmm, I'll have to teach you more of my words instead.'

He went in search of the unfortunate fowl.

Chapter Seven

'Don't look, but I think we have a visitor.' Sara continued to eat the piece of roast chicken she was holding, but tried not to make any sudden moves.

Rurik's head came up, his expression wary as his eyebrows knitted. Slowly he reached for the axe hanging off his belt. 'Where?' He sounded frighteningly intense, and Sara was glad he was on her side. Having seen what had happened at this farm, she'd come to realise just how dangerous a situation she was in. Staying in the Viking era was definitely not going to be a walk in the park. These were violent times and none of the rules or laws she was used to meant anything here. But she had Rurik to protect her, thank goodness; she wasn't alone. There was no need for violence now, though, and she smiled as she replied.

'No axe. It is a dog. Behind you.'

Rurik relaxed and put the axe back. 'Oh.' He turned his head and looked at the shaggy creature regarding them warily from the open doorway. 'At least someone escaped with their life,' he muttered, then held out a piece of chicken. 'Here, boy, do you want some? You must be starving.'

The dog's head came up and its nostrils flared as the smell of food reached it. Sara couldn't see if the canine was hurt, but she guessed the attackers might have scared it at the very least. 'Come,' she said softly, holding out some more chicken. 'We will not hurt you.' She added in English, 'Come on, sweetie, we want to help you. It's OK, I promise.'

Rurik raised his eyebrows at her. 'You sound like a temptress. I hope you never speak to me like that.'

'Temptress?' Sara didn't know that word in Old Norse.

'A woman who is trying to entice a man,' Rurik explained with a smirk.

'Huh!' She wanted to punch him again, but was sitting too far away. Instead she countered, 'Why would I want to do that?' Although seeing him prepared to share his meal with a starving dog had definitely made him go up in her estimation, she had no intention of trying to seduce him. She'd sworn off men altogether.

'True.' Rurik turned his attention back to the dog, and eventually the promise of something to eat proved too much for it to resist. He – Sara could see it was a hound now – quickly snatched the morsel out of Rurik's hand and gulped it down, then tiptoed over to Sara. When she crooned at the animal and held out her hand for him to lick, his wariness lessened. After several more treats, he lay down next to her, putting his head on his paws and gazing at her adoringly.

She almost snorted. If only it was that easy to attract human males and keep them, Anders wouldn't have . . . But she wasn't going there.

'Here, he can have the leftovers.' Rurik had found wooden platters in one of the outhouses, and now he dumped the parts of the chicken neither of them wanted to eat on to one of them. The dog wolfed down the skin and gristle in seconds, then burped.

That made Sara laugh. 'Good boy,' she said, tentatively stroking the fuzzy head. 'Look, he has . . .' She pointed to the dog's neck.

'A collar,' Rurik supplied.

'Yes, a collar, so he is not wild.'

'No, I expect he belonged to whoever lived here.'

'Sad. What's your name, boy?'

'*Hundr*, most likely.' Rurik rearranged his cloak and made himself more comfortable, leaning back on his elbows while glancing at the dog, who did seem to raise one ear at hearing the word.

Sara squeaked with outrage. 'No! He cannot have the name "dog".' That would be too sad for words. This creature was clearly more than just his species. He seemed lovable and intelligent.

Rurik shrugged. 'Well, we'll never know, will we?'

'He needs a name.' She was adamant. 'I name him Beowulf.'

'Beowulf?' Rurik spluttered with laughter, startling her. She hadn't heard him laugh before, and it was an unexpectedly wonderful sound that made her feel all warm inside. Which was ridiculous really. He shouldn't be affecting her at all.

'It is perfect,' she declared.

He shook his head, still chuckling. 'It sounds like a king. In fact, I have heard a tale about a hero called that . . .'

'Yes! Me also.' At last, something they had in common. Sara had read a translation of the famous poem a few years ago. 'This dog is a king of dogs. Look! Beautiful head.'

'You are . . .' He said a word she didn't understand, but she guessed it meant 'deluded'.

Too bad. From now on, Beowulf was what this dog was called, and if Sara had anything to do with it, he was coming with them when they left the following day.

Rurik woke early, his senses on full alert, but all was quiet, apart from the dog – Beowulf, honestly! – who was snoring softly, curled up next to Sara. The two of them looked so peaceful, and something stirred in the region of Rurik's heart, but he shook his head. He mustn't let them affect him in any way. No one was ever going to pull his heartstrings again; he was determined about that. And especially not someone from the future who could disappear at any moment.

Still, he sat and watched the woman and the dog for quite a while before going outside to wash in a bucket of water from the well. He dunked his whole head, shivering as the coldness hit his scalp, and used a torn-off piece of an old shirt to wash his torso. Despite the early morning chill in the air, he allowed the breeze to dry his skin while he used a comb to untangle his hair. He'd shaved before leaving Ribe, which meant he only had stubble on his chin as yet, though it was itching as it grew and he scratched it absently. As he pulled on his shirt, he turned around and found Sara and the dog watching him from the doorway. She quickly averted her gaze, but not before he'd caught a strange expression in her eyes – half yearning, half hatred – that he didn't understand.

What was that all about?

'Good morning! Are you wanting to wash yourself too?'

She stepped into the yard, closely followed by Beowulf. 'Yes please, and I think he is thirsty.' She pointed at the dog.

'Ah yes, of course.' They'd forgotten to give the hound anything to drink the previous evening, although presumably there was a stream nearby where he could have gone if he was dying of thirst.

Rurik pulled up another bucket of water and poured some on to one of the wooden plates he'd found yesterday. Beowulf drank gratefully, and the plate had to be filled several times. At least the water in the well looked clean, which wasn't always the case in Rurik's experience. He wouldn't drink it himself, but it was probably fine for a dog.

'Here, you can go and wash inside,' he said to Sara, pulling up another bucketful of water, which he handed to her.

'Can I have that, please?' She pointed at the cloth, looking slightly embarrassed, as if she didn't want to talk to him about washing. Rurik found this endearing, but again tried to suppress any feelings of warmth towards her. She was just a woman he was protecting for now, nothing more.

'Oh, yes. And here, use this for drying.' He gave her a length of linen he hadn't needed himself, and handed over the wash cloth. He didn't think she'd want to stand half naked in the breeze to dry off the way he had. And he definitely didn't want to even contemplate such a thing. 'You might need my comb, too.' He took it out of his leather pouch.

'Thank you. Soap?'

'No, you'll have to make do without.' He'd had some lye in his kist, but the sea water had turned it to mush and he'd had to throw it away and rinse it off his clothing.

Sara and Beowulf disappeared back into the building and Rurik waited impatiently for their return. Just in case anyone came back to this place, he wanted to leave as soon as possible. Another, more thorough, search of the outbuildings and yard yielded six eggs, which the attackers must have overlooked, and he quickly made a fire and set them to boil in the cauldron. He almost groaned at the thought of having to feed the dog as well now, but from the way Sara's hand had rested on the shaggy beast's head earlier, he was sure Beowulf would be travelling with them. Two eggs each would have to suffice for now.

They ate them quickly – Beowulf swallowing his in two bites – and set off again. Sara looked rested, if a bit wary still, and Rurik decided she must be over the first shock of ending up in his time. He'd seen her push some hay into her shoes to make them fit better, which showed her to be a practical person. That was good. But if she was staying, she had to improve her language skills, and to that end he started talking to her almost as soon as they were under way.

'Are you well this morning?'

'Yes, thank you.'

'Your leg does not pain you after walking all day yesterday?' He'd wondered whether it ached when overused, but she'd shown no signs of it nor complained.

'No. It is healed.' She hesitated and gestured towards the dog. 'You do not mind?'

Rurik smiled and shook his head. 'No, I like dogs. And he might be useful for guarding us; he'll warn of anyone approaching.'

Sara smiled back. 'Yes, I think that too.'

'Where did you learn my language? From the Christian men?' He'd heard of places where men like that Ansgar, the so-called 'Bishop' he'd met in Ribe, taught children all manner of things. Apparently the followers of the White Christ liked to share their learning in a variety of subjects, and not just their beliefs, or so Rurik had been told.

She frowned. 'Christian men? Oh, no, in a . . . *school.* Um, a different place of learning. But I need to practise more.'

'Yes, but you are doing tolerably well. You are already speaking better than yesterday. Just talk to me and you will learn quickly. Tell me about your time.'

'My time? What do you want to know?'

He spread his hands. 'Everything!'

She began haltingly to describe the world she had come from, and whenever she floundered, he tried to guess. It became a sort of game between them and kept them entertained while they walked. Beowulf ambled along behind them. He hadn't hesitated for an instant when Sara had called him as they set off, and Rurik could see he'd already bonded with them. Dogs were wise creatures, and no doubt the canine knew his former master or mistress was gone for good.

Halfway through the morning, they found themselves on a

much bigger track, partly paved and wide enough for two wagons to pass each other. Rurik knew of only one people who had created such things – the Romans – but he was surprised to find the track here in the land of the *Engilskir*, and said so.

'Oh, the Romans lived here for four hundred years,' Sara told him.

'Really? How do you know that? Are they here now?' He'd come across Romans – or at least people descended from them – when he'd travelled to Miklagarðr with his brother, and didn't much like them.

'I read it in a . . . well, I read about it. And no, they are gone. Maybe another four hundred years ago?'

'Oh, good.'

Sara laughed. 'Why is that good?'

'They like to control everything,' Rurik muttered. 'So many rules.' The Gríkkjar in Miklagarðr had driven him crazy with all their laws and restrictions.

'I see. They were a great . . . *civilisation*.'

'Clan? People?' he guessed.

Sara shrugged. 'They were very good builders. Look how straight this is.' She indicated the road that stretched ahead of them as far as the eye could see, and she was right. Not the slightest kink could be detected. It was as though they had laid it out with string, forcing their way through any obstacle. Rurik had to admit this was impressive.

'If it takes us to Jorvik faster, then good!'

Being on such a large road had its downsides, however. They started to meet other people, locals who were using it to transport goods in wagons or carts, scurrying from one place to another. Very few of them returned Rurik's friendly greeting, and he began to wonder what it was about him that made them so wary. His clothing was more or less the same as theirs, though they seemed to keep their hair shorter. He glanced at Sara – possibly it was the fact that she was so obviously a woman dressed in men's clothes that were too big for her. That wasn't a common sight and might be frowned upon here. He'd have to find her a gown soon. And new shoes.

'I do not think they like us much,' he whispered to her when yet another farmer had walked past with a scowl.

'Maybe they think we burned that house?'

'Just the two of us? Hardly likely.' But perhaps she had a point. The locals clearly saw enemies everywhere, and no wonder.

During the afternoon, they managed to find a farm where the family were willing to sell them some barley, vegetables and smoked lamb. Rurik tried to engage the head of the household in conversation, but as soon as he'd handed over some silver, the door was shut in their faces. He sighed.

'I suppose I can't blame them, but I sincerely hope it will not be like this in Jorvik, or else I might as well go straight back home.'

Sara touched his arm. 'At least we have food now.'

'Yes, that's true.' And there were plenty of streams to drink from, so who cared if they had to go without ale for a while?

Sara felt as though her head was going to explode. All day Rurik had talked to her, asking questions, correcting her vocabulary and grammar. It was exhausting, but she had to admit it was improving her Old Norse language skills quickly. When you'd been corrected for the third time on the conjugation of a certain verb, your brain got the message. And it was amazing how much it all made sense when you were actually using the language to communicate with someone, rather than just trying to learn in a classroom. Everything she'd been cramming into her brain during lessons came bubbling to the surface, and the more they chatted, the more she remembered. A lot of the words were similar to the Swedish ones she was used to as well, which helped.

However, when he'd asked the umpteenth question about the twenty-first century, she'd had enough for today. 'Why do you want to know so much?' she demanded. 'You said you know another . . . person like me. Why don't you ask him?'

'Her. And I don't want to.'

His sudden scowl puzzled her. 'Why? She is not nice?'

'Yes, very, but she is married to someone and I can't be bothering another man's wife with questions.'

'Oh, I see.' Although he looked like he'd wanted to, very much. Sara found herself wondering who this woman was and why she'd chosen someone other than Rurik to marry. If she herself had the choice . . . but she didn't want to marry anyone. Still, as far as she could see, Rurik ought to be a pretty good marriage prospect – handsome, easy-going, strong and considerate, and with a good profession. She was sure being a silversmith meant you were quite well off in Viking times. But there was no accounting for taste, and perhaps the woman in question had fallen in love with an even better man. 'Well, no more questions today, please. I am very tired.'

Rurik looked as though he was going to protest, but then shrugged. 'Very well, but your speech is so much better now and you must learn more quickly. We will talk every day and soon it will be perfect.'

'I hope so.'

It was a dry evening, and as there weren't any buildings in sight, they made camp near a small river. Sara watched Rurik put bits of vegetable and smoked lamb into the cauldron, boiling this for a while before adding barley grain and some mushrooms he'd picked nearby. She wondered vaguely if she ought to be doing the cooking. Presumably it was women's work in his time, but she didn't know how, so he'd have to teach her. Still, she was all for equality, so it was a good thing that he could cook.

In fact, on the whole, he seemed remarkably tolerant in his attitude towards her. Not only had he accepted with only a small amount of surprise her claim that she was a silversmith, but he hadn't attempted to make her his thrall or subjugate her in any way. From what Linnea had told her, the man she'd ended up with had immediately taken her captive, whereas Rurik treated Sara more or less as an equal. It would seem she'd been incredibly lucky.

Linnea. Sara couldn't help but wonder if she was in the same era as her friend. Linnea would be hundreds of miles away, but at least if she was there, it meant a possible ally. How long had it taken her to fit into her new surroundings? To stop feeling like an outsider who knew nothing? Sara was fully aware that without Rurik she'd be as helpless as a small child, and just as vulnerable. Well, thank goodness he wasn't mistreating her in any way.

When the stew was ready, he divided it between two bowls and a large plate he'd brought from the burned-out farmstead, and then produced a couple of horn spoons from his travelling chest. The plate was for the dog to use. 'Here, Beowulf,' he said, blowing on the food to cool it down a bit before giving it to him. The dog fell on it, grateful for anything.

'This is very good!' Sara was surprised at how delicious it was, but maybe she was just ravenous, having walked all day.

'The word you want is "tasty",' he told her. 'And don't look so surprised. I have cooked before, you know, when I travelled.'

She smiled. 'Sorry. It's just . . . I don't know what to . . .'

'Expect?'

'Yes, expect. Thank you. You are very kind to me and Beowulf.'

'Think nothing of it.'

But she did, and she thought again how lucky she'd been in coming across this particular man. It could have been that grumpy farmer instead, and then where would she have been? That didn't bear thinking about. It also made her feel guilty, because she knew Rurik didn't really want her tagging along, and that she'd more or less forced her presence on him. Not that she'd had much of a choice . . .

When it was time to sleep, she was surprised to find Rurik spreading his cloak next to hers. In the barn the previous night, and the cave before that, he'd kept his distance, but now he was close enough to touch. A tendril of unease shot through her. Had he been lulling her into a false sense of security so he could attack her now? The thought made her jittery, and her anxiety must have shown in her face, because he sent her an enigmatic look.

'I shall sleep close by in case you need protection during the night,' he explained.

'Oh, right. Thank you.'

Protection from what? He was the only thing remotely dangerous around at the moment. She remained wary, all her senses on full alert, but he rolled himself into the cloak and curled up on his side facing away from her. Beowulf, perhaps sensing her tension, squeezed himself into the small gap between them and lay down. Sara relaxed and put an arm round the big dog. Even though the ground was uncomfortable to sleep on, at least they were warm enough with him around. 'He's like a fire,' she muttered before falling asleep. 'Good dog.'

She couldn't believe she'd already spent nearly two days in the Viking era. What would tomorrow bring?

Chapter Eight

In the morning, they took turns to wash in the river. Sara muttered about something she called a 'shower', and Rurik gathered she was used to bathing every day. Personally, he felt that once a week on the *laugardagr* – bath day – was enough, but he'd gathered that people in the future were obsessed with cleanliness and smelling good.

'Can you buy soap soon?' Sara asked him before heading to the water.

'Depends on the locals, doesn't it?' Rurik was sure they'd sell him some lye if he gave them enough silver, but he didn't particularly want to waste his resources on that. 'Use sand to scrub your skin,' he advised her. 'Works just as well.'

'Huh.' Sara didn't look convinced, and when she came back, she was frowning. 'How do you clean your teeth?'

'My teeth?'

'Yes, my mouth tastes bad in the morning.'

'Try chewing some of this.' Rurik bent to pick some wood sorrel and held it out to her. 'It is edible and gives a fresh taste.'

'Thank you.' Sara chewed thoughtfully for a while, but Rurik noticed she didn't swallow the leaves and spat them out instead, even though they were perfectly safe to eat.

They walked southwards for one more day, chatting as they went along.

'You still want to stay here?' Although he was becoming used to her presence and didn't resent it quite as much, Rurik would still prefer it if Sara left. She didn't belong here, and he couldn't help but worry what would happen when they reached Jorvik. How would she fit in? And what was he to do with her once they arrived there? As an unmarried woman, she couldn't live alone, and he doubted she'd ever been anyone's servant. Besides, judging by Linnea's non-existent housewifely skills, Sara wouldn't know how to perform even the simplest of household tasks either.

That meant only one thing – she'd have to live with him. But as what? His apprentice? Pretend sister? Or mistress? No, definitely not the latter.

'Yes.' Sara didn't elaborate, and Rurik felt bad for pestering her about it. She must have her reasons, and no doubt it was all the fault of the gods. They were toying with these humans, and were probably thoroughly amused by the predicament they'd placed Rurik in. Perhaps he ought to make an offering to try and appease whichever god or gods had created this situation? Difficult, though, as he wouldn't know which one to appeal to.

He could always just give her the *seax* and try to make her realise it would be best if she went back to her own era. Something held him back, though. If he was truthful, he was enjoying their exchanges, and learning about a future that sounded like the most amazing *skald*'s tale. She could be making it all up, of course, but somehow he didn't think so. Her voice and expression were sincere when she described everything, and she never once faltered or contradicted herself. That would point to it being the truth, or at least as she saw it.

It was nice not to have to walk alone, too. If he'd been by

himself, the locals might have been tempted to attack him, but the sight of a woman walking by his side gave them pause. It probably made him seem less threatening. Surely allowing her to stay just a short while longer wouldn't hurt? Then hopefully by the time they reached Jorvik, she'd have had enough of his world. Perhaps the lure of those showers, whatever they were, would be enough to tempt her. Then he could give her the knife.

They spent another night under the stars. Not ideal, but Rurik was grateful that at least the weather stayed dry. As they bedded down, he tried not to touch Sara with any part of his body. He'd noticed that she jumped every time they came into contact even slightly, and although he wasn't sure whether this was out of fear or attraction, he wasn't unaware of her as a woman. How could he be? With her luscious shape outlined by the male clothing and the occasional brush of her hair on his skin as it escaped confinement, she was very feminine. Tempting. And he was only human. But no good could come of trying to seduce her. It might make her want to stay in his time for good, something he was keen to prevent. No, once they reached Jorvik, the sooner she was gone, the better. Thank the gods for Beowulf – the dog was an asset, his warm body like a furnace against their backs as he lay down between them, acting as a barrier.

He had other uses as well, as they found on their fourth day.

They'd been continuing along the Roman road – it made sense to follow it, as it seemed to be heading straight for the south – when a group of men appeared without warning from a forest on their right. One moment the road was clear, the next they were standing in front of them. Rurik and Sara didn't have a chance of escape.

'Hello, what have we here? More travellers?' The leader of the group guffawed, but Rurik ignored that and focused on the fact that he'd been speaking Norse, not *Enska*. Presumably this was one of the bands of marauders going around these parts. Maybe even the ones who had ransacked that farmstead. He hoped not, as that had seemed like a particularly vicious attack.

'You could say that,' he replied, doing his best to sound affable and unconcerned. 'But seeing as how we are apparently fellow countrymen, I would hope you aren't intending to stand in our way?' He put a hand on the axe hanging at his belt, making sure that they could see him doing it, but didn't pull it out yet. There were a dozen men facing him, and he knew he'd never be able to fight his way out of this situation, but still, it was good to show that he wasn't averse to using violence if he had to.

Sara had shrunk back behind him, standing close to his shoulder, and a quick glance showed that she'd had the sense to grab Beowulf's collar. The big hound was baring his teeth and growling low in his throat. Excellent. At least that might make the men think twice about accosting her. He saw the leader frown when he caught sight of the dog; the man didn't come any closer, but he returned his gaze to Rurik.

'Well, well, a *Svíar*, are you? I can hear it from your speech. Holger over there is the same.' He nodded towards a large red-headed man, who grinned briefly in acknowledgement. 'I'm Asmund and these are my men. We are part of Hálfdan Hvítserk's contingent, on our way to meet up with the others by the coast further south. We've been gathering provisions.' He gestured towards the forest, where Rurik could now glimpse several carts filled with goods, and also a group of well-laden packhorses.

He vaguely remembered Sigvardr mentioning a man called Hálfdan, one of the leaders of a great army that was rampaging through Saxon lands, he'd said, and had been for some years now. Apparently, Hálfdan was one of the sons of a legendary warrior by the name of Ragnar Loðbrók. Sigvardr had been on his way to join them. 'Best way to make your fortune quickly,' he'd joked, but Rurik didn't agree. He much preferred to make a living by honest work, but he wasn't stupid enough to mention that now.

'I see. And we are on our way to Jorvik. I am a silversmith, hoping to ply my trade there.'

'Hmm.' Asmund didn't look convinced. 'Show me the contents of your kist.'

Rurik resented this order, but he had nothing to hide. 'By all means.' He'd already placed the chest on the ground when the men appeared; now he bent to open the lid. Asmund waved one of his men forward, and the oaf rummaged for a while, then shrugged.

'Looks like he has the tools of his trade and nothing much else,' he commented.

'How were you intending to work as a silversmith without silver?' Asmund asked, not unreasonably, although Rurik could have done without the accompanying smirk.

'I will have to start small, with commissions from people who have their own silver and want it melted down,' he replied. 'Unfortunately, my wife and I were in a shipwreck on the way here, and the silver I'd brought is now at the bottom of the sea.' He made a face. 'Not an ideal start to our new life, eh, *ást mín*?' He sent Sara a sad smile and she played along.

'No,' she said, looking downcast.

'Is that why she's dressed strangely?' Asmund looked Sara up and down, and Rurik had to force himself not to react to the man's blatant ogling. Although she cut a somewhat comical figure in the overlarge clothing, as he'd noticed for himself there was no denying her feminine shape, which was undoubtedly what had caught Asmund's eye. She was a very pleasing sight, the tunic straining across her chest.

'Yes, her kist disappeared too and her clothes were ruined.

We've been trying to buy items from the locals, but they don't appear to be very friendly.'

There were chuckles from several of the men at that comment. 'I wonder why,' Asmund said with another smirk. 'There's a better way for you to obtain garments for your wife and silver for your trade – you'll join us.'

Rurik had half expected this and was debating with himself how to reply. He wasn't averse to fighting when he had to, but these men were engaged in warfare, and it wasn't for a cause he'd chosen. 'I think my wife would rather have me in one piece in Jorvik.'

Sara stepped closer to him and grabbed his arm with the hand that wasn't holding on to Beowulf. 'Yes!' She sounded genuinely frightened, which was no wonder really.

But Asmund just shook his head. 'It wasn't a request. Either you come with us willingly, or we take your wife captive and kill you. We have no use for cowards, but camp followers are another matter.' He glanced at the dog with another frown. 'As for the mutt, I have a spear here somewhere.'

Rurik heard Sara gasp in outrage, and clenched his fists, livid at being called a coward and furious with himself for not being more vigilant. They should have avoided this road and kept to the smaller tracks. That wasn't cowardice, just plain caution. But it was too late now; the trap had closed around them. If only he hadn't allowed Sara to come with him, she wouldn't be in this situation. He should have insisted on sending her back to her own time immediately, but it was too late now. Perhaps later, if they could snatch a moment alone somewhere. For now, he had to protect her as best he could.

'Very well, we'll join you,' he said. 'But my wife is not for sharing.' He put as much steel into his voice as he could. 'Anyone who touches her is a dead man, and the same goes for the dog.'

Asmund laughed, but he seemed to like Rurik's bravado. 'Well said! Come then, you can help pull the first cart.'

Rurik took Sara's hand and hissed, 'Keep holding on to Beowulf, and if anyone approaches you, let him attack. I don't trust these men at all.'

'Do we have to go with them?' Her eyes were large pools of anxiety and he could feel her hand shaking in his.

'For now. We'll leave them at the first opportunity. Stay close to me.'

He had a feeling that last admonition was unnecessary. To Sara, he was probably the only safe thing in the world right now.

Sara hadn't liked the way Asmund looked her up and down earlier. His gaze made her skin crawl. It was as if he had X-ray vision and could see right through both her shirt and tunic and had realised she wasn't wearing a bra. Not that he'd know what one of those was, but still . . . He seemed more relaxed now that Rurik had agreed to join the group, but how could she trust that none of these men would attack her after dark? She and Rurik had to sleep at some point and anything could happen then. She swallowed down bile and tried to breathe slowly so as to dissolve the knot of fear in her stomach.

This wasn't an adventure any more, this was harsh reality. And it didn't look as though they'd be going to Jorvik any time soon, unless that was where Asmund was heading.

She remembered jokingly referring to the Great Heathen Army a couple of days ago when Rurik told her about marauders. From her reading, she recalled that this had been one of the biggest armies ever to invade mainland Britain. No one knew exactly how big, but figures of between two and three thousand men had been suggested, arriving in a hundred ships or more. The thought made her shudder. They had roamed the countryside for years, enticed by the wealth that supposedly existed in Britain, and also what must have seemed like very lush farmland to them. Compared to places like Norway and Sweden, where arable land had to be coaxed out of the landscape by hard toil, the fields here were amazing.

The Heathen Army had conquered huge swathes of the country – or rather, countries, as Britain was divided into many kingdoms during the Viking age. Sara had no way of knowing whether this had already happened, though, or if the army had only just arrived on these shores. She would have to listen to their conversation to try and find out. In a way, that would help her, as then she'd know roughly what year she had ended up in. But it wouldn't get her any closer to Jorvik. Or Linnea in Sweden.

And she might not survive the day, let alone long enough to go anywhere . . .

The feel of Beowulf against her right thigh as she walked gave her some hope. The big dog seemed to have gone into instant guard mode and was sticking very close to her, baring his teeth at anyone who came near them. 'Good boy,' she muttered, giving him a surreptitious stroke on his soft head.

A small lifeline also appeared in the shape of Holger, the large red-headed Swede who'd grinned at Rurik earlier. He drew up alongside them, pulling another handcart, and struck up a conversation with Rurik.

'Good to have some more *Svíar* with us. Well, they call me a *Svíar*, but I was born and raised on Gotland. The Danes can't tell the difference. Where do you hail from?' Sara could hear that his dialect was different to that of Rurik, but both also deviated from the Norse spoken by Asmund and some of the others.

'Birka,' Rurik replied. 'That's where I trained as a silversmith.'

'Ah, yes, I've only been there once. We tended to go in a more southerly direction for the most part.'

'Understandable. I travelled to Aldeigjuborg a couple of years ago and we stopped off on Gotland first.'

'A great trading place, or so I hear.'

Sara had no idea where Aldeigjuborg was – she'd never heard of this town – and she tuned out as the two men went on to talk about other places they'd been. At one point she did hear Holger whisper that they didn't need to worry about Asmund, adding, 'As long as you're on his side, he won't harm you. Just likes to bluster a bit. Saves his violence for the locals. Either way, stay near me and I'll make sure no one touches either of you. We *Svíar* have to stick together, eh?'

'Thank you,' Rurik replied. 'If you need anything made out of silver, just let me know.'

A shudder rippled through Sara as she thought about the poor people at the farm where they'd found Beowulf, but if Holger was telling the truth, there was some comfort to be had in his promise of protection. The man had giant fists and was pulling his cart effortlessly, while Rurik was having to put his back into it. Having Holger shielding them would be a blessing for sure.

'So where are we heading? The coast, did Asmund say?'

Sara, Rurik and Holger sat together on a boulder in the shade of some trees, eating coarse bread and cheese. The whole group had stopped at midday to rest and water the horses, and someone had handed out the food. Most people only ate in the morning and evening, but Rurik supposed it made sense to have a morsel or two now in order to keep their strength up. He also assumed the bread and cheese had been looted from somewhere, but he tried not to dwell on that.

'Yes, at first. We have ships waiting there, guarded by some of our men while we went to gather provisions. But we'll be sailing south and then inland along one of the rivers. Hálfdan and the others have agreed to aim for the heart of the Mercian kingdom next – that's the one in the middle of this large island – and take it once and for all. We'll find somewhere to make camp and strike out from there. It's a weak kingdom, unlike the one in the south.' Holger shook his head. 'Stubborn lot, the West Saxons. Best left alone if you ask me. Nothing would make me go down there again, I can tell you.'

'I see. That makes sense.' Rurik knew they were currently in the former kingdom of Northumbria – or Norðimbraland, as the Danes called it – which had been taken over by Norsemen some years back. He'd heard that Jorvik was the centre whence this part of the island was ruled, although there was some sort of Northumbrian puppet king still on the throne. His enquiries had been quite thorough – he'd specifically wanted to avoid walking into a conflict, and he'd made sure that Jorvik was a safe place to put down roots. But he hadn't counted on being blown off course and ending up much further north.

'How do you know the Mercians are weak?' he asked Holger.

'Oh, they've made peace with us several times by paying us off. That means they haven't the strength to withstand us in battle and they should be easy to defeat.' Holger chuckled. 'Don't know why anyone would think we'd stay away as long as there's still more riches to be had.'

Rurik nodded. The men surrounding him were clearly not the type you could buy off for long, and the locals had been foolish to think that would work.

'Besides,' Holger added, 'there appears to be a rival claimant for the Mercian throne. An ambitious nobleman who is willing to work with us in order to achieve his aim. Says he's descended from another royal line and ought to be the rightful king. Who knows? It matters not.'

Work *with* the Norsemen or *for* them? Rurik didn't ask.

Presumably it would mollify the Mercian people if they ostensibly had one of their own as king. Whether he had any real power or not was irrelevant.

He absently fed Beowulf half of his meal and noticed that Sara did the same. They needed the big dog, and the way to his loyalty was definitely through his stomach, although Rurik had seen the way Beowulf almost purred with pleasure whenever Sara caressed him. Good. The stronger the bond between them, the better.

'Have you been here long, Holger? Done much fighting?' He was curious about this Gotlander, who seemed so easy-going and yet must be a formidable warrior judging by the size and strength of him.

'Oh yes, I was one of the first ones here. Must be about seven, eight winters ago now. Always up for a good fight, and as the fourth son of a poor farmer, there wasn't anything for me at home.' Holger shrugged. 'I heard that the sons of Ragnar Loðbrók – Ívar the Boneless, Hálfdan Hvítserk and Ubba – were putting together a *here* – an army – and went to join them. I wasn't the only one, as I soon found out. I reckon there were at least three thousand men who set out together, quite a sight I can tell you! We sailed to East Anglia first, where the people seemed reluctant to fight us. Well, they were probably overwhelmed by the sheer number of our ships. Instead they gave us their valuables and supplies so we'd leave them alone. Their king, a weakling by the name of Edmund, gave us even more, including horses. That set us up nicely for the first campaign.'

'You didn't take over that kingdom then?'

'Not immediately, no, although a couple of winters later we went back, and that time Edmund was stupid enough to try and fight us.' Holger snorted. 'The *fifl* was just asking to get himself killed, and he did. But that first year we went north instead and conquered these parts, Norðimbraland.' The big man laughed and pointed at the Roman road they'd been following. 'These amazingly straight roads run all over this country and make it very easy to move swiftly when you need to. I'm told they're hundreds of years old, but they still serve their purpose.'

'They have certainly survived remarkably well,' Rurik replied drily, and again cursed himself for not realising that he should have stayed well away from these roads.

Holger continued, obviously in an expansive mood. 'Most of our ships followed along the coast, in case we needed a quick escape route, but they weren't necessary. We met with little resistance – I don't mind telling you I got a bit bored for a while there – but then we came to Jorvik, or Eoforwic as the locals call it, and that was a different matter. Plenty of fighting spirit there, but we captured it in a great battle and stayed there for the winter. Ah, those were the days . . . The *skalds* sing about it even now.'

'Was there a Northumbrian king? Or was he as weak as that Edmund?' Rurik was curious as to why this conquest seemed to have been so easy.

Holger laughed. 'There were two: one the rightful king as far as we could make out, but not well liked by half his subjects; the other a usurper. We watched them fight each other for a while, but both were killed when they tried to take Jorvik back from us, and then we stepped in and took over the entire kingdom. Our leaders appointed someone as ruler, but in truth they made all the decisions and Ecgbert just danced to their tune.'

Rurik frowned. 'I was told there was a different king in Jorvik, one Ricsige?'

'Oh yes, Ecgbert died last year, I believe. Don't know much about the new one, but trust me, he's powerless.'

'Good to know.' And it was – the more power the Norsemen had, the better as far as Rurik was concerned. It would make it easier for him to set up in Jorvik and ply his trade.

Always assuming he ever made it there, which didn't seem at all likely now.

And what about Sara? What was he to do about her? He'd instinctively claimed her as his wife in order to protect her – in accordance with Norse laws, most men were honourable enough not to molest another man's spouse, and he'd counted on that – but thinking about it now, this could prove more problematic than helpful. If he gave her the *seax* and she went back to her own time, how would he explain her disappearance? A husband wouldn't simply send his wife off by herself, and in the middle of enemy territory at that. Asmund would believe he'd hidden her away on purpose, and probably punish him in order to find out where she'd gone.

And that was one secret he would never be prepared to divulge.

He swallowed a sigh. For now, the best option was to keep her close. Hopefully a time would come when they could both sneak away from this band of brigands, and then he wouldn't hesitate for an instant to send her on her way, back where she belonged.

Chapter Nine

As everyone was getting ready to leave again, Sara disappeared into the forest to attend to a call of nature. She brought Beowulf with her – better safe than sorry – and walked as far in as she dared while still sure of the direction back. The last thing she needed was to get lost here in the middle of nowhere, and in the wrong century to boot.

When she'd finished, she heard the sound of running water and walked towards it. After only twenty yards or so, she came upon a small stream, where she bent to wash her hands and face before cupping her hands to drink. She assumed the water would be clean enough – no pollution from factories or chemicals in this century – and it tasted wonderfully refreshing. Beowulf agreed and lapped noisily by her side, making her smile.

'You're a bit of a clown, aren't you, sweetie?' she murmured. He wasn't a pretty dog, but still very appealing, with a pair of soulful brown eyes under bushy eyebrows, and an equally bushy moustache that was now full of water droplets.

Just at that moment, however, he raised his head and started growling, with his gaze fixed on the other side of the stream. Sara froze, wondering if Asmund or one of his men had snuck up on her, but instead her eyes met those of a pale youth with a shaved head. He was standing stock still, staring at her while holding on to a thin tree trunk as if he needed support. Sara's first reaction was one of relief, and she was just about to wave at him with a smile when she caught sight of his clothing. An ugly brown tunic that reached more or less to his sandal-encased feet, with a coarse rope serving as a belt. Together with the shaved head, this could only mean one thing – he was a monk.

Sara's thoughts whirled. A monk would indicate that there was a monastery nearby. And a monastery was probably exactly the sort of place Asmund was looking for – full of valuables and presumably with stores of provisions. And easy prey – men who didn't fight back because they'd been taught to turn the other cheek. Didn't the Vikings specialise in looting holy places? Yes, who hadn't heard of Lindisfarne and Jarrow? *Damn!* There was going to be a bloodbath, and judging by the look on the youth's face, he'd figured that out too.

Glancing behind her to make sure she hadn't been followed, she waved at him with both hands, indicating that he should flee. '*Northmen!*' she hissed, hoping he could hear her. '*Danes!* Run! Warn everyone!'

She had no idea if he understood her. Although Rurik had said the Anglo-Saxon language was similar to Old Norse, it might not be enough. But by the widening of the youth's eyes, she gathered that he understood the first word at least. She pointed behind her and then held up her hands to show him that there were about a dozen of them, then motioned again for him to run. He nodded and took off, disappearing as if all the hounds of hell were after him. Sara only hoped he could run fast enough all the way back to wherever he'd come from.

'Sara! *Sara?*' She heard crashing in the forest behind her and Rurik calling her.

'Here! I am coming.' Taking Beowulf by the collar, she ran

towards his voice and then straight into him as she rounded a large tree trunk. Her chest collided with his much harder one and she bounced back, almost stumbling on a tree root. 'Oof! Sorry, took longer than I thought.' She could feel her face heating up at the thought of such close contact between them, but tried to ignore it. It was just an accident. No need to be embarrassed.

Rurik grabbed her upper arms to steady her, a scowl on his face. 'You shouldn't be wandering around on your own. Tell me next time and I'll come and keep guard, yes?'

'Fine. I had Beowulf, but . . . very well, I'll tell you.'

'Make sure you do. You could have run into any one of the men rather than me.' He was still frowning, and although Sara knew he was right, being scolded like a small child annoyed her.

There were more important things to consider, however, and she swallowed her irritation. As they walked back to the others, she quickly whispered to him about seeing the monk. Rurik groaned out loud. 'Odin's ravens! Asmund won't leave a prize like that alone, which means we'll have to help loot the place. Exactly what I don't want.'

'At least the monks have a chance to escape with their lives now that I've warned them. Their valuables can be . . . bought again.' She didn't know the right word for what she meant, but Rurik filled it in.

'Replaced. Yes, I suppose you're right.' As they emerged on to the road, he smiled at Holger, who was looking impatient. 'Here she is. Got a bit lost, but no harm done.'

'Good. Let's go.'

The monastery was clearly visible from the road, and as Rurik had guessed, Asmund wasn't about to pass it by. He laughed in glee when he spied it, then, leaving a couple of men to guard their carts and horses, he beckoned everyone else forward to join him in looting the place.

'The perfect end to our journey,' he declared, the light of battle and greed shining in his eyes. 'No idea how we missed this on the way north. Come! You too.' He indicated Rurik and Sara.

Rurik was about to protest, but realised he couldn't leave Sara unprotected with the men by the carts as he didn't trust them. He was still annoyed with her for going off on her own like that, and cross with himself for registering how tantalising her curves had felt when she'd bumped into him. He didn't want to notice anything about her; he should never have let her come along in the first place. He'd been a fool to allow it. Time enough to think about that later, though.

'Coming,' he said, grabbing Sara by the hand. Her fingers gripped his convulsively, and despite everything, he couldn't resist giving them a reassuring squeeze. He'd make sure she didn't have to do any actual looting or, the gods forbid, killing.

Holger had given them a length of rope, which Sara had tied to Beowulf's collar so that she didn't have to hold on to that all the time. It made it easier for the dog to move freely, and he trotted along beside them. It wasn't long before they reached the monastery, a large, low stone building with a tower at one end and a gatehouse. The gates were barred, but it didn't take Asmund and a couple of his men long to hack them to pieces with their axes. Rurik helped – he'd rather use his axe on wood than on someone's body, and reckoned Asmund would get through with or without his assistance. Best to show willing.

With loud yells of excitement, Asmund and his men poured into the serene courtyard beyond the gates, scattering a few unwary hens, who dispersed in a flurry of feathers and affronted cackling. 'This way!' the leader shouted, heading unerringly for the corner where the tower was situated. 'They always keep the best things in their holy places.'

Rurik hung back and followed more slowly, scanning the other buildings. They seemed empty, but he noticed a couple of pale faces staring out of the windows on the far side of the courtyard. Why were they still here? 'Go over there and get those fools out,' he whispered to Sara. She nodded and disappeared in that direction with Beowulf, while Rurik continued into the chapel with the other men.

A couple of monks were kneeling on the stone floor, their voices raised in some sort of chant or song that was beautiful in an eerie way. The sound echoed round the walls and lofty ceiling. They stared at a wooden cross with a crude figure of a man attached to it, hanging on the wall above a table. Although it wasn't a very good carving, Rurik could see the man's face contorted in agony, and on his head he had some kind of spiky crown. He assumed this was the so-called White Christ, or Jesus, that he'd heard about in Birka. Why he'd been nailed to a cross he had no idea. He'd never bothered to listen to that part of the story.

The table was covered in an embroidered cloth, again with the figure of Jesus, together with what looked like a flock of sheep. Perhaps he'd been a shepherd rather than a carpenter? Rurik was sure it was the latter, but he could have misheard. There was a circle of light behind the man's head, as though the sun or moon encased him. Rurik didn't know what this meant either.

'Move, you fool!' Asmund shouted as one of the monks, an older man, got to his feet and went to stand in front of the table, on top of which Rurik glimpsed an array of silver items. 'Do you really think you can stop us, old man?' Asmund laughed and shoved the monk out of the way.

The old man shouted, 'No!' and tried to charge at him. Rurik shook his head, wondering if he had a wish to die, because that was surely where he was heading. This was confirmed when, moments later, Asmund pulled out his sword and ran the monk through without further ado. Blood gurgling out of his mouth, the old man sank to the floor, his eyes fixed on that wooden cross and his mouth contorted into a strange smile. Rurik thought he heard him muttering something about 'our father', but then the life force ebbed out of him and he was silent.

The other monks, who had stayed on the floor, screamed at this gruesome sight and leapt to their feet, but Asmund's men caught them easily before they reached the doors. They suffered more or less the same fate as their leader, although the mortal blows were inflicted with axes this time. Rurik considered it dishonourable to kill men from behind without giving them a chance to defend themselves – even if these monks clearly had no idea how – and wanted nothing to do with such actions. Instead, he ran forward and started gathering up the silver items on the table.

'Do you have a sack?' he asked Asmund, who grinned and pulled one out from inside his tunic.

'Of course. What do you take me for?'

Together they piled everything they could find into the sack, and Rurik made no protest when Asmund hefted it on to his shoulder. He didn't want the loot in any case. The man was welcome to it.

'Let's look through the rest of the buildings. They've probably tried to hide more of their valuables elsewhere to fool us. And where is everyone? They must have seen us coming and fled out a back door, the cowards.'

Asmund led the way outside and Rurik followed. He hoped Sara had managed to chase out the rest of the monks. Why hadn't they left already? If, as she claimed, she'd told the young one to warn them, there shouldn't have been anyone here. But he'd heard that some of these Christians actively wanted to sacrifice their lives for their beliefs, as it gained them something in the afterlife. That seemed foolish in the extreme to him, as everyone knew that the best way to die was to do it fighting, but perhaps that was their way of reaching Valhalla, or whatever their equivalent was.

Just then, Sara appeared at the door opposite. 'In here, come! See what I've found.' She waved them over, and Asmund smiled and clapped Rurik on the back.

'She's a feisty one, your wife. See how she's enjoying this life already? You did right to join us.'

As if I had a choice . . . But Rurik didn't say that out loud.

Sara had found four terrified young monks in what looked to be a writing room: there were tall desks in rows, lots of pieces of parchment, as well as quill pens and ink. Along one wall stood a long table with a beautifully embroidered cloth that swept to the floor, and displayed on top were the most amazing illuminated manuscripts. They were similar to the ones she'd seen at the British Library in London when she'd gone there to study the designs. A quick glance showed vividly coloured drawings and meticulously inscribed letters, with some of the pages embellished with gold leaf. Real, exquisite works of art.

It pained her that Asmund would probably ruin these, but there wasn't much she could do about it. The monks were another matter.

'Why are you still here? Run! Go!' Even if they didn't understand her words, they ought to get the message as she flapped her hands at them, wearing her sternest expression. They stared alternately at her and Beowulf, who wasn't growling but still looked fierce.

'Can't. Abbot said to stay. Many gone, though. Hiding in forest. We were chosen. Suffer for our Lord.' One of the young men had stepped forward to answer her, his Adam's apple bobbing nervously but his stance resolute.

Sara shook her head and hissed, 'The Northmen only want gold and silver. That's not worth dying for. Now leave!'

But they all shook their heads. 'No way out from here.' They indicated the long room, which she could now see only had the one door. If they went back into the courtyard, chances were they'd be killed immediately.

'Damn it all!' she muttered in English. Asmund and his men would be here any second, and she couldn't bear for these poor monks to die just to protect a few books, no matter how valuable. Her gaze fell on the display table and she had an idea. 'Go under there, quickly! I'll say there's no one here. *Come on!*' She motioned for them to crawl underneath the tablecloth, and after looking at each other and hesitating for a second, they did as she ordered.

When the last sandal-clad foot had disappeared beneath the cloth, she ran to the door and shouted for Asmund and the others to come. They charged into the room, and she raced over to the display table and slammed shut the open books, pointing at the covers. 'Look! Gold, isn't it?'

She'd noticed that the illuminated manuscripts had covers made of wooden boards, on to which were fastened the most amazing decorations, in both gold and silver. There were also jewels or semi-precious stones embedded in the metal, making them not only beautiful but probably extremely valuable. The silversmith in her longed to examine them more closely, but this was not the time. As she'd guessed, Asmund's eyes lit up at the sight, and he didn't so much as glance underneath the cloth. His whole attention was focused on what was on top of the table.

'Indeed! Excellent! Let's pull them off, men,' he ordered.

Sara tried not to flinch as these works of art were ripped apart, but she knew that the real value lay in the manuscripts themselves, each of which would have taken months or even years for the monks to complete. The covers could easily be replaced, whereas the many hours of toiling with a quill could not. And she'd much rather sacrifice the bindings than the lives of the men who were hopefully keeping very still not three feet away from Asmund's toes.

A couple of his henchmen, overexcited and whooping with glee, overturned some of the writing desks and materials, spilling ink all over the flagstone floor, but as soon as he had all the bindings, Asmund called them to join him in searching the rest of the monastery. Sara was the last to leave, and she hissed a final warning to the monks. 'Stay there and don't come out until we've gone!'

She sincerely hoped they'd understood and weren't stupid enough to disobey her. As she stepped outside, she thought she heard someone whisper, 'May God bless you, lady.'

Chapter Ten

'We should have burned the place to the ground. Those *aumingi* deserve nothing better,' one of Asmund's men grumbled on the way back to the carts.

'No time,' Asmund growled. 'We need to get to the coast by nightfall. Do you want the others to leave without us?'

Rurik was extremely grateful they hadn't had time to torch the place, and hoped that the rest of the monks could soon return from wherever they were hiding. Sara had told him of the monks under the table and he appreciated her resourcefulness. Asmund hadn't suspected a thing, thank Odin. And the man was well pleased with his booty – on top of the valuables, the men were carrying as many sacks of grain as they could manage, and a few other victuals besides. It had been a successful raid.

They continued on their way with the carts precariously laden. Some of the sacks had to be tied down so as not to topple off, and even Holger was huffing a bit as he pulled his burden. 'I'll be glad to get back to the ship,' he muttered. 'A bit of rowing will seem like entertainment after this. Never thought I'd end up as a beast of burden.'

Rurik smiled at the man. 'At least you're strong enough. The rest of us are going blue in the face.'

Holger guffawed. 'Nah, you're not doing so badly. Anyway, not far now. I can smell the brine. Can you?'

As he sniffed the breeze, Rurik caught the tang of salt water. The thought of setting foot on a ship again was not an appealing one, but the weather was fair and it sounded as though they'd merely be hugging the coast this time, not crossing any large seas. 'Well, as you say, rowing will make a nice change. I look forward to it.'

Thankfully, they didn't have to do any rowing this day, since they arrived just as darkness fell. In a small bay, spread out along the sandy beach, lay the largest number of ships Rurik had ever seen in any one place, apart from in Miklagarðr. It was an impressive display, no doubt about it, and probably a terrifying sight to any locals. No wonder some of them had tried to pacify the invaders rather than fight them.

There were fires and torches along the half-moon of sand, with men, women and children milling about, talking, laughing and joking. Some of the little ones were still playing chase, even though they should have been settling down by now. But there was excitement in the air, an atmosphere of anticipation and exhilaration that was contagious. Rurik understood why those children couldn't sit still.

'You have a tent?' Holger asked, as they left their carts near a ship that apparently belonged to Asmund.

'No. As I said, we were in a shipwreck. I'm lucky my kist floated ashore with all my tools in. It's all we own now.'

'I'll find you a spare one. Always some around. We lose men every time we fight.' Holger cast a speculative glance at Sara. 'Should I try to obtain some clothing for your wife, too? If you can pay, there might be women willing to sell you various items.'

'Yes please.' Rurik sincerely hoped that by wearing women's garments, Sara would stand out less. He'd noticed she had garnered quite a few lascivious glances during the afternoon, and he was sure this was partly because of her strange attire. For some reason, the male tunic emphasised her feminine attributes despite the fact that it was too big for her. The loose fit allowed her breasts to sway in a most alluring fashion as she walked, something he'd rather not think about himself . . .

Holger nodded. 'Stay here and I'll be back shortly with a tent. There'll be food for everyone soon too.'

That was good news. Cooking smells were wafting across the beach, making Rurik's stomach growl, and he was sure that Sara and Beowulf would be just as hungry. He sank down on to the sand next to the cart he'd been pulling, and Sara followed suit, with Beowulf curving himself around her side. Without thinking, he took her hand and plaited his fingers with hers, giving them a squeeze. He'd forgotten his earlier annoyance with her and knew she wasn't to blame for their predicament. No, it was all his own doing.

'Are you coping?' he whispered. 'I can't tell you how sorry I am that we are in this fix. I should have been much more vigilant and—'

She stopped him by putting a finger over his mouth. 'Shh, it's not your fault. You could not know. And I think I trust Holger, he will keep us safe, no?'

'I hope so.' Rurik sighed. Who knew if the man's friendliness was genuine? It certainly felt like it, but only time would tell.

In the meantime, he was suddenly extremely aware of how soft Sara's finger felt on his lips, and how tiny her other hand seemed encased in his big, callused one. He also noticed that she was leaning against his side, her breast brushing his arm and tendrils of her hair caressing his cheek. Something like a small shock shimmered through him. She was very appealing, and her hair was beautiful, the dark brown shining with red highlights in the glow from the nearest fires. Although she'd plaited it loosely that morning, a lot of this had come undone, and the wavy tresses floated freely in the sea breeze.

Rurik cleared his throat and abruptly pulled his hand away from hers. He wasn't interested in any woman other than the one he couldn't have. Perhaps one day he'd take a wife for real, but right now a pretend one was as far as he was prepared to go. He almost groaned at the thought that he had to make everyone here believe Sara was his beloved, but it was the only way to keep her safe from other men. He stopped another sigh from escaping. He should never have let her come with him. It was too dangerous. What had he been thinking?

And he still couldn't give her the *seax*, surrounded as they were by people at all times. This was neither the time nor the place; that way lay danger for them both. For now, they'd just have to keep up the pretence.

Holger returned and interrupted his gloomy thoughts. 'Here, found you a tent and some clothes. A man's wife died of a sickness yesterday; these are hers.' He dumped a bundle on the ground in front of Sara before depositing the various parts of a tent next to Rurik. 'Might be best to wash them first, aye?'

Rurik felt Sara recoil slightly as she stared at the garments, but she managed a stiff smile for Holger. 'Thank you, that's very kind. I'll do that.'

'And thank you for this.' Rurik indicated the tent. 'Will make a nice change not to sleep with just the sky above our heads.'

'Don't mention it. I'll hold you to the promise of silver-smithing soon.' Holger grinned. 'Now come with me and we'll find a meal, then I'll introduce you to my woman and some of our countrymen.'

*

The food was basic, but tasty – meat stew with onions, mushrooms and root vegetables, as well as the ubiquitous barley, and flavoured with some kind of herb. The woman who'd cooked it was pleased to see that they had their own bowls, and filled them with generous portions. Rurik offered her silver but she shook her head.

'All provisions are shared and none of them are paid for,' she told them. Sara guessed she meant it had all been stolen in the first place, but she was so hungry she couldn't summon up the energy to care right now.

Holger was true to his word and introduced them to the group of men and women around this particular campfire. They proved to be mostly Swedes – no surprise there – although from different parts of that country, and Sara knew they didn't identify themselves as one people. The kingdom of Sweden hadn't been born yet; that was still several centuries into the future. Here they were *Svíar* or *Geats*, sometimes not even that, like those from Gotland. But they clearly differentiated themselves from the Danes and Norwegians, who also claimed to stem from various smaller kingdoms or areas rather than the modern countries she knew, and their dialects were distinct. From what she could observe, they were making Rurik and herself welcome, but she couldn't immediately remember any of their names.

'How long have you been married?' The woman sitting closest to Sara smiled at her while rocking a toddler to sleep on her lap.

'What? Oh, er . . . not very long.' Sara felt her cheeks heat up and hoped it didn't show in the darkness.

'I can tell from the way you're sitting so close to each other. I'm Eadgyth, by the way. Holger is my man.'

Sara noticed she hadn't said 'husband' but wasn't sure whether that meant the couple weren't married or if this was the normal way of referring to your partner. 'Oh, yes, he said, didn't he. I'm Sara.'

'*Sah*-ra? That's unusual.'

'Yes, I know. My parents had strange ideas.' She smiled and shrugged, hoping that would end this particular topic of conversation. A change of subject might help. 'Is this your only child, or do you have others?'

There were still overexcited kids running riot along the beach, and any number of them could have been Eadgyth's.

'Just this one so far. He's enough trouble, I can tell you. Never still for a moment except when he's asleep.'

'He's lovely.' Sara put out a hand to stroke the downy reddish-blond tendrils on the sleeping boy's head. She'd always wanted children and had hoped that she and Anders . . . but that wasn't going to happen now. Just as well, given the fact that he was a lying, cheating bastard. He would have made a terrible father.

'Thank you. Every mother thinks that about their own child.' Eadgyth hugged the little one and changed his position slightly while he slumbered on peacefully. 'You'll see. And your man will be as besotted as Holger – they can't resist having little copies of themselves.'

Sara didn't tell her that there was absolutely no chance of that happening unless she had an immaculate conception. Rurik wouldn't become a father any time soon, at least not with her as the mother of his child. A thought occurred to her – perhaps he already had a wife and children back where he'd come from? She hadn't asked, and when he'd told her to play along, pretending to be his wife, she'd never given it a thought. It might be a good idea to find out.

'You are not a *Svíar* like your husband?'

'Er, no. I'm still learning his language.' Sara winced. It must be fairly obvious.

But Eadgyth surprised her. 'Me too. I'm *Engilskr* from Vestrsaxaland, the West Saxon kingdom. I was captured during a raid four winters ago and forced to be a thrall.'

'What? You mean you're Holger's thrall?' Sara was confused, as the woman didn't look too upset about it.

Eadgyth laughed. 'No, no, I'm a free woman now. The man who captured me died in battle soon after, and Holger, who was his right-hand man, told me that meant I could go home if I wanted to, as my owner had no family or relatives to claim me.' Her smile turned coy. 'But he also suggested I might like to stay on as his woman, and . . . let's just say, he can be very persuasive, so I said yes. I haven't regretted it.'

'Oh, good.' It was a relief to know that Eadgyth wasn't someone's slave, although Sara supposed she'd have to get used to dealing with that sort of scenario here.

'It means *Danskr* isn't my language either, really, but it's similar to mine so was fairly easy to pick up. You'll soon get used to it.'

'I hope so.'

With this conversation in mind, Sara whispered Rurik's name as they lay down back to back inside their newly acquired tent – although it was very far from any tent worth its name that Sara had ever seen, consisting only of some canvas and a few supporting uprights.

'Yes?' Rurik half turned. Some of the nearby fires were still casting a faint light through the tent material, and she could see him glancing at her over his shoulder.

'Do you . . . I mean, are you married?'

'What? No!' His whole body swivelled round and he raised himself up on one elbow. 'Why do you ask?'

'I just want to know if I am taking someone's place, although I know this is not real.'

'I don't have a wife and I don't want one either.'

'Right.' Sara was surprised at his vehemence. 'No children?'

'No! If I had any, I would have brought them with me, not left them behind. Honestly, what do you think of me?' He sounded quite irritated now, and she figured maybe she should leave the subject alone. It seemed to be a sore point.

'Sorry. I just . . . Never mind.'

'What? Tell me.'

'I was surprised, that's all. You are . . .' She hesitated, not wanting to inflate his ego, but he must know his own worth already, so she plunged in. 'Well, you are handsome and a smith – a good occupation, yes? – and I thought many women would want to be your wife. Forget I asked. Goodnight.'

But Rurik stayed on his side, looking down on her. She sensed it, even if she refrained from looking at him. 'Thank you,' he said. 'I am honoured that you should think that, but as I said, I don't want a wife. Not now. Perhaps not ever. The one I wanted was taken.'

Unrequited love? Sara's interest was piqued, but she was sure he wouldn't discuss this any further with her. Best to keep her curiosity contained. 'I see,' was all she replied, but he'd stirred up memories, so she couldn't help adding, 'And the person I wanted was not the man I thought. He was a . . .' She tried to remember a word she'd heard earlier today. What was it? Oh yes. 'An *aumingi*.'

Rurik chuckled at that and seemed to relax. 'Then we are almost even. Goodnight, Sara.'

Chapter Eleven

Rurik was still mulling over Sara's words the following morning as he helped to load all the looted provisions on to Asmund's ship. She thought him handsome, did she? Well, that was flattering, and perhaps it meant she'd be willing to let him take some liberties, but he wouldn't. Now that he was getting to know her, he'd realised that that way lay danger. If he needed relief of that sort, it was probably better to visit one of the camp followers who were bound to be around. At least then he'd feel nothing other than lust.

That thought gave him pause. Why was he worried about feeling anything else for Sara? He couldn't, not when the only woman he would ever love was Linnea. Still, he and Sara were becoming friends and he wanted it to stay that way. No complications.

He had always thought love was a notion dreamed up by *skalds* – until he met Linnea. Most people married whoever their parents chose for them and there was never any mention of love. Land, possessions, social status and forming powerful alliances with other families, these were the most important considerations. Love, or at least mutual respect and liking, might or might not come later. But in Rurik and his brothers' case, there were no elders to matchmake for them, unless you counted their aunt Estrid, although she had no authority over them as such. Which left them free to make their own choices.

Not that this was much use to him, since the woman he would have liked to marry was taken.

If he wanted a family – and he might, eventually – he would have to accept a more prosaic type of marriage. The normal kind. It was a means to an end, that was all. Everyone wished for descendants, and being in love was not necessary. Sara was not the right woman for him, though. She didn't really fit in here and she could disappear at any time if the gods chose to take her away. He still had no idea why they had sent her to him in the first place, but perhaps if he was patient, he'd find out.

He threw a glance at her as she knelt by a small brook with Eadgyth, Holger's woman, washing the clothes she'd been given the night before. At her request, Rurik had bought some lye soap from another woman, and she'd happily followed Eadgyth with her pile of dirty garments. She was laughing now at something the other woman said, and he watched as her whole face lit up, those amber eyes twinkling. They were framed by thick dark lashes, which emphasised their appeal. She was very pretty altogether, there was no denying it, but in a completely different way to Linnea's cool golden-haired beauty. Sara was shorter and curvier – no mean feat, as Linnea was certainly well rounded in the right places – and somehow more colourful, with her shining hair, glinting with red highlights, and sun-kissed skin. Rurik found himself thinking of the two women as gold and copper – both beautiful, but while gold just gleamed, the copper gave off a warm, flaming sheen.

Whereas Linnea had a regal look to her, Sara seemed softer and more feminine. Rurik found his protective instincts coming to the fore whenever she was near, and although he'd often wanted to protect Linnea too, she'd always been self-sufficient and capable.

He shook his head. What was he doing comparing the two? There was no point. Sara was his pretend wife for now and that was all. She'd make some other man a great wife for real, he was sure, and although she'd been badly let down by someone by the sound of it, there would be others wanting her. He had no doubt about that.

It just wasn't going to be him.

'Your man keeps glancing over here. He's clearly besotted.' Eadgyth giggled and gave Sara a friendly push.

She felt her cheeks heat up but tried to laugh along, even though she knew this was far from the truth. 'Well, our marriage is quite new,' she murmured. Just how new, or how fake, she wasn't about to tell the woman.

'Always the best time.' Eadgyth rinsed out some cloths she'd been using as nappies. Sara looked away and tried not to grimace. It was a good thing she wasn't going to have babies in this age. How did anyone survive without disposables? Washing off faeces every day would not be her preference, that was for sure. The smell was revolting even from a distance. To be fair, though, she had been told by friends that when it was your own child, you didn't mind such things. It became the norm.

It occurred to her that she would have to deal with this sort of thing in a way when she had her periods. There were no sanitary towels here; presumably the women of this age used cloths similar to Birger's nappies. She'd have to find out. Thank goodness she'd only just had her monthly curse and didn't need to think about this quite yet.

She rinsed the clothes she'd been washing one last time and

wrung them out, shaking them to get the worst of the creases to disappear. 'Right, I'm finished. Should we help with loading?' She nodded towards the ship, where the men had formed a line, passing goods from one to the other.

'No, just pack up your things. We'll be off soon, but you have time to let the washing hang over a bush for a while first. I bet you'll be glad to get back into women's clothing again.'

'Mm.' Sara wasn't convinced, actually. Wearing a dress all the time – and a long one at that – would restrict her movements and take some getting used to, but of course she couldn't tell Eadgyth that. And it might stop everyone from staring at her. She'd noticed that she was receiving quite a few looks from both men and women in the camp, and she could do without being the centre of attention. She would be especially pleased if Asmund stopped ogling her – she'd caught him at it several times already this morning. It made her uneasy.

Packing wasn't difficult, since she didn't have anything other than the wet washing, which she draped over the nearest bush as instructed. She hoped the clothes would be dry soon, as she didn't know how to transport them wet. It wasn't as if she could put them in a plastic bag. Hopefully she'd also find an opportunity to wash her body before putting the clean garments on. She was beginning to feel distinctly grubby, and shuddered to think how many days she'd worn the same things now. How did these people cope without deodorant, soap, shampoo and toothpaste? Although she had to admit, she'd not recoiled from anyone yet, so they must manage to keep themselves fairly clean even without such modern items. Or maybe her nose had adjusted to the smells already.

While they waited to board the ship, the women sat on the sand playing with little Birger, who was quite fast if a bit unsteady on his chubby legs. Sara smiled at the sight of him dressed in a miniature version of the adult male Viking clothing – he looked very sweet.

'Just as well to let him run now, as he'll have to sit still on board the ship.' Eadgyth sighed. 'Prepare yourself for screaming. He doesn't take kindly to being confined.'

'Let's collect a few things to keep him occupied then,' Sara suggested. 'Sticks and rocks, perhaps? Shells?'

'Good idea.'

Soon afterwards, they were finally allowed on to Asmund's ship, which seemed loaded to the gunwales. 'You'll have to sit in the middle, next to those sacks,' their leader growled. 'There's not much room.' He threw a look of acute dislike Beowulf's way, which the big hound responded to by growling softly in his throat.

'Here, Beowulf, ignore him,' Sara whispered, indicating the planks next to her. She put an arm round the dog while she and Eadgyth made themselves as comfortable as they could on a couple of sheepskin rugs. Four other women and more children joined them, and Sara felt very crowded. Would the boat really be able to carry all this weight? But no one else seemed bothered, and soon the men had pushed it into the water and jumped on board.

She watched as they fitted the oars into loops of rope and, at a signal from Asmund, began to row as one. Their synchronicity was impressive, as was the fact that they didn't appear to be straining much. The ship was riding low in the water, the waves only a foot or so below the top of the sides, but their progress was smooth, with no bobbing up and down, and Sara relaxed. When, further out from shore, the sail was hoisted, she ducked with the others to avoid the bottom of it, or getting tangled in the ropes, then smiled at Eadgyth when the wind caught the sail and the ship took off. It gathered speed almost instantly and it was like flying along across the sea, a lovely sensation.

A thrill went through her, and she looked over to where Rurik was putting his muscles to good use. He was clearly in his element and looked at ease, skin glowing and sun-kissed, his golden hair tousled by the breeze. Their eyes locked for a moment and some kind of spark passed between them. She felt her blood sing and couldn't help but smile at him. He smiled back, as if he'd felt it too.

She hadn't expected to enjoy the journey, but she turned her face towards the sun now and prepared to do just that.

Rurik had positioned himself on a bench near Sara so he could keep an eye on her in case she became frightened. He didn't know if she'd ever travelled by ship, and the expanse of sea could appear daunting. After his recent escapades, he wasn't all that keen himself, but as he'd expected, they stayed close to the coast and the sea was calm. And he needn't have worried about Sara – she looked as though she was relishing the experience, as was Beowulf. The hound turned his nose towards the sun, the same way his mistress was doing, and his ears flapped in the breeze. The sight made Rurik smile. For an instant, as he and Sara exchanged a glance, he felt a connection with her, but he told himself it was only a shared joy in sailing on a calm sea on a beautiful autumn morning.

He'd wondered how Beowulf would deal with having so many strangers crowding around him, especially children, but the dog submitted patiently to being leaned on, having his fur and ears pulled, and generally being mauled by Holger's little son. Soon he was receiving attention from some of the other children as well. Rurik concluded that the animal must have been used to the youngsters at the farmstead where he'd lived. It was good to know he could be gentle when necessary and yet fierce in his defence of Sara. That was exactly how a hound should be.

Sara must have been thinking along the same lines. 'He's wonderful, isn't he?' she called over to him. 'So patient.'

Rurik's smile widened at the proud tone of her voice, as though Beowulf was her child and she was taking credit for his behaviour. 'Yes, indeed.'

The sail did most of the work and it wasn't until late afternoon that they had to pick up the oars again to steer the boat into an estuary. A long spit of land had to be passed first, then they turned sharp right into the mouth of the estuary and carried on along the right-hand – or northern – side. As dusk wasn't far off, the man in charge of the lead ship apparently decided to make landfall, and everyone else followed suit. Soon the long line of ships was pulled up on to a sandy beach, just like the day before, and the passengers jumped out to stretch their legs and set up camp for the night.

Rurik hadn't been introduced to the leader of this army – or *here*, as the others called it – but Holger pointed him out in the distance. 'That's Hálfdan Hvítserk,' he said. 'A strong and decisive jarl, one we're all happy to follow. He's not led us wrong so far.'

That was also good to know, but Rurik didn't comment that this assumed a wish for fighting and plunder on his part, something that wasn't true. He believed there were better ways of gaining wealth and recognition, but there was no point mentioning that here.

'So is he the overall leader of this *here*? A king?' he asked. Hálfdan seemed to be deep in conversation with a group of men dressed in colourful tunics, the garments ostentatiously decorated with woven bands that included gold and silver threads that flashed in the fading light. This usually indicated high status.

'No, I don't believe we have just one jarl or king in charge at the moment. Hálfdan used to share that role with his brother, Ívar Ragnarsson, known as Ívar the Boneless.' Holger chuckled at

Rurik's raised eyebrows. 'I know, strange name, eh? But the man was a legendary warrior, as fast and agile as they come. Although exceptionally tall, you wouldn't have believed his flexibility and speed. I saw it for myself several times.' He shook his head, his expression changing to one of deep sadness. 'But Ívar went off to fight elsewhere, and unfortunately, he died a year ago, in Írland. Ever since, the leadership has been split between Hálfdan and the lesser jarls. They don't always see eye to eye, more's the pity.'

Although Rurik had no wish to take part in any battles, he felt a fleeting regret at never having met the amazing warrior. 'I see. Who are the others?'

'Hálfdan's brothers Bjōrn Ironside, Ubba and Sigurd Snake-in-the-Eye, as well as their allies Guthrum, Oscetel and Anwend. There were others, but some have fallen in battle, and Ívar's greatest ally, Olaf the White, who was his co-ruler in Írland, is up north somewhere at present. I believe they'll be bringing Ívar's body over and we're to bury him as soon as we have found a suitable resting place.'

So many deaths. Rurik wondered if it was really worth it, but to these men it must be, or else they'd never have set out on this quest to conquer and plunder. And as they appeared to be the winners overall, everyone looked happy, at least for now. He swallowed a sigh. Even if he'd made it to York without mishap, who was to say he wouldn't have become caught up in this fighting at some point anyway? Perhaps it was just as well he was part of it now.

But somehow it all felt completely wrong.

Sara stood for a moment on the sandy beach of the Humber estuary and stared at the incredible view of the sun going down to her right. She recognised this wild and beautiful place, having been here recently with some friends for an outing. Then, as now, she couldn't help but be in awe of nature – the sea stretching into the distance, with rolling clouds above that made you feel extremely small and insignificant, almost weighing you down. It was like being part of a Turner painting, one you'd want to stare at for hours and at the same time lose yourself within. Behind her the flat landscape, covered in long grass, stretched for miles. Seagulls whirled overhead, and a curlew's call echoed over the landscape, while at the water's edge further along, banks of reeds danced in the wind. Sara's hair was being blown around too, becoming impossibly tangled, while the fresh salty breeze stung her nose. She didn't care – it was a magical place.

'Sara, are you coming? I could do with some help putting up our tent.' Rurik's voice drew her away, but until the sun had disappeared below the horizon, she kept sneaking glances at the sight. It was such a strange thought that this part of the world would be more or less unchanged after a millennium. And that she had been given the opportunity to see both.

If only she could have told her grandpa about it. He of all people would have truly understood the reverence and wonder she felt. But she might never see him again . . .

Best not to think about that now.

As they bedded down for the night in their tent, with Beowulf by their feet, Rurik told Sara what he'd learned earlier about the collection of warbands and their various leaders. When he mentioned Ívar the Boneless – whom he called *Ívar Beinlausi* in his language – she drew in a sharp breath.

'Even I have heard of him.' She remembered the stories she'd read and the speculation as to whether his name was because he had some illness, or even if it was an oblique reference to impotence. 'You are saying he was very . . . what?'

'Flexible. Able to bend and stretch in all directions. And fast, even though he was very tall.'

This was another new word for her, but she memorised it as she was doing with everything else she learned on a daily basis. A giggle escaped her. 'So it wasn't that he couldn't . . . er, sleep with a woman.'

'What? Oh, I see, "boneless".' Rurik laughed. 'No, I've not heard that mentioned.' He was turned towards her, leaning on one elbow, and although she couldn't see his expression, she heard him chuckle again. The sound did funny things to her insides, making her want to shiver, and she was supremely aware of how close he was in the darkness. She shouldn't have mentioned sex; it was giving her body ideas. It would be so easy to reach out and touch him, and just . . .

He interrupted her wayward thoughts with a question. 'Does that mean people in the future joke about such things too?'

'Of course. Although it is not funny really. Not for the man it happens to, anyway.' Sara could feel her cheeks heating up, because of both the subject under discussion and her own stupid reaction to Rurik. What was wrong with her this evening? Sleeping with him would be a very bad idea, even if he'd be willing, which he clearly wasn't, since he was fixated on some other woman. He hadn't tried to touch her a single time since they'd met.

'I should think not! Was that what happened to your man? You said he was an *aumingi*.'

'My man? Oh, Anders, no . . . quite the opposite.' Sara snorted. 'He was only too ready to sleep with anyone, including a woman I thought was a good friend.' And she hadn't had a clue until the day she came home from hospital . . .

After the road accident that claimed both her parents' lives, Sara had been in hospital for months with internal injuries and a broken leg, as well as a couple of cracked ribs. It had taken ages to heal and then she'd needed physiotherapy to help her learn to walk again. Anders had appeared to be the devoted boyfriend, visiting often and trying to cheer her up with his tales of life at the design company where he worked. Not once had he shown any impatience at having to wait for her to recover, and she'd been so grateful.

She was due to be discharged at last at the end of June, but the physio had been pleased with her progress and the doctor agreed. So much so that a few days early he'd said, 'I think you might as well go home now and just come in once a week for your physiotherapy sessions. Is there anyone who can collect you?'

'No, they're working.' Sara knew that both Anders and her grandfather were busy during the week. 'But I can take a taxi. I still have my keys.'

She shared a flat with Anders, and although she knew he'd probably have preferred some warning so that he could tidy up and do some cleaning, she was eager to get away from the hospital and didn't care about the mess. She'd even clean it up herself; anything to be home at last. She was heartily sick of hospitals. It was also the day before Midsummer, and she was really looking forward to celebrating that with friends and family.

But when the taxi dropped her off, and she'd made her way slowly up the stairs to the flat, the sight that awaited her was much worse than a bit of dust . . .

'You saw them?' Rurik's voice brought her back from the painful memories, which, strangely enough, seemed very distant now and not quite as raw.

'Yes. I found them in my bed.' Well, it had been Anders' bed too, but definitely not Marie's. She sighed. 'Maybe it was good. Better to find out before I married him, my grandfather said.'

Rurik put out a hand to stroke her cheek, and the gentle caress made her hold her breath. 'That man was a *fifl*. He did not deserve you. I'm sure you'll find someone much better.'

'Maybe. We will see.' For that, she'd have to go back to her own time, and right now she didn't want to. Right now, she wanted Rurik's hand to stay where it was, because it was sending a tingling feeling all the way down to her stomach. When he took it away, she had to force herself not to grab it and pull it back.

No, he definitely wasn't the answer to her problems. And she was determined to get home somehow. She took a deep breath and tried to pull herself together. Not every man was like Anders, and if . . . no, *when* she returned to her own time, she'd find someone better. Someone she could trust. Although how you knew a person was trustworthy was a mystery.

She turned over and stared into the darkness. Perhaps not going back at all was the answer. What was there to return for after all? Apart from Grandpa Lars, not much.

Chapter Twelve

Rurik watched Sara the following morning, wondering if she'd be brooding over the past. She had sounded so hurt the night before when she told him about her betrothed's perfidy, and although he'd never experienced anything like that himself, he could understand how painful it must have been for her to find the two lovers. And in her own bed too. He unconsciously made a fist, wanting to thump that Anders so hard his nose smashed. The *níðingr*.

Sara definitely deserved better.

She seemed fairly cheerful this morning, though, helping Eadgyth prepare a meal of barley porridge and playing with the little boy, Birger. Her only complaint before they packed up the tent had been about washing.

'Isn't there anywhere we can bathe?' she'd asked him.

'Swim, you mean?' Rurik frowned. It was a blustery day and the wind off the North Sea wasn't exactly warm. No one in their right mind would go swimming on a day like this.

That made Sara laugh, though. 'No, *fifl*, to wash. In a tub with soap. I feel so dirty. I've worn the same clothes for days, and now that I'm going to put on the clean ones, I want to be clean under them too.'

Rurik lifted his eyebrows at her. 'So have we all.' What was wrong with that? 'I'm sorry, but I doubt there will be any bathing until we are settled somewhere for the winter. I hear we are heading inland. If we pass any lakes or streams, however, I'll see if we can sneak off to bathe if that is what you wish.'

'Thank you, that would be wonderful.'

In the meantime, she'd have to make use of a bucket and cloth like everyone else. Rurik had managed to acquire a few additional things for them, since it appeared they were stuck with this group of people for the foreseeable future: a bucket, some more lye soap, a few extra blankets, a couple of sheepskins, some decent shoes for Sara that actually fitted, and a waterskin. It was as well to start preparing for winter, even if it was still a few months off.

He'd considered sneaking off during the night with Sara and Beowulf, but since he wasn't sure exactly where they were and in what direction Jorvik lay, it would be foolhardy. Besides, he wouldn't put it past Asmund to come after them, and his threat of taking Sara captive was enough to make Rurik think twice. It wasn't worth leaving until he could be sure they wouldn't be followed and punished.

Offering Sara the choice of travelling back to her own time with the magical *seax* still wasn't sensible either. Not just because it could get one or both of them killed; Rurik found himself reluctant to do this now for several other reasons. The first was that he'd placed the knife in a secret compartment in his kist and he didn't want to risk anyone finding out there was such a thing. Inside it were other valuable items he would need in the future. Secondly, he found that he liked spending time with Sara, and as long as she wasn't in any imminent danger, what harm could there be in her staying a while? At least until Asmund stopped paying attention to them. And every time he mulled it over, he reached the same conclusion as before – that it would be extremely difficult to explain her disappearance when they'd been at pains to show everyone they were newly married and supposedly in love.

No, best if they carried on as they were for the moment.

After the morning meal – the *dagverðr* – everyone piled into the ships again, and the men began to row into the estuary, heading west. At first it was wide, but as the hours passed, the shores on either side came closer, the distance narrowing. Rurik took turns with other men to row, but he wasn't really tired. It was nice to sit with Sara and Beowulf from time to time, though, and just watch the passing scenery.

'It's pretty here,' Sara commented, 'but not like home. I love this, but I still like big forests and lakes best.'

'Where is your home?' Rurik felt safe asking about Sara's past, as Eadgyth was busy chatting to some of the other women, and the children were particularly noisy today. He doubted anyone would hear her except him, although he'd looked around to make sure and leaned forward to catch her words.

'I grew up in Svíaland, not far from Birka, like you,' she said quietly. 'But for the past year, I've lived in Jorvik.'

'Really?' He looked at her. 'How strange. Is that where you were when you . . .' He didn't want to say it out loud, but she caught on anyway.

'No, no, I had travelled north to look at something.' She leaned even closer, making tendrils of her chestnut hair blow across his cheek. He pushed them away, noticing their silkiness as he did so, but her next words made him forget about that. 'Someone had found the grave you made for your friends.'

Rurik blinked in confusion. 'And what were they doing with it?' He couldn't imagine why finding a grave was of significance.

'Digging it up.'

'Eh? What for?'

Sara looked uncomfortable. 'Um, to learn about your time. Your friend had an *Ulfberht* sword and a beautiful gold pin like a bird, yes? And his head was hurt. We thought he'd been killed in battle.'

'They dug Sigvardr's bones up?' Rurik scowled. That wasn't good. How was the man supposed to enjoy his afterlife if someone was tampering with his remains?

Sara put a hand on his arm, her gaze troubled. 'I'm sorry. They didn't mean any harm. We . . . they just want to learn more. There isn't much writing about your people, you see, only buried items.'

It was a struggle for Rurik to understand this concept, but he could see from her eyes that she was apologetic; she clearly hadn't thought there was anything wrong with what they'd been doing. 'I see,' he muttered. 'Will they put Sigvardr back?'

'Yes, I'm sure they will,' she replied, but she wouldn't look at him and Rurik didn't believe her. Still, it was a long way into the future and there wasn't anything he could do about it. 'Whose was the bird pin?' she asked. 'Was it his?'

'No, mine, actually. I made it. Sigvardr had quite a few possessions to be buried with him, some of it plunder. That *seax* was definitely plunder, and I'm sure he'd taken the sword from an enemy in battle too. But the other two had nothing, so I decided to give them a gift each.' He shrugged. 'The bird and a silver Thor's hammer.'

'That pin was beautiful! Could you show me how to make one, please? I was going to try to do it in my time, but it would be so much better if I watched you first.' Sara's eyes were shining now, and Rurik found himself itching to find out whether she really was capable of such craftsmanship. She seemed confident in her own abilities.

'When we make camp for the winter, we can set up a forge,' he mused. 'There should be quite a few customers for us here.' He glanced around at the other ships, upwards of a hundred if he wasn't mistaken. With all the looting these people had been doing, they ought to have a surplus of metal items, ready to be smelted down and fashioned into jewellery, belt buckles and the like. If Rurik and Sara could tap into that market, they would make a good income. 'We'll need to buy some bellows and we will have to construct a hearth, but I know how to do that,' he told her. 'As long as there's suitable clay nearby.'

'Clay?' She looked dubious.

'I will show you.' And he was excited about that – he realised he would actually enjoy working with her as long as she was as skilled as she claimed. Time would tell.

The estuary became a river, and after another half a day's rowing, the procession of ships reached a fork where you could either continue straight on or turn left. Sara was pretty certain that they were currently on the River Ouse and this was where the Trent joined it. Holger's next words confirmed it.

'Straight on would take us to Jorvik,' she heard him tell Rurik, and she winced inwardly on his behalf. That meant they were indeed very close to his original destination – and hers too, of course – and yet so far from reaching it, with no hope of going there at the moment.

'But we're heading south?' Rurik sounded resigned, although Sara might have been the only person to register his regret.

'Yes, south-west,' Holger confirmed. 'We'll stop at Torksey first. It's where we spent last winter. A good place, with plenty of room for us all.'

The cavalcade turned left, which proved trickier than it looked, as there were strong currents swirling about here. Sara vaguely remembered that this part was called Trent Falls, although she couldn't see any actual waterfalls or rapids. She was familiar with this area of the UK in general, having lived in York for a year now, but she'd never gone as far south as the Trent. As the long line of ships progressed in a southerly direction, she looked around her with interest. Whenever they passed any houses, people would invariably scurry indoors, consternation or alarm on their faces. They must have been relieved when the ships passed by without stopping.

A few hours later, they came to an area of flat land on top of a low cliff near the river's left-hand side. The edge of the cliff facing the river was almost vertical, perhaps as high as between five and ten metres, but on the northern side of what looked almost like a small island, there were sandbanks sloping gently towards the higher ground. The boats were dragged up as far as possible on to a sliver of beach there, which Sara assumed would become wider when the tide ebbed. Rurik jumped out and asked her to hand him their things. Beowulf managed an elegant leap on to the beach by himself, but Sara hesitated. This beach was different to the dry one of the previous day, and she didn't particularly want to get her shoes wet and muddy.

'Here, lean over the edge and put your hands on my shoulders,' Rurik instructed. After a slight hesitation, she did so, and he grabbed her waist and lifted her bodily over the gunwale. A little squeak of surprise escaped her when he didn't put her down, but swung her into his arms, carrying her to where the sand was dry. Without thinking, she twined her arms round his neck, and couldn't help the tingle that shot through her at being so close to him. She could feel the muscles in his chest and arms, warm and firm against her even through their combined clothing, and he smelled of sea and fresh air. She swallowed hard and resisted the strong impulse to lean her cheek against his shoulder.

'There you go.' He put her down and hung on to her a moment

longer as she stumbled slightly. 'Whoa, careful.'

'Th-thank you.' Her voice sounded breathless, which was silly, as he was the one who ought to be out of breath.

'My pleasure.' He didn't appear to have been affected at all by her nearness, so she told herself to stop being such an idiot. But she couldn't help a small sigh from escaping her as he turned away to go and fetch the rest of their belongings.

Soon everyone made their way up to the camp site, which turned out to be more or less oval in shape. The area seemed vast, about five or six normal fields joined together to form a whole. There were tents and huts spread out across this northern part of the area, perhaps left behind from the previous winter, with fires lit and sounds of workmen hammering and shouting. Once the entire army arrived here – and they were still missing a few contingents as far as Sara could make out – this place would be a lot more crowded.

On the opposite side to the river, the camp was bordered by wetlands, probably marsh, and with so much water the site was virtually an island, exactly as it had looked when they approached it. 'A good defensive position,' Rurik muttered, looking around. 'I can see why they chose this place for their *wintersetl* last year. You'd be safe from flooding and sudden attack here. No need for fortifications.'

'How long are we staying?' Sara whispered, keeping close to him, as there seemed to be a lot more people milling about here than at their previous camp on the beach. Women and children, as well as men who were clearly not warriors. She felt an urge to grab hold of his hand, but resisted. Although it would be consistent with their roles as man and wife, he probably wouldn't like it. And she wasn't sure demonstrations of affection between couples were the done thing here.

'Who knows? Until everyone is assembled, I should think.'

'And then what?'

'Then we are apparently taking the kingdom of Mercia. Just like that. Holger says it's ripe for plucking.' Rurik's mouth tightened, as if he didn't approve of this plan, but they were both aware it wasn't up to them. 'Let us find a good place to pitch our tent. I can hear the sound of a hammer on anvil – perhaps we can also buy what we need to do some business.'

They claimed a small plot next to Holger and Eadgyth, with the latter volunteering to watch their things while they went to investigate the smith activity. There turned out to be quite a few traders who had stayed behind when the army moved off, apparently doing business with the local population. Now that the army was back, they were set to do even better. After a year of looting, the returning warriors would be laden with items that could be melted down and made into new objects.

'Holger said some of these men have been roaming for years, plundering as they went,' Rurik told Sara. 'Not just on this island, but in places like Frankia and Írland and lands further south. Even as far away as the Grikklandshaf. That should guarantee plenty of work for us smiths.'

Others were profiting from the influx of people as well, with merchants crying their wares and craftsmen setting up stalls. A man carving beautiful things out of antlers caught Sara's eye and she itched to have a closer look. Next to him another man fashioned various items out of leather. Perhaps better to come back another day, though; they needed to get settled first.

'So all this new-found wealth is from looting?' she commented, as they walked, not entirely happy about that. It seemed wrong, and she had no doubt she'd be asked to melt down stunning objects like those book decorations Asmund had taken from the monastery. Sacrilege.

'No, there are other ways of obtaining it.' Rurik shrugged.

'I heard Holger say they've done some trading in thralls along the way. Then there's all the tribute the local kings have been paying, of course – that's been shared out. And I should think there have been quite a few hostages held for ransom, which is always lucrative.'

She stared at him. 'Trading in thralls? Hostages? That's . . . that's . . .' How did you say 'barbaric' in Old Norse? It wasn't a word she'd learned yet.

'What? It's entirely normal practice.' Rurik scowled at her. 'The locals would do the same to us, given half a chance.'

'Yes, but . . .' Words failed her. It was abhorrent, despicable even, and she was going to have to work with the proceeds from these activities? That didn't sit right with her.

Rurik sighed. 'Don't tell me – this would not happen in your time?'

'No.' She hesitated, suddenly thinking about criminal gangs who operated in many parts of the world. They engaged in human trafficking, theft and violence. But they weren't the norm.

He put a hand on her arm. 'Look, it is not something you can change, Sara, so let it be. You are here now and your rules don't apply. Remember that.'

She sighed and nodded reluctantly. It wasn't as if she was likely to forget, but he was right – she couldn't fight the entire system single-handedly, and she was the odd one out here.

The first couple of smiths they approached were none too friendly and seemingly not keen on the competition, but the third was a Dane apparently called Grim – a name that didn't suit him at all, since he was extremely jovial – who listened to Rurik's explanation of the shipwreck without interrupting him.

'Bad luck,' the man commented. 'But illness was rife here recently and I happen to have a few items for sale that might be of use to you. Belonged to a good friend of mine who sadly succumbed.' He led them over to a large kist that proved to contain a small anvil, a sturdy pair of bellows and some tongs and other paraphernalia. 'Would you be interested in buying these?'

'Yes, absolutely. That's exactly what I need.' Rurik grew serious. 'But what are you asking in return? I don't have much silver left.'

Grim scratched his beard and considered for a moment. 'How about you help me with my work until such time as I judge that you've earned those items? These next few weeks are going to be incredibly busy, and I reckon I'll receive more commissions than I have time for.'

'Could we make it a fixed number of days?'

Sara was glad Rurik was canny enough not to agree to just any old deal. Who knew if this Grim would cheat them?

'Very well. Say ten days? I hear tell the *here* is staying for at least that long before moving off again.'

'Ten days it is.'

The two men swore some complicated oath, which Sara didn't follow, but she gathered it was binding for them both.

Rurik was smiling as they headed back to their own tent. 'Ten days will go quickly, then we can start trading on our own account.'

She was pleased he had said 'we', but that seemed to mean she wasn't included until those ten days were up. 'What will I do while you work? Can I help?' She envisaged endless days sitting around with Eadgyth doing nothing but babysitting. If Birger had been her own child, that would have been one thing, but he wasn't, and she wanted to be learning the Viking age techniques of a silversmith, not childminding.

'I suppose you could be my assistant.' Rurik hesitated. 'You don't mind doing menial work? Just for now? It might be best not to tell Grim that you are a smith in your own right.'

Sara sighed. 'Very well.' She knew he was right, but it was galling. There was a lot to be said for twenty-first-century equality, that was for sure.

That evening, she sat outside the tents with Eadgyth and watched as Holger played a noisy game of *hnefatafl* with some friends. He'd found a barrel of ale, so spirits were high as the drink flowed, and the men seemed to be gambling on the outcome as well, which added to the excitement.

'How does it work?' she whispered to the other woman, curious about this board game. It looked simple enough, played on a chequered board with gaming pieces that seemed to be made of lead. Each one had a little peg at the bottom that fitted into holes on the board.

'I don't play it myself,' Eadgyth told her, 'but I gather there is a king piece with a sort of army surrounding him, and the aim is to make him escape to a corner or the edge of the board. The opponent has to stop that from happening, obviously. Holger is very good at it. Look, he just won again,' she added with a proud smile.

'I see.' Sara kept watching and itched to try it herself. She'd have to ask Rurik to teach her some time.

Rurik himself was busy next to her, fashioning two aprons out of large pieces of leather he'd bought that afternoon. 'Mine wasn't salvageable after the shipwreck,' he'd explained before he started. 'And you'll need one as well.'

He'd used a very sharp knife to cut out the basic shape, and now he was adding ties and straps by fastening them with coarse thread, sewn through holes he'd made with an awl he had borrowed from someone. He seemed to know exactly what he was doing, his movements deft and assured. Sara couldn't help but admire his skill. There was something very appealing about a man with dexterity, and he had nice hands, strong and long-fingered.

He'd pushed his shirtsleeves up to expose muscular forearms too, and her gaze lingered until she realised what she was doing and shook herself mentally.

She shouldn't be admiring anything about him. He clearly belonged to someone else, even if that someone didn't want him in return. Besides, she wasn't ready to open herself up to more heartache. It was simply too painful when things went wrong.

'Can I help?' she asked him. Eadgyth had gone inside the tent to soothe a fractious Birger, and Sara was bored.

'If you wish. Here, fasten this strap, like so.' He showed her what to do and it wasn't difficult, just a bit fiddly.

They worked together and it felt companionable. Neither seemed to feel the need to talk and Sara couldn't help but contrast this to her evenings with Anders. He'd always wanted to discuss his day, tell her about everything he'd achieved, and make plans for the future. Plans she now realised all hinged on him hanging on to her coat-tails. He'd been on the same design course as her at uni, but he'd never been more than mediocre while Sara had won prizes and awards. It should have made alarm bells ring, but he was also good-looking and charming, and she'd been flattered that he had singled her out.

What an idiot she'd been.

But she'd learned that lesson. She'd never trust a silver-tongued man again.

Chapter Thirteen

Grim's workshop was in a small hut that had been partly dug into the ground. It had a hearth built up of stones and clay, with two clay ridges either side of the actual fire. Into one of these ridges a pair of bellows had been inserted, its nozzles emerging through a hole to fan the flames. Next to the hearth stood an anvil on top of a huge tree stump, and several buckets of water. Grim had hung his various tools in orderly fashion on the wall, and there were also two workbenches where one could sit to do polishing and finishing. Rurik was glad to see the man seemed organised and knowledgeable.

The front of the hut had a large opening that could be covered by a flap at night. It let in plenty of light and helped to cool the hut, as the immense heat from the hearth tended to make it sweltering otherwise. The roof was made of thatch – presumably reeds from the nearby river – which wasn't ideal, but a type of tent made of hides had been rigged up above the hearth to catch any sparks.

'I see you have been busy already,' Rurik commented, when he and Sara arrived the following morning. She'd not been best pleased to be roused when it was barely dawn, but he wanted to make a good first impression on Grim and had ignored her grousing. 'I hope you don't mind my wife helping? She acts as my assistant.'

He handed Sara her apron and donned his own. The leather fastenings were a bit stiff as they were so new, but they'd soon soften. And he couldn't possibly work without protection. That would be foolish in the extreme.

'Not at all. Many hands make less work. Welcome, er . . . ?'

'Sara.'

'Right. *Sah*-ra. And who is this?' Grim's eyebrows rose at the sight of Beowulf, who'd slunk in behind her skirts.

'Oh, sorry, that's our hound.' Rurik frowned at the dog. 'I thought I told him to stay with Eadgyth.'

'He's, um, not very obedient yet,' Sara muttered. 'Can he stay, please? I will keep him in a corner.'

'Yes, very well. As long as he's not underfoot.' Grim finished laying out an array of thin silver arm rings and small amulets on a piece of blue cloth on the bench nearest the large opening. He was probably hoping these would catch the eye of any passers-by. There were also some rings in a heap on a flat ceramic plate, and a couple of long neck chains, as well as belt buckles and an ornate sword hilt. 'Now then, I've received some commissions already, with men bringing me their loot. This is what we need to work on first . . .'

The two men settled down to their day's work, and Rurik was pleased to find Grim easy to get on with. They complemented each other well, and produced the required items faster than if they'd been working alone. Sara was initially given some pieces of jewellery to polish with a cloth and some vinegar, but when a ring needed the addition of relief decoration, she volunteered to do the punch work.

'Are you sure you know how?' Grim asked, his bushy eyebrows once again heading upwards.

'Yes, I . . . er, Rurik has taught me.'

Rurik hid a smile at this lie and hoped she knew what she was doing. Fortunately, that proved to be the case and Grim pronounced himself satisfied with her work. She also dealt with a couple of female customers who'd been lured into the hut by the glimmer of silver. They seemed more comfortable talking to another woman, and Grim obviously had the sense to realise this, as he just whispered the prices of each item to her.

When the ladies had left with their purchases, he clapped her on the shoulder. 'Well done! I expected them to haggle more, as the price I gave you was too much, but you kept it high. Excellent!'

Sara beamed back and shrugged. 'If they want to pay that much, up to them.'

At midday, Sara asked if she could take a break to walk Beowulf round the camp. The big hound had been very patient all morning, but he probably needed exercise. She headed back to their tent first, hoping to find a morsel of something to eat. The Vikings only seemed to have meals twice a day, but she was used to breakfast, lunch and dinner, and her stomach growled in protest at having to wait so long.

'Sara, how goes the smithing?' Eadgyth was, as promised, sitting outside her own tent and keeping an eye on theirs, at the same time as trying to keep her little son out of mischief.

'Very well, but I'm hungry. Is there anywhere to buy food?' Rurik had given her a handful of *stycas*, little Northumbrian copper-alloy coins, as well as a few bits of hacksilver for emergencies and a leather pouch to keep them in. She'd been fascinated to see that the silver consisted mostly of cut-up Arabian coins – *dirhams* – that seemed to only be used as bullion. No one here appeared to care whether you paid with coins or pieces of metal; both types of payment were acceptable.

'I had Holger fetch us some supplies and put half of it in your tent.' Eadgyth waved a hand in that direction and smiled. 'There should be some flatbread in there if you need to eat.'

'Thank you, that's wonderful!'

'It was nothing. You have been kind to me. Not everyone is.' The woman's expression clouded over momentarily, but she was soon back to her normal sunny self.

Sara had noticed that some of the Scandinavian women mostly ignored Eadgyth and other English wives and camp followers, who seemed to stick together. 'Why is that?' she asked. 'You are not the enemy now.' In fact, they'd been victims of this war or invasion, whatever you wanted to call it.

'I'm still not one of them, but they'll get used to it. Besides, they don't all come from the same place either and tend to cluster in their own groups.'

That was certainly true. Sara had heard Rurik say that the army was made up of men from many different parts of Scandinavia, as well as some who had settled in places like France, the Netherlands, Ireland and Scotland. They all had a common goal at the moment, but only worked together when they felt like it, not because they were all Danish, Swedish or whatever – there was no such concept as yet. It therefore followed that the women and children they brought with them weren't a homogenous group either. They spoke various dialects of Norse, had their own particular fashions and customs, and were definitely not all the same.

'Don't look so worried, Sara.' Eadgyth smiled. 'Things improved when I had Birger – now I'm the mother of one of their kind. I hope you have a child soon, as that will help you to fit in too.'

'Hmm.' Sara dived into her tent to avoid answering that. She found the promised flatbread and shared it with Beowulf as they made their way towards the edge of the river to give him a run. It wasn't exactly dog food, but he seemed to eat anything and everything, grateful for every morsel.

'Gut-bucket,' she teased him with a smile, and received a doggie one in return, complete with tongue lolling to one side.

The countryside around them was fairly flat in general, with the occasional tree and lots of bushes and reeds by the river. Banks sloped down towards the water to the north and south of the camp, and Sara decided to head south to explore that part. She skirted the cliff edge facing the river, and looked out across the glittering surface. The Trent was tidal here, and at the moment it was ebbing, leaving smooth muddy beaches on either side. It was quite wide even so – maybe thirty to fifty metres – and they'd been able to row two ships side by side yesterday without any problems. A few of the ships had been dragged up the banks and turned upside down, where men worked to repair them or add caulking. She avoided some vicious-looking brambles and rosehip bushes, but resolved to come back and pick some fruit later in the afternoon. The dark berries glistened in the sunlight, ripe and ready.

'If only I had some apples and custard to go with them,' she murmured. But perhaps blackberries went well with barley porridge?

There were also nettles, equally vicious, to avoid. Sara kept to the grassy areas that had been trampled by the people over-wintering here previously, and was pleased to see Beowulf had the sense to do the same. She let him find his way down the slope to the river's edge, and watched as he drank his fill then dashed about with great loping strides. It was lovely to see him happy. He must have been very confused and afraid when those marauders attacked his former master and family. Now he'd accepted her and Rurik as substitutes and given them his whole loyalty, a gift she appreciated.

She was just looking at the clouds, which were turning a bluey grey, with feathery white bits at the top, perhaps presaging a coming rain shower, when a voice rang out behind her.

'Out walking on your own? Is that wise? You might become lost.'

She swivelled round and there was Asmund, standing much closer than she'd like. He had grey eyes, chilling and intense, and they were fixed on her while crinkling at the corners as if he found the situation amusing. His thinning mane of light brown hair was flapping in the breeze, with long tufts sticking out on either side of his head, making him look faintly ridiculous, but she didn't so much as smile at the sight. A frisson of fear shot through her. Why was he here? And where was everyone else? She hadn't noticed how alone she was, nor how far from the camp she had strayed.

'I'm walking the dog and I'm not lost,' she replied curtly, gesturing to Beowulf, who came bounding up the bank to stand next to her. The hound let out a low growl, watching Asmund intently. The man glared back, but thankfully didn't come closer.

'You should take more care, is all I'm saying. I am concerned for your welfare, er . . . Sarey, was it?'

Yeah, right. She didn't believe that for a second. 'Sara,' she corrected him automatically.

'Well, Sarey,' he continued as if he hadn't heard her, 'if you ever need any help, come to me. I'm a reasonable man.' He smiled, but his eyes stayed cold, making her want to shiver.

'Thank you, but I have a husband. I don't need help.'

'Things can change.' Asmund smirked. 'There will be fighting, and your man might not be very good at it. There are always casualties in battle.'

Sara fumed inwardly, since the man appeared to relish that thought. 'Oh, I think he is, but we will see. Thank you for your . . . concern.' And thank goodness she'd just learned that word so that she could answer him. She took a step back and grabbed hold of Beowulf's collar, as the dog had now bared his teeth. She'd have to remember to bring his makeshift leash next time. 'I must be going back. Good day to you.'

She nodded and passed Asmund on the narrow path, making sure Beowulf was closest to him. To her relief, he just inclined his head and made no move to detain her. As she walked away, however, she thought she heard him chuckling.

Hateful man! What was his problem? He was the last person she'd run to for protection.

'Are you good at fighting, Rurik?'

'What?' Rurik looked up from his evening meal and noticed that Sara wasn't eating. Instead she was pushing her food around in her bowl in a distracted fashion. He put his own spoon down and took her hand, as she was clearly in need of reassurance. 'Yes, I believe I can hold my own in most clashes. I've been trained with a sword, axe and bow and arrow since I was a child. Why do you ask?'

'Oh, just something Asmund said earlier.'

'Asmund?' A shimmer of unease skimmed down his back. 'Why were you talking to him?'

'I met him while walking Beowulf. He . . . was in my way. And he said he was concerned about my . . . welfare? Yes, that was the word he used.' Rurik felt her hand trembling. 'I don't like him. He looks at Beowulf like he's going to kick him, or worse.'

Never mind the way he looked at the dog – Rurik was more annoyed about the man accosting his pretend wife. 'The *aumingi*. Don't listen to him.'

'But he said there will be battles, and what if you . . . ?' Sara turned her face away and shook her head. 'No, I must not think like that.'

'No, indeed. I'll be fine. I helped my brothers fight the Pechenegs in Garðariki and I think I can handle a few Mercians. If there is any fighting, I'll stick with Holger. He's survived seven or eight winters here, and countless skirmishes.' He gave her hand a squeeze and let go. 'As for Asmund, ignore him. He seems the type who likes to cause trouble. And from now on, don't walk anywhere alone. I'll come with you.'

'What are the Pechenegs? I know where Garðariki is, but I've never heard of them.'

Rurik was happy to enlighten her, as it changed the subject, and soon afterwards, she was back to eating her meal. As for that *fifl* Asmund, he'd have a word with Holger to sound him out. If the man was targeting Sara in particular, he'd have to be dealt with, but if he was merely stirring up trouble with anyone for the sake of it, they'd just keep an eye on him. He was clearly trying to rile Rurik, or perhaps he was testing him in some fashion? He'd made a point of gathering his men together earlier to divide the spoils from their latest raids, but although he'd insisted on Rurik's presence, he hadn't given him so much as a *styca*, the tiny coins that were barely worth the metal they were made of.

'You're not part of my *lið* yet,' he had told Rurik. 'You'll need to swear an oath of allegiance before you receive your share.'

They both knew that wasn't going to happen. A *lið* was a close-knit group of warriors sworn to their leader; a brotherhood almost, and more like kin than just comrades in arms. Nothing on earth would make Rurik want to belong to Asmund's retinue in such a way. Bound to him by oath and acknowledging him as his chief? Never. But there was no point antagonising the man outright, so he just shrugged and replied, 'I hadn't expected any part of this as I wasn't around when you . . . captured it.' He didn't say 'stole', as that wouldn't help matters.

'Well, we'll have to see about the oath-taking soon.' The smirk Asmund had sent him made him seethe, but he was determined to be long gone before he could be made to swear to anything.

He carefully broached the subject with Holger over a tankard of ale later that evening, while Sara was busy being taught a board game by one of Eadgyth's West Saxon friends. The clatter of the lead gaming pieces, and the women's laughter when she made a mistake yet again, made sure she couldn't hear his words.

'Ah, up to his tricks again, is he?' The big Swede shook his head. 'Anyone would think the man was related to Loki, the way he goes on. Pretend it's nothing and he'll soon tire of the game and find other prey. He gets bored easily. As for swearing an oath to the man – never.'

Rurik was surprised. 'You haven't? But I thought you were part of his retinue?'

'Oh, I choose to fight with them, aye, but I never swore allegiance to Asmund and he didn't insist. Knows I'm my own man; I made that clear. I only agreed to stick with his group until I find something better. Not that I told him that, mind.'

'I see.' But perhaps Holger's circumstances were different. He was so big and strong, any leader would want him in his *lið*, oath or not, whereas Rurik would be dispensable.

'Prove yourself a good fighter and he'll learn to respect you,' was Holger's advice. He gestured around the camp. 'Besides, there are plenty of other groups here, and Asmund can't force anyone to join him if they don't want to. As long as you don't disappear entirely, because then he'd go after you.'

That was probably true.

'And are we going into battle?' Rurik was, as he'd told Sara, good with any kind of weapon, but he still felt this wasn't his fight. He'd not come to this country to conquer its people or forcibly appropriate their land. At the moment, however, he seemed to have no choice but to do both.

'I should think so. We're heading for the heart of the Mercian kingdom, and even if the people along the way don't put up much of a struggle, their king will probably make a stand near his stronghold.' Holger clapped him on the shoulder. 'We'll soon dispatch him and then we can settle down for the winter.'

Rurik wasn't as sanguine, but he chose not to voice his concerns. There was, after all, nothing he could do about it.

'Speaking of battles, do you need a shield? There were some spares, so I grabbed one for you. Perhaps you can get your woman to repaint it for you?' Holger dived into his tent and emerged with a round wooden shield covered in a garish red pattern. 'Unlike some of the other leaders, Asmund doesn't insist on us all using his colours, so you're free to do what you want with it.'

'Thank you, yes, that might come in handy. I'll see what I can do about finding some paint.' Rurik put his hand through the handle at the back, testing the feel and weight of the shield. 'Perfect,' he declared. It was exactly like one he'd used at home.

'You're welcome. Always good to be prepared.'

He showed it to Sara later on and tried to ignore the startled look she gave him. The sight of such accoutrements obviously brought home to her the reality that battles were likely. But she soon rallied, and when he muttered about having to repaint it, she said, 'Would you like me to decorate it for you? I'm told I am quite good. What sort of motif do you want? A dragon, perhaps? Or does your family usually use something else?'

'A dragon would be nice, but I'm happy with anything.' He

smiled at her, glad she was taking this well. 'I'll obtain some paint for you. Thank you.'

'My pleasure. I love painting!'

He was looking forward to seeing what she'd come up with.

Sara threw herself with heart and soul into decorating the shield. She'd been dismayed at first when he'd showed it to her, because it made her realise that fighting wasn't just likely, it was probably inevitable. The *here* wasn't in England on a pleasure jaunt; they had come with the intent to conquer and plunder. That wasn't going to happen without bloodshed, obviously.

And now it looked as though Rurik had no choice but to take part.

It was good that he had a shield – any kind of protection was welcome – and it was sturdy and well made. The dreadful red paintwork didn't suit him at all, though, and she was determined to give him something more fitting. Something he could be proud to carry in battle. Why this was so important to her, she didn't stop to analyse. It just was, and she stayed by their tent the following day in order to concentrate on the task.

'I'm sure you and Grim can do without me for one day,' she told Rurik.

'Of course. Here, I've obtained some blue and grey paint for you, and a little bit of green. Will that do?'

'Perfect, thank you.'

She began by taking the shield down to the river and scrubbing off the old paint with sand and water. Eadgyth happily came with her, as she had baby clouts to wash, and little Birger enjoyed splashing at the water's edge with Beowulf on guard.

'He's wonderful with him!' Eadgyth glanced at the dog. 'Look, he's preventing him from straying too far out. It's as if he understands that it's dangerous.'

Beowulf did indeed seem to be herding the toddler closer to shore, standing in the water to physically prevent him from venturing out. Sara smiled. 'He is amazingly good. Whoever raised him must have trained him to watch over their children.'

Back at their tents, Sara shared a quick meal with the hound while she waited for the shield to dry out in the sunshine. It didn't take long, as it was a lovely day. Then began the actual work of painting a suitable motif on to it. First she took a piece of burnt charcoal from their cooking fire and started to sketch the rough outline of a dragon. Its head was placed at the top, above the shield boss, and she made the body snake around in a circle so that it was almost biting its own tail.

'That is amazing, Sara!' Eadgyth watched in awe as her friend picked up the grey paint pot to fill in the outline of the mythical creature. 'Where did you learn to paint like that?'

'Oh, a . . . um, learned man taught me. He said I had a . . . skill for it.'

'Aptitude,' Eadgyth corrected.

'Yes, that.'

'Well, you certainly have. Rurik will be so pleased.'

Sara felt her cheeks heat up and bent over her work so it wouldn't show. She hoped he would like it and be proud to carry the shield into battle. It felt important to her to contribute in some small way, and as she couldn't fight alongside him, this was the best she could do. If she painted it with love, perhaps it would protect him?

The thought brought her up short. No, what was she thinking? It wasn't love, just concern for someone she had come to like and, perhaps, admire. A good friend. Nothing more.

He deserved her best work, and that was what he would have.

*

'Sara, that is incredible!'

Rurik had returned from a long day in Grim's forge and wanted nothing more than a drink and a meal, then sleep. But the sight of his new shield motif made all thoughts of tiredness fall away, and he gazed at it in wonder. Sara had leaned the shield against their tent frame, presumably to dry, and he hunkered down in front of it, studying the amazing dragon that now crawled its way around the central iron boss. Outlined in dark grey, its body was blue but highlighted in turquoise and green, making it seem as though the creature's scales were shimmering in sunlight. It had sharp talons and a fierce expression, and its wings were edged with lethal-looking spikes. Around the rim of the shield, Sara had added a decorative pattern alternating the same colours, which added to the overall impression of sumptuousness.

It was a shield any man would be proud to bear.

'You like it?' She knelt next to him, and the look she sent him was almost shy, and definitely uncertain.

'Like it? I love it! I don't think I have ever owned such a fine shield in my life. You were being exceedingly modest when you said you are skilled at painting. This is very good work indeed – I feel as though he might leap off at any time to devour me.' He smiled at her, then on impulse pulled her in for a bear hug. 'Thank you. Thank you so much!'

'It was nothing,' she muttered into his shoulder, but she briefly hugged him back with a fierce strength that told him the shield mattered to her. She had clearly wanted to do him proud, and there was no denying she had. 'I hope it brings you luck,' she added.

'I am sure it will. How could it not? Such a magnificent creature will scare away all opponents.' He was joking, but at the same time he felt as though the love and care she had put into this painting project must give him good fortune.

It warmed him to think that she wanted him kept safe, that his welfare mattered to someone here. That meant a lot, especially since his family was so far away and might never find out what had happened to him should he fall in battle. Sara was the closest thing to kin he had at the moment, and he was glad he hadn't sent her back to the future yet.

He should probably find a way to do that, and a twinge of guilt shot through him, because it was his fault that she was still here. His actions and lack of foresight had put her in danger, and it was up to him to dispatch her to safety. But it seemed impossible here among the thousands of people camping all around them, and deep down he knew it would be better to wait for an opportune moment when no one would notice her disappearance. And there was one other – rather selfish – reason why he hesitated.

He wanted her to stay a bit longer.

'That is very pretty work you're doing.'

Grim had come up behind Sara and was peering over her shoulder as she added minute filigree details to a pendant Rurik had fashioned earlier. It was in the shape of a Thor's hammer – Mjōlnir – and she was decorating it with a swirling pattern made up of tiny silver beads and twisted silver thread. After a whispered conversation, where he ascertained whether she'd done such work before, Rurik had entrusted her with the silver solder, tweezers and a pair of tongs. For each added piece of the pattern, she had to coat the base – the flat piece of silver in the shape of a hammer – with a solution made up mostly of silver and copper. This acted as a sort of glue when she put the beads or silver thread on top and heated it up. The added copper gave the solder a lower melting point, which was essential so that she didn't melt the entire object she was trying to add the filigree to. It was slow, painstaking work, but Sara loved it.

'Thank you.' She smiled at Grim.

'Did your husband teach you?'

'Er, yes.' She thought it best to lie. The smith would never understand about art school, jewellery-making courses and design degrees, although she smiled inwardly at the thought of what his expression might be should she try to describe them to him.

Rurik, who was behind Grim, raised his eyebrows at her and grinned, but she pretended not to see him. If she could only have her normal tools, she'd show him a thing or two. Doing this work with a blowtorch was much easier, but for now, she was stuck in his time, where he was the master craftsman.

'Perhaps you'd like to continue with this ring when you are finished? The lady who ordered it said she wanted something beautiful.' Grim held out a ring that was nothing but a flat hammered piece of metal at the moment, although the ends were nicely shaped and filed.

'Of course. Could I add leaves, perhaps, so that it is like a . . . ?' She searched for the word but couldn't come up with it. Fortunately, Rurik came to her rescue.

'Vine,' he supplied. 'Like ivy.' He was becoming very good at guessing whenever her vocabulary knowledge faltered.

'Yes, that's it.'

'Excellent idea!' Grim beamed. 'Do whatever you like. We can always smelt it down if it is not to the woman's liking.'

Sara winced at the idea of melting something she'd spent hours slaving over, but let it go. Hopefully the customer would be so satisfied she'd tell all her friends. Only another week, and then she and Rurik would be able to set up on their own. If they had gained a reputation for excellence by that time, so much the better.

She had to admire his skills too. Having expected his technique to be clumsy in comparison to her modern ones, she found that he could create the most delicate of items despite the primitive conditions. Grim was going to miss having them around.

As if he'd been thinking along the same lines, Rurik asked him, 'Are you coming with us when we leave? If so, perhaps we could continue to work together.'

'No, I've decided to stay here, as before. I've built up a good circle of local customers in these parts, and they'll come back once the army is gone. Some of the *here* will be left behind to guard this place as well – the leaders can't risk losing it, and they need to maintain control over the area. Very strategically situated, is Torksey. There's the river crossing point just to the north, a Roman road, and the river itself, of course, giving easy access to the sea and to Jorvik, as well as inland. I like it here and have already acquired a dwelling house.' He grinned and winked. 'And possibly a wife.'

Rurik smiled back. 'In that case, we wish you well. We will have to fend for ourselves, wherever we end up.'

Sara was sure he didn't mind. He'd always intended to set up on his own and had probably only asked Grim out of politeness. As for herself, she couldn't wait until they could work by themselves so that she could get properly stuck in. Doing filigree was all very well, but she was used to creating pieces of jewellery from start to finish, and that was what she would do.

As long as nothing happened to Rurik along the way.

Chapter Fourteen

Exactly ten days after arrival, the convoy of ships set off again, heading up the River Trent and into the centre of Mercia. Rurik wasn't sad to go, although he'd miss Grim. The man had been pleasant and easy to work with, and he'd been as good as his word. Rurik was now the owner of the anvil, a pair of bellows and an assortment of extra tools, as well as two buckets. Everything he'd need, in fact – the silver he would find elsewhere.

As they had come with Asmund, they were forced to continue to travel on his ship, something Rurik didn't relish. The man had kept his distance from Sara since that day by the river, but he appeared to glance in her direction a lot more often than was necessary. Almost every evening he'd passed by their tent, even though the site was huge and there must have been another route he could take. As this was probably designed to irritate Rurik, he tried to ignore it, but it was galling nonetheless. And he found that he didn't like other men ogling Sara, even though she wasn't really his wife. He still felt responsible for her. Protective. Possessive, even? No, he had no right.

'Does he stare at all the women like that?' he growled to Holger, who was sitting beside him on the rowing bench when Asmund yet again turned his lustful gaze on Sara. Luckily she seemed oblivious, as she was playing with Birger.

'Who? Oh, Asmund. Yes. Always has an eye to the comely ones.' Holger sighed. 'Just as well we're forever capturing new thralls, or we'd have our work cut out keeping him away from our women.'

'Hmm.' Rurik vowed silently to be extra vigilant. 'So where exactly are we going? Just upstream?'

'Yes, but it's going to take a day or two to reach the Mercian king's sacred place. Hreopandune, they call it, and it is said there is a building for worshipping the White Christ where many of the Mercian kings are buried. Special followers of their god also dwell there, both men and women, like those fools we saw on the way to the coast. It's a powerful site and there's bound to be some valuable items for the taking. In fact, I've heard it is the richest prize in the whole kingdom.'

Rurik wasn't planning on stealing anything and hoped the current king would have the sense to take his valuables and leave. If not, he might soon be joining his ancestors in that special building.

'The richest prize, but not the king's main stronghold?'

'No, that is elsewhere, a place called Tamworth. Perhaps we'll go there afterwards.'

'So the *here* hasn't fought the Mercian king before?' Rurik was curious and wanted to know everything he could. It always paid to be well informed.

'Oh yes, several times.' Holger chuckled. 'The first time we attacked, he made peace with us, but I heard tell he wasn't happy about it. We spent the winter in his kingdom, then moved on and captured a fortified site to the east. Meanwhile, he'd sent for help and brought allies from the south to take us on – King Aethelred and his brother Alfred. I think they're kin through marriage, or so I understand. Either way, their combined forces couldn't breach our defences, and in the end they gave up and went home.'

'I see.' Rurik didn't think much of a king who didn't fight to the last man, but as he hadn't been present, and didn't know the exact circumstances, he decided to reserve judgement on the man for now.

While he rowed, he gazed at the procession of ships progressing up the river. It was an imposing sight, and probably an intimidating one as well for anyone not connected with the Norsemen. He reckoned there were upwards of a hundred vessels, carrying perhaps as many as three thousand people altogether, possibly more, stretched out along the waterway as far as the eye could see. Some were travelling side by side, others singly. No one seemed in any great hurry, and there was an atmosphere of expectation and suppressed excitement in the air. Singing and laughter, joking and talking echoed across the water. If he hadn't known they were heading towards bloodshed, he'd have thought they were on a pleasure outing, going to a feast. The rowing itself wasn't very onerous either, despite the fact that they were travelling upstream, but it became harder when the tide turned. He felt as though the whole situation was surreal.

Their progress wasn't wholly without incident. There were a few 'minor altercations', as Holger called them. In a couple of places, the locals had gathered in large groups – sometimes in the hundreds – to defend their lands. They put up a spirited defence, but in the end they didn't stand a chance, and word must have spread upriver, since these instances became less and less frequent. Rurik wasn't called upon to fight, as the clashes were over before Asmund's ship reached them.

Finally, those in the lead ships, who knew the lie of the land, halted just east of their final destination to allow everyone to catch up. The riverbanks on either side became clogged with ships and people, but the shouting and laughter stopped. An eerie silence fell over them all – no point warning the enemy of their approach if they weren't aware of it already. Although how they could fail to be, Rurik had no idea.

'Nearly there.' Holger was beaming with anticipation. 'We'll be making our way to Hreopandune soon.'

'Will there be much resistance?' Rurik couldn't imagine the men and women of the Christian god would put up much of a fight. Judging by the ones they'd come across in Norðimbraland, they were more inclined to just stand there and await slaughter. He couldn't understand that attitude at all. Why would you do such a thing? There was no honour in it.

'I hope so! The king and his men should defend what is theirs, at the very least.' The big Gotlander clearly relished a battle, and Rurik wondered what the man would do if and when this army ever disbanded. At some point, surely, the leaders would realise they'd conquered enough lands. Perhaps Holger would settle down somewhere with Eadgyth and their children, but if he thrived on excitement and adventure, no doubt he'd soon be off again. For men like him, there were always other destinations, new places to attack and plunder.

Rurik himself had never hankered after that type of adventure, but he had every intention of surviving the fighting. Whatever happened afterwards, he had plans for his future that didn't include this *here*.

'Hreopandune?' Sara frowned and repeated the word a couple of times. 'Ah, wait, I think he means Repton. I've heard of that place.'

Rurik shrugged. 'The name makes no difference. As soon as everyone is here, we will fight to take it from the Mercian king. I must sharpen my weapons.'

They had disembarked while they waited, taking the opportunity to cook some food and rest. He was sitting cross-legged on the ground, using his whetstone to transform his axe into an extremely deadly weapon. Sara could see the sharp edge from near the circle of stones where she was attempting to start a fire. She still hadn't quite got the hang of the fire iron, and it always took her a lot longer than him to make enough sparks, but she refused to give up or ask for help. This was a necessary skill for survival here and she was determined to master it.

'Slant it a bit more,' Rurik advised, ignoring the glare she sent his way.

'I am.' Finally the dry grass caught fire, helped by her blowing on it. 'See, I can do it.' She hung a small cauldron, half filled with water, on a tripod and added some bits of meat she'd been saving.

He just smiled, but after smoothing the whetstone over the axe one last time, he grew serious. 'Sara, there is something I must tell you, in case anything happens to me during the battle.'

She swivelled round, her whole attention focused on him now. 'What?' The thought that he might be hurt – or worse – had been trying to worm its way into her brain ever since she first heard about the coming attack. But she'd done her best not to think about it, because what good would it do? None of the other women voiced any fears and she wouldn't either. In fact, she'd even heard some of them egging the men on, stirring them up to be extra heroic. That seemed crazy to Sara, but what did she know? Perhaps it gave them added courage.

But dear God, what if Rurik doesn't come back?

She'd be lost without him here. And quite apart from the whole being-stuck-in-the-scary-past thing, there was no denying she'd miss him. She liked him more and more each day. He was an exceptional man. And attractive, though that was neither here nor there.

He wasn't *her* man for real, although when he looked at her with those amazingly clear eyes, she couldn't help but wish that there was something other than concern in their depths.

'Don't look so serious, I'll be fine. This is just a precaution. Come, I need to show you something.'

He led the way back on to the ship and over to his kist, which was stowed under the seat he shared with Holger. There was no one nearby, but he still bent to whisper in her ear as if what he was about to say was extremely secret. 'You mustn't tell anyone about this, understand? Our future depends on it. Do you swear an oath?'

'Yes, of course. I swear not to reveal your secret.' She was curious now. 'What is it?'

He knelt by the chest and pushed some of the clothing and other items inside, then beckoned her closer. 'Give me your hand.' She did, and, after checking that no one was watching them, he guided her fingers down to the bottom of the chest. In one corner, cunningly disguised by a natural mark in the wood, was a small hole. When you inserted one finger into it and tugged, a panel came loose.

'Oh!' Sara stared in awe at the items revealed underneath. At first glance it looked like a lot of tangled uncarded wool, but she could see that nestled inside this was an array of glittering stones, pieces of amber and hacksilver.

'This was what I was going to start my new life in Jorvik with,' Rurik whispered. 'I'm still hoping to do that, but should anything happen to me, I wanted you to know it was there in case you have need of it.' He closed the panel and stuffed the other items back on top of it. Turning to put his hands on her shoulders, he looked into her eyes. 'Promise me that if I don't survive, you'll take these things and run.'

'Where to?' Sara's heart was suddenly pounding with fear she could no longer suppress.

'Home. There's everything you need in there to get you where you want to go, but you'll have to be away from here. Understand? No one must see you. Take a small rowboat and slip away at night. Even if you're not very good at rowing, the currents should carry you swiftly downstream.'

She nodded. If she just followed the river, she'd reach the turning for York – Jorvik – and from there she could buy passage to Sweden with the riches in Rurik's kist. 'I-I'll try.' That chest was heavy, but she ought to be able to carry it a short way.

He gave her shoulders a little shake. 'You must! It would be dangerous for you to stay here without me.'

'I know. But Holger and Eadgyth—'

'They have no obligation to you.' He shook his head impatiently. 'Oh, they're nice enough and probably wouldn't allow any harm to come to you, but we can't be sure. And who's to say Holger will survive? The man has had the luck of the gods so far, but it might run out at some point. That day could be today.'

She swallowed hard. 'Very well, I'll run. But please try not to . . . g-get hurt!' The word 'die' was too harsh; she couldn't say it. Her whole body was shaking now at the mere thought, and she took some deep breaths to try and calm down. He'd said he was good at fighting – she had to believe him.

Because the prospect of having to slip away secretly at night, with a stash of valuable items, and without him, was not one she wanted to contemplate. Rurik just had to survive.

The ships slid on to the low-lying banks of the river, the only sound the hiss of their keels against sand, mud and grass. Groups of men vaulted over the sides and into the shallow water, splashing their way on to dry land. The groups became a steady stream of warriors, all running full tilt towards the Mercian king's settlement. Rurik was wearing a leather cap and overcoat to give him some protection from blows, and he carried his axe in one hand and shield in the other. Others had spears or bows and arrows; any weapon was acceptable. Personally, Rurik wasn't fond of fighting with a spear and he was glad he didn't have to today. His favourite was the axe, as he could do a lot of damage with that in a short space of time.

The buildings of Hreopandune came into sight as they ran closer, and it became obvious they had been spotted. To Rurik's surprise, the defending force looked woefully small and there was no sign of anyone with royal bearing. It could, of course, be the case that the Mercian king – Burghred by name – was unprepossessing, but surely he would at least be wearing costly clothing so that he'd stand out? Apparently not.

'Which one is the king?' he hissed at Holger. 'You've seen him before, have you not?'

'Yes, but I don't think he's here. Must be in Tamworth still, if he hasn't run away.'

'Run away?' What kind of leader didn't stand and fight for what was his? Rurik couldn't understand it, but there was no time to think about that now.

The settlement, which incorporated the building sacred to the White Christ, was situated on a bluff next to the river on the southern side. Rurik had heard the *here*'s leaders talking about the satisfaction they'd feel at capturing such an important and central site. It obviously held great significance for the people of Mercia, and by taking it, the Heathen Army would show them that they were in control in every way. The defenders were gathered on the slope leading up towards the settlement, but although they had the advantage of higher ground, the attackers had far greater numbers.

'Stay on my right,' Holger hissed. He was also wielding an axe with a long handle, and Rurik pitied anyone who got in his way.

'Why?' He glanced at his friend, wondering what difference it made which side he was on. They could fight together either way, and it didn't look as though it would be a lengthy or difficult battle.

'Because Asmund is to the left. He's been glancing at you and I wouldn't put it past him to try something underhand. Someone told me he's been bragging about taking Sara away from you soon, and I know the only way he could do that is over your dead body.'

'You're right about that. The trolls take him!' Rurik scowled and peered past Holger to check for himself. Asmund was indeed looking in their direction, but quickly turned away as if it had been coincidence. 'Thank you for the warning. I'll move even further away once the battle starts,' Rurik muttered, clenching his jaw. 'Hopefully the Mercians will keep him busy. Not that I'm afraid of him, but I really don't want to have to kill one of our own men.'

'Good idea. I'll follow you.'

The fighting began with a roar of war cries, imprecations and taunts, as well as banging of shields. The noise was deafening, ramping up the tension and excitement and stoking the attackers' courage. Not that this was necessary really, as they were not afraid. Dying gloriously while fighting was generally held to be the best way to go, and Rurik felt calm about the prospect. It wasn't an end, just a new beginning, and if it happened, so be it. He'd avoided drowning in the North Sea, and he'd do his best to stay alive today, but the Norns would have decided long ago whether he'd succeed or not. No point fretting about it. His only regret would be leaving Sara unprotected.

With an almighty roar, they headed for the nearest group of Mercians, who had taken up position on the slope leading to the sacred building. Rurik wasn't sure if he imagined it, but some of his opponents seemed rather lacklustre in comparison and not quite as eager. They must have known they stood no chance against the greater force of the Northmen. He was soon in the thick of things, lost in concentration as he began to fight. He used his shield effectively and managed to deflect several blows, while wielding his axe to advantage. He knew the shield design was irrelevant to his survival, but still felt that Sara had imbued her painting with luck, which helped to make him feel confident about his chances of survival. Perhaps it even contained some of the magic that had brought her to him. There were screams and shouts, gurgles of men in the throes of death, war cries and the clang of steel on steel. The smell of fear and death was in the air, as well as the tang of blood, and dust clouds rose to tickle his nostrils. It was chaos, but at the same time he was aware of their side making steady forward progress.

Holger was next to him at first, but after a while, men eager to fight pushed in between them and he lost sight of him in the melee. It didn't matter, as he was working his way towards the right, as he'd said he would. The battle raged all around him and everything became a bit of a repetitive blur – swing the axe, parry attacks, sidestep falling men, wield the axe again. He didn't feel tired, a strange fizzing and tingling in his blood keeping him going. And it was best not to think about what was going on or why he was even in this fight – that would make him lose concentration.

One moment of inattention could be fatal and he drew in a steadying breath, focusing on the task at hand. He'd promised Sara he would come back and he intended to keep his word.

Just as this thought flitted through his brain, someone barged in from his left and with a single sword thrust killed the Mercian he'd been about to fight. Rurik skidded to a halt, ready to turn on the next enemy, but the man who'd killed his opponent swivelled round and raised his sword again. Asmund. The *aumingi* was pretending to have gone berserk, slashing out at anyone and anything, red in the face and spitting with rage, but Rurik glimpsed the calculating look in the man's eyes, and the slight smile. This was no berserker; this was a man bent on taking what wasn't his – Sara.

A wave of fury surged through his own veins and galvanised him into action. He used his shield to deflect the powerful blow from Asmund's sword. It reverberated all the way up his arm to his shoulder, but he barely noticed the resulting pain. Instead he continued the shield's trajectory so that it hit the other man's sword arm, making him falter for a moment. At the same time Rurik raised his axe and prepared to kill the coward, but before he could bring his weapon down, someone came barrelling into Asmund's right side and shoved him out of the way so that he stumbled and fell to the ground.

'What did I tell you?' It was Holger, panting slightly from his efforts, but he didn't stop to hear Rurik's reply. Instead he nodded in the opposite direction. 'Let's head over to that side. The Mercians can deal with him.'

Rurik hadn't really wanted to kill one of their own, so he followed Holger's lead and soon found himself caught up in fighting on the *here*'s other flank, although it wasn't long before their opponents were either dead or running away. At least half the *here* were by now busy rampaging through the Christian buildings, and Holger ran off to join in the looting. Rurik stopped and took stock of his surroundings. He had thought the inhabitants long gone, but some must have stayed on, and screams of terror pierced the air as men and women in long white tunics tried to flee for their lives. Most were killed, and the ones who had been cowering inside their sacred buildings soon met the same fate. There was no shelter to be had anywhere. Not a single one of them tried to defend him- or herself, and Rurik left them alone. They weren't worthy opponents, in his opinion.

The buildings themselves were either going up in flames or being ransacked, apart from the ones that presumably contained food and other provisions. Statues, stone crosses and other artefacts were smashed to pieces, with bits of masonry and plaster flying everywhere. Amazing coloured windows were systematically shattered, the glass scattering into a thousand shards and raining on to the ground. It was as if the rainbow itself was fragmenting and descending to earth. Soon it was all more or less over, and men gathered around Hálfdan and the other leaders, watching as a Mercian nobleman came riding towards them with a group of retainers. Hálfdan held up a hand to stop anyone from attacking the newcomers.

'That must be the rival who's been wanting to take over the throne,' Holger muttered, having rejoined Rurik. 'Ceolwulf, was it? Something like that.'

It certainly seemed as though there was some sort of understanding between him and the conquerors, although it took a while before the looting and wrecking stopped completely, as the men were still fired up. In the end, silence descended on the scene and the invaders found themselves masters of all they surveyed, while Ceolwulf and his men approached warily. Locals of lower ranks began to appear from wherever they'd been hiding in the surrounding village and stood watching the proceedings, eyes wide with apprehension. Some bowed; others remained defiantly upright, but the terror was clear to see in their flickering eyes and panic-stricken expressions. Most of them looked to Ceolwulf as if waiting for directions, and he made calming gestures that appeared to settle them somewhat.

Rurik wasn't sure what would happen next. He'd heard many tales by now of past attacks, where no one was left alive and buildings were razed to the ground. It wasn't for him to decide, however. He watched as Hálfdan Hvítserk and his two brothers, Ubba and Sigurd Snake-in-the-Eye, jumped up on to a stone wall so that they could be seen and heard by everyone. They beckoned the Mercian to join them, and he tried his best to look regal and in control as he dismounted and did as they asked.

Hálfdan raised his hands and his voice. To Rurik's surprise, he began to speak *Enska*; presumably he'd learned it during the many years he'd spent in these lands. Holger, who was standing next to Rurik, translated quietly; he had picked up the local language from Eadgyth.

'He's saying, "People of Hreopandune and Mercia, if you are willing to accept us as your overlords and cooperate, you will not be harmed further. Ceolwulf here will be your king from now on, but he will be swearing an oath of fealty to us. Do not forget it! Now where are the hostages?"'

'This Ceolwulf is giving us hostages?' Rurik watched as two young men dismounted and came forward at a sign from their new king.

Holger nodded. 'Yes, it's the only way to assure his complete submission. I'm guessing those two are relatives of his.'

'I take it the other king isn't going to fight him for his throne?'

'No, he's probably halfway to the sea by now, unless he's run to his brother-in-law in the south again. Much good that will do him.' Holger spat on the ground. 'Not much of a leader, was he?'

'No, indeed. Are you hurt?'

Holger shook his head. 'A few scratches, that's all. You? There's blood all over your tunic.'

Rurik was surprised to see that his friend was right, but he was sure it wasn't all his own blood. He had a few cuts on his arms, and his right eye throbbed from where he'd been punched by someone's sword hilt, but other than that, he was in one piece.

'I'm fine.' He grinned. 'Sara will be pleased.'

The big Gotlander laughed. 'And Eadgyth.' He gave Rurik a friendly shove. 'Nice to have a soft woman to go back to after a day like this, eh?'

'Yes.'

But of course it wasn't quite that simple.

And glancing over his shoulder, he saw that Asmund was still alive. That was unfortunate.

Chapter Fifteen

Sara sat on the planks at the bottom of the ship with one arm around Beowulf's shaggy neck. They'd packed up all their belongings at dawn and loaded the ships, just in case disaster should strike and they had to make a quick getaway. And they were moored downstream, safely out of the way of the enemy. Everyone had assured them it was just a precaution and it wasn't expected that they'd have to flee. That didn't stop her from worrying, though.

Eadgyth was nearby with a sleeping Birger on her crossed legs. Neither woman felt like talking, but Sara took comfort from her friend's presence. She stared at the peaceful river scene all around them, reflecting on the strangeness of her life. There were no dwellings here, and if she hadn't known that she was in the Viking era, she could have just been on a pleasant outing in her own time. The view was the same, the early October sun reflecting in the water, which was flowing sluggishly at this point. Graceful reeds lined the banks, interspersed with weeping willows, bushes and short stretches of beach. It was serene and as far from discord as you could get, and yet not a mile from this place there would be chaos and carnage by now. She shivered.

'Have you ever seen a battle?' she asked Eadgyth.

'Not a big one, no, but I've been present at quite a few skirmishes. I've seen bloodshed, if that's what you mean, and I've seen the aftermath.' The woman's expression grew bleak.

'Your family?' Sara guessed.

'Yes. All gone, or at least I think so. I was the only one left alive at our settlement, but some of my brothers were away fighting for the king and it's possible they have survived and will come home one day.'

Sara took Eadgyth's hand and gave it a brief squeeze. 'Let's hope so.'

Time dragged on, slower than a snail at half-speed, or so it seemed. It was weird to think that women had waited since time immemorial for their menfolk to return from various battles, and all they could do was hope. Sara felt helpless, frightened and insignificant. There was nothing she could do to influence the outcome. If only she was the kind of girl who enjoyed martial arts and outdoor pursuits, perhaps she could have joined in the fighting. In Sweden, girls were allowed to do military service if they wanted to, but Sara hadn't even given it a second thought. She was into art and creative activities, not bloodshed and destruction. Now, she regretted this – it would have been good to at least know how to defend herself.

What would she do if Rurik didn't come back?

She'd promised to run, but it might not be that easy.

At last, exclamations from some of the other women heralded the return of the men. They came walking along the riverbank in groups, some talking and laughing loudly, others groaning, limping or supporting injured comrades. Sara and Eadgyth jumped out of the ship and on to the shore, scanning the groups with anxious gazes. They spotted Holger first, as he was so tall, and Eadgyth let out a sigh of relief. 'Thank the Lord,' she murmured, surprising Sara, who hadn't known the woman was a Christian.

'I couldn't bear to lose him, not now.' She hefted the still sleeping Birger on to her shoulder and walked forward to greet him.

Sara barely noticed. Her whole focus was on the man next to Holger, who was covered in blood and sporting a black eye. He didn't seem to be limping, but the sight of him all gory made her heart stop for a moment. Then, without thinking, she ran forward. When she reached him, she threw her arms around his neck, nearly knocking him over. 'You're alive!'

Rurik's own arms came around her instinctively and he found his balance. A chuckle rumbled through him. 'I told you I'd be fine.'

Sara suppressed the sob of relief that was trying to escape. She knew she was probably making a spectacle of herself, but she'd never been so thankful in her life. Before Rurik had time to say anything else, she yanked him close and kissed him fiercely, her mouth finding his as if it was the most natural thing in the world. His eyes opened wide in shock, and she stared into the turquoise depths, which showed that he was as startled as she was herself by her bold action. But the shock lasted only a fraction of a second, and in the next instant he was kissing her back as if his life depended on it. He crushed her to his chest, his mouth moving over hers, caressing, demanding, until she opened her lips to let him kiss her more deeply. Fireworks went off inside her veins, making her whole body fizz and tingle, and she responded wholeheartedly because it felt so good. She lost herself completely in the kiss until Holger's laughter brought her to her senses.

'Now there's a proper welcome for you. Eadgyth, my sweet, where's mine?'

Breaking apart, Sara and Rurik watched as Holger swept Eadgyth into his arms and kissed her soundly. They were both slightly out of breath, and Rurik still had one arm around her waist, but they weren't looking at each other. Birger, who'd become sandwiched between his parents, ruined the moment by waking up and starting to howl.

'Ah well, it was nice while it lasted.' The big Gotlander grinned. 'Come here, young man, none of that mewling now, please.' He hefted the boy on to his shoulder and jiggled him until he started giggling instead.

'What an affecting little scene, to be sure.'

The whole group had started to move off in the direction of the ship, but stopped and turned as one at the sound of the harsh voice behind them.

'Asmund. Good to see you survived the skirmish.' Holger said the words but didn't look as though he meant them. In fact, his expression was distinctly frosty. 'After you.' He indicated that his leader should precede them to the shore, and after a slight hesitation, Asmund strode off.

'What is *wrong* with that man?' Sara wondered out loud.

'Who knows? Always some discontent festering inside him. I've had enough of it.' Holger took Eadgyth's hand. 'I'll find someone else's group to join when we leave this place in the spring, *ást mín*. I'll not stay with a man you can't trust.'

'What do you mean?'

'He tried to attack Rurik during the battle and he knows I saw him. That's not going to make for a good relationship. Besides, I never swore an oath to him, so I'm free to go wherever I want.'

Sara's blood froze at the thought of Asmund trying to hurt Rurik, but the latter seemed to be in one piece, despite his bloodstained clothing. From now on, they'd be even more vigilant, though. She looked him up and down and made a face. 'We'd better get you cleaned up. Shall I wash your wounds? And I'm not sure that tunic can be saved.'

She was still trembling slightly from that spectacular kiss, but she knew it had been a spur-of-the-moment reaction and was best forgotten. She had to get her unruly body under control and try to act normal. But dear God, she'd been so afraid of losing him. It was only now, when she had him back safe and sound, that she realised just how much he'd come to mean to her.

Too much. But it made no difference in the overall scheme of things, because she couldn't stay in his era, and he was still in love with someone else, no matter how willing he was to kiss her. Besides, it wasn't as though she'd given him much choice – she'd practically flung herself at him. From now on, she'd have to act more sensibly.

Rurik took her hand and she played along for now, as it would have looked odd otherwise. They followed Holger's lead and started walking again. 'I'll clean myself up, but thank you.'

When they reached the ship, he let go of her hand, and Sara felt bereft even though she was sure he'd only held on to her for show as well. At least he was alive, though, and she wasn't alone.

Rurik ran into the river wearing nothing but his linen undertrousers. The water was freezing, but his whole body was on fire, so that was no bad thing. What on earth had he been thinking, kissing Sara like that? He should have just given her a brief peck and left it at that, but the instant their lips met, all rational thought fled. There was only sensation, her body crushed to his, her luscious mouth so enticing he'd just had to delve in. He couldn't help but kiss her thoroughly and she'd responded with an abandon that had him reeling.

Odin's ravens! The woman could kiss. And she was a very tempting armful, no doubt about that.

If it hadn't been for Holger breaking the spell, they would probably have continued for an embarrassingly long time. Thank the gods for the Gotlander.

He'd have to be more careful in future. Keep his distance, so as not to give her ideas.

He scrubbed every limb with fine sand from the edge of the river, dunking his head and using lye soap to clean his hair, which was matted with blood – not his – and perspiration. It felt wonderful to clean off the stench of gore, and he sincerely hoped he wouldn't have to take part in any more fighting. The Mercians seemed to have more or less rolled over and surrendered. Presumably, with their old king gone and the new one in place, they'd not give the invaders any more trouble.

'What now?' he asked Holger as the two of them stood on the bank, drying themselves with pieces of linen cloth. 'We won't all fit in the Mercian king's sacred buildings, if there's even anything left of them.'

'No, we'll camp around them, I expect. First thing to do is to bury our dead and then build some sort of defences and a long-port. You know, mooring all the ships next to each other so that no one can get through. Hálfdan and the other jarls will give us directions later, I expect.' He sighed. 'I sometimes feel as though I've done more digging than fighting during this expedition. But I suppose it's necessary. Burghred might come back with his brother-in-law in tow again, and we'd best be prepared.'

'King Aethelred, was it? From the West Saxon kingdom?'

Holger shook his head. 'No, not him. He died and his brother Alfred is king now. A dangerous man, that. I told you, I'd not go back and fight him again.'

'I see. Well, let's hope he doesn't aid the Mercians this time.'

Either way, the southerners wouldn't come during winter, and it was now almost *Gormánaður*, the slaughter month, and first month of the winter season. At its start, the first feast of the year would be held, the winter *blōt*. The jarls would want to be firmly entrenched here by then, although Rurik wasn't sure these precautions were necessary. The Mercian people were probably tired of bloodshed.

'I'd prefer not to spend the winter in a tent,' he mused out loud. 'If only we could find a hut of some sort, I could set up a forge there.'

'That sounds good. I'm sure there will be as much demand for your skills here as there were in Torksey. I'll keep my eyes and ears open and will let you know if I hear of anything suitable.'

'Thank you.' Rurik put a hand on Holger's shoulder. 'And thank you for coming to my aid on the battlefield. I think I'd have been able to best Asmund, but you knocking him out of the way like that showed him he couldn't get away with murder.'

'Think nothing of it. I'm sure you'd do the same for me.'

Holger was right. He'd proved to be a true friend, and there was a bond between them now that would be hard to break.

'Who's that?' Sara looked up from where she was kneeling by the side of the river, trying to scrub the blood out of Rurik's tunic. Luckily he'd worn a dark green one, and the stains weren't so bad. Cold water and lye soap were working wonders.

'That's the new Mercian king, Holger says.' Eadgyth wrung out yet another linen clout, the stinky nappy mess gone. 'His name is Ceolwulf and he used to be one of the former king's men. I think he was secretly in cahoots with our leaders even before the battle. Made things easier. He didn't appear until all the fighting was done, apparently.'

Sara frowned. 'But . . . why is there a Mercian king? I thought we, I mean, the Northmen, were in charge now.'

'Oh, we are. Ceolwulf was just appointed to appease the locals, I think, but he'll do as Hálfdan and his brothers say. He's sworn an oath and given us hostages so we can be sure he doesn't go back on his word. Besides, we're only staying here for the winter, and they'll need someone in charge when we leave next spring, although naturally a small garrison will be left behind. It's the same in Jorvik and other places.'

'I see.' She supposed it made sense, but she had no idea how the Norsemen knew they could trust this Ceolwulf, hostages or not. Still, that wasn't her problem.

She looked over to where Rurik, Holger and a whole host of other men were busy digging a huge ditch and rampart to enclose their camp. It looked to be at least three or four metres wide, and just as deep. This would eventually form a D shape, with the river as the straight part of it on the northern side. Most of the longships had been moored side by side there to create a barrier along the water's edge, although some had been dragged up further in order to undergo repairs. She supposed some of them had been in use for quite a few years now, and there was bound to be wear and tear. Carpenters and other workmen were busy with various implements, making quite a racket. And a couple of blacksmiths had set up makeshift forges, presumably to produce nails and whatever else was needed to fix the ships. The clang of their hammering was even more deafening.

The greater part of the army had gone to camp on a hillside a few miles east of here, and Sara wondered whether that was a better place to be. It would be less cramped, for one thing, although not as secure. Here there wasn't much in the way of privacy, and she felt hemmed in.

The church of St Wystan, which stood on a bluff behind them, was being incorporated into the defences as a sort of gateway. The church doors were to be used as guarded entrances to the fortified area, and a lot of the tents had been put up inside the ramparts. That made sense, as it meant less digging, but she was sure the Mercians wouldn't be happy about it and would see it as sacrilege. It was apparently the place where their kings had been buried for decades, as well as the saint it was named after. She'd been told some of their bones were still in a crypt under the altar, but whether they'd be allowed to stay there was anyone's guess. There were rumours of miracles, relayed to her by some of Eadgyth's friends who were Christians and clearly excited to be near such a holy place. Apparently Wystan – or Wigstan, which was his real name – had been the grandson of a king, but hadn't wanted to be one himself. For some reason he'd been killed anyway and buried here, and that was when the miracles had started and he'd been declared a saint.

Sara didn't believe in miracles or saints, although she couldn't help but reflect that she hadn't put any credence in magic either, and look what had happened to her.

There were a few other buildings here as well – most of them totally wrecked, leaving them as mere husks. They had apparently belonged to a monastic community. Those poor souls had been killed or fled before the Norsemen even arrived, and what was left of their dwellings were now being used by Hálfdan and the other leaders, or so Sara had heard.

She was curious as to what a ninth-century church would look like, and once she'd finished the laundry, she decided to head up the steep slope from the river and take a quick peek.

'Could you keep Beowulf with you for a short while, please?' she asked Eadgyth. It didn't seem right to bring him into a holy place, so it was best he stayed behind.

'Of course. He can help me keep an eye on Birger.' The big hound didn't seem to mind being used as a nursemaid, and Sara was glad. Perhaps he missed the children of his former family.

The religious building wasn't far from the water, but it was about fifteen to twenty metres above it. She noticed some newly dug graves near the church walls and wondered why a heathen would want to be buried here of all places. There were people going about their daily business all around her, but no one stopped her or said she couldn't enter, so she sneaked inside the church. It was a peaceful place, other-worldly, but it was a complete mess, with bits of broken sculptures and stucco strewn across the floor. There had evidently been some sort of mouldings on the walls, but these had mostly been hacked off, and hardly anything remained of what used to be multicoloured glass windows. The walls were built out of different-sized stones. Some effort had been made to make them smooth, but it still looked a bit higgledy-piggledy. There were no pews, just a large area laid with huge floor slabs, so she assumed the congregation stood up to hear the sermons. That must be tedious.

At one end, a Gothic pointed stone arch, just a little wonky and out of alignment, led to a raised area with an altar. This was bare apart from debris, and she assumed that was because anything that had stood on it had already been looted. A shame. Beyond the altar was another window with broken glass panes, and chilly air wafted in. Two crude candelabras had miraculously been left intact and were placed on either side of the altar.

To the left of this raised section a narrow, slightly curved staircase led down towards a small door. The crypt? It had to be. There was no one around at the moment, and she decided to have a quick peek. As it was bound to be dark, though, she grabbed one of the candles from the candelabra, and shielded the flame with one hand as she made her way down the steps.

The door wasn't locked, but creaked slightly as she opened it. She had to duck her head to avoid some spiderwebs at the top of the opening, and shuddered. Stepping into the crypt, she felt a chill in the air that she wasn't entirely sure was due to the fact that it was underground. Another shiver snaked down her spine. This was creepy. It wasn't a large space, maybe four or five metres square, with a vaulted ceiling held up by four stone columns. These had a carved spiral pattern from top to bottom. There was stone flooring, worn smooth as if trampled by many feet over time. Alcoves were set into the walls, and some of these held caskets, which Sara assumed contained the remains of the Mercian kings and the saint, although if the monks and nuns had had any sense, they would have taken their saint with them and fled. The kists must have been richly decorated, but now showed signs of having been hacked about. She guessed any gold or precious adornments had been looted.

It might have been her imagination, but she was suddenly convinced she could feel the animosity of these long-dead royals, and she couldn't wait to get out of the place. Spirits ought not to be disturbed, and she shouldn't have come. When she turned to leave, however, she found her way blocked by a large man, who must have entered very quietly.

'Asmund!' The word squeaked out of her, and she took a step back in fright, almost losing her grip on the candle. It illuminated his face clearly, and the smile she saw hovering on his lips was not a nice one. Her throat went dry, and for an instant she couldn't seem to suck enough air into her lungs as they constricted with fear, along with her stomach muscles.

'Did I not warn you against going off on your own?' He crossed his arms over his chest and regarded her with his head to one side. He didn't sound as though he was unhappy about the fact that she hadn't heeded his advice. She mentally compared him to a spider watching the fly it has just caught, knowing it's stuck.

And she was, because he was standing in front of the only way out.

'I . . . just wanted a quick look.' She tried not to show the terror that was paralysing her, but she was sure he could probably see her heart beating so hard it was nearly jumping out of her chest.

The hand holding the candle shook, making the flame tremble, and Asmund's smile grew wider.

'Well, I hope you've seen enough.' He glanced around. 'Personally I don't see anything special in here . . . except you.' His gaze returned to her and he moved forward slowly while looking her up and down. 'I shall enjoy having you.'

'I'm n-not yours to have.' She made her voice as firm as possible, despite the fact that it sounded weedy and shaky. Her eyes roamed the small space, trying to find something to defend herself with, but then she realised that she was holding the perfect weapon already. And she'd read somewhere that attack was the best defence. Time to find out if that was true.

Asmund's eyes were now firmly fixed on her chest, and that was to her advantage. She sprang into action, taking him by surprise when she lunged towards him, candle first. She thrust the flame as close to his left eye as she could, at the same time letting out a scream that she hoped someone would hear. He'd left the door half open, and as he brought both hands up to his singed cheek with an angry growl, she ducked past him and tore up the staircase. So intent was she on escaping the bastard in the crypt, she barrelled straight into someone with their foot on the first step, and the pair of them went tumbling to the floor.

'What in the name of . . . ? What is occurring?'

Sara looked up to find that she was sitting on the stone slabs next to Hálfdan Hvítserk, who was blinking at her in confusion. She was still holding the candle, and saw its flame flicker one last time before it died. 'I . . . he . . . I need to leave.' She waved a hand in the direction of the crypt, just as Asmund came charging out, one hand still holding his cheek and what appeared to be a severely singed eyebrow.

'Asmund.' Hálfdan got to his feet and held out a hand to pull Sara up as well. She wanted nothing more than to dash out of there, but he held on to her wrist. 'Is this your woman?' The question was directed at the other man, who'd stopped dead at the sight of his leader.

'Er . . .'

'No! No, I'm not. I'm Sara, Rurik's wife. The silversmith. I just wanted to see the crypt. The saint, you know? I didn't know Asmund was going to come after me. I . . .' She was aware that she was babbling, but the shock of the encounter was making her shake from head to toe, and she had to swallow down a sob.

Hálfdan scowled at Asmund. 'I've warned you about this before, have I not? If you wish to be a part of this venture, you leave other men's womenfolk alone, understand? Otherwise you can go elsewhere. Wives are firmly out of bounds, as you well know, though to be sure, it is the husband's duty to keep them safe.'

'She was asking for it. Has been since we first met,' came the surly reply.

'I never!' Sara's outraged gasp made Hálfdan narrow his eyes at first her, then her would-be attacker.

'That must be why she burned you, then?'

Asmund's cheek was bright red, the skin already starting to blister, but he bit his teeth together. 'A small misunderstanding, that's all.'

'I'm sure I was very clear in my refusal,' Sara muttered.

Hálfdan's frown didn't let up. 'Well, Sara doesn't seem to want you now, so from this moment on you will leave her alone, is that clear?' Asmund looked mutinous, and his jarl clarified, 'If I hear that you've so much as looked at her, you'll be cast out from the *here*.'

'Fine. She's not even worth the bother. Stupid woman.' Asmund came up the stairs and pushed past them, barging into Sara's shoulder hard. If Hálfdan hadn't been holding on to her wrist, she would probably have stumbled and fallen over.

After the man had gone, her legs gave way and she sank to the floor, still shaking. Hálfdan knelt before her. 'If you have any more trouble with him, you're to come to me directly. I'll deal with him once and for all. He's a nuisance, has been since he arrived on these shores. And tell your man to be more vigilant.'

'Th-thank you, Jarl Hálfdan. You are most kind.'

'Not a bit of it. I detest men who can't follow simple orders and I won't have it in my *here*. Now, let me escort you back to your tent.'

She took his outstretched hand for a second time, very grateful for his support.

'Thank you anyway. I appreciate your help.'

Chapter Sixteen

Rurik was taking a break and had gone to find Beowulf, intending to go for a walk along the riverbank. He was astonished to see Sara walking towards him holding on to Hálfdan Hvítserk's arm as if her life depended on it.

'What on earth . . . ? Sara, are you well?'

The dog bounded over to her and danced around emitting a series of short barks of pleasure at seeing his mistress. She bent to fuss him and murmur a greeting, but seemed very subdued.

Meanwhile, Hálfdan stopped before Rurik and looked him up and down as if trying to judge what manner of man he was. 'Your wife has had a fright. That oaf Asmund tried to attack her.'

'In broad daylight? The trolls take the man! I'm going to—'

'Calm down.' Hálfdan held up a hand. 'I've dealt with it. He shouldn't bother her again. If he does, I'll want to know about it immediately.'

Fury rose within Rurik, but he tried to suppress it and listen to what the jarl was saying. He wanted to wring Asmund's thick neck with his bare hands, bash his skull with his axe and then ram a sword through him, but that would be foolish. That wasn't how justice worked in their society, at least not where he came from. He had to trust that the man would do as Hálfdan had ordered, or else be punished by his superiors. But he'd make sure Sara was never alone for a single moment from now on. The thought of that man's big hands on her made him want to go berserk. He took some deep breaths and attempted to reply in a reasonable tone of voice.

'Thank you, Jarl, I appreciate it. I thought she would be safe here within the enclosure during the day, but I will definitely guard her better in future.'

'You're welcome.' Hálfdan was about to leave, then turned back as if he'd just thought of something. 'Did I hear Sara say you're a silversmith? I have need of one of those.'

'I am, but I have no forge as yet. I've been looking for a suitable dwelling.'

'There is a cluster of buildings not too far from here to the east at a place called Foremark, near the other encampment. I had earmarked them for storage, but perhaps one of those would be suitable, if you don't mind not being here in the thick of things? We can't all fit within the ramparts anyway, and some of my men have been ascertaining which of the locals have fled and left buildings we can use.'

'That sounds perfect, thank you.' Rurik was still too angry to fully appreciate what Hálfdan was saying, but moving anywhere away from this place sounded good. Away from that *argr* Asmund.

'I'll send someone to take you there tomorrow morning. You're excused digging duties from then on. Come and tell me as soon as you are ready to commence work and I'll let you know what I require.'

'I will. Thank you again.'

Hálfdan strode back towards the church, leaving Rurik to turn to his pretend wife. 'Are you hurt? Did the *aumingi* touch you?' The rage simmering inside him threatened to erupt at the thought, but Sara shook her head.

'No, I burned his cheek with a candle and fled. Then the jarl came to my rescue. I'm fine. Just a bit . . . shaken.' Her voice trembled on that last word, and without thinking, Rurik opened his arms and she went into them with a strangled sob. He could feel her shivering, and held her until he judged her to be calmer. From time to time he kissed the top of her head, and it felt like the most natural thing in the world.

'Well done for your quick thinking,' he murmured. 'Let's hope he sets his sights on someone else from now on, or I won't be answerable for the consequences.'

'I think he understood, and he's afraid of Jarl Hálfdan, I could tell.' Sara snuggled closer and something warm stirred inside Rurik. Something he didn't want to feel. Couldn't allow himself to feel.

'I sincerely hope so.' He gently untangled himself from her and focused on the dog, who was sitting patiently by their side. 'I'd better . . . um, walk Beowulf.'

She looked up at him, her cheeks turning a bit pink. 'Yes. Yes, of course. And I'll see about some food. Thank you for . . . well, thank you.'

As she ducked into their tent to gather up the cooking utensils, he stood for a moment staring after her, but then nodded to the hound. 'Let's go.' He needed a long walk to sort out his muddled thoughts.

Their new home turned out to be part of a group of buildings huddled together on a hillside a couple of miles east of Hreopandune. The large encampment was nearby, but it was mercifully out of sight. Instead there were fields all around in a tranquil setting, and Rurik spotted traces of old fortifications in the landscape. The settlement was reasonably high up and far enough away from the river not to be affected by any possible flooding, which was good. He had a suspicion the River Trent – as Sara called it – could be temperamental in spring and autumn.

The man sent by Hálfdan to escort them to this place pointed to the building on the far right. 'That one's not being used yet. Will that do you?'

Rurik let go of the handles of the cart he'd borrowed to transport their belongings and went to look inside. It had clearly been someone's dwelling, but whoever it was had left in a hurry. There was a hearth with a few utensils lying around it and a chain coming down from the rafters to hang a large cauldron on. A bucket looked as though it had been kicked over in the haste to flee, and a couple of kists stood with their lids open and what was left of the contents spilling out. Around the walls were benches, and he glimpsed two smaller rooms at the back. One still had a bed in it, while in the other he could see shelves. He nodded at Hálfdan's man. 'This will be perfect, thank you.'

'Good, I'll leave you to it then.'

When he went back inside the house, Sara was standing in the middle of the beaten-earth floor, gazing around her. 'How much lye soap did you bring?' she asked.

'What? Soap?'

'Yes, we'll need to clean this place from top to bottom. There could be all kinds of vermin.' She pointed at the benches, which were covered in greasy-looking furs. 'I'm going to start by burning those.'

'Is that wise? We don't have much to replace them with.' He wasn't fond of bed bugs himself, but they were preferable to being cold.

'If we . . . I mean you, start trading, you'll soon have enough silver to buy new ones. I'd rather spend the winter in our tent than sit or sleep on those.' She shuddered dramatically.

'Very well, let's see if the former owners left a broom behind.'

He was impatient to start making his forge, but he could see her point. They were going to live here for months, and it was best to make it comfortable first.

They spent the rest of the day cleaning the little house, including taking the bed outside to scrub it thoroughly in a nearby brook. Sara looked around with satisfaction and smiled at Rurik. 'That's better. Now I've stopped feeling itchy just looking at this place.'

He returned her smile. 'Does that mean I'm allowed to start creating my forge?'

'Yes, of course. Thank you for helping me first. I suppose I ought to have done it by myself . . .' She trailed off, never quite sure what the unwritten rules were here when it came to her role as his wife. But he shook his head.

'No, it was faster this way. Tomorrow you can help me instead.' He pointed to the section of the room by the door. 'I thought we could remove the benches from over there and set up a work space. I'll need to find stones or bricks, and some clay, then we can lengthen the legs on one of the benches to make it into a table. I'll put nails on the wall to hang our tools and then I'll see about obtaining some soapstone to make moulds.'

'Sounds good.' He'd thought of everything. 'I don't suppose we can buy a tub of some sort as well? I'd love to have a bath.' He opened his mouth, but she forestalled him. 'And don't tell me to go in the river. It's the month of *October*, you know.'

He gave her a lopsided grin. '*Gormánaður*? Yes, but the chill isn't that bad yet. Still, I'll see what I can do.'

She sank down on to a three-legged stool next to the hearth and added another log to the fire they'd just started. 'It's going to be very quiet without Holger, Eadgyth and Birger around. I hope they don't have to spend all winter in a tent. Can't be good for a small child.'

'We could always ask them to live here with us.' Rurik hesitated and stared out of the door, as if he couldn't quite meet her eyes. 'I was going to sleep on one of the benches here, but if you don't mind me sharing the bed with you, there's room for them. I expect Holger will only be around at night in any case.'

Sara bit her lip. On the one hand, it would probably be a good thing not to share a bed with him. That seemed a lot more intimate than just lying next to him in a tent, rolled up in her own cloak and blanket. And yet she was used to having him near at night and realised she'd miss that. It made her feel safe and protected.

Pretending a nonchalance she didn't feel, she said breezily, 'Yes, why not? I'm sure Eadgyth would be pleased. I know she was worried about Birger's cough yesterday.'

Rurik nodded, still without looking at her. 'Very well, I'll ask them when I go in search of building materials. I'd best fetch us some water now.' He grabbed the pail and headed outside without saying anything further.

'Well, that was awkward,' Sara muttered to Beowulf, who tilted his head as if he understood what she was saying. 'Let's hope I don't come to regret it.'

Because just the thought of sharing an actual bed with him made her tingle all over.

Rurik wasn't sure he'd done the right thing in suggesting they should sleep in the same bed. He'd been determined to stay on one of the benches in order to be away from Sara's nearness, but the thought of little Birger dying of cold in a tent made him reconsider. And what was the problem? They'd slept next to each other for weeks now.

It was becoming more and more difficult not to turn around and take her in his arms, though. *Admit it!* He sighed.

Yes, it was true. After that kiss they'd shared, it was as though his body had woken from a deep slumber and was suddenly supremely aware of her. He'd tried to tell himself it was just the fact that he hadn't had a woman in a long time, but whenever he looked at any of the available ones – and there were quite a few throwing him inviting glances, it had to be said – he felt no desire to take them up on the offer.

It was ridiculous.

Perhaps it was because she'd activated his protective instincts. He did feel responsible for her. Several times he'd contemplated asking her if she wouldn't rather go back to her own time, but she seemed so content, he couldn't do it. She'd said she wanted to stay for a while and experience life here, and he'd agreed. Now that all danger appeared to have passed, where was the harm?

Except to his own equilibrium and peace of mind.

Sleeping with her would be a very bad idea, though. She wasn't the kind of woman you trifled with; she would want complete commitment and he wasn't sure he could give her that. Not now, perhaps not ever. He couldn't offer her love, and from what she'd told him, it seemed she wouldn't settle for anything less, as apparently in her time that was what marriages were based on. No, she would only end up being hurt again, and she deserved better.

From tomorrow onwards, they wouldn't be alone in the house, so there was just the one night to get through before that. To make it as easy as possible, he lingered by the hearth long after Sara and the dog had retired for the night. He didn't climb in beside her until he heard her even breathing, showing that she was fast asleep. As he lay down, however, he couldn't help himself – he pulled her against his chest and held her close for a long while before letting go.

She'd never know.

*

Holger and his little family moved in the following day, and Eadgyth gave Sara a fierce hug. 'You're a godsend,' she whispered. 'We were so cold last night and Birger wouldn't stop coughing.'

The toddler did indeed look under the weather, his nose runny and cheeks very red and blotchy. Sara caressed his strawberry-blond hair. 'Poor little one. We'll soon make you better. I've got some warm broth. Why don't you feed him a bowl of that while I give Rurik and Holger a hand?'

The men had brought stones and clay, and Holger helped them build a square base on which they could construct the two parallel clay ridges to keep the fire contained. Before this was dry, the nozzles of the two bellows were inserted so that they stuck out on the inside. This way they wouldn't catch fire when the charcoal grew incredibly hot. It also ensured that the air they generated would be blowing into exactly the right spot.

'Excellent! Thank you for helping, Holger.' Rurik clapped his friend on the back. 'Hopefully this will be properly dry the day after tomorrow. There's just one thing I need to tell you both.'

'Yes?' Holger stopped in the middle of picking up a spare piece of clay that had landed on the floor.

'Sara will be working with me as a smith in her own right. Even though she's female, she's been trained the same way I have and not just as an assistant to her husband. I know that might sound strange, and we won't go into the reasons, but we would appreciate it if you'd keep that to yourselves. It's probably best if we don't advertise the fact.'

Holger's eyebrows had shot up, but he nodded. 'Fine by me.'

Eadgyth echoed this assurance, and Sara breathed a sigh of relief. There wasn't anything to actually stop her from working as a smith, and apparently it did happen that women took over their husbands' businesses if they became widowed, but she'd rather not draw attention to herself, so it was better this way.

'In that case, I'll do the cooking for all of us,' Eadgyth offered. 'Makes sense if Sara is going to be busy working with you.'

'Thank you, that would be wonderful!' Sara smiled at her friend. It wasn't just the fact that she'd be spared the extra work, but she still wasn't very good at cooking Viking food, and had been struggling for days now. Poor Rurik must be heartily sick of the few dishes she knew how to make.

'Good, that's settled then.' Rurik went outside and brought in a load of soapstone. 'We may as well start making moulds,' he said to Sara. 'That way we can produce some amulets and round brooches first and start selling them.'

She was happy to do that, and picked up a sharp knife and a stone. 'What are we making first? Thor's hammers?'

'And crosses. There are all sorts of people here. Probably best to try and cater to everyone.'

They worked hard, and by supper time, Sara was famished. Eadgyth ladled stew into wooden bowls and added mashed turnip with butter, a real treat. Little Birger seemed reluctant to eat, and after a few spoonfuls, he turned his head away, grizzling.

'You need to eat a bit more, Birger *mín*. Please?' Eadgyth cajoled, but to no avail.

Sara put a hand on his forehead and didn't like that it was burning hot. 'Is there anything you can give him for the fever?'

'I have some willow bark. I'll steep it now.'

The toddler had to be practically force-fed this concoction, but after a while it did seem to have some effect and he fell asleep, only to wake everyone in the middle of the night when his cough started up again. Sara was listening from the back room, but when the coughing started to sound like the bark of a seal, she got up and pulled her cloak around her, tiptoeing into the main room.

'Eadgyth?'

'Here.' The woman was sitting by the fire, which she'd stoked and added wood to. Sara could see that she was rocking Birger on her lap, while tears coursed down her cheeks. 'He . . . he's very unwell.'

'I know, but we'll make him better.' Sara was sure she knew what ailed him, because she'd helped a friend, Jenny, whose baby had sounded just like that. 'I think he has *croup*, and I've heard of something that might help.'

'*Kroop*?' Eadgyth dashed away some tears. 'I don't know what that is, but I'm willing to try anything.'

'Right then, here's what we have to do . . .'

Sara filled a small cauldron with water and hung it over the fire. Then she fetched a large blanket, which she wrapped around Eadgyth's shoulders. Birger continued his seal-coughing, sounding as though he was having trouble drawing breath. 'Poor baby. We're going to help you breathe more easily.' She used a folded cloth to lift the now boiling cauldron off the hook and placed it on the floor in front of Eadgyth. 'Now, I'm going to put the blanket over you and Birger like a tent, and I want you to try and hold him as close to the steam as possible so that he breathes it in. Try wafting it towards him if you can. Here, use this.' She held out a flat piece of bark for Eadgyth to utilise as a fan.

'Very well.'

She draped the blanket over mother and child, and prayed that this would work. Rurik had come out of their room and was sitting next to Holger now, both of them staring at her intently. The big Gotlander, who was normally so happy and boisterous, wore a sombre expression, his shoulders slumped. It made her feel nervous, but there was no time for doubt. Either the steam would help Birger or it wouldn't – at least she had tried something. Her friend Jenny had resorted to sitting in her bathroom with the shower on full blast. Hopefully the steam emanating from the cauldron would have the same effect, though it might take longer.

Although infants dying seemed to be a fairly common thing here, and people were used to it happening – prepared for it even – Sara was sure Birger's parents would be dreading such an outcome. Especially as he was their firstborn son and obviously much loved. There were many dangers to small children in this era, things that were so easily avoided or cured in her own time, but croup needn't be one of them. And it wouldn't be, if this worked.

At first, nothing happened, and Sara hung up another pot of water to boil. When she'd exchanged the first one for the second, however, Birger's cough started to sound more normal. Sort of loose and phlegmy, rather than barking. 'I think it's starting to work!' came Eadgyth's muffled voice from inside the blanket. 'His breathing is easier.'

'Good. Let's keep going for a while longer, though.'

Rurik and Holger exchanged looks of relief, but Sara was barely aware of them as she swapped cauldrons several more times. Eventually Eadgyth pushed the blanket off herself and smiled at Sara, her face red and damp from the warm steam. 'He's asleep,' she whispered. 'And he's breathing almost normally. I don't know how to thank you enough!' There were tears glistening in her eyelashes, and Sara almost felt like crying herself.

She shook her head. 'It was nothing. I just happen to have a friend whose child went through the same thing. She told me what to do. I'm glad it worked.'

The relief was making her slightly dizzy, and as if he'd noticed, Rurik came over to help her empty the cauldrons and fold up the blanket. Eadgyth had gone back to bed by this time, with Holger cocooning her and the little one inside a warm cloak. Rurik took Sara's hand and led her back to their own bed.

'Well done,' he breathed, putting his arms around her to give her a fierce hug. 'You probably saved the child's life.'

'Like I said, it was pure chance that I knew about this illness.'

'Chance or not, they will be forever grateful. Come, you need to rest now.'

He pulled her down on to the new sheepskins he'd purchased that day, and made Beowulf move over. The dog's tail thumped a welcome, but he was good at fitting into whatever space was available and didn't complain about having to shift himself.

The last thing Sara felt before she sank into a deep sleep was Rurik's strong arms around her, and a profound sense of well-being.

Chapter Seventeen

'How is he today?' Sara emerged from the bedroom feeling rather bleary, but she didn't mind. Staying up half the night had been in a good cause.

'Much better, thank you.' Eadgyth beamed at her and pointed at her son, who was busy playing with a small duck carved out of wood. 'He ate some porridge, and although he's not as energetic as usual, he's taking an interest in things at least.' Birger's cheeks had lost their red flags, and although his gaze wasn't quite as bright as normal, he definitely looked a lot healthier than yesterday.

'I'm glad.' Sara settled down on one of the benches with the bowl of porridge the other woman handed her. 'Where are the men?'

Rurik hadn't been in the bed when she woke up, only Beowulf, who was now busy slurping his own porridge before settling next to Birger. It made Sara smile to see the protective look on his face as he gazed at the little boy. She was sure now that he must have been used to guarding children back at the farmstead. Amazing how dogs could survive something like the horrific attack on his owners without it affecting their trust for other humans.

'Rurik was going to speak to Jarl Hálfdan, and Holger went

along with him to see if he was needed for more digging.'

Rurik appeared shortly afterwards, carrying a bulging sack. When he dropped it on to the floor, it made a clanging noise. He beckoned her over. 'Come and see, Sara. We're to create some beautiful grave goods for the jarl.'

She was confused. 'Is he dying?' He'd seemed perfectly healthy the day he rescued her from Asmund.

Rurik laughed. 'No, it's not for him. It's for his brother.'

'Which one?' She'd heard he had several, and Eadgyth had pointed two of them out to her during the journey.

'Ívar the Boneless. As I think I told you, he died a while back in Írland, but his brothers have brought his remains here for a fitting funeral. Holger stayed behind to help with the preparations. Ívar is to be placed in a special chamber and surrounded with the remains of hundreds of warriors who fought with him. Women who followed the *here* too.'

It sounded like they were trying to make some sort of major statement, creating a lasting memorial to one of their own heroes so close to all the Mercian kings and their saint. But Sara was mostly focused on one fact that struck her as revolting. 'Eeeuuww! They're bringing loads of dead people here? Hundreds, did you say? That's going to smell dreadful!'

'No, no, they are just the bones of people who are long gone. They've been collecting them along the way here. Didn't want them buried in hostile territory. Much better here, with their leader.'

That seemed incredibly macabre to Sara, but as long as she didn't have to deal with it, it shouldn't matter to her. She focused on the task at hand instead as Rurik tipped the sack's contents on to the floor. A small mountain of metallic items landed in a heap – chalices, plates, book bindings, jewellery, as well as assorted pieces of hacksilver and gold. '*Oh my God!* That's half a monastery there. What does he want us to do with all this?'

'Melt it down and create a sword hilt, a knife hilt and a magnificent brooch. I thought perhaps you could try your hand at the latter?'

That made sense, as she'd never had to create parts of weaponry before. 'I'd be happy to, and I'll do my best. How big should it be?'

He went over to his kist and rummaged around, bringing out a simple bronze brooch. 'Perhaps twice the size of this? You can copy the shape and then embellish it any way you want.'

'Very well.' How she wished she had some paper and pencils in order to draw ideas, but she'd just have to wing it.

'I'll get started on the other items. The new hearth seems ready and I've bought some charcoal. I'd better make a mould first, though.'

They worked solidly for days, and Sara felt more content than she had in ages. Without her modern tools, she had to adapt her working techniques and often asked Rurik for advice. He showed her how he would tackle it and he was incredibly patient with her. She was grateful that he didn't patronise her in any way, just accepted that she knew how to do these things, albeit not the way he was used to doing them. The hammering, smelting, shaping and decorating was mostly the same; the smells and sounds of the forge familiar and safe. And the pure joy of doing what she loved best made happiness fizz in her veins.

'That's truly beautiful, Sara!' Eadgyth admired the finished brooch, turning it over to study the intricate details. It was a so-called penannular brooch, which meant that it was in the shape of an incomplete ring with a very long, sharp pin to fasten it. This particular one was huge and very heavy; she'd used masses of silver in its making. As it was available, what was the point in stinting? It was more in the style of a Celtic brooch than the plainer Viking ones she'd seen, but as Ívar the Boneless had apparently spent time in Ireland, she thought perhaps it was fitting to mix the two types.

Sara had been told that Ívar's battle banner featured the image of a raven, and she'd made each open end – the terminals – into the head of such a bird. Their curved beaks were slightly open, their eyes made of glittering crystals. The top of the brooch was also a raven, its head to one side and the wings spread out along the curve of the circular shape. She had added a feather pattern, inlaid with more crystals, and the one eye visible on the central bird was made out of a large garnet. The sparkling effect of the whole piece was stunning in the sunlight coming in through the door.

'Yes, exquisite workmanship, Sara.' Rurik admired it in his turn and smiled at her.

'Thank you both. I hope Jarl Hálfdan will like it.' She felt her cheeks heat up at this praise and realised she'd wanted to impress Rurik, rather than the jarl, although she didn't want to contemplate the reason behind that. 'A shame it's to be buried.'

'But it will go with Ívar to the afterlife.' He sounded so confident, she didn't want to contradict him. They each had their own beliefs, and Eadgyth wisely didn't voice her doubts either. Besides, Sara could always hope that modern archaeologists would one day excavate Ívar's grave, find the brooch and display it in a museum. The thought made her smile. How weird would that be when it had actually been made by a twenty-first-century woman?

She became conscious of the fact that she hadn't thought about her own time for days now, and she wasn't missing it much. Well, she missed the people, of course, her grandfather especially – she often wondered what he was doing – but it had been ages since she'd hankered after modern food or conveniences. Quite simply, she was beginning to feel at home here. Who would have thought?

There was no way she could stay for good, though. Rurik would want her gone as soon as possible, she was sure. Although he never said as much, she was aware of being an added burden for him. Someone he had to look out for when really he'd just wanted to start a new life by himself. Why would he want her around? Still, at the moment they were both stuck with the situation and had to make the best of it.

'Shall I help you with the other items now?' She wrapped the brooch in a piece of felted wool and put it aside.

'Yes please. If you wouldn't mind doing some of this filigree work for me?'

For the rest of that day, they worked together in perfect harmony, each complementing the other. Towards evening, Rurik turned to her and smiled. 'I've never had a partner before. I've been someone else's apprentice, following orders, but I haven't worked together with anyone apart from that brief spell with Grim. I quite like it.'

'Me neither, and yes, it's nice.' That was an understatement, but she didn't want to sound too gushy. Since graduating from art college, she had always been a one-man band, choosing to set up her own business and try to make it on her own. Anders had attempted to inveigle himself into her workshop, but she'd made excuses such as telling him it wasn't big enough for two, although the truth was that she hadn't wanted to share with him. She now realised the pleasure of proper teamwork with a man whose skills were equal to her own, and the quiet enjoyment of not being all alone, and found herself smiling back at him.

'Let's hope Jarl Hálfdan is pleased with what we have created for him. That should bring in a lot more business.'

*

The following week everyone made their way back to Hreopandune. The day of the big ceremony had dawned cold and crisp, with a thin layer of frost on the ground. Everyone's breath emerged as clouds of mist while they walked, and the cold air stung their cheeks. Rurik wondered if Sara was missing that thick tunic she'd been wearing when he first met her. And the sturdy shoes that stank when they tried to burn them.

Perhaps she was missing her own time altogether?

But she hadn't mentioned anything about going back for ages now, and he was reluctant to bring up the subject. He told himself it was just that he was becoming used to having her around. She had certainly eased the loneliness he'd felt at leaving his own family. The fact that he hadn't actually dreamed about Linnea for days now – weeks, even – was another reason for keeping her here. Strangely, whenever he thought about holding a woman in his arms, Sara's shape was the one that sprang to mind first, rather than his sister-in-law's.

He shook his head. It was probably merely the fact that Sara was here and Linnea was not. If he saw the two of them together, surely the latter's cool blonde beauty would win out? A tiny voice inside his head asked if he was absolutely certain about that, but he ignored it.

'Thank you again for the mittens and hat, Eadgyth. I would have frozen to death today without them.' Sara, who was walking next to him, beamed at her friend. Holger's woman had busied herself making hats and mittens for them all using the *nålbinding* technique. This created thick, warming woollen items that kept their extremities from turning blue.

'And thank *you* for the extra garment for Birger. Doesn't he look sweet in it?'

Sara had fashioned herself a small tool that looked like a thick metal stick with a hook at one end. Using a technique similar to *nálbinding*, she'd made the little boy what she called a *crocheted sweater*, an added layer to protect him against further illness. He was wearing it now on top of a thick woollen tunic, and with a small cloak over that was lined with squirrel fur.

'It's not as thick and warm as the things you've made,' she protested.

'Every garment helps.' Eadgyth sent a look of love towards her son, who was riding on his father's shoulders.

A pang of envy shot through Rurik, taking him by surprise. He'd left Birka determined never to have a family, since he couldn't have one with the woman he wanted. Instead he was going to dedicate his life to creating beautiful silver and gold items. Watching Holger and his family, however, made him jealous. The bond that child had created between them was something he suddenly wanted for himself. One day.

He glanced almost instinctively at Sara. He'd watched her with Birger; she would make a wonderful mother. But she wasn't of his time and there was no point setting his sights on her. Besides, as he'd told himself before, it wouldn't be fair of him to marry a woman when he could never truly be hers. What would happen if he ever took her home? She'd be bound to notice his awkwardness around Linnea. Women were good at spotting these things.

No, best to leave things as they were.

'Is that Ívar the Boneless?' Sara grabbed Rurik's arm so she could stand on tiptoe to see better.

'Yes, that's him.' He put one hand over hers as if to steady her, and she resisted the urge to lean on him even more. It was becoming harder each day not to touch him at every opportunity, but she knew she mustn't. He wouldn't welcome it, she was sure, as he still slept with his back to her each night. Except for the night of Birger's cough, when they'd gone to sleep spooning. It had been wonderful, but he'd made it clear it was a one-off.

They were standing among the crowds on the riverbank as a huge ship came gliding towards them. The raven banner fluttered from the top of the mast and the front was adorned with a carved raven that screeched soundlessly at the spectators. A row of colourful shields hung along the gunwales on either side, all sporting the same bird motif, and the rowers were working in silent tandem. The vessel came to a stop near a newly built jetty, and Sara saw the men stow away the oars before standing up to form a line either side of a large box.

The coffin containing Ívar the Boneless.

Slowly, respectfully, they picked it up and carried it to shore. Hálfdan Hvítserk and his brothers Ubba and Sigurd Snake-in-the-Eye – who reputedly had the pattern of a snake in one iris – greeted the men, and then took up positions at the front of the coffin to help transport it up the slope. A fourth brother, Björn Ironside, who had arrived on Ívar's ship, joined them. Before they set off, Hálfdan placed the newly commissioned silver items on top of the coffin – Sara's brooch, together with a sword and a dagger with the new hilts Rurik had produced – along with a whole load of other treasures. Well polished as they were, the objects shone in the pale sunlight and cast reflections at those standing closest. A procession of sorts was formed, and the people on the opposite side of the river scrambled into boats to quickly row across and follow it.

Sara and the others also started walking, and eventually everyone was crowded into an area outside the newly created defences to the west of the church. A lot of people, including them, climbed up the side of the rampart in order to have a better view of the proceedings. She could see that a mausoleum of sorts was being created, with the lower part of the walls of a small building forming the base. Rurik had told her it was an old tomb that was being reused, and she hadn't asked what had happened to whoever had been buried there originally. Once the ceremony was over, it would be covered over and turned into a grave mound.

The inside appeared to be divided into two, with a stone sarcophagus in one part, placed on a base layer of red marl. She blinked as she caught sight of the hundreds of human bones that were neatly stacked in piles along the insides of the space surrounding the stone kist. There were skulls on one side, and longer bones – from arms and legs perhaps – on the others, with smaller bones in between. A truly macabre sight. 'Jesus!' she breathed. 'Where did they get those?'

'I told you – they've been collected from temporary graves all over the country.' Rurik barely glanced at them; his gaze was mainly on the procession, which was nearly at the mausoleum now. Sara noticed a group of four people waiting just outside, their wrists tied together, their eyes slightly unfocused, as if they were drunk or stoned. Next to them a sheep stood patiently, seemingly unfazed by the noise around it.

'Who are they?' she whispered, nodding towards them.

'Thralls. They're to go with Ívar. Sacrificed. The sheep as well.' Rurik's voice was clipped, as if he knew she wouldn't like this. When she gasped in outrage, he took her hand and squeezed it hard, sending her a steely glare. 'Don't say a word, please. It is not something you can influence.' He sounded harsh, quite unlike the easy-going Rurik she dealt with most days, and a shiver went through her. This was a major difference between them – his attitude towards life, death and killing, things that were abhorrent to her. It highlighted how out of her depth she really was in his time. No way would she ever condone human sacrifice, while he took it for granted.

'But that's—'

'Tradition,' he hissed. 'And it isn't done very often. Only for a truly special person, like Ívar.' His voice was even more implacable, a definite warning to stay silent, and his grip on her hand tightened.

Sara wanted to argue with him, tell him exactly where he could stuff his 'traditions', but instead she gritted her teeth, knowing that he was right. There had to be over a thousand people around her, and if she protested, she'd just make a spectacle of herself. They might even decide that she would make a good sacrifice too. She shuddered again, suddenly feeling sick to her stomach. It was barbaric, but she was helpless to prevent it happening.

'I'll tell you when to turn your gaze away,' Rurik whispered, as if he at least understood the turmoil inside her even if he didn't agree with her. 'Don't think about it.'

But how could she not?

The wooden coffin was lowered into the sarcophagus. Both were long; it would seem Ívar had been an exceptionally tall man, as Rurik had said. The rest of the grave goods were placed on or around the coffin by the deceased's brothers. While they and a few other strong men added a stone lid to the sarcophagus, a woman dressed in a flowing black gown and a dark cloak sewn with crystals began to chant in a loud voice. Others joined in, copying her words. Sara was still thinking about the four unfortunate souls awaiting their gruesome fate and didn't really listen. She watched the proceedings as if in a dream. It was surreal.

Two pits had been dug either side of the mausoleum, and sacrificial offerings were burned in those. Sara tried not to look, so had no idea what went in there, although she thought she heard clucking and squawking at one point.

Men began to bring forward more baskets and boxes full of bones, laying them out with the others and stacking them on top of each other in an orderly fashion. Were they hoping the skeletons would accompany their leader into the afterlife? It was an extraordinary sight, and she still couldn't believe they'd gone to the trouble of exhuming bodies to bring them here. The mere thought made her shudder in revulsion, but no one else seemed to think it strange.

'Are those Ívar's warriors who died in battle?' she asked quietly.

'Not all of them. I understand some are women and children, the wives and families of the men who followed him, killed by the enemy.'

Some of the skeletons seemed to have been buried with their own grave goods, and these were added to the pile – axes, swords, knives, jewellery, even coins. The men laying out the dead were meticulous about not forgetting anyone's possessions. Sara marvelled at the forethought and work that had gone into the ceremony. They must have spent months collecting these remains and transporting them here. And it was done out of respect for their former leader.

Ívar the Boneless must have been quite a man.

Why would he want to be buried here, though, and not in his homeland? Although, come to think of it, conquering parts of England and Ireland had been his life's work, so perhaps it was fitting. Here at Repton, he was at the heart of his new kingdom, symbolically taking the place of those he'd vanquished. Or even lying alongside them, if the Mercian kings hadn't been removed. Yes, it was a grand gesture, with the mound probably clearly visible to anyone passing by on the river. A statement, as she'd thought when she first heard about it.

But she couldn't wait for it to be over.

Chapter Eighteen

'Thank you again for making the items I asked for so quickly. I particularly liked that brooch – it was perfect. I hope Ívar appreciates it when he wears it in Valhalla.'

After the mound had been covered over with soil – quite an undertaking, which took ages despite the dozens of men who helped – a huge feast began, with most people bringing their own food and drink. Eadgyth had prepared theirs, and they were sitting together with some of Holger's other comrades and their families, enjoying the fruits of her labour. Hálfdan Hvítserk, wearing a snowy white linen undershirt as befitted his name, since Hvítserk meant just that – a white shirt – had come up behind Rurik without him noticing, and clapped him on the shoulder now as he praised the silversmith's skills.

'The brooch was my wife's handiwork,' Rurik replied. 'I told her about the raven motif and she created it to suit.' He wasn't sure what Hálfdan's reaction to this would be, but to his credit, the man didn't bat an eyelid. Instead he smiled and bowed in Sara's direction.

'Then I thank you also, Sara. I appreciate your efforts.'

'You're very welcome.' She was blushing, but her amber eyes shone with joy. 'I was in debt to you,' she added quietly, and smiled for the first time since the ceremony. Rurik was aware that she was still upset about the sacrificed thralls, but he felt she was overreacting. It was nothing to do with them what Ívar's brothers chose to do in his honour. That was their prerogative.

'Not at all. I wish you all good feasting.'

The jarl moved off, and Rurik followed him with his eyes. He noticed Hálfdan walking past Asmund, who was with a raucous crowd not far from them. The annoying man was staring at Sara again, a sour expression on his face. Hálfdan must have seen it too, however, because as he passed the man, he smacked Asmund over the back of the head and leaned down to whisper something in his ear. The warrior turned puce and spluttered a protest of some sort, but then turned away and concentrated on his ale. Rurik stifled a laugh.

He didn't think they'd have any more trouble with Asmund.

The weeks and months flew by, and they were exceedingly busy with commissions from people who had noticed the items they'd created for Hálfdan. Sara heard with satisfaction that Rurik's stash of hacksilver and other forms of payment in the secret compartment at the bottom of his kist was growing, although she didn't look for herself. She trusted him to keep it safe. If and when she left to travel to Sweden, she wanted him to keep most of it anyway. All she needed was enough of her share to pay for her journey.

After the burial of Ívar the Boneless, her relationship with Rurik had been slightly strained for a few weeks, but she came to recognise that she was being silly in taking out her frustration on him for something he'd had no control over. He hadn't personally decided to sacrifice four human beings, and although the proceedings seemed not to affect him, that wasn't necessarily because he was a callous and uncaring man. He was simply acting and thinking the way he'd been conditioned to since birth, just as Sara was. The fact that their attitudes were polar opposites had nothing to do with him as a person. Humanity had moved on in its thinking during the thousand years since his birth, but she couldn't expect him to share her beliefs any more than she shared his. In the end, she let it go. There was simply no point brooding about it.

Gradually they regained their camaraderie in the forge, and Sara was content to work alongside him. She was learning a lot, but also teaching him a thing or two. Sketching out rough ideas on pieces of bark using charcoal was one such.

'I need to see the design before I make it in silver or gold,' she explained.

At first he disagreed. 'I can see it in my mind. What need is there to draw it on bark?' But he gave it a try, and after that she found him doodling several times, as if he'd realised he enjoyed it.

Eadgyth had been talking about the midwinter festival – Yule – for weeks, and was busy preparing large amounts of food and ale for this. It was to be celebrated in mid January, if Sara had understood correctly, and not around the time of the winter solstice in December.

'Everyone has to bring their own dishes to the feast,' Eadgyth told her. 'It's only fair; we can't expect the jarl's thralls to provide everything for us.'

She and Holger had slaughtered a bullock and a sheep, and she seemed intent on using every last part of these animals in her cooking. Sara tried not to look too closely at what she was eating, and for the most part she was so hungry after a hard day's work, she'd have consumed anything.

Time passed quickly, and by her reckoning, December had come and gone. She was surprised to find she didn't miss the traditional Christmas celebrations as much as she'd thought she would, but there was still a pang of regret. What was her grandfather doing right now? Had he even bothered to celebrate? With her gone, he might be too depressed. He'd already been mourning the loss of his son and daughter-in-law, Sara's parents, and although he had other children, that kind of grief was hard to shake off. The previous year, neither of them had been in the mood for tradition. Instead, Sara had taken him on a trip to Japan, where people concentrated on New Year, rather than Christmas. It had been a refreshing change for both of them and helped them cope with the festive season.

A wave of sadness and longing engulfed her whenever she thought about him. If only he could have come with her to the Viking era, how much fun they would have had. He'd have been like a child in a sweetshop, eager to absorb everything and find out every minute detail of life here. What if he became ill, or worse, and she wasn't there to be with him? She swallowed down a lump of misery at that thought. But he was a strong and robust man, usually healthy as a horse – a strange expression if ever there was one – and she was probably worrying about nothing. The best thing she could do was to store up as much information about the Vikings' everyday life as possible so that she could tell him all about it when she returned. And make sure she could go back somehow. Yes, as soon as possible she'd have to try and reach Jorvik, and from there, Sweden. She ignored the little voice in her head whispering that it would be a wrench to leave this place, to say goodbye to Rurik and her friends. *And Beowulf!* It shocked her to realise how at home she felt here now, almost as if she belonged.

Nothing would happen until spring, though, as the weather was too cold for travelling any long distances. For the moment, it was best not to think too much about it, so she threw herself into the Yuletide preparations as a distraction.

'Do you exchange gifts during the midwinter feast?' she asked Rurik in a whisper. 'If so, I want to make something for Eadgyth. Can we spare some silver?'

'Of course. Take whatever you want.' He bent to whisper back. 'But just so you know, Holger has asked me to fashion her a neck torc.'

'Good, I'll make an arm ring then.'

There was no need to hide what she was doing, as her friend would assume she was working on a commission for someone else. She spent the next two days creating a bracelet made of plaited strands of silver with a pattern etched into the surface. There was a narrow gap in the circle to help with putting it on, and she made each end into the head of a fox. This felt appropriate, considering Eadgyth's vivid red hair, and Sara had often heard Holger refer to her affectionately as his 'beautiful fox'.

She did try to hide the fact that she was also making a small present for Birger – a silver chain long enough to go around his wrist twice, with a flat bit in the middle on which she chiselled his name in runes. When he grew older, he should be able to grow into it. She couldn't make anything for Rurik, because he kept a close eye on everything she made and would have asked who it was for. Instead, she spent her evenings learning how to do band weaving – or tablet weaving, as Eadgyth called it. Once she'd mastered the art, she produced lengths of the stuff, and whenever Rurik went out with Holger to spend time with their comrades, she sewed the colourful bands on to a plain blue tunic Eadgyth had helped her buy.

'Do you think he'll like it?' she asked her friend, having just put in the last stitch.

'Hold it up and let me see. Oh yes, that looks wonderful! How can he fail to be pleased with that?' Eadgyth smiled. 'If he doesn't appreciate it, he'll have me to deal with, since I was the one who taught you.'

Sara laughed. 'Very well, I'll refer any complaints to you.'

As it turned out, she need not have worried. They all exchanged presents on the morning of the feast, and Rurik's eyes lit up at the sight of the tunic. 'Thank you, that's exactly what I needed today. Is that the band you've been weaving? I wondered what you were going to use it for.' He smiled at her and leaned over to give her a hug. 'I shall put it on in a moment, but first – this is for you.'

He held out a very tiny parcel wrapped in red cloth, and Sara opened it carefully. It was so light, she wasn't sure there was actually anything inside, but once she'd unwrapped it, she could see why. She gasped with delight. 'Oh Rurik, you remembered! Thank you so much!'

Nestling on the cloth was a tiny gold shawl pin in the shape of a bird, very similar to the one Robert had showed her all those months ago. It had a tiny eye made of a garnet and its wings stuck up, the feathers outlined in silver.

'I'm not sure it's exactly the same, but it's as near to the original design as I could make it.'

'It's perfect, thank you.' It was her turn to lean over, but instead of a hug, she gave him a kiss on the cheek, which seemed to discombobulate him slightly.

'I, er . . . I'll go and put my new tunic on now.' He hurried off to the back room and came back shortly afterwards wearing his new garment. The blue colours made his eyes look even more turquoise than usual, and Sara thought he was extremely handsome. Dangerously attractive, in fact. She turned away to hide the fact that she thought so.

She pinned her shawl with the little bird, joy flowing through her. She was so touched that he hadn't forgotten her admiration of the pin. It seemed to show that he paid attention to what she said, and that he cared about her happiness, at least a little. And whatever the future brought, she would always have this reminder of him and their time together. That made the bird doubly precious, in every sense of the word, and she would treasure it. She swallowed down a sudden lump in her throat at the thought that this might all come to an end soon. Today was a day for celebration, not for maudlin thoughts. And she was determined to enjoy the festivities to the full.

Holger, too, had donned a new tunic, made by his wife with a border that was even more intricate than the one Sara had managed. But she reasoned that Eadgyth had had many years of practice, so it was only fair that hers should be better, although she was inordinately pleased when Rurik bent to whisper that he liked the colours of his more.

Eadgyth was thrilled with her gifts – both the torc from Holger and the bracelet from Sara. 'And I love Birger's wrist chain. So clever of you! Does that really say his name? Holger says it does.'

'Yes.' Sara hadn't thought about the fact that Eadgyth might not be literate, but thankfully Holger was.

In return, they gave her a silver bangle, which she told them she would treasure.

They were all in a festive mood as they set off towards Repton, everyone carrying either a basket of food or a cask of ale.

'We've missed the *blōt*,' Rurik whispered to Sara. 'I thought you might prefer not to see it.'

'Thank you.' That was thoughtful of him. He'd obviously realised that she didn't relish the thought of animals being slaughtered in honour of the gods any more than she did thralls. It seemed just as pointless and cruel to her, but she knew it was the norm for these people. They believed it necessary in order to ensure luck and a good harvest in the coming year. To each his own. She still hadn't forgotten those poor sacrificed thralls, but there was no point dwelling on things she was unable to change.

'Just to warn you, most people will be spattered with blood, as that is a part of the ritual. Try not to take any notice.'

'I won't.' Good thing he had told her, though, or she might have wondered if there had been some sort of big fight.

The feast was in full swing when they arrived, with singing, dancing and storytelling, and Sara was soon caught up in it all. It might not be Christmas, the way she was used to, but it was certainly a celebration worth remembering, and Rurik had told her it would continue for three nights in a row. There were toasts to the gods – Odin especially, but also Thor, Njorð, Freya and Freyr – and to victory and success during the coming year for the *here*. The leaders were toasted as well, and mugs of ale raised in tribute to the dead, especially Ívar the Boneless.

'These are called *minni*,' Rurik told her. 'Memorial toasts so that these men are never forgotten. The day people stop remembering you is the day you truly die.'

That made sense, and Sara was happy to toast them all, adding a quiet one to her parents as well. Naturally she would never forget them, and had she been back in her own times, she would have gone to the cemetery to light candles for them and lay a pretty wreath on the snow by their headstone. She was sure her grandfather would do it on her behalf, though, as well as his own.

A lot of ale was consumed – apparently everyone was expected to partake of copious amounts – and Sara had her fair share. She'd always enjoyed ale and beer of all kinds, and she wasn't the only one by the sound of it. There was chatter, laughter and raucous singing, the festive mood contagious. The celebrations were taking part inside a large hall that must have belonged to the Mercian king, although some people were sitting elsewhere, as it was a dreadful crush and they couldn't possibly all fit in. Sara sat next to Rurik on a bench by a trestle table, just taking it all in and enjoying the feeling of being a part of this big, noisy crowd.

'Is this how you celebrate midwinter too?' He must have noticed her gazing around at everyone and nudged her shoulder.

'What? Oh, no. It's usually just the family, nothing on this scale.'

'You never have gatherings where people come from far and wide to be together?'

Sara thought of music concerts and outdoor festivals. It wasn't quite the same, but similar enough. 'Yes, sometimes, but not like this.'

'Move up! We need more space at the end here,' someone shouted, and Rurik shuffled closer to Sara. A frisson went through her as she became aware of just how near he was, their bodies squashed together from shoulder to knee. Whenever he bent to tell her something, his hair brushed her cheek in a silken caress. It smelled clean and she was glad he had shaved his beard off for the occasion, as his chiselled features were revealed to advantage. She itched to draw a likeness of him, but instead stored the image in her mind for the future.

'Have you tasted this?' He held out a piece of flatbread dripping with honey, and without thinking she opened her mouth. He grinned and fed her a bite. 'Good, isn't it?'

'Mmm.' But it wasn't the honeyed bread she found delicious, it was the way his eyes sparkled in the light from a nearby oil lamp, the way his gaze seemed to linger on her mouth and then travel up to lock with hers, and the feel of his hard biceps and warm thigh against her. She had to swallow several times to get the bread down her throat.

'More?' When she mutely shook her head, he reached out and brushed some crumbs off her cheek. 'Messy,' he murmured. The brief touch almost made her jump – it was as though an electric shock ran through her right down to her toes. She wanted to grab his hand and hold it there, perhaps twine her fingers with his and . . .

Thankfully, before she could make a fool of herself and say or do something she'd regret, Holger claimed Rurik's attention and the moment was lost. For the rest of the meal, however, Sara was supremely aware of his every movement, her body fizzing with anticipation. Which was ridiculous, as nothing was going to happen between them.

By the third day, the ale was making her head swim and her vision a bit fuzzy, but it felt good and she allowed herself to relax and just enjoy herself. Everyone else was in the same state, so where was the harm?

The leaders of the *here* had apparently had considerably more to drink than she had, though, as late on the third evening, a commotion broke out. All those within hearing distance, including Sara's group, stopped talking and turned to eavesdrop. Hálfdan Hvítserk seemed to be arguing with his brothers and a couple of other jarls, whose names were Guthrum, Oscytel and Anwend, according to Rurik's whispered comment. Sara had a feeling she knew the name Guthrum from somewhere, but her brain was too foggy with ale and she gave up trying to remember why.

'We've done what we came here to do,' Hálfdan was shouting. 'We control Mercia, Norðimbraland and the land of the East Angles. What more do you want? Let the king of the West Saxons keep his domain. We have more than enough for everyone here to share.'

'But we came to conquer all,' one of the others yelled back. 'It was Ívar's dream, his goal. And that Alfred needs to be taught a lesson.'

'It's you who'll be vanquished. I don't want any part of it. As for Ívar, he's not here any longer, is he? *Our* dreams and goals are what matter now.' Hálfdan crossed his arms over his chest and looked decidedly mulish. 'It's eight winters since we arrived on these shores, and I grow weary. I say we secure the northern border properly, then portion out the land.'

'And I say we head south.'

Hálfdan's brother Sigurd Snake-in-the-Eye held up his hands, trying to calm the flaring tempers. 'Can we not agree to differ? There are more than enough of us here to do both. Hálfdan? It's a good idea to secure the north, so why don't you do that. Let these hotheads take on King Alfred again if they've a mind to. I'll go with you.' He turned to his other brothers. 'Ubba? Bjōrn?'

'Nah, we've decided to go to Írland for a spell. It's a great place for trading. But we'll be back. Save us a nice little settlement somewhere.' Ubba laughed.

Sigurd nodded. 'Very well. Guthrum?'

The man who'd spoken earlier replied. 'I'm definitely going south, but I'm happy to let Hálfdan head north and settle down if he so wishes. As he said, there's plenty of land to go round. I'll find mine elsewhere. Oscytel, Anwend, are you with me?'

The two men nodded.

Hálfdan raised his drinking horn, which Sara suspected might have been the Mercian king's until recently, as its decorations looked decidedly Saxon. 'Come spring, we'll go our separate ways then and you may all choose your preferred direction. To our success, north or south, and may we always be welcome in each other's lands!'

That was a diplomatic way of putting it, and a great cheer went up. 'Hear, hear!'

Sara frowned, having trouble following. 'So does that mean the *here* is split in two?'

'Yes, but that's not to say it won't grow again. Who knows?' Rurik grinned. 'Our choice is easy, though – we go with Hálfdan and persuade him to let us stay in Jorvik. I doubt he'll force anyone to fight, the way Asmund did. He's a reasonable man.'

'Oh good. When do we leave?' She took another large swig of ale and felt it swirling round her veins. Getting back to York sounded good. Home territory at last, even if it was a thousand or so years too early.

He laughed. 'Not until spring, but that can't come soon enough for me.'

'*Amen* to that,' she muttered.

It would seem the Great Heathen Army was no more, but just at that moment, she didn't care.

Rurik watched with amusement as Sara stumbled out of the privy and wove her way towards the door of their hut. Holger and Eadgyth had already retired to their sleeping bench, but he'd stayed outside to make sure she was safe.

'Here, let me help you.' He took her hand and guided her towards their little room at the back. In order to give the other couple some privacy, they'd installed a proper door, but he realised now that it worked the other way as well. He was suddenly very aware of being alone with Sara and extremely close to their bed, which was empty for once. Beowulf seemed to have decided to sleep by the fire and hadn't stirred as they passed him.

'That was fun.' She giggled and stumbled over something on the floor.

Instinctively he reached out to catch her, and she ended up in his arms, her soft breasts rubbing against him. He drew in a sharp breath. 'Sara, let's get you into bed. Have you never had ale before?'

'Yes, but not quite so much. And definitely not for three days in a row. Tasted good, huh?'

'Mmm, very,' he agreed. He had an urge to taste it again, but on her tongue. Perhaps one kiss wouldn't hurt . . .

He'd had quite a lot of ale himself and his usual caution seemed to have flown out the door. Without thinking about it further, he dipped his head to kiss her enticing lips, sucking gently on the bottom one before demanding entry with his tongue.

Sara giggled again, but didn't seem to mind. She joined in with great enthusiasm, so much so that he found himself almost reeling from the onslaught. *Odin's ravens, but this woman likes kissing!* Tracing the outline of his lips with her tongue was a bold move, but one he enjoyed to the full. He pulled her closer and the kisses began to spiral out of control. Somehow he found himself pulling his tunic over his head and helping her to divest herself of her over-gown. With nothing but linen between them, he could feel the hardness of her nipples, showing clearly that she was as aroused as he was.

He ought to stop. This was not a good idea.

But it *felt* insanely good.

He gave in to yet another urge and cupped one breast in his hand. It filled his palm to overflowing, luscious and firm. As he caressed the underside, then slowly drew his thumb across the nipple through the thin material, she moaned. Her hands found their way in under his shirt and she lightly raked her nails down his back and round to his chest. All the while they continued to kiss, deeply, passionately, creating a sizzling tension that flowed through his veins and headed south. He put both hands on her perfect behind, pushing her even closer. As if she knew exactly what she wanted, she rubbed herself against his hardness.

'Sara . . .' He really ought to stop, and some semblance of reason tried to rear its head when she pushed him backwards towards the bed. 'We really shouldn't . . .' But another light shove had him tumbling on to his back, and she laughed as she sank down on top of him.

'I know. But we're not hurting anyone, are we?' She kissed her way up his chin and cheek, murmuring, 'We're just two lonely people, enjoying some time together. No one needs to know.'

When she put it like that, how could he refuse? Perhaps the ale had clouded his judgement, but just in that moment, it sounded eminently reasonable to him.

'Are you sure? You've done this before?' But he could tell she had, because she was pulling her *serk* over her head now. She was no frightened maiden, but very much a willing participant. In the pale moonlight coming in from a hole near the roof, he could see her naked torso and it took his breath away. She was incredibly beautiful. More so than he could have imagined. 'By all the gods, Sara, you're a temptress and no mistake.'

She smiled and tugged at the hem of his shirt. 'I'm also very impatient, so please take this off.' She sounded a lot more sober now, not to mention demanding. He liked it. He liked it a lot.

He chuckled and complied. Although it was refreshing being ordered about like this, he wasn't going to put up with it for long. Only his trousers remained, and he made short work of removing those after the shirt, then he flipped her down on to her back and leaned over her. He caressed her from neck to thigh, but when he tried to move his hand further down her leg, she stopped him.

'Not there. That bit is ugly,' she muttered.

'What? Oh, your scars. They're not ugly, they're a sign of courage.' He overrode her hand and stroked her leg, then kissed the scars one by one, tantalisingly slowly. 'In fact, you're lovely all over.'

Soon the time for words was past and there was only sensation. Her velvety skin under his hands, her sighs of pleasure, the way she responded to his caresses, returning the favour and stoking his desire to breaking point. When he entered her at last, she joined in the rhythm of his lovemaking without hesitation. Her abandon and enjoyment added to his in a way he'd never experienced before. When the world shattered into a thousand pieces for both of them, he felt his head spinning out of control.

There was only one thing he could do – hold on to her as if he'd never let go.

Chapter Nineteen

Dear God, what have I done? Sara woke the morning after the feast with a head full of pounding drums and a foul taste in her mouth. And wearing no clothes. Blurred images from the night before swirled round her mind, and her body trembled with remembered ecstasy. It had been incredible.

It had also been a huge mistake.

She shivered and opened her eyes. What had she been thinking? A one-night stand with a man who was born a thousand years before her? She must have been mad. Or drunk. But a tiny voice inside her head told her she couldn't blame it on the ale – she'd sobered up rather quickly once Rurik started kissing her, as it felt so incredible. If she was being honest with herself, she simply hadn't wanted to stop.

And he'd been so irresistible. She'd wanted to kiss him for weeks, months even. Ever since that explosive kiss after the battle, she'd longed to do it again. And there was no denying the fact that she had a crush on him. A great big giant useless crush. Because it couldn't lead anywhere. She wasn't planning on staying in the Viking age for ever if she could help it, and he certainly wouldn't fit into her world. Linnea had told her that her husband, Hrafn, had offered to try, but it would never have worked. It would be the same for Rurik. And why would he want to anyway? They'd had sex, that was all. It wasn't like they'd entered into a marriage contract.

'Oh get a grip! It wasn't a big deal,' she muttered. She'd had one-night stands before. Well, just the once, but still . . . It was embarrassing, but quickly forgotten if you didn't allow yourself to dwell on it. Nothing to get uptight about. *Unless you get pregnant.* The sudden thought made her draw in a sharp breath and swallow hard. She hadn't even considered that last night. While she was with Anders, she had been on the pill, so contraception wasn't something she'd had to consider in a long time, and she hadn't dated since. But of course she should have thought about it. Becoming pregnant was a distinct possibility, and then what would she do? She had no idea.

'Don't get ahead of yourself,' she whispered. No point getting het up about it until – if – it happened. She'd know soon enough.

For now, she and Rurik were both adults, they could handle the situation. His space in the bed was empty and cold, and as he wasn't here to discuss the matter, she assumed he was going to pretend it hadn't happened. Fine, she'd do the same. She certainly didn't want to hear him voicing any regrets. That would make the whole thing so much worse.

Shivering, she jumped out of bed to try to locate her clothing. She found it neatly folded on a chest near the bed, and realised that Rurik must have done that before he left. He obviously didn't want her stumbling half naked into the other room. Her hair was a tangled mess, and she spent some time with his comb trying to tame it. When she'd succeeded in getting rid of all the knots, and had made a loose plait, she stood up and made her way to the door. The floor undulated slightly – or maybe that was her feet – but she didn't feel sick, thank goodness, and hopefully the headache would go away if she drank some water.

'Sara, how are you? Rurik said you weren't feeling well this morning, so we left you to sleep.' Eadgyth looked unnaturally cheerful, even though Sara was sure the woman had consumed just as much ale as she had.

She grunted in reply. 'Head hurts.'

'That's not good. Would you like some willow bark infusion?'

The mere thought of it made her nauseous, but it seemed impolite to refuse. She nodded slowly, so as not to move her brain too much. 'Just need some water first.'

Soon after they had moved into the house, she'd instigated a system whereby they always kept a cask of cooled boiled water to hand. She didn't want to drink ale on a daily basis, but she was well aware of the dangers of drinking contaminated water. Things she'd read about dysentery and typhoid in Victorian times due to dirty water made her stand her ground. There was a well serving all the nearby dwellings, but God only knew what bacteria lurked in there. So far her scheme had worked – no one had gone down with diarrhoea a single time, even though their neighbours often had upset stomachs.

After several mugs of water, half a cup of willow bark infusion, and a piece of newly baked flatbread, she started to feel more human. That was just as well, because her biggest test came soon after, when Rurik walked into the house carrying a sack of charcoal. 'Good morning,' he said breezily, glancing at her for a brief moment then turning away to deposit his load on the floor near their workbench. 'Feeling better?'

'Yes thank you.' Sara hoped that Eadgyth would think her burning cheeks were due to embarrassment at having a hangover. 'Are we working today?' She tried to adopt a cheerful tone, but wasn't sure she succeeded.

'No, it's a rest day. I thought I'd take Beowulf for a long walk. Want to come?'

His offer sounded lukewarm and Sara got the message – he'd rather be alone. She shook her head, something she regretted instantly when the pounding inside started up again. 'Er, no thanks. I think I'll just . . . sit here for a bit.'

'Very well.' Rurik whistled for Beowulf, who jumped up with alacrity.

She tried not to wince at the sharp sound, but must have flinched anyway, as Eadgyth put a hand on her arm. 'It will soon pass,' she murmured. 'Why don't you lie down again? I always find headaches go away faster that way.'

'Thank you. Good idea. I'll do that.'

And if a great big hole could open up under the bed and swallow her, that would be even better.

Rurik wasn't sure what to say to Sara when they went to bed that evening. He knew he should have been sensible and not given in to temptation last night, but he didn't regret it. How could he, when it was one of the best experiences of his life? They had both drunk a little too much ale, but not to the point where they had no control over their actions. Either one of them could have stopped it happening at any time. But they hadn't. There was no denying it complicated matters between them, though. He didn't know whether to apologise or tell the truth – that he'd love to do it again. And should he offer to marry her? It wasn't as though she'd been a maiden. No, she'd clearly made love before. But she was under his protection and he should have kept his hands – and other parts of his anatomy – to himself.

'What do you think, Beowulf? Would you like me to marry Sara?' The dog's tail thumped and he grinned, but since that was his usual expression when out for a walk, Rurik was none the wiser. He sighed.

Everyone retired early, as they were all still tired from the feast, and he steeled himself to talk to her. Before he could say anything, however, she closed the door and started speaking in a low but intense voice. 'Just so you know, I don't want any speeches about honour and guilt. What happened last night shouldn't have, but it did, and now the best thing is just to forget about it. There was no harm done – well, unless . . . but we won't think about that now. And I don't hold you responsible. *OK?*'

He blinked. 'But I—'

She held up a hand. 'No, don't. I know you don't love me, because you're pining for someone else, so even if you'd taken it into your head to offer me marriage, I'd refuse. As far as I'm concerned, we are friends and work comrades, nothing more. Is that clear?'

Frowning, he nodded. 'Don't I get a say?' Although she'd let him off the hook with regard to marriage and he ought to feel relieved, he was unaccountably annoyed. She'd dismissed his proposal without even listening to it. Yes, she had a point about him not being in love with her, but how many marriages were based on love? Theirs would have been a practical union – and intensely pleasurable, judging by last night – but only lasting until she decided to go back to her own time. Unless he could persuade her to stay . . . He was beginning to think that marrying Sara would suit him very well. They were well matched in most respects. And was love really necessary? Friendship and mutual goals would be more practical.

No, he was being foolish. Why would she want to stay in his era? After all the things she had told him about the future – her time – there was no doubt she'd leave as soon as they could get away from this place.

'I'd rather not hear it.' She put her hands up to clutch her head, as though it still ached. 'I'm sorry to be so direct, but it's better that we know where we stand, don't you think? And if you remember what I told you about my former betrothed, you'll understand why I could never be someone's second best.'

'I see.' And yet . . . *was* she second best? He wasn't even sure about that any longer.

Every time he'd closed his eyes today, the vision of a naked Sara bathed in moonlight had tormented him. Try as he might, he couldn't even conjure up Linnea's face, let alone the rest of her. Not that he'd ever seen her unclothed, but still. A dark mood settled on him like a wet blanket. Perhaps he would have come to love Sara in time, if only she'd given him the chance. But she wasn't going to. She wanted them to forget what had happened. So be it.

'Very well,' he said. 'A truce, then? And we go on as before?'

'Yes. And no more ale. Ever.' She shuddered. 'Vile stuff.'

He almost smiled at that, but then recalled the taste of it on her lips. Delicious and sinful. The trolls take it, but he wanted her again, seductive and willing the way she'd been the night before. He was fairly sure he could have persuaded her too. Just one kiss had ignited her desire; it probably would again. But unlike some men, he could take no for an answer. He wanted her to desire him wholeheartedly, and not because he was good at seduction. And that clearly wasn't how she felt.

He turned away and lay down with his back to her. 'Goodnight.'

Spring came at last, and with it a thaw that melted all the snow that had fallen during February. Sara was heartily sick of being cooped up indoors, but at least in the forge it was nice and toasty. If only she hadn't had to spend nearly every waking hour with Rurik, watching him, yearning for his touch and knowing he was not for her.

It was unbearable.

At least she wasn't pregnant, thank goodness. After an anxious wait that lasted a week longer than it should have done, she had started bleeding, and although she'd felt relief, there was also a nagging sense of regret. She told herself not to be so silly. Although a part of her would have loved to have Rurik's child, it would have made matters incredibly difficult when it came time for her to leave.

They continued to work together every day, and as the work space was fairly cramped, he was much too close for comfort. She spent a lot of time trying *not* to notice his muscular forearms as he hammered the metal and worked the bellows; his deft fingers fashioning exquisite items; the broad shoulders straining against his shirt and his golden hair continually escaping the leather thong he tied it back with. She longed to run her fingers through it again and pull him against her, the way she'd done that one, glorious night.

But it would be a huge mistake and lead to even more heartache.

Soon they'd be on their way to Jorvik, and then she'd enquire about passage to Sweden. Aiming for Birka first, she was sure she'd be able to find someone who could take her to Hrafn's settlement. Linnea had said he was well known in his area, a big landowner. How hard could it be to find them? And she knew now that she was in roughly the same year as the one when her friend had ended up in the Viking age. She had remembered why the name Guthrum rang a bell – he'd fought King Alfred of Wessex and later been converted to Christianity. This had happened roughly in the late 870s, which was near the year Linnea had claimed to live in. Perfect.

The hardest thing for now proved to be saying goodbye to Eadgyth, Holger and little Birger. They'd decided to follow Hálfdan up north, while Sara and Rurik would be joining a shipful of people heading for Jorvik. 'God, but I'll miss you!' She couldn't hold back the tears as she hugged her friend and the sturdy toddler, who was growing stronger every day.

'And I you. I hope we meet again, but if not in this life, I'll find you in the next, I swear.'

Sara gave a watery smile. 'You're starting to sound like Holger. Aren't you a follower of Christ any longer?'

'Yes, but there's no harm in adding a few more beliefs, is there?' Eadgyth smiled back, just as tearful.

'No, maybe you're right. Well, let's pray to all the gods that they keep us safe.'

Rurik was giving Holger a man hug. 'If you change your mind, come and find us in Jorvik. Or if we're not there for some reason, go to my brother Hrafn's house. I told you where he lives, not far from Birka, remember? He'll tell you where I am.'

'Will do. The gods be with you.' Holger was in a good mood, as he'd been itching for some action for months. Sitting still and doing nothing didn't suit him at all.

'And you.'

As she and Rurik boarded the ship with their belongings, Sara felt a prickling on her neck, as though she was being watched. Turning, she found Asmund staring at her from his own ship, which happened to be moored nearby. When he saw that she'd noticed him, he grinned and mouthed a few words: 'I'll see you again.'

Although she couldn't hear him, it was as if he'd shouted to her, and she was sure the blood drained out of her face. Since the midwinter feast, he'd kept his distance, although she had sometimes felt his gaze on her whenever she had occasion to visit the camp at Repton. She'd thought Hálfdan had knocked any stupid thoughts out of his head, but it would seem not. Hopefully he was heading north with his leader, and with any luck, someone would kill him in a battle. Although she felt guilty for wishing such a horrible thing, right then she didn't care.

She gave him her best death glare and turned away pointedly. A chuckle floated across the water, and she shuddered. If she never had to meet him again, it would be too soon.

It was strange to be travelling down the river, back out towards the Humber. She felt her spirits lift the further they went, and told herself she'd be fine. Soon she would be on her way home and then she could forget all about Rurik. After Anders, she'd sworn off men – well, this time she'd keep her promise.

Jorvik, when they finally reached it, was a much bigger town than she had thought. Situated on the north-eastern side of the River Ouse, it was surrounded in part by old Roman walls. As high as five metres in places, these had been fortified with wooden ramparts. Where there were bits of wall missing, the spaces had been filled in with timber palisades and earthworks. She was surprised to see what must be Roman gateways on each side, giving entry to the streets inside. She glimpsed a large stone building – possibly what would one day become York Minster, she guessed – and in one corner, on the western side looking towards the river, she also recognised an angular Roman tower. She pointed it out to Rurik.

'That still exists in my time,' she told him, 'although only the bottom part remains. Isn't it amazing that it has survived for millennia?'

He looked awed by this. 'Indeed.'

Holger had told them that the Vikings had taken the city at the beginning of their invasion, some six or seven years ago. As always, he'd been in the thick of things, and happy to give an eyewitness account of the fighting. When the Northumbrians tried to regain it, most of their forces managed to enter the city fairly easily, but that turned out to be a ruse by the Vikings, as they then found themselves trapped inside the walls. They'd been soundly defeated, and that was the end of their resistance – from that moment on, Jorvik and Northumbria were in the hands of the Northmen. The *skalds* still sang about these events, obviously proud of what had happened. Sara doubted the original inhabitants viewed it in quite the same light.

There was little sign of strife now, however, and Jorvik looked to be a very prosperous city. Seemingly thousands of people were scurrying about their business, with tradesmen crying their wares from every side. Craftsmen of all types proliferated – leather and textile workers, joiners, smiths, potters and cupmakers – each one a specialist in their own trade.

The River Ouse was obviously central to daily life, with much activity along its banks, including boatbuilding. It was tidal, and linked to the North Sea via the Humber, as she had already experienced for herself. The wall-enclosed city was on the northern side, but new buildings were springing up in the south as well, where the land sloped gently upwards. The Ouse was joined with the Foss, a smaller river coming down from the north. Sara knew that at this time, in the ninth century, the city was a port with well-established links to the Continent. She'd seen some of the imported goods in a museum in her own time, and they came from as far afield as the Middle East. Apparently the people here had had a taste for luxury items such as silk, wine, amber and ivory.

As they disembarked and walked into the town, she had to take shallow breaths, as there was a foul stench hanging over the place. This was no modern city with proper plumbing – each house would have a cesspit, open to the air, and there was no escaping the noxious odours. Some of the manufacturing businesses, such as tanning, were also smelly, and the houses were crammed in tightly together, which meant a lot of people in not very much space. Each property's boundaries seemed to be marked by a fence, mostly of wattle. Most of the houses faced the street gable end on, and these were no more than five or six metres wide. She assumed there was no running water, and any wells were bound to be unsanitary. If she was going to drink any water here, she'd have to boil it for as long as possible or she'd catch cholera or dysentery or something equally unpleasant fairly quickly.

She heard quite a few languages along the way: what Rurik called *Enska* – Old English – and Norse, something that sounded vaguely Latin, and even Welsh or Gaelic of some type. Irish perhaps? But everyone seemed to be getting along just fine. It was as if they'd all decided to forget the fighting and try to prosper. In most cases, she could tell who was Anglo-Saxon and who was Scandinavian by the way they were dressed and their various hairstyles, but some people sported a mixture. They were obviously integrating and copying each other.

'When I first met Holger, I thought his hair unkempt,' Eadgyth had confided. 'Most of the males I'd known wore theirs short, at least at the back. Holger looked quite wild, with a fringe hanging over his eyes. Now I find it appealing, and he does keep it clean and neat.'

Sara could see what she'd meant; many of the men here had what she would term a short-back-and-sides style, while others wore their hair long, either loose or confined somehow. It was true that a lot of them sported a long fringe. That was obviously the fashion. She had to agree with Eadgyth – it was very attractive. Especially Rurik's, but she suppressed that thought.

'How do all these people get enough food?' she wondered out loud, needing to redirect her thinking. 'Is there really sufficient for everyone?'

Rurik threw her a glance, as if it had never occurred to him to worry about such things. 'I should imagine most of the produce is brought in from the surrounding area.' He pointed to a bridge that spanned the river. 'See those carts over there? They look laden with all manner of goods. But Holger said a lot of the inhabitants also have small plots outside the town where they grow some of what they need. If we're staying, we should probably look into that, or we'll be spending far too much on provisions.'

Sara had never been into gardening, but somehow the thought of growing their own vegetables appealed to her. 'Good idea.' A sort of Viking allotment – how quaint.

They passed stalls selling jewellery of every kind. As this was her own specialist field, she eagerly studied the items on display – everything from cheap copper alloy brooches, crystal and glass beads and silver buckles to objects carved out of amber and jet. She couldn't wait to take a closer look once they were settled here. As an expert on Viking and Anglo-Saxon designs, she was fascinated to see that in this town the craftsmen appeared to have merged the two in many cases, creating a unique Jorvik style. There were also distinctly Celtic-looking things, such as cloak pins with a little ring at the top called ring pins. She would have liked to dawdle, but Rurik was in a hurry and took her hand to hurry her along the streets, some of which were paved or cobbled. The touch of his warm palm against hers was enough to distract her, and she instantly forgot the jewellery.

'We'll lodge at an alehouse first while I make enquiries about renting premises,' Rurik said. It turned out to be some type of inn, and Sara didn't like it, as it was a noisy place, packed with people. They were in luck, however, and he came back the following afternoon smiling broadly. 'A smith died not long ago and his widow wants to sell their house and go back to her family across the sea. I've negotiated a good price and we can move in next week.'

'Oh, I'm glad,' she mumbled half-heartedly.

He regarded her with a frown. 'You don't sound very pleased.

Are you tired of life here? I thought you said you wanted to experience Jorvik and see what the craftsmen here produce.'

That was true, she had said that. 'Yes. I just . . . I was longing for home,' she admitted.

For the first time in ages, he took both her hands in his and looked her in the eye. 'You can go any time, Sara, but I would be really grateful if you'd stay just a little longer to help me set up my business. The customers like your designs and you have a light touch when making intricate things. Can you bear it?'

She swallowed hard. Her main goal upon reaching Jorvik had been to leave as soon as possible. To escape from Rurik's distracting presence and the unwanted feelings he stirred up in her. The truth was she would have been happy to stay here for ever if that was what he really wanted, but not as his business partner. There was no denying she was in love with him, and the longer she remained by his side, the harder it would become to leave. Working alongside him, brushing against him in passing, sharing banter, laughter and advice, watching him frowning in concentration or beaming with pleasure when one of his creations turned out well . . . it was driving her crazy. No good could come of staying and prolonging the agony, and yet, gazing into the aquamarine depths of his eyes, she found it impossible to say no. Taking a deep breath, she nodded. 'Very well. A few weeks more won't make a difference.'

That was a lie, but she couldn't refuse him anything.

He smiled and squeezed her hands, clearly oblivious to the battle that had raged inside her. 'Thank you, I appreciate it. Now, do you want to come and see the house? Meet the widow? She has some furniture and other household goods she'd like to sell as well, but I wasn't sure how much of it to buy. Perhaps you can choose.'

'*OK.* Let's go.'

He held on to one of her hands again as they wove their way through the busy streets of Jorvik, and Sara allowed herself to pretend that it was because he wanted to, and not just so he wouldn't lose her in the throng.

It was a nice daydream.

Chapter Twenty

Their new home turned out to be very similar to the buildings around it – a dwelling house and workshop all in one. It was situated in one of the streets that hadn't been cobbled yet. Instead, the surface consisted mostly of mud, albeit thankfully fairly dry at the moment. Made of timber posts and wattle screen walls, the house was daubed with what looked like a mixture of mud, straw and – judging by the smell – dung, in order to keep out the cold and the rain. The floor was of stamped earth, and the roof thatched; Sara hoped that too was waterproof. A stout wooden door led straight from the street into a long room, perhaps four metres by seven or eight. In the middle of the space, a large rectangular hearth had been placed, its perimeter built of stones. A couple of these had Roman writing carved on them so had clearly been looted. Benches lined the walls, and there were no windows apart from a few tiny openings.

Another door at the back opened on to a long yard – it was too overgrown to be called a garden, but at least it gave a sense of space. It didn't smell very nice and Sara deduced this had to be where the privy was, and the rubbish pits or middens. A handful of chickens were picking through the dirt, clucking contentedly to themselves. Some were doing the same inside the house itself, making Sara wonder what was lurking in the floor for them to eat.

The widow selling the house greeted them politely. 'I've packed everything I want to take with me. I thought you might like to keep the rest, for a price, of course.' She gestured to various items. 'There are some cooking utensils, a lockable chest, woollen wall hangings to keep out draughts, a couple of pottery oil lamps and my late husband's tools and forge.'

Sara took one look at the woollen hangings and declined those – they looked like they'd been there for donkey's years and could be crawling with fleas, although she didn't say that out loud.

The widow's mouth turned down, but she inclined her head. 'Very well, I'll find another buyer for them.'

'We'll take all the rest, though, thank you,' Rurik hastened to add, as if he didn't want to offend the woman. She could always change her mind and sell everything to someone else. 'Can we look out the back?'

'Yes. There's no dog house, though.' She glanced at Beowulf as if she didn't want him in her home. 'You'll have to build one.'

Sara didn't reply. Probably best not to mention that the dog slept with them, usually at the foot end of their bed.

They exited the door and the odours grew worse. Sara tried not to wrinkle her nose; it wasn't just their cesspit that stank, but all their neighbours' too. These privies were nothing but a hole in the ground with a wooden seat, surrounded by wattle screens to give some privacy. Once it was full, another hole was dug nearby and the first one covered with soil. She was used to it by now, but at Foremark at least there hadn't been so many of them in close proximity. She resented having to use such facilities during cold weather, but needs must. It certainly didn't encourage anyone to linger.

The properties were divided by wattle fences and the people on the right had a couple of funny-looking little pigs in a pen, which didn't help. Was there anything smellier than pig manure? On the other side, a woman was hanging out dyed woollen skeins to blow in the breeze – yellow, red, blue and green – and Sara marvelled at the myriad of colours. She knew by now that most of them were made using natural dyes, although a few needed imported colours.

Narrow gaps between the buildings showed a glimpse of the main road, but it would be difficult to squeeze through there. The yard itself was also narrow, but a lot longer than she'd thought – perhaps thirty or forty metres. It sloped down to the river, where each house had a small piece of frontage.

'You don't grow anything here?' Sara asked, surveying the sea of stinging nettles, brambles, docks and tall grass, bisected by a walkway of old planks. It was a mess, quite frankly, and she'd take her shears to it the minute this house was theirs. Perhaps she'd even ask Rurik to borrow a scythe from somewhere.

'No, we had a small plot of land outside of town. Someone else has bought that though, sorry. There are some herbs growing next to the house.' The woman pointed them out, then turned towards the river. 'And I've left you a small rowing boat, in case you want to catch fish. There's plenty of shad and grayling to go round. And eels, naturally.'

Sara shuddered at the thought – she'd never liked eating eel, as she couldn't rid herself of the feeling she was chewing on a snake. As for the other types of fish, she hadn't heard of them, but she liked any kind so she was willing to try. She'd spotted dill among the herbs and that went well with seafood. Excellent.

'Thank you.' Rurik smiled at the woman. 'Where is the nearest well?'

'Just at the end of the street.' She pointed in the opposite direction to the one they'd come from.

'That's good. Will the hens be staying?'

'Oh yes, no point dragging them across the sea. They're laying well at the moment and mostly fend for themselves, but they appreciate scraps and some grain occasionally.'

Having chickens of her own appealed to Sara. She was looking forward to collecting their eggs. 'Do you leave them out at night?'

'No, that would be foolish. There are foxes around and they'd kill them all. Best to bring them indoors in the evening. They'll roost in the rafters, that's what they're used to.'

In the rafters? How very unhygienic, but if that was the price you had to pay to keep them safe, so be it.

They moved in the following day and Rurik wasn't surprised when Sara insisted on thoroughly cleaning the house from top to bottom. Her fastidiousness was something he'd become used to by now, and he had to admit he'd not had a single stomach upset since she'd insisted on using boiled water for everything. Why, he had no idea. Having a clean house also seemed to help. Little Birger had been sick far less often than any of the other infants back at Repton. He'd frequently seen Sara wash his wooden toys.

'We're burning these for a start,' she muttered, making him carry the widow's straw mattresses out into the back yard. 'The gods only know what's living inside them.'

'I'll buy some more sheepskins to sleep on instead,' he offered. He didn't share her fear of bed bugs, but he had to admit he would rather not be forever scratching.

He'd bought lye soap as they needed it immediately, although by now Eadgyth had taught Sara how to make her own. He helped her to heat water for scrubbing in a large cauldron, and did his fair share of cleaning to make the work go more quickly. The sooner the house was ready, the faster he could begin to trade and use the forge.

'It does smell a lot nicer in here now,' he commented, when all the benches had been washed down and the floor swept to within an inch of its life. The disgruntled hens had retreated outside, clearly unhappy with this new regime. A rat and several mice also disappeared, fleeing the broom, not to mention the watchful eye of the hound.

'Move, Beowulf!' Sara ordered. The dog scurried out of the way, perhaps wary of being bathed. He'd been subjected to that ordeal several times since they'd found him, especially whenever he rolled in something disgusting.

Rurik smiled and retreated to the front part of the room, the workshop, which they'd also cleaned and tidied up. 'I'm going out to buy some charcoal now. Will you manage on your own for a while?'

'Yes, of course.' She paused for a moment. 'Can you purchase some food as well, please? We'll need all the basic things – barley, some kind of meat or fish, flour if there is any, and I suppose you'll want ale.'

'Definitely.' He grinned. She wasn't averse to ale herself and they both knew it, although since the midwinter feast he had noticed that she mostly stuck to water. The few times she'd accepted a cup of ale, she had refused to have more than one. A shimmer of awareness seemed to pass between them, like a current in the air, and her eyes widened as if she remembered clearly what effect too much ale had on her. For a moment they stared at each other, as though unable to look away, but then she broke the spell by closing her eyes. Rurik felt something akin to frustration well up inside him, but knew he had no right to any such emotion. 'Very well,' he said curtly, 'I'll see what I can find. Beowulf, guard your mistress!'

The hound barked, as if confirming that he would, and Rurik knew that he could trust him.

When he returned, he was carrying a sack of charcoal – the

merchant had promised to deliver more tomorrow – and another sack with provisions. 'Here you are.' He put it on the table by the back door. 'Some beef, barley, turnips and onions. Will that do for now?'

Sara sent him a smile, throwing out the last of the scrubbing water into the back yard. 'Perfect, thank you! You're an *angel*.'

'A what?'

'A being from . . . er, the sky.' She shook her head. 'Never mind, but I love you right now.' She stood on tiptoe and kissed his cheek. 'I'm so hungry I could eat a whole cow.'

He stilled, her words echoing in his ears and the imprint of her luscious mouth burning his cheek, but he knew she wasn't serious. He found himself wishing that she was. But did he really want her to be in love with him? He wasn't sure. All he knew was that he would like her to stay a bit longer so that he could understand his own feelings. Shaking his head at himself, he went over to the small hearth they'd be using to melt metal.

'Let me know when it's ready. I'm going to get started over here.' He busied himself lighting the charcoal and taking some silver out of the secret compartment in his kist. All the while, he watched Sara as she went about her chores, humming as she chopped the ingredients for their meal. A fierce longing to be allowed to call her his woman – his wife – for real swept through him. She looked so contented, so beautiful.

He wanted her to stay for ever.

But she was longing to go home.

'Who said we needed another silversmith in this town? We've got plenty, don't we, Alfr?'

Rurik looked up from the anvil, where he'd been busy hammering out a silver bowl. He exchanged glances with Sara, who looked as astonished as he himself felt at hearing such an unfriendly greeting. Two men stood outside the hatch that faced the street, reaching inside to pick through the various items on display. One of them, the man who'd spoken, made a face as he held up a particularly fine ring in the shape of a snake. Sara had spent hours embellishing it with filigree, and no one should have cause to look at it as if it was shoddy work.

'Can I help you?' Rurik asked, putting down the bowl but retaining his grip on the hammer as he moved to stand behind the table.

'Yes, by leaving.' The man guffawed and dug an elbow into his friend's side as he joined in the laughter.

'Excuse me, but have I missed something? I was under the impression that all tradesmen were welcome in Jorvik. It is a centre for free trade, is it not? No one said anything about needing permission to set up a business here.'

In fact he'd been informed that the Northumbrians, Mercians and Danes mingled amicably here, finding common ground in their resentment of the kings of the West Saxons who had tried to take control of this part of the country. Newcomers were quickly assimilated, and so far everyone had been nothing but friendly. Not these two, apparently.

'Well, see, there's unwritten rules that aren't necessarily known to everyone. I'm Knud and I'm the chief silversmith in this town.' He indicated his friend. 'This here is Alfr, the second-best one.'

If Alfr minded being referred to in this way, he didn't say anything.

'And your point is?' Rurik crossed his arms over his chest, noting with satisfaction that Knud was past his prime and sporting a large gut. That meant he could be easily bested if it should come to a fight man to man.

'My point is that there's not enough trade to go round if we keep getting too many newcomers. Therefore, you'd do better to move elsewhere. Your services aren't needed here.' Knud's cheeks had been ruddy before, but turned an even darker red now, as if he didn't like being argued with.

Too bad.

'Rubbish,' Rurik said succinctly. 'There are people coming and going all the time, giving plenty of trade for everyone. Now if you're not interested in buying anything, I'd thank you to move out of the way so that my customers can see my wares properly. Good day to you both.'

He nodded and turned back to his anvil, giving Sara a small shake of the head as she opened her mouth to say something. That would definitely not help matters.

'Well, you've had a friendly warning. The next one won't be,' Knud growled behind him, but Rurik pretended he hadn't heard and carried on hammering.

'They're gone.'

He looked up to find Sara still staring towards the hatch.

'Good. I hadn't expected it to be easy to set up a new business, but I could definitely do without that sort of welcome.' It was galling in the extreme, and irritation fizzed inside him, making his movements jerky. He had to will himself to take a deep breath to steady his hands, else he'd ruin the bowl.

She shuddered. 'They were horrible. What reason could they possibly have for not wanting competition? Surely that's healthy and good for the customers?'

'Jealousy. I bet he's getting lazy in his old age and the items he produces are probably not as well made as they should be.' Rurik sighed. 'We'll have to be on our guard. I didn't like the implied threat.'

'Me neither. *Bastards.*'

'What does that mean?' He was intrigued by the foreign words she sometimes let slip when they were alone.

'Sons of women who weren't married when their child was conceived.'

'Er . . . and what is wrong with that?'

'You clearly haven't listened to the Christian priests. Where they rule, men and women have to be married in order to produce children. If they are not, those children are said to be *bastards*, and that is not a good thing to be. Or at least that used to be the case. In my time we no longer pay much attention to that sort of thing, but the word has lived on as an insult.'

'I see. Strange. Well, any insult sounds good to me when it comes to those two. Let's hope we don't see them again.'

Sara had been in Jorvik for three weeks now, and had been intending to raise the subject of travelling to Sweden, but she could never find the right moment. Just like at Foremark, they'd cleaned the newly acquired house from top to bottom, then set up the business. They'd brought quite a few items already made, which meant they could start selling goods right away, but before she left, she'd wanted to help Rurik build up a good stock. That work was almost done now, but as he didn't have anyone else to help him as yet, he still needed her around to watch the shop whenever he had to go out and about.

'Um, shouldn't you have an apprentice?' she ventured to ask. At least if he had one of those, she wouldn't be leaving him in the lurch.

'No, why?' He stopped what he was doing to scowl at her.

She held up her hands. 'Only asking. I thought most craftsmen did. And you know I won't be here for ever.' In fact, she was itching to get away. She had been right: it was agony staying here. Every day that passed, she fell more deeply in love with him, and since her feelings weren't reciprocated, the best cure would be to escape from his presence altogether. She didn't know how much longer she could bear it. They didn't share a bed now, as the widow had left two behind in the back room, but he was still too close for comfort. Since the midwinter feast they'd lived in a sort of uneasy truce, almost tiptoeing around each other, and it was seriously frustrating. Although she was the one who'd told him their relationship had to be platonic, she couldn't stop her dreams from featuring heated images of their night of passion, and it was driving her insane. Sleeping with him wasn't the answer, though. A relationship based purely on lust would simply never be enough. No, the sooner she left, the better.

A wet nose nudged her hand and she looked down. *Beowulf!* How on earth was she going to say goodbye to him? She knew Rurik would take good care of him, but she'd miss him unbearably. Almost as much as she'd miss his master. But neither of them could be part of her future. It was impossible.

Said master was now rubbing the stubble on his chin, making Sara long to touch it too. Her fingers clearly remembered how it felt – soft yet slightly harsh – and the rasping noise was sending shivers down her spine, in the nicest possible way.

'Perhaps you're right,' he said. 'We might both need to be out at the same time occasionally. And I'll need someone to help when you leave. That was what you meant, right?' His scowl deepened. 'I'll ask around.'

Two days later, he arrived home with a big, burly teenager. 'Sara, this is Tryggve. Tryggve, Sara. And Beowulf.' Rurik indicated the dog, and the youth, who'd given Sara the merest nod, fell to his knees in front of the hound and held out a hand to be sniffed. When he seemed to pass muster, he proceeded to scratch Beowulf behind the ears and generally make a huge fuss of him. His expression turned into a goofy grin that matched the dog's, making Sara want to laugh.

Instead, she smiled. 'Welcome, Tryggve. I can see you're going to fit in well here.' Anyone who loved dogs as much as she did had to be a good person. And Beowulf was a good judge of character, so his immediate acceptance of the young man boded well.

Rurik shook his head, as if in exasperation, but looked pleased too. 'He's been training with a blacksmith, but the man died last week and there's no one else to take him on at the moment. Isn't that so?' He raised his eyebrows at the teenager, who got to his feet after one last pat.

'Mm-hmm.'

'I'll show you where you can put your belongings, then we'll get started.'

'Fine.'

Clearly not a man of many words, but Sara was pleased. Now Rurik would have someone to help him keep an eye on things after she'd gone.

Chapter Twenty-One

'*Woof! Woof-woof!*'

Rurik sat up in bed, startled awake by Beowulf's barking. A crash and some muffled swearing coming from the back yard had him out from under the covers in an instant. 'Tryggve!' he shouted as he raced past the sleeping bench in the main room. 'Out the back, now!'

'Huh? What?'

He didn't stop to see if the youth lumbered after him. Instead he threw open the back door that led to the long, thin garden backing on to the river. Sara had insisted he clear the space of nettles, and she'd swept the path made of planks that led to the privy. He quickly scanned the area, but there was no one in sight. Beowulf shot out from behind him and took off into the darkness, vaulting the fence while barking furiously, but there was no time to worry about that now.

The first thing Rurik saw as he exited the door was fire. Someone had placed a heap of twigs against the back wall, and these were slowly being consumed by flames. There wasn't a moment to lose. 'Water,' he yelled, almost colliding with Tryggve, who was coming the other way. 'Take a bucket and fetch water from the river. Quickly!'

They both ran inside and Rurik grabbed two of the buckets he kept near the forge to dunk hot metal into. They were both nearly full, while another bucket nearby was empty. Tryggve grabbed that one and sprinted out the back and down towards the river, while Rurik ran to dump the contents of the other two on the fire.

'What's happening? Oh no!' Sara had come outside in just her *serk* and stood frozen in the doorway. 'Are there any more buckets?'

But her help proved unnecessary. When Tryggve returned with his contribution, it was enough to douse most of the flames. It needed only one more trip to the river from both of them to extinguish it altogether.

'That was close.' Rurik leaned forward with his hands on his thighs and breathed deeply, shaking with shock and fury.

Sara voiced his thoughts. 'Who would deliberately do such a thing?'

They looked at each other and spoke in unison. 'Knud.'

'The *jōtuns* take the man!'

Tryggve blinked. 'You mean you didn't put that pile of sticks there?'

She snorted. 'No, and we certainly wouldn't set fire to it if we had.'

'No, I suppose not . . .' The youth frowned. 'You know Knud? He's trouble, my late master swore.'

'I wouldn't go so far as to say we know him,' Rurik muttered. 'Rather, he introduced himself to us and then threatened to get rid of us if we didn't leave.' He ground his teeth together. 'Well, if he thinks this is the way to go about it, he's wrong.'

Beowulf came bounding back across the fence and up the path with a piece of cloth between his teeth.

'Ah, there you are. Good boy! You bit one of them? Thank you!' It was Rurik's turn to fuss the dog, who had probably saved their lives. The house and the business at the very least.

The hound was given a large marrow bone Sara had been saving for him as reward. 'And there will be more of those,' she promised. Glancing at the others, she added, 'At least now whoever it was knows we have a guard dog. Hopefully that will deter them from trying again.'

'Indeed. And if it doesn't, I'll be ready for them. Tryggve, do you know how to handle a weapon of any kind?'

'Yes, I have an axe. My uncle taught me how to use it.'

'Good. Make sure you sleep with it next to you from now on.'

A week passed without further incident and business was brisk. Word seemed to have spread through the town about the new silversmith, and Sara found herself so busy she barely had time to think about leaving. Just a little while longer, she kept telling herself. After all, what difference did it make? And the thought of leaving Rurik and Beowulf was hugely depressing.

Tryggve was becoming more talkative, and had proved to be good at his work. Despite his big hands, he was capable of copying the intricate filigree and punch work that Sara did – particularly the latter – and she enjoyed teaching him, as he caught on quickly. He didn't seem to miss the heavier blacksmith's work he'd been doing before.

'My mother's been telling everyone about the pretty things I'm making,' he commented one day. 'Those are some of her friends.' He nodded towards the hatch, where a group of women were oohing and aahing over a basket of rings, trying them on in turn.

'Really? That's very kind of her. It's certainly helping.' Sara smiled at the teenager.

He shrugged. 'People can see for themselves when something is well made.' Glancing at Rurik, he added in a whisper, 'And I like working with Rurik much more than Uve. He hasn't hit me a single time yet.'

'Hit you?' Sara stared at him. 'Why would he?'

'Well, if I didn't learn fast enough . . .' Tryggve didn't seem to feel this was anything out of the ordinary, but she was appalled and very glad the youth was away from such a violent employer. She realised Rurik might be unusual, as he seemed to be a peace-loving man, not prone to hitting anyone unless he had to defend himself. This was a harsh era, after all, and life was tough for a lot of people. It made her thank her lucky stars yet again that she'd ended up with him.

Later that day, however, she almost changed her mind.

Rurik was rushing to finish a commission for some warrior who was off adventuring and wanted a knife handle done quickly. As soon as it was done, he downed tools and wrapped it in a piece of material. 'I'm going to deliver this in person. I won't be long.'

'Very well.' Sara barely spared him a glance, as she was working on a soapstone mould and wanted to get it just right.

'Oh, I almost forgot – please can you put this away in my kist? You know where I mean.'

He handed her the small wooden box containing the takings for the day, a mixed pile of various payment types – hacksilver, a tiny piece of gold, some coins that looked to be Islamic and a few bits of bronze and copper.

'Yes, in just a moment.' She put it on her lap, assuming he meant she was to hide it in his secret compartment.

'Thank you.'

A little while later, she blew away any loose bits of soapstone, pleased with her handiwork. 'That will do,' she muttered. Tryggve was busy hammering out a piece of silver with a view to stretching it into thread, and seemed to be in his own little world. The perfect time to go and hide today's gains.

Beowulf followed her into the back room, and she pushed the door shut. Best not to let anyone see what she was doing. Rurik's kist was under his bed, and she grunted as she pulled it out. 'This is a lot heavier than it used to be, eh, boy?' she commented to the dog. As usual, he put his head to one side, as if listening intently to her words. She smiled at him and ruffled his ears. 'You're such a good boy, aren't you? How I will miss you!'

But she didn't want to think about that now.

There were a lot of clothes in the chest, as well as shoes and a spare belt, and she took everything out and put it on the bed. The little hole in the wood was exactly where she remembered it, and she had no trouble lifting the secret bottom enough for her to be able to add today's hoard to what was already in there. When she went to close it again, however, it wouldn't quite fit, no matter how much she jiggled it. Something was in the way.

'Oh bother!'

With a sigh, she decided to take the entire fake bottom out and try to reorganise what was underneath. As she pulled it off, something moved and caught the light. She gasped. 'No, I don't believe it!'

For a moment she didn't dare touch the object that had caused the jam, but then she reached out and picked it up. The magical *seax*. How on earth had it ended up in here? She'd seen Rurik throw it into the sea, and when she'd searched for it, it was gone. Had he found it before her? That was the only explanation she could come up with. But in that case, why hadn't he told her?

She'd said it was important to her, hadn't she? And yet he had hidden it away, making her believe she was stuck in his time all these months. 'Why, the sneaky lowlife bastard . . . I could have gone home at any point!'

Beowulf whined, obviously sensing that something was wrong. 'No, not you, Wulfie, your master. I'm going to have words with him and you might want to cover your ears.'

With fury surging through her in great drowning waves, she reorganised the secret compartment, leaving the *seax* on top where she could easily find it again. She should have been pleased that there was no longer any need for her to travel all the way to Sweden to find Linnea, but she was too angry to be relieved. How *could* he? And what had he hoped to gain by it? It wasn't as though he wanted her as anything other than an unpaid assistant. Sure, they worked well together, but he didn't really need her. He could get by perfectly well on his own with just Tryggve to help him.

She couldn't understand it, but come evening, she was going to get to the bottom of this, and he'd better have a damn good answer.

Sara was very quiet during their evening meal and seemed in a bad mood. Rurik knew that women sometimes took umbrage at the slightest thing, and the best course of action was to leave them be. Hopefully she'd get over whatever it was and be her usual sunny self in the morning.

When they'd gone into their bedroom for the night, however, she closed the door and rounded on him, her eyes lit with barely controlled rage. Rurik took a step backwards and blinked when she poked him in the chest.

'I found it! Why didn't you tell me? Why would you keep it hidden from me all these months? It makes absolutely no sense.'

'What are you talking about?' He frowned. 'Hidden?'

'The *seax*!' she hissed, and gestured at his kist. 'It was in there all along!'

'Er, yes . . . and what of it? I was keeping it safe for you.' He took another step back to avoid her accusing glance, not sure what he'd done wrong.

'You knew that I wanted it! I told you I needed it to travel back to my time.' She was trying valiantly to keep her voice down, presumably so that Tryggve wouldn't hear them, but he could see that she was longing to yell at him. Her eyes were dark pools shooting sparks of anger.

'Yes, but you didn't *want* to go back straight away, you said. In fact, you begged me to let you stay for a while and I agreed. I did tell you it was in the kist the day before the battle of Hreopandune, but since then you've seemed content to remain. Well, until we arrived here at Jorvik and I asked if you'd wait for just a few more weeks.'

'You did *not* tell me that. I would have remembered.' Her scowl had grown to fearsome proportions.

Rurik closed his eyes and tried to recall his exact words. 'I showed you the kist and told you that everything you needed to go home was in there.' Relief flooded through him. He *had* said that, he remembered it clearly now.

Her mouth fell open. 'Everything I needed to . . . ? And from that I was supposed to deduce that you meant the knife? For the love of Odin! I thought it was still in the sea!' She threw up her hands and stomped over to her bed, throwing herself down so hard the wood creaked in protest.

'Well, perhaps I should have clarified, but I thought you understood. And you would have found it in there if I'd died in battle.'

She didn't reply, just lay down and turned her back on him. Beowulf, ever the peacemaker, jumped up beside her and snuggled down as if to comfort her. Rurik heard a sniff, and then her arm came round the shaggy dog's neck, pulling him close.

Jealousy shot through him. Jealousy of a dog. *Odin's ravens!* This was insane.

'Sara, I swear I did not keep the *seax* from you on purpose. Why would I? I was only trying to do what you wanted. If you'll recall, I was very dubious at first, but you insisted.'

Perhaps that wasn't quite true. He could have asked her at some point whether she wanted to go home and reminded her that he had the knife, but he hadn't. Because he wished her to stay. He couldn't bear the thought of her leaving, but now he seemed to have made matters worse and she would leave for sure.

'Sara?' he tried again when there was no reply.

'I don't want to talk about it. I need to think this over,' came the muffled reply.

Rurik sighed and lay down on his own bed after removing his tunic and woollen trousers. He was desperate to talk things over with her, but he could tell it would be futile just now. Perhaps by morning she would have calmed down and then she'd be more reasonable.

With another, even deeper sigh, he tried to settle down to sleep, but his thoughts wouldn't give him any respite. Instead, he resigned himself to an endless night of staring into the darkness.

Chapter Twenty-Two

A crash and a cry of pain woke Sara, as well as Beowulf's frantic barking. The dog shot off her bed and over to the closed door, which Rurik was already opening.

'What's going on?' She sat up and scrambled to her feet, about to follow him.

'No, stay there. This could get ugly,' he whispered, motioning for her to back away. 'Close and bar the door. Please, Sara. Now!'

She reluctantly did as he asked, because the urgency in his voice had brooked no argument, but not before she'd peered out to see four men wreaking havoc in the main room. They had dark scarves or pieces of cloth tied over the lower part of their faces like bandits, and were obviously keen not to be recognised. At the moment they were throwing tools and smaller pieces of furniture around, smashing soapstone moulds and pulling down a shelf above the workbench. Dear God, what was happening?

There was a small hole in the door, and she peered through it to watch the scene that was unfolding. From what she could see, poor Tryggve had been hit over the head, as he was clutching it and didn't seem quite steady on his feet. Rurik pushed him out of the way and picked up a piece of wood from near the cooking hearth, going on the attack without hesitation. The four men were advancing on him from all sides, brandishing knives of various sizes, and although he managed to disarm one of them by hitting his hand, another slashed him on the shoulder.

'*Niðingr!* You won't get away with this,' Rurik hissed, head-butting another of his opponents while neatly sidestepping a swipe from the man's knife.

Beowulf sank his teeth into the rear of a third man, who howled in pain and tried to kick the dog. Sara couldn't stand this. Rurik's own weapons were hanging on the wall in the main room, and he couldn't reach them. Fighting four armed men with a piece of wood was never going to work. She had to do something. Scrambling under his bed, she pulled out the kist and pushed the clothes to one side so that she could open the secret compartment. Her fingers fumbled at first, but on the second try she managed to lift the cover and retrieve the *seax*. She hurried to close it again, just in case those men succeeded in overpowering everyone – she didn't want them to know about the silver and other valuables. As soon as she'd pushed the kist back under the bed, she rushed over to the door and opened it.

'Here, Rurik, catch!' she shouted. He spun around after jabbing one of his opponents in the stomach, and she threw the *seax* to him handle first. Thankfully he caught it, and managed to swivel and draw blood from one of his assailants.

Tryggve seemed to have rallied and was busy trying to fight someone with the help of a pair of heavy tongs. He wasn't inflicting much damage, but at least it kept him from being stabbed himself. Sara ran over to the hearth and picked up a medium-sized skillet, one she normally used for baking flatbread. Hefting it with both hands, she lunged at the nearest man and bashed him as hard as she could. It almost made him drop his knife, but unfortunately he was made of stern stuff and she'd mostly succeeded in riling him. She cried out and started backing up with the skillet held in front of her as he advanced. This was not going to end well. She should have hit him with even more force.

'I'll make you regret that,' the man muttered, but Sara barely heard his words because she'd recognised the voice. *Asmund!* Was she never to be free of the bastard?

'You!' she spat with loathing, but that only made him chuckle. As he continued to move towards her, she tried to hit him again, but he grabbed the skillet and wrested it out of her hands, flinging it away.

'Sara, didn't I tell you to stay out of this?' Rurik rushed over to help her, clearly exasperated. He fooled Asmund into thinking he was going to attack from the right, then changed direction and brought the *seax* down from the left, slicing the man's right arm almost from top to bottom. A long red line appeared on Asmund's shirtsleeve, and he dropped his knife.

'Get him!' he urged the others, while clutching at his now useless appendage and shouting a string of curses.

Sara had meant to help, but had forgotten that she might be a distraction. In rushing to her assistance, Rurik had turned his back on the others. The moment's inattention gave the final attacker the chance to jump forward, and Sara cried out when she saw him punch Rurik on the jaw. The blow sent him reeling back towards Asmund, who'd rallied yet again and bent to retrieve his knife from the floor. Rurik reacted quickly and swivelled to deal with him, but he was a fraction too late. Before he could move out of the way, the man calmly stuck his knife into Rurik's lower abdomen. The latter froze as his assailant pulled the knife out and stood there staring at him, breathing heavily.

'*Nooooo!*' Sara's scream reverberated around the room, echoed by a disbelieving noise from one of the other men.

'What have you done?' he growled. 'That was not what was

agreed. You were only supposed to wreck the *aumingi*'s workshop and maybe rough him up a little.'

Asmund spat on the floor. 'He had it coming.' He turned towards Sara, pointing at her. 'As for you, I'm going to—'

His words were cut off by a howl of pain. Beowulf had taken the opportunity to jump up and sink his teeth into the man's hand, hanging on even when Asmund tried to shake him off. 'Let go, you foul beast!' He aimed a kick at the dog, but the hound danced out of the way before finally releasing the mauled hand.

'Come, let us leave before all this commotion brings the neighbours.'

Asmund, still spluttering curses and threats, was hustled out the door by two of the other men, who sent worried glances in Rurik's direction before disappearing into the night.

The last man stood motionless for a moment, his eyes wide with shock, as if he hadn't bargained for murder to be a part of this night's work. Tryggve rushed over and hit him on the arm with the large iron tongs, causing the man to shriek then stumble backwards and out through the door. Tryggve slammed it shut behind him and shouted, '*Argr!* I hope I broke his arm, the coward. Rurik, are you . . . Oh no!'

The youth's eyes opened wide as he and Sara both took in the rapidly spreading stain on Rurik's shirt. Rurik groaned and bit his teeth together, swearing under his breath. Sara's heart constricted, and she tried to stem the tide of panic rising inside her.

'I'm so sorry! I just wanted to help. I didn't realise . . . Forgive me!' She blinked away tears, trying to make her brain think what to do.

He shook his head, and she wasn't sure if he was giving forgiveness or withholding it. He was clearly badly hurt, and a knife wound to the stomach could be fatal. She'd done a first aid course, and with all the stabbings happening in the UK on a regular basis recently, she'd read up on how to treat such injuries. It all depended on where the knife had gone in, but in the first instance she needed to try and stop the bleeding as much as possible.

'Lie down on the bench,' she ordered. They could argue about whose fault it was later. If there was a later. Her own blood went cold at that thought, but she pushed it aside and concentrated on leading him over to the nearest bench. Tryggve cottoned on and helped her by pushing his master on to his back.

'Best do as she says,' the youth muttered.

'Get me a blanket, please, Tryggve. We have to keep him warm.'

They wrapped Rurik up, leaving his abdomen free, and Sara put her hands on the wound and pushed as hard as she could, applying pressure where she thought it was most needed. 'I've got to stop the bleeding,' she said. He grunted and hissed in a breath of pain, but didn't protest.

It wasn't going to work, though. He wouldn't survive without a doctor. Proper treatment. Blood transfusions. Antibiotics. She stifled a sob and attempted to order her panicked thoughts. There was nothing like that here. What did you do in Viking times when you'd been stabbed? Waited for death probably. She couldn't sew the wound up herself, and even if she did, he had to be bleeding internally. She needed to get him to a twenty-first-century surgeon, and fast, or she would lose him.

No, I can't lose him! Not now. Not like this. Especially not when it was her fault.

His face was noticeably paler; she could see that even with just the light from the fire, which Tryggve had stoked. His skin was also chilly and clammy to the touch, and his pulse was fluttering at an alarming rate. She knew what that meant. If he didn't receive medical attention soon, he'd go into shock. She made a decision and instantly felt calmer. It would be all right. It had to be.

'Tryggve, I have to get help for Rurik and I know how, but I will need you to keep an eye on Beowulf and this house until we come back.'

'Come back? Where are you going?'

'I, um . . . can't tell you that.' She beckoned him over and whispered, 'Can you keep a secret? Swear an oath never to reveal what I'm about to tell you?'

'Y-yes, I swear by all the gods.' The youth's eyes were huge, but he was listening intently.

'I'm a *vōlva* and I'm going to take Rurik to another realm – a, er, spirit realm – where some of my fellow shamans can treat him. I don't want you to watch when we leave, as I'd have to kill you if you saw anything. That is strictly forbidden.' The boy's eyes widened even further, and he was hanging on her every word. 'So please can you take Beowulf into the back room and close the door. Lie down on the bed and wait until everything is quiet out here, then you can come out again.'

'Very well.' He took hold of the dog's collar and pulled him away from where he was leaning his muzzle on Rurik's legs. 'Come, Beowulf, it will be fine.' He hesitated and gazed at Sara. 'It will, won't it?'

'Yes, I hope so, but I must hurry. We will come back, I promise. It could take a while, weeks even, so in the meantime, just stay here and keep the shop closed and protected. And keep Beowulf safe. Can you do that?'

'Aye, I'll get a few of my uncles to come and help. Those cowards won't get away with this. I know who at least one of them was. I caught a glimpse of his face.'

'Good. Thank you. Now go, please.' She shooed him away and he did as she'd asked.

As soon as the youth had closed the door, she grabbed the *seax* off the floor and shook Rurik. '*Hey*, stay awake. I need you to say the magic words with me. Please, even if you only whisper them. Say after me – *með blōð skaltu ferðast*.'

He was so pale now, she was afraid he'd lose consciousness any second, and she knew she would only have one chance at this. As he murmured the words, she said them with him while gripping his hand so that she could slash at their fingers at the same time. The horrible spinning motion she remembered from last time assailed her, but she tried not to cry out. Instead she concentrated on continuing to apply pressure to his abdomen with their joined hands, while gripping the knife with the other. He'd need it to get back to his own time.

If he survived.

For a while everything went black, and when she came to, she found herself lying diagonally on top of him, still gripping the *seax*. Thank God. At least she hadn't lost that.

But had it worked?

She looked around her and saw that they were on a pavement. There were street lights nearby – *street lights, hurrah!* – and she could hear traffic in the distance. 'Yessss!' She wanted to punch the air, but this was not the time. Rurik needed an ambulance, right now. Although he was still breathing, his pulse felt faint and he was even paler than before. Not good.

Someone came walking towards her and she shouted, '*Help!*' for all she was worth.

'What's happened?' A middle-aged man came rushing over to kneel beside them.

'This man's been stabbed. I think someone tried to mug him and it went wrong. Please, call 999. We have to get him to hospital immediately!'

'Yes, yes, of course.' He fumbled with his mobile and she was vaguely aware of him talking and giving directions while she continued to put pressure on Rurik's wound.

In a surprisingly short space of time, which still seemed like aeons to Sara, he was being lifted on to a stretcher and pushed into an ambulance. The paramedics were calm and precise, asking questions, sticking needles into him and doing all sorts of checks. She was bundled into the back with him and then they were off.

As they whizzed through the streets of York at top speed, the siren blaring, she held his hand and prayed to every god she could think of. *Please, let him survive. Please!*

A strange noise woke Rurik, and at first he thought he'd ended up in some alternative afterlife.

Beep, beep, beep.

Out of the corner of his eye he could see a square metal object with a piece of glass at the front where an other-worldly green light was bobbing up and down, making a pattern. He frowned. What *was* that? Some type of magic? A will-o'-the-wisp? He'd heard of those but never seen one before.

He took a deep breath and pain sliced through him. Everything hurt, but especially his lower abdomen. Only shallow breaths were bearable; anything else was impossible. And he felt weak, like a newborn. Weren't you supposed to be rejuvenated when you died and go back to how you were in your prime? He'd still been in his, but right now his body was useless.

Everything else around him was white, as if he was inside a cloud. Although he could make out walls and a ceiling, so perhaps it was a massive kist or grave chamber. Had his soul not progressed any further yet? He was definitely not in Valhalla. There were no warriors, no handmaidens, Valkyries or mead, and he couldn't hear any sounds of feasting. But maybe his last fight didn't count as a battle – it was more of a brawl, after all – and therefore he hadn't been honoured with access to that august establishment. A shame.

Glancing at his arm, he suddenly noticed see-through snakes attached to his skin and possibly disappearing inside him. *What in the name of . . . ?* What dark magic was this? His head was swimming and he was having trouble focusing, but he didn't like those snakes. They had to go. Intending to rid himself of them once and for all, he tried to sit up and reach for them, only to feel a cool hand pushing him back.

'No! You have to lie still. It's vital that you don't move too much.'

'Sara?' he croaked. His eyes widened as her face came into focus. 'Oh no! Are you dead too? Did those cowards kill everyone?' He clenched his fists. 'I swear I'm going to go back and haunt them. I'll appear as a *draugr* and scare the wits out of them.'

Astonishingly, that statement made her laugh, and her hand gripped one of his. 'No, no, you're not dead, and you can go back and deal with them as they deserve eventually, although not as a *zombie*. You're badly injured, but the, er . . . healers say you'll live. You have to do as you're told, though, and rest.'

'*Zom-bee?* Not dead? But . . . where are we?'

She leaned forward and whispered so quietly only he could hear. 'In my time.'

'What? Why? How?'

'Shh, I'll tell you later. For now, you have to pretend you don't know me. I told them I found you bleeding in the road. You'd been attacked and you were talking *Icelandic*, which I happen to understand. I've stayed to translate for you. Even if you manage to make yourself understood, you have to say that you don't remember anything except your first name. Nothing, understand? You can't let on that you don't know what any of this is.' She gestured at the green light and other unidentifiable objects.

'*Icelandic*?'

'It's a language similar to yours. They won't know the difference, as it's not common here. Please, do as I say. It's important or we might get in trouble.'

'Very well. But first I'm going to sleep. Can you take away the snakes?'

She frowned. 'What snakes?'

'In my arms. Don't like them.'

'Oh!' She gave a gurgle of laughter. 'They're not snakes. I'll explain later, but trust me, they are keeping you alive and they won't hurt you. I swear.'

'Fine.'

He was too tired to argue and just closed his eyes.

Chapter Twenty-Three

'You are sure he doesn't remember anything other than his Christian name? There was no trauma to his head, but perhaps the shock and blood loss . . .' The nurse was looking at Sara sceptically, and tapped her pen on her clipboard.

'Yes. He says it's all a blank.' She didn't add that his name was heathen, not Christian, as that wouldn't help matters.

'Was he here for the festival? He was certainly dressed that way. As were you, I recall.'

Sara nodded. 'Looks like it, but he must have got the dates muddled up, as that was months ago. As for me, I'd been to a party. We, er . . . had to dress up and it was the only costume I had.' There was a Viking festival held in York every year, but it was usually in February, and they were now in late April, so it wasn't plausible they'd both got it wrong. She had changed into modern garments and was grateful that no one else had remarked on the way she'd been dressed when Rurik was brought in.

Getting into the flat had been a performance in itself, and required some acting on her part. One of her neighbours, Mrs Morris, had a spare key to her front door, but as Sara had been away for over six months, the woman was shocked to see her.

'I thought you'd been in an accident or something! No one seemed to know where you were.' She goggled at her as if she was looking at a ghost.

'Er, not an accident, but I did become very ill. I've, um . . . been in hospital and then my grandfather looked after me,' Sara lied.

'Goodness! What kind of illness?'

Sara cursed her neighbour's curiosity. Mrs Morris had always been one for gossip, and she should have thought of a better story. She pasted on a vague smile. 'Oh, the doctors aren't sure. They're still doing tests, but at least I feel better now. Some sort of virus, maybe a bad case of glandular fever? I'll be sure to tell you as soon as I know. Now, if you wouldn't mind giving me my key, please? I'm dying to have a shower.'

At least that last part had been true, and she'd rushed off without giving the old lady a chance to ask why she was wearing a Viking outfit.

The nurse at the hospital was still regarding Sara through narrowed eyes. 'Hmm. Well, I don't know what to do about payment. He's had several blood transfusions, expensive surgery and a lot of medication. The NHS will need to claim that from someone if he isn't British.'

'I know.' Sara shuddered at the thought of everything Rurik had gone through. The doctors said he'd been very lucky and the knife had only penetrated his lower intestines, missing anything more vital. But it had still been touch and go. 'I've called the Icelandic embassy and they're making enquiries. I, um, promised he could stay with me for a while after he's been discharged so that they'll know where to find him. We've become friends.'

'I see.' The woman's mouth was a thin line of annoyance and disapproval, but there wasn't anything she could do about the situation.

'And if he starts to remember anything at all, I'll call you straight away, I swear.' Sara's fingers were firmly crossed behind her back. It was probably criminal to defraud the UK health system in this way, but technically speaking Rurik had been living and working here for nearly a year. It was just that the year in question was a millennium back in time.

'OK, fine, see that you do, please. This is highly irregular and I don't know how to fill out this form.' The woman swept out of the room, clipboard clutched to her chest.

'What was that all about?' Rurik's voice from the bed sounded stronger now, more like his usual self, although his face was still pale. He had lost a lot of blood, and despite the transfusions, it would be a while before it was fully replenished.

'They're suspicious. All this has to be paid for.' Sara indicated the machines that surrounded him, although to his intense relief the snakes had been removed that morning, as he was eating and drinking well and didn't need a drip any longer.

'You didn't bring any silver?'

She shook her head. 'There wasn't time to think of such things. I could pay them myself, but I'm not going to.'

'You have your own wealth here?' He was studying her intently, but lay very still, as though he was continually wary of his surroundings.

'Yes. I inherited quite a lot from my parents when they died.'

'Ah, so you're an heiress. Why didn't you say? I'd have married you on the spot,' he joked with a half-smile.

'Ha, ha, very funny. I didn't bring it with me to your time, did I?' She'd arrived there with nothing and he had been kind enough to provide for her ever since. Now it was her turn. 'But I could do when we go back.'

'We?' His eyebrows shot up. 'You're not staying in your time?

What about your family and your life here?'

'I'll go back to them eventually. First I want to make sure you return safely. And I'm going to get that *bastard* Asmund once and for all, if it's the last thing I do.'

'Asmund? What has he to do with anything?'

'He was the one trying to attack me when you came to my defence. I recognised his voice. And then he stabbed you.'

Rurik shot up in bed, then winced and put a hand to his abdomen. 'The complete and utter *argr*!'

'Yes. We have to find a way to get rid of him without actually killing him. That would make us as bad as he is.'

'He deserves to die,' Rurik muttered, but she ignored him. They weren't murderers and he knew it. As if he'd heard her thoughts, he added, 'I'll challenge him to a fight to the death. That way it is not murder. It's fair and just.'

'I don't know about that . . .'

It was probably crazy to even contemplate going back, she was fully aware of that, and taking revenge on her nemesis wasn't really a good enough reason. Being hopelessly in love didn't count, because it was not reciprocated. She should stay here and get on with her life, but she knew she'd never settle back into it unless she found out what happened to Rurik. What if she sent him back and those thugs were waiting for him again? Was Tryggve safe? And Beowulf? Asmund and his henchmen were low enough to take out their spite on a defenceless dog. It didn't bear thinking about. No, unless she knew for sure, she'd spend the rest of her life wondering about it.

As for her family, there was only her grandfather. The moment she knew Rurik was safe and would live, she had rushed off to find a phone in order to contact him. Luckily she'd had a spare credit card back at the flat and used it to buy a pay-as-you-go mobile, since hers was presumably still buried in the cave in Marsden Bay.

When her grandpa answered and she heard his voice, she had barely been able to get the words out, her emotions getting the better of her. Eventually she'd croaked, 'Hello, Grandpa, it's me, Sara.' He was, of course, incredulous and rather emotional too at first, having feared the worst when she'd disappeared all those months ago, but he told her to go with her gut instinct when she broached the possibility of returning to the ninth century.

'If you want to return with that young man, do so. At least now I know you're alive and well somewhere. As for the rest, I'm with the Vikings – I'll see you in the next life, if not before. And you could visit occasionally, couldn't you? Like Linnea.'

She could, now that she had the *seax*.

'I think you should stay here. It will be dangerous for you in the past.' Rurik brought her thoughts back to the present, his turquoise eyes narrowed and his gaze troubled. 'It was my fault you had to remain as long as you did.'

'No, I understand how it happened now. It was just a misunderstanding. And I want to come. I miss Beowulf and . . .' She'd been about to confess that she couldn't bear the thought of never seeing Rurik himself again, but that had to remain her secret. Perhaps if they spent more time together, he'd start to forget that other woman, whoever she was. He hadn't looked as though he was pining for anyone for a while now. And if there was even the slightest chance that he could come to love her, she had to take it.

But no, she was fantasising again. That wasn't going to happen.

'I see.' Her words had made him frown and she wasn't sure why. 'How soon can we leave?'

'You'll need to regain your strength first. If there's going to be a reckoning when you get back, the stronger you are, the better. A few more weeks should do it. But we are going to my house soon. No more of this place, or disapproving women.'

'You have a house all to yourself?'

'Not exactly. Part of one – it's called a *flat*. It's not very big, but it's enough. I've borrowed it from a friend who doesn't need it any longer.' Linnea would probably never set foot in it again, and the rent Sara paid went to her parents for safe keeping. She knew they bought gold and silver items with the money, which they gave Linnea whenever she visited. It could be melted down and added to her and her husband's wealth in the past.

'I look forward to seeing it.' Rurik wrinkled his nose. 'I hope it smells better than this room.'

Sara laughed. 'That depends on what you consider better.' There was no stench of antiseptic at her place, but it wouldn't be the kind of environment he was used to – woodsmoke, cooking, damp . . . Still, she hoped he would like it. It was her home.

Or it used to be. Somehow it just felt like a temporary place to stay now, and she had no attachment to it whatsoever.

Rurik held on to some sort of handle as the strange carriage transported them to Sara's house at last. She'd called it a *taxi*. The speed was amazing, faster than the strongest of horses at full gallop, and everything outside the glass panels passed by in a blur. She had tried to explain to him how it worked, with no visible means of propulsion, but he'd had trouble taking it in. However it was being pushed, it was exhilarating and he enjoyed every moment.

The healers had pronounced themselves satisfied with his progress, and when the stern older woman had found him exercising in his room, she'd been outraged, going straight to whoever was in charge.

'Hanging off the door frame? Honestly, whatever next?

Nothing wrong with you, young man. Time to let someone else have your bed.'

He'd understood a few of her words, as Sara had spent some time trying to teach him a bit of her language, and the rest he read in the woman's sour expression. Soon after, he'd been told he could leave. The strength was quickly returning to his limbs, thanks to the amazing food they'd brought him every day at regular intervals. They had also made him swallow little round things, which Sara claimed were healing potions, and whatever magic was inside them, they'd helped no end.

Sara's dwelling turned out to be up one flight of stairs. These were covered with some sort of rug, well worn in the middle of each step and dirty in places. There was a rail to hold on to – why, he had no idea. The walls were painted the colour of oxblood, but with white wooden bits at the top and bottom that had a shiny surface. There was no plain wood anywhere, as he was used to, other than a small table inside Sara's home that was recognisably pine.

'Lie down on the *sofa* if you want.' She gestured towards a piece of furniture that appeared to consist of a mountain of giant cushions all stuck together. 'I'm just going to make a cup of *tea*. You must be used to that by now.'

Rurik grunted and lowered himself on to the cushion pile. It was incredibly malleable, and he sank down feeling as though he was in the lap of an enormous goose. It was comfortable, he had to admit, and he was tempted to just lean back and close his eyes, but he was too curious about his surroundings to do that. Instead he stared at the roof, which was low and flat, painted all white but with some sort of pattern picked out around the edges and in the middle. Where were the rafters? And how did the smoke from the hearth escape when there were no holes up there? Not that he could see a hearth, but still . . . Through the big window, perhaps. It was unbelievably large, actually, and covered with flawless sheets of glass. The first time he'd seen this was when they moved him to a different room at the place of healing, one he'd had to share with three other men. He'd asked Sara about it and she had explained about the way glass was used in her era. Amazing.

As for the tea, he'd been awash with the stuff for days, since it was served morning, noon and night in the place of healing. He couldn't say he liked it exactly, but it was drinkable.

Sara returned shortly afterwards with a mug made of burnished pottery. 'Here. I put lots of *sugar* in it, as that is good for you. It helps to give you strength.'

'What is *sugar*?'

'Something sweet, like honey. Perhaps you would prefer that?'

'No thank you. A good tankard of ale would be better,' he muttered under his breath.

She obviously heard him. 'You can't have that until you've finished taking the *penicillin*.' At his raised eyebrow, she clarified. 'One of the healing potions. You still have two days left.'

Two more days without ale. He sighed. If they even had ale here. 'I suppose I'll survive.'

He looked around the room, noting how cluttered it was. If all these things were Sara's, then she was indeed an heiress. He'd never in his life seen so many items in one place. 'What do you do with all this?' Sweeping a hand to indicate it all, he took a sip of the tea. It was a lot sweeter and stronger than the type they'd given him in the healing place, and it was delicious.

'Um, I just own it.' She looked slightly bewildered, and glanced around. 'Do you know, I actually have no idea why I've bought so many things. It's not as though I need them, is it?' She laughed. 'I survived six or seven months in your era with just some clothes and a few other items. And I didn't miss any of these. Weird.'

'I would like a proper home one day,' he surprised himself by saying. 'Somewhere I know I'm going to stay for a long time, perhaps for ever. Then I too might amass a wealth of items.'

'I doubt you'll have as many as I do. In fact, I'm going to sort through it all and get rid of most of it before we go. Anything absolutely vital I'll send to my grandfather for safe keeping. The rest – who needs it?'

'You might want it when you come back for good,' he ventured, not daring to look at her as he said the words. He'd been extremely pleased to learn that she was intending to return to his era with him, but he knew it was only temporary. Unless he could persuade her to stay. He knew that was what he wanted, but it had to be her wish too. Surviving the near-fatal stabbing had focused his mind, and he had realised that he didn't just owe her his life; he was head over heels in love with her. Before, he'd been clinging on to his belief that it was Linnea he wanted, but truth to tell, he couldn't even summon up an image of his sister-in-law's face now when he closed his eyes. Only Sara. She was constantly in his thoughts and dreams, and he wanted a future with her.

'Mmm,' she replied vaguely.

Tentatively he reached out a hand to touch her arm. 'Sara, how long do you think you might stay?'

She jumped and turned to look at him. 'Er, I'm not sure. Why?'

'Because I'm thinking of returning to Birka and I'd like you to come with me. If you want. I'll be starting over again, but we've done it twice already and it shouldn't be too difficult. It's for the last time, I swear. After my near-death experience, I've realised I want to live closer to my family. Going to Jorvik was a mistake, even though business was brisk.'

She nodded. 'If you need me to help, then I will. I owe you.'

'Owe me what?'

A flush crept over her cheeks. 'It was my fault you almost died. I should have listened to you and stayed in the back room. You wouldn't have been distracted then, giving that *bastard* a chance to—'

He made an impatient noise, cutting her off. 'Don't think like that. Who knows what would have happened? It was fate, that's all. And you saved me – I'm still alive, aren't I?'

'I suppose so, but—'

He reached out to put his fingers under her chin and turned her face towards him, looking deep into her eyes. 'There is no but. And you owe me nothing. Either come with me because you want to or don't, but not due to any feelings of obligation, do you hear?' That was the last thing he wanted her to feel for him, but he didn't say that out loud.

'Very well.' She gave him a small smile, her expression brightening. 'Then yes, I want to.'

'Good. Now is there anything to eat here? I'm starving.'

Sara chuckled. 'That sounds more like the Rurik I know. Stay there and I'll see what I can find.'

He leaned back and closed his eyes, smiling and sinking into the feathery embrace of the sofa.

He wasn't going to lose her quite yet. Not ever, if he could help it.

Sara had been shopping before bringing Rurik home, and she rustled up some pasta carbonara. It was quick and easy to do, and one of her favourite dishes. It felt strange to be cooking on a hob and not over an open fire, but it was so much faster and cleaner. She'd never appreciated modern appliances before, but she certainly did now. For dessert she'd bought chocolate ice cream, which she hoped he would like. It would certainly be different to anything else he'd ever tasted.

'Mmm, this is delicious!' He'd cleared his plate of pasta in record time and held it out. 'Is there any more?'

'Yes, a bit.' She grinned at him. 'You definitely seem to be getting back to normal if you're this hungry.'

'Actually, I'm not sure I have room for more, but it tasted so good I can't resist. I'll need to do some weapons practice soon or I will grow exceedingly fat.'

She wagged her finger at him. 'Uh-uh, no exercise yet. The doctor said you have to keep still until that wound is completely healed. You're to stay in bed or on this sofa for at least another week.' Peering at his abdomen, she added, 'Does it hurt?'

'Not as much. More the occasional twinge if I move the wrong way.' He scowled. 'I hate being inactive. I want to be doing things. And there's nothing wrong with my arms or legs.'

'Well, I think I can keep you busy without you moving so much as a muscle. Hold on and I'll show you.'

She introduced him to the dubious delights of television and enjoyed his reaction, a mixture of awe and confusion. After trying unsuccessfully to explain how it worked, she gave up and just told him to take her word for it that it did. 'Here, this is how you change the *channels*. See at the top? There are various types of *programme – news, music, documentaries* . . .'

'*His-to-reh*,' he said, startling her. 'What does that mean?'

'You can read? But those aren't runes.' She stared at him.

He grinned. 'I know. When I travelled with my brother, we learned this way of writing too. It's one of the types they used in Miklagarðr. Although I'm not very good at it.'

'Mik— Oh, you mean Istanbul. I see. Well, you're full of surprises. And that word means tales about the past, like your era.

I know you don't understand much of what they're saying, but if I put on the *music channel*, you can just watch the images and listen. I'll leave you to it while I wash up.'

She picked up their plates and cutlery and got to her feet, but before she could move off, he grabbed her hand and looked up at her. 'Thank you, Sara. For the food, for everything. You are being . . . wonderful.'

Was she imagining the appreciation in his eyes? Maybe not, but it was probably just a basic gratitude for looking after him, nothing more. Still, she couldn't stop a warm feeling from spreading through her at his words, and her fingers tingled where they were joined to his. 'You're welcome.'

When they'd had a chance to digest the pasta, she brought out the ice cream and laughed at his expression of utter bliss as he tasted the first spoonful. 'What *is* this? You're sure I'm not in Valhalla after all?'

'No, definitely not. This is *ice cream* and the taste is *chocolate*. If I had to name one thing I missed the most when I was in your time, this would be it.'

He nodded with his eyes closed as he savoured another spoonful. 'That I can understand. I'd stay here just for this.'

She shook her head at him but was pleased at his reaction. 'We'll have to eat so much of it during the next couple of weeks that we get sick of it. That's the only way to cure the craving.'

'Hmm. Somehow I don't think it will work.'

Eventually it was time for bed. 'You might want to have a shower first to wash off the *hospital* smell,' Sara suggested. 'It always clings to your skin.'

'A shower? But there is no rain.' He glanced out of the bedroom window with a frown, and she burst out laughing.

'Sorry, I shouldn't laugh. I can't expect you to know everything. The kind of shower I meant is like having a bath but standing up. I'll show you.'

'Huh. As long as you don't try to wash me with little cloths.' He glowered.

'Um, no, I'll let you manage on your own. Come, I'll show you how it works.' She felt her cheeks turning pink at the thought of washing any part of Rurik's body. Best not to let her mind stray there. She almost giggled again, though, at the memory of his indignation when he'd told her how the nurses had tried to give him a bed bath. Apparently he'd snatched the cloths out of their hands and insisted on doing it himself, pain or no pain.

'I've not been bathed by anyone since I was a small babe in arms,' he'd muttered when he recounted this tale. He was nothing if not fiercely independent.

She helped him remove the tracksuit trousers and hoodie she'd bought him before he left the hospital. He was fascinated by the zipper and had pulled it up and down for ages when she first showed him. The elastic in the trousers also intrigued him, although he claimed to have seen something like that before. She'd purchased underwear and some plain T-shirts, plus socks and trainers in roughly the right size. She figured he could sleep in his boxers and T-shirt for now, although she almost changed her mind when he stood before her wearing only those garments after his shower. The thin cotton moulded itself to his muscular frame, showing every ridge of the six-pack he hadn't lost despite his recent ordeal. As for the strong arms, shoulders and legs, displayed in all their glory . . .

Her mouth went dry and she had to swallow a few times before she managed to make him follow her back into the bathroom. 'I'm going to show you how to brush your teeth,' she croaked, and busied herself with toothbrush and paste.

'Ah, so that's what you were talking about,' he muttered, but he copied her movements without grousing and squeezed out some extra toothpaste to eat. 'I like this taste.'

She snatched the tube out of his hand. 'It's not food, Rurik!' But he just laughed.

'Can I have a shower again tomorrow?' he asked. 'That was the most amazing thing! I could have stayed in there all evening.'

'I noticed,' she replied drily. She'd had to practically force him out of the cubicle. Not an easy thing to do without looking at him through the glass door. 'But yes, of course you can. As often as you like. Most people here have one every morning.'

'Excellent.'

Afterwards, he sank into her queen-size bed, making a noise that was not dissimilar to that of a purring cat. Sara smiled, but having finished her own nightly routine – which felt strangely alien now – she got in beside him under the duvet and suddenly felt discomfited. 'Sorry, we have to share the, er, blanket,' she murmured.

'That's fine.' He cleared his throat. 'Any chance we can share more than that?'

'What?' She whirled round to stare at him.

'I would like to hold you, if I may. Just for tonight.' His gaze slid away from hers, as if he was regretting having mentioned it.

'Hold me? That's all?'

He chuckled at that. 'Yes, don't look so suspicious.' He gestured to his midriff. 'It's not as though I'm in any state to do much else, is it?'

'Oh. No, I suppose not. Um, *OK*, I'd like that.'

Carefully, so as not to bump into his wound, she turned her back towards him and scooted up against his tall frame. He felt warm, and the hairs on his legs tickled just a tiny bit. The hard plane of his chest against her back was like protective armour, and they fitted together beautifully. His arm came around her and she heard him sigh with a contentment that was echoed inside her. This was nice. No, it was more than nice – it was sheer bliss.

And if she had a choice, she'd want to go to sleep this way for the rest of her life.

Chapter Twenty-Four

'. . . and this is a *blowtorch*, which is what I use instead of a hearth most of the time.'

'Incredible! Show me again?'

Sara was giving Rurik a tour of her workshop, which was just a small rented room at the back of a jewellery store. The owner, Peter, had nearly had a heart attack when she'd walked in earlier, but accepted her explanation that she'd been taken ill suddenly all those months ago, and had therefore been unable to communicate with anyone. The lies tripped off her tongue quite easily, as did the information that she'd decided to give up her business here and relocate to Sweden.

'I'll be packing up all my stuff and shipping it home in the next few days. Would you be OK with one month's notice?'

Peter nodded. 'Sure. In fact I've got someone who's interested in taking the room straight away, so don't worry about paying any more. It's fine.'

'Are you sure? Thank you, that's really kind of you.'

She gave the man a hug, as he'd been a good friend to her during her year in York. When she turned back to Rurik, he was scowling at Peter. Was he jealous? Of a middle-aged man old enough to be her dad? That thought made her want to giggle, but she was probably completely wrong. Why would he be jealous when he didn't want her for himself? That made no sense. Thankfully Peter became busy with customers after that and Sara was free to show Rurik all her modern tools.

'This is really delicate work.' Rurik picked up some of the jewellery she'd made before ending up in the past. 'And I like the patterns.' He turned the pages of a couple of her sketchbooks, where she'd doodled designs. She would have to remember to buy some paper and pencils later to show him how much easier it was than trying to do it on bark. He was sure to enjoy that, since he was as creative as she was.

'Thank you.' She was absurdly pleased that he admired her handiwork. He'd seen her in action in his era, but in the twenty-first century she could do so much more. 'Have a look at this. It makes everything look huge so it's much easier to do the tiniest of pieces.' She showed him a big magnifying glass in a frame and heard him suck in a breath of astonishment.

'By all the trolls, this is amazing!' He peered through it for a while, then turned to look at her. 'You'll miss this.' He was back to frowning again.

'Yes, in a way, but I've spent a lot of time trying to copy the motifs from your time, so now I can just do the real thing instead. And I can always come back, remember? Now I have the *seax*.'

He didn't look entirely convinced, but he made no further comment.

'Come, let's go for a walk. I want to show you Jorvik as you've never seen it before.' She took his arm and led him outside. So far he'd been stuck in her flat since he was released from the hospital, and she had ordered a taxi for the short journey to the workshop. But they were going back to the past soon. She wanted him to see and learn as much as possible while he was here. Perhaps that way he would understand her better.

And forget that other woman? She pushed that thought away. Not going to happen.

'Very well, but you'll have to feed me more of that *ice cream* if I'm to keep my strength up.'

Sara laughed. 'I'll see what I can do.'

They walked down a road that Sara called a *street*. 'That's a Roman word, I think, although it might amuse you to know that in Jorvik, your countrymen made such an impression that some of the roads are still called *gate*. That's a *Danskr* word, isn't it? See?'

She pointed up at a sign fixed to a nearby house. He read it slowly. '*Peh-ter-gah-teh*. Peter? Is it named after that man we just met?'

That made her laugh out loud, and her eyes sparkled in the spring sunshine. They were beautiful, like dark honey, and he almost forgot what they were talking about as he gazed at her. In this era, she was more confident and outspoken, never shrinking into the background as she'd often done in his time. Here she was in charge, and it suited her. Not that he wanted to be ordered about by a woman all the time, but neither did he want to spend time with a mouse.

'No, no, it's named after a Christian *saint*,' she was saying. 'A holy man. There's a big church over that way.' She pointed. 'Let's go and have a look at it.'

They entered what she said was the Jorvik – or York as it was now – Minster. It was an enormous stone building, worthy of a king, with all manner of embellishments and carvings. The lofty ceiling was vaulted high above them, the floor perfectly smooth and polished. A proliferation of wooden benches surrounded them, and there were lights along the walls, lit even though it was daytime. He couldn't take his eyes off the amazing windows, where bits of coloured glass seemed to form images. 'By all the gods, this is incredible! I've only ever seen one other place like this, the Hagia Sophia.'

'Oh, of course. I'd forgotten that must have existed already when you went to Istan— I mean Miklagarðr.'

'Yes, I snuck inside one day, although I wasn't sure if I was allowed.' He looked around once more, turning slowly to take it all in. 'This is beautiful, but I don't know why your god needs houses like this in our realm. He must have his own, like Odin has Valhalla.'

She smiled. 'Perhaps. Let's go and look at the rest of the town.'

As they ambled along, he tried to take it all in. There were thousands of people around them, all dressed in the same strange way as them. Although he found these clothes comfortable, they were a bit too clingy for his liking. Anyone looking at him would be able to see the outline of every part of his body with ease, not something he was used to. Thank the gods Sara had sent for some proper clothing for him. She'd bought it somewhere she called *the internet*, saying there were people who made Norse garments and they would arrive soon. His own had apparently been cut off him when he arrived at the place of healing, and the stern woman there had taken it upon herself to throw them away. Such a waste – he'd been rather annoyed about that and inclined to press for compensation, but Sara had told him to let it go.

Quite a few of the passers-by stared at him in a way that made him uncomfortable. He blinked at the sight of the amount of female flesh on show as well, although when he commented on it, Sara said it was normal.

'They're not camp followers or women for sale?'

'No, definitely not, so don't even think about it.' She gave him a fierce scowl, which he found endearing.

He chuckled. 'I wasn't looking to purchase their services.' She was still frowning, though, making him wonder if she was jealous. But that would mean she cared, and he hardly dared to hope for that. 'Unless you want me to?'

She stopped dead, and, as she was holding on to his arm, yanked him to a halt too. The sudden movement hurt his abdomen, but it was healing remarkably well and he bore the pain by sucking in a hasty breath.

'What? Why would I want that?' she said.

'Well, I might be a burden to you right now. I could spend a night with someone else, if you would rather. And quite a few of them seem to be giving me come-hither looks.' He had no intention of doing so, but he wanted to gauge Sara's reaction to such a suggestion.

'No!' Her reply was gratifyingly vehement, and her cheeks turned pink as she seemed to realise she was overreacting. 'I mean, it's fine. You're not a burden. And they're probably just looking at you because . . .' She tailed off, blushing even more furiously.

'Because what?' It was his turn to pull her to a stop.

'Nothing.' She glared at him, then shrugged. 'Oh, very well. I'm sure you already know that you are exceedingly handsome. You've probably had women looking at you like that all your life. Now do you want to see the sights or not?'

With a small huff, and without waiting for a reply, she dragged him on, and he hid a big grin as he allowed her to tow him along the road. She thought he was handsome. And she did care, he'd swear to it. The question was only: how much? But he wouldn't ask. He'd teased her enough for now.

The exchange made him feel optimistic, though. If Sara cared enough about him to be jealous, perhaps he'd be able to persuade her to stay in his time long-term. He knew now that he wouldn't be depriving her of her future here, because she'd have the choice to come back any time she wanted to. It was up to him to make sure she'd rather live in his time. He'd definitely have to give this more thought when he was on his own back at Sara's house. For the moment, there was too much to take in, and the noise and bustle all around him was very distracting.

'Are those all *taxis*?' He gestured towards the noisy metal carriages that kept passing. The smoke coming out of them was noxious, and he had to cough a couple of times, something his abdomen wasn't very happy about. Coughing and laughing still gave him twinges of pain, although it was improving daily.

'No, they're called *cars*. A taxi is one you can hire to drive you somewhere, but most people have their own.'

'Do you?'

'Yes. Or at least I did before I ended up in your time. I forgot to ask my grandfather what happened to it.'

They wandered around for quite a while, with him asking endless questions and Sara quietly explaining everything they saw. All the other strange wagons and metal horses for riding on, the many tall houses tightly packed together, with glass openings so large Rurik had no idea how they stayed in place. Not to mention all the goods for sale – thousands of unfamiliar items, and even the food on display was different. He tried to take it all in, but it really was incredibly noisy and he was having trouble concentrating. It was like being in Miklagarðr over again, only with all these new things added.

'I must say, you're remarkably calm,' Sara commented, glancing at him.

'There's nothing threatening here, is there? I can't see anyone carrying a weapon.' He'd been glancing at the passers-by to make sure, but everyone seemed peaceful.

She laughed. 'No, I suppose you're right about that. I think perhaps you've had enough for one day, though. Shall I buy you that *ice cream* I promised you?'

'Yes please!'

'In here, then.'

She ushered him into one of those glass-fronted houses and found them a table with two chairs. Both were made of metal, which he found odd, but the chair was comfortable and he was happy to rest for a while.

'What flavour would you like?' She held out a parchment with images on it of glass beakers filled with coloured balls of food.

'Er, a little bit of everything?' He grinned. 'I might as well try it while I can.'

'Good idea.'

Sara ordered a selection of five ice-cream scoops for Rurik and something called a Pavlova cup for herself. She was in awe of how he was taking everything in his stride, although she didn't know what he was thinking, of course. He'd always seemed laid-back, though, and nothing fazed him in his own world.

'Is it true that people in your society are only afraid of one thing – dishonour?' she asked while they waited for their order.

'Yes. What else is there to be scared of?' Those aquamarine eyes of his were twinkling at her, as if he was teasing.

She narrowed her own gaze at him. 'You must be afraid of losing loved ones, of becoming sick, of dying, starving, of pain . . .' She thought about Asmund and shivered. 'Personally, I'm not keen on being raped or beaten.'

He shook his head. 'Of course no one wants those things to happen, but it is up to the gods and the Norns, who weave the strands of fate. There really is no point thinking about it. The end result is always the same – we go into the afterlife, where nothing can hurt us. Naturally not everyone ends up in the same place, and I would be sad never to see my brothers again, should we be separated. But I doubt any of it bothers us when we're dead.'

'Hmm.' He had a point, but only if everyone's souls really did end up in an afterlife. Who knew if that was true? This wasn't really the time for a theological debate, though, so she decided to drop the subject.

Her hand was resting on the table and he put his on top of it, giving it a squeeze. 'You fret too much, Sara. Just live instead and enjoy it.' The smile he gave her made her want to grab his hand in return and tell him she'd be perfectly happy to enjoy it with him. In any way he wanted. As if he'd read her mind, he added, 'I'd be happy to help.' There was a deliciously wicked glint in his eyes, giving the impression he was talking about the pleasures to be had in bed, but she was probably imagining it. Before she could turn her palm upwards, he'd removed his and she almost felt bereft.

Damn it all, she had to get a grip.

Their ice cream arrived, and she told him about the various flavours she'd chosen. 'Chocolate you've already tried, but I know you liked it so I ordered some anyway. Vanilla is a very basic flavour but one most people love, me included. Then there's strawberry, lemon sorbet and mango.'

'Thank you.' He dug in and she smiled as a lot of appreciative noises emanated from his side of the table. He ate with complete single-mindedness, not looking up once. Finally he leaned back with a satisfied grin. 'That was extremely tasty. All of it.'

'So you don't have a favourite?' She was busy finishing hers, a mixture of vanilla, raspberry and strawberry, sprinkled with tiny meringues.

'I think the first one you gave me was the best, although the pale one had a wonderfully delicate flavour.' He gave his bowl one last scrape before licking the spoon. 'Mmm.'

He closed his eyes, and the look of utter bliss on his face reminded her of their one and only night of passion. Her memories were a bit hazy, but she was pretty sure he'd had that exact same expression then.

Without thinking, she blurted out, 'It all tastes great if you lick it off someone's skin, or so I've heard.'

Oh shit! Where had that come from? He choked on the final small amount he'd just put in his mouth, and his eyes opened wide, staring at her as he coughed.

Holding his abdomen, he grimaced. 'Ouch! What did you just say?' He pinned her with an intense look; one that reminded her distinctly of a smoulder. She'd certainly caught his attention.

'Um, nothing. Forget it. I don't know why . . . I mean, I must be very tired.' Her cheeks were flaming, she could feel it, and she wished she had some ice cream left over to cool them down with.

He tilted his head to one side and raised his eyebrows. 'You have tried this?'

'No! No, I haven't actually.' It was true. Anders was more of a 'wham-bam-thank-you-ma'am' type of guy. He'd never bothered much with foreplay. That didn't mean she hadn't fantasised about such things, and suggested them occasionally. At least until he'd laughed one too many times.

The grin Rurik sent her could have melted any number of ice-cream scoops. 'Perhaps it's about time then? It sounds . . . intriguing.'

She shook her head, embarrassed beyond belief. 'I wasn't talking about me. Just what I've heard other people say.' Standing up so abruptly she nearly overturned her chair, she said, 'I'm going to pay now. Wait here.'

Rurik stared after her, his mind filled with visions of something he'd never even contemplated before. Intriguing didn't even begin to cover it. Licking food off a woman's body? He'd be nothing loath to try licking anything off Sara's skin, provided she'd allow it. But by the way she'd scurried off just now, she didn't seem willing.

That was a shame. For a moment there he'd thought she was suggesting . . . But no, clearly not, although she must at least have been thinking about such a thing. That in itself was food for thought.

He stayed in his seat until she came back and picked up the containers she'd been carrying with items they had bought. The tight clothes he was wearing bothered him even more right now, as he was sure they would reveal to the world exactly what he'd been thinking about – Sara, naked and covered in ice cream.

'Let me carry some of those.' Before she could refuse, he'd grabbed a few of her containers and held them strategically in front of himself as he followed her out of the eating place. If they were going to do any more walking, he had to get his thoughts – and his body – under control, or he'd be extremely uncomfortable.

'Shall we go down to the river?' she suggested, without looking at him.

'Yes, why not? Has that changed too?' He tried to keep his tone normal, although even he noticed there was a certain husky note in it. *Sweet Freya, what is this woman doing to me?* Hopefully he could steer his thoughts in another direction, although not if he was walking behind Sara. He could see the enticing sway of her hips with every step she took, as her trousers clung to her backside even worse than his own clothing did. It was as though she had encased herself in blue skin. He had to make a monumental effort not to reach out and turn her around in order to kiss her senseless.

No, this had to stop.

Perhaps he should throw himself into the river for a cooling swim?

'It's more or less the same,' she was saying now as they came to a stop in the middle of a bridge. 'Just a lot more buildings on either side.'

That was an understatement. He would have had a hard time even getting to the edge of the water, had he wanted to swim. 'I suppose I'll have to bathe at your house then,' he muttered.

Laughter gurgled out of her. 'You want to swim? It's April! It'll be freezing.'

Freezing would be good. Just what he needed. But he could see this wasn't the place. He shrugged. 'I've bathed in the middle of winter on occasion. Can we go back now, please? I believe I've seen enough for one day.'

Her expression turned immediately to one of concern, and she put a hand on his arm. He gritted his teeth as even this small touch sent a shock wave of lust through him. *The trolls take it!* What was the matter with him?

'Of course. I'm sorry, I've tired you out.'

'No, not at all. But you have shown me many things today. I need time to think, that is all.' Well, not quite all. He would go and stand for a very long time under that shower; man-made rain coming from a metallic head. It was fast becoming one of his favourite things about her era, and he knew he was going to miss it enormously when he left.

She didn't look as though she believed him, and it was easier not to protest. If she wanted to think him an invalid still, very well. It saved him having to explain what really ailed him.

Chapter Twenty-Five

Although he wasn't allowed to do any heavy lifting yet, Rurik spent the next few days helping Sara to sort and pack up her jewellery tools and finished products, as well as everything in her flat. She'd booked a removal company to take some of it to Sweden, and the rest she either took to nearby charity shops or threw away.

'What about the tables and benches?' He stood looking around the now almost empty flat.

'They're not mine. Everything that's left belongs to the owner. I was only borrowing them.' She didn't know what Linnea's parents planned to do with it, but the place had been rented to her furnished and she assumed they would just find another tenant. Her grandfather had promised to explain the situation to them, as she didn't feel like talking to anyone else yet. 'Now, how are you feeling? Ready to go back?'

'Yes, I am almost back to full strength. As long as no one hits me in the stomach, I'll be fine.'

Sara shuddered. 'I hope there won't be any fighting at all, but I suppose it depends on whether Asmund and his men returned. Tryggve said he was going to enlist the help of his uncles.'

'We will see. No point fretting about it.'

They'd decided to leave at three in the morning from the exact same spot where they had ended up on arrival. She remembered the street and the place clearly, and just hoped that poor Tryggve didn't have a heart attack if they suddenly materialised in front of him. The youth was a heavy sleeper, though, and with any luck, he'd be out for the count. If he was even there.

The hardest part was saying goodbye to her grandfather. She settled down to FaceTime him late in the evening.

'I'm so sorry to do this to you,' she told him. They'd always been close, and even though he had other family members nearby, she knew he missed her dreadfully. As she did him.

'Don't be silly. I can tell that this is something you really want to do. Haven't I always told you to follow your dreams? There's no other way than to live life to the full. I'm an old man and I believe in fate. If we're meant to see each other again, we will. If not, well, as I told you, I'd like to believe the Vikings were right and we'll meet in the next life. We may not go to Valhalla, you and I, but we can feast in Freya's hall instead.'

'Oh Grandpa.' She shook her head at him, but a part of her was starting to believe too. How else had she ended up in this strange situation? It was some sort of magic, that was for sure. Who was to say an afterlife didn't exist as well?

'Now, just you look after yourself and your young man, OK? I want to picture you happy and content.'

She wanted to protest that Rurik wasn't her young man, but Grandpa knew her too well and had obviously read between the lines. No point disillusioning him by telling the truth – that the love was very one-sided. 'I'll do my best.'

'Good, now can I have a few words with him, please?'

She did a double-take; she hadn't expected that. 'You want to talk to Rurik?'

'Yes, just briefly.'

She stared at him suspiciously. 'Er . . . OK, but don't say anything embarrassing, will you?'

'As if I would!' Her grandfather managed to look offended and mischievous at the same time.

'Hmm. Rurik? Could you come here for a moment, please?' She'd left him in the sitting room while she talked to Lars, and now she called out to him.

'Yes?' He appeared in the doorway with his eyebrows raised and she held up the screen.

'This is my grandfather, Lars. Grandpa, meet Rurik.'

'Good evening to you.' Lars grinned as he tried out his best Old Norse.

Rurik's gaze flickered briefly to Sara before he replied politely. 'Good evening, Lars. I trust you are well?'

'Very well, thank you. And you are recovered. I will not speak long, but I ask you please to have a care for Sara. I believe you are a good man and I depend on you.'

She cringed and muttered a protesting 'Grandpa!' but he ignored her and fixed his eyes on Rurik, who nodded.

'You have my oath I will protect her to the best of my ability.'

'Thank you, that is all I can ask. May the gods be with you both.'

'And you, Lars.' With that, Rurik disappeared back into the sitting room, closing the door behind him. He'd understood her need to say her final farewell alone.

'A nice young man. Don't let him go.' Lars beamed at her, his eyes sparkling.

'That may not be up to me, but anyway . . . Love you and miss you!'

As she hung up, she couldn't stop the tears from falling, and she sat on the bed, unable to move. Silent sobs racked her body and doubt coursed through her. Was she doing the right thing? Shouldn't she just let Rurik go back alone? She was only going to give herself more heartache, and maybe she'd even be in the way.

'Sara? Please don't cry. You will see him again.'

She looked up to find Rurik kneeling in front of her. He reached out and took her in his arms. There was a box of tissues on the bedside table and she plucked one out to blow her nose and wipe her eyes. 'You're right. I will. Somehow.'

He smiled and stroked her cheek. 'That's better. I've always loved your courage. It's why I allowed you to stay with me in the first place.'

'Really?'

'Yes. That and the fact that you undressed in front of me so fearlessly.' He chuckled as she punched him on the arm.

'*Fifl!* As if I had a choice. At that time I didn't know if you would kill me if I didn't comply.'

'Mmm.' He drew one finger slowly across her lower lip. 'I don't suppose you'd do it again, would you?'

She stilled. 'Un-undress? What, now?' Her whole body trembled as he continued the caress, his gaze seemingly fixed on her mouth as if he was mesmerised.

He nodded. 'I want you, Sara. Very much. You are an amazing woman. It is agony sleeping next to you every night and not being allowed to touch you. And who knows what tomorrow will bring?'

His words seemed to echo those of her grandfather – live in the moment and enjoy it while you can. And hadn't Rurik himself said the same thing as well, earlier in the week? Yes, why not? There was nothing to stop her really, other than the fact that she wanted so much more from him than just his body. It was better than nothing, though. She looked into his eyes and saw desire and tenderness. They hadn't cuddled again after that first night, and she'd assumed it was because he didn't want to. It would seem she'd been wrong.

'I . . . *OK*.'

She stood up, not wanting to overthink this. He said he wanted her, and it was mutual, she couldn't deny that. And this might be her last chance, as who knew what awaited them in the past? 'But please turn off the light.'

'Why?' His expression turned puzzled.

'My scars are so ugly. It was dark last time, and—'

He cut her off with a sudden, fierce kiss, then gave her a stern look. 'Nothing about you is ugly, Sara. I told you before that your scars are marks of honour. I want to see every last part of you with the light on. Please? From what I remember, you are incredibly beautiful, scars and all.'

'I . . . Really?' She couldn't believe he thought so, but his words went straight to her heart and affected her more than she'd care to admit. He sounded as though he truly meant it, and if he'd only wanted to sleep with her, there would have been no need to say such things.

'Yes, really.' A sudden mischievous grin lit his features. 'Was there any *ice cream* left, perchance? I can always cover your scars with that, if you like.'

A wave of pure lust rocked her, and she drew in a sharp breath as she grinned back. 'Um, yes, I do believe there was a little bit left.'

'Excellent. I'll fetch it.'

He came back in record time and drew her close, kissing her cheek, her jaw and moving down her neck towards her shoulder, where he pushed aside the material of her T-shirt. She forgot about being embarrassed and just revelled in the sensation of his softly stubbled face rubbing against her skin. When he turned her around and pulled the garment over her head, she didn't protest. She allowed him to trail his fingers over the scars on her torso as his hands made their way around to cup her breasts. She wasn't wearing a bra, as she'd become used to going without.

'I remembered correctly. You are unbelievably beautiful, *unnasta*,' he whispered, his voice sending a shiver deep within her. He still sounded sincere, and she was too entranced by his gently moving fingers to care about the marks on her body. If they didn't repulse him, so much the better.

She turned and tugged his T-shirt off, taking her turn to explore. The hard planes of his chest, with hair tapering down towards his new scar and the boxers he'd complained were too tight. They definitely were now. When had he removed his trousers? She hadn't even noticed, but he was pushing hers off and she kicked out of them to help him.

Careful not to touch the site of his wound, she allowed her fingers to stray downwards. He was doing the same to her, and his caresses were tantalising, enthralling, so that she found it difficult to concentrate. He knew exactly how to excite her, his fingers finding all the right places until she thought her legs would give way and she'd just melt into a puddle at his feet.

'Lie down and let's try this then.' He picked up the ice-cream tub and a spoon, dropping tiny amounts along her stomach and across her breasts.

She gasped at the cold sensation, but that was quickly followed by the warmth and delicious friction of his tongue. 'Hey, leave some for me,' she protested, but it was an effort to think at all and she almost had to force herself to return the favour. It was worth it, though, to see his expression and the desire burning in his eyes.

'Enough! Let me love you, Sara *mín*,' he breathed, pulling her down on to the bed. 'I can't wait any longer.'

A vague thought about contraception flitted through her brain, but she pushed it away. She hadn't conceived the first time they slept with each other, and now she no longer cared if she became pregnant. She'd been broody ever since meeting Eadgyth and little Birger, and she realised that she would love to have his baby. A mini Rurik – what could be more wonderful? So if it happened, that was fine by her.

'Me neither.' She wanted him so much it almost hurt, and when he claimed her, she forgot everything else. There was only the here and now, and if she'd had a choice, she would have wanted this to last for ever.

'I'm ready. What were those words again?'

Rurik stood on a dark road with Sara, his body still pleasantly languid from their lovemaking. They'd ended up doing it twice, because being sticky with ice cream necessitated a visit to the shower, and to his surprise, Sara had joined him.

'Let me cover you with soap,' she'd whispered, proceeding to do just that before he even had time to reply. Having her deft hands roaming his body had proved almost as pleasurable as the ice-cream licking, and he'd had his first taste of making love under a spray of water. It had been amazing.

'I do believe I'll have to take you outside in the rain when we return,' he'd murmured.

'What? Naked?' She'd sounded scandalised and amused at the same time, which made him chuckle.

'Yes, but we'll find somewhere private.'

'Mmm, I like the sound of that.' She'd seemed to enjoy their shower time as much as he had, especially when he'd returned the favour with the soap.

He was finding it difficult not to grin from ear to ear now, or pull her back to the house to pleasure her again, but he knew he had to focus on what they were about to do. If they were successful, he could try to entice her into his bed later. For now, they needed to concentrate.

'*Með blōð skaltu ferðast.* And we have to say it at the same time, remember?'

He nodded. 'Very well. Can I hold the knife, though, in case I need to use it the moment we arrive?'

'Yes. Just make sure you cut both our fingers more or less at the same time.'

It seemed a strange way of doing magic, but he didn't question it. If a blood sacrifice was necessary, so be it. The gods worked in mysterious ways, and mere humans were but pawns in their games. Right at this moment, he was pleased they had placed him in this particular game, as they had brought him Sara, but the next few days might not be as pleasant.

'One, two, three . . .'

They knelt on the ground and recited the words in unison, while Rurik slashed at their fingers and then gripped Sara's hand. He'd been too far gone last time to notice the extreme dizziness and nausea that roiled through him, but he couldn't avoid it now. Gritting his teeth, he tried to hold on to his evening meal. There was a horrible susurrating noise invading his head, loud voices, and spinning, always spinning. It was becoming unbearable, but she had told him this would happen, so he wasn't unduly concerned. They just had to suffer through it.

The world went black for a while, and when he surfaced, it was still very dark. Much darker than the street they had been on, where big lights on top of a pole spread their muted sheen. He jumped when something wet was thrust into his face, but then he laughed softly. 'Wulf, my friend, you're still here!' he whispered, unaccountably glad to find the hound in one piece. He must be going soft in the head if he was that relieved to see his dog again.

Or rather, Sara's dog, as Beowulf had now thrown himself at her with a small bark of joy.

'Shh! Yes, yes, I'm very happy to be back with you too. Urgh, no, don't lick my face!'

She was trying hard not to giggle, Rurik could tell, but they both knew this wasn't the time for levity. He swiftly looked around to check for any danger, his eyes adjusting to the darkness. They were on the floor next to the hearth, and he assumed it was their house since the dog was here. The fire had been banked for the night and only gave off a very faint glow, but it was enough to see that they were alone in here apart from a snoring bundle on the nearest bench. Tryggve, thank the gods.

'Let's go into the back room,' he whispered, and took Sara's hand to help her up. They tiptoed into their bedchamber, with the dog at their heels, and shut the door. It was a bit brighter in here, with moonlight streaming in from the hole up near the roof. 'All seems well. If Tryggve is asleep, he can't be too worried about anything.'

'No. Perhaps his uncles helped him, as he said they would.'

'We should get some sleep. There won't be any answers until morning.'

'Yes, you're right. Good boy, Beowulf.' The big hound had already settled down on the floor, his tail thumping contentedly as he watched his humans.

Rurik was more intent on watching Sara as she wriggled out of her over-dress. She was back to wearing Norse clothing – as was he, thank the gods! – but although her garments were nowhere near as clingy as the ones from her century, he could still clearly see the outline of her luscious body as she sat down on the bed. The sight sent a bolt of desire coursing through him, so fierce it almost made him gasp out loud. After what had happened earlier, there was no way he'd be able to go to sleep without touching her again. He pulled off his own tunic and sank down next to her. 'Sara?'

'Yes?'

He was wondering how to ask whether she'd mind another bout of lovemaking when he saw her beautiful mouth curve into a grin. She leaned forward and put her lips on his, giving him the lightest of kisses that still managed to resonate all the way down to his toes, despite the fact that it barely touched him. He felt his eyes widening as she placed her hands on his chest and pushed him down flat on his back. 'I don't think we were quite finished, were we? It must be my turn.'

She crawled on top of him and straddled his thighs, bending down to slide her body slowly up his. He felt her lush breasts rubbing against him every inch of the way and swallowed hard. 'Your turn?' he croaked.

'Mm-hmm. To make love to *you*.' She captured his mouth with hers once more, drawing a response from deep within him. He didn't think he'd ever get enough of kissing her. It was sheer bliss.

'Do whatever you want. I'm all yours.' He put his hands behind his head and watched as her grin widened.

'Good. You won't regret it.'

No, he was quite sure he wouldn't.

Chapter Twenty-Six

'You're back! And you are healed! How is that possible? The blood . . . your stomach . . . that knife . . . Everyone thinks you're dead!'

Tryggve had jumped several feet into the air when they emerged from their bedroom the next morning, and Sara couldn't blame him. It must seem like magic – well, it *was* magic of some sort – and to a youth from the Viking era, Rurik's survival would appear to be a miracle.

'The wound wasn't as deep as we feared,' she lied. They could never explain about hospitals, surgery and antibiotics. Far better to make up a different story.

'Oh, well, that is good. I'm so pleased.' The youth beamed at them. 'I'll, er, make some porridge.'

'No, let me. Why don't you sit down and tell us what has been happening here instead.' Sara knelt by the hearth, her movements practised now as she realised how routine this type of cooking had become for her. So different to making twenty-first-century dishes on her ceramic hob, but enjoyable nonetheless. And this morning, nothing felt like a chore. She was floating on a little cloud of happiness. Making love with Rurik was the most amazing thing that had ever happened to her. It had never felt like this with

Anders, and she couldn't believe she'd ever thought herself in love with him.

This was what it was supposed to be like.

Of course Rurik hadn't said he loved her, but he was considerate and tender, and she was hoping she might make him forget the woman he'd been pining after, whoever she was. She'd certainly do her best. He'd looked more than content with her efforts so far.

'Ah, yes.' Tryggve was squirming slightly and bent his head to stare at the floor. 'I, um, went to my uncles at first light and they came back here with me to see the damage.' He sighed. 'They wouldn't come with me to Alfr's house though. Nor Knud's. Said that as you weren't here to accuse anyone of trying to kill you, and there was no body, there was nothing they could do. I'm sorry.'

'Not your fault. You think two of those men were Knud and Alfr?'

'Yes. I recognised Alfr. His voice is very distinctive. And he always follows Knud's lead, so it had to be the two of them. In fact I'm fairly certain the man whose arm I broke was Knud. He's been going around with a sling, saying he fell over and hurt himself. I'd say that's too much of a coincidence, wouldn't you?'

'Definitely.' Rurik's eyebrows came down in a fearsome scowl. 'So this was all Knud's doing? He tried to kill me just because he doesn't want competition? Unbelievable!'

'Not him, he's too much of a coward,' Tryggve sneered. 'I believe he'd hired two others to do his dirty work for him. They were just going to ruin your forge, make a mess, you know?'

'Yes, he must have paid Asmund, another man who hates us,' Sara put in. 'I'm sure he was more than happy to help.' It would have been the perfect scenario for him – someone else paying him to hurt the man he wanted out of the way. Only he'd gone too far, judging by what she'd heard Knud or Alfr say that night.

She saw Rurik clench his fists, and his eyes were shooting

sparks of anger. 'We will go and confront them. Would your uncles back us up? The *níðingr* will rue the day he tried to have me murdered, and as for Asmund, I'll challenge him to *einvígi* to settle this once and for all in combat. I'm tired of him following us wherever we go.'

'Yes, I'll run and find my kinsmen.' Tryggve stood up and handed his now empty bowl to Sara with thanks. 'Knud's a wily coward and there's no saying how he'll react.'

When the youth had left, Sara put a hand on Rurik's arm. 'Be careful, please. I'd like you to stay in one piece this time.'

He gave her a grim smile. 'Don't worry, I intend to.'

'Good.' She whistled for the dog. 'Beowulf, let's go. You might be needed to help.'

She would swear the hound knew exactly what that meant, and he was very happy to come with her.

Two of Tryggve's uncles came hurrying in his wake. Rurik had met them before, coming to an agreement with them when he took the youth on as his apprentice, and they both smiled when they recognised him.

'You really are healed! From what Tryggve told us, we thought you'd be in the afterlife by now for certain.'

'Not yet.' He smiled back and greeted them. 'Thank you for coming. I could take on Knud any day, but his henchman Asmund is another matter. He's bound to do something underhand.'

'We'll watch him, if he's still around.'

The group moved down the street with purposeful steps, heading towards Knud's workshop. Halfway there, however, a voice calling his name made Rurik stop. He looked up, astonished to find Hálfdan Hvítserk coming towards them. 'Jarl Hálfdan? I thought you were up north.'

The jarl stopped before them and thumped Rurik's shoulder, looking extremely happy to see him. He acknowledged Sara before replying. 'I was, but we decided to come back here for a while. I needed to check on the puppet king. I was going to visit your workshop but was told you'd been killed. A knife wound?' He looked Rurik up and down. 'Not true, obviously, I'm happy to see.'

'No, I was badly wounded, but Sara and, er, some healers helped me. I'm almost back to full health.' Rurik unconsciously rubbed his new scar, and scowled as he remembered where he was going. 'As a matter of fact, I'm just on my way to sort the matter out.'

'How so? Confront the culprit, you mean?'

'Exactly. We believe the man behind the attack on myself and my property was another smith, Knud, but he's a coward and will be easily dealt with. Asmund is another matter.'

'Asmund?' It was Hálfdan's turn to frown. 'The one in my *here*?'

'The very same.'

The jarl uttered a string of oaths. 'Then I'm coming with you.'

'You don't have to—'

Hálfdan held up his hand. 'I do. And what's more, I know where both men are, because I've just left them playing dice. We've set up camp on the spit of land between the two rivers. Most of the men are resting there. Come, I'll show you.'

Rurik and the others followed. He wasn't sure what to think about the jarl's intervention. On the one hand, it was a stroke of luck that he knew where the two culprits were to be found, but on the other, he wanted to sort this matter out by himself. He couldn't exactly tell the leader of the *here* to go away, but he hoped the man would have the sense to just watch.

This was his revenge and no one else's. He'd stop Asmund from taking Sara away from him once and for all. And from ever hurting anyone else.

If the matter hadn't been so serious, Sara would have laughed at the expressions of horror and shock that crossed the features of Asmund and Knud when they caught sight of Rurik and his group coming towards them. Their faces drained of colour, leaving their cheeks deathly pale. They grew even more troubled as their gazes flickered towards Jarl Hálfdan. The two men stood up hastily, overturning the board game they'd been intent on, as well as a tankard of ale that spilled its contents over the grass and one of Knud's shoes.

'M-Master Rurik, you're alive!' Knud took a step back and brandished his arm, which was indeed in a sling, as though it gave him an excuse for not defending himself.

'Should I not be?' Rurik's tone was silky, but deadly. 'And Master is it now? That's not what you said the night you and your men tried to kill me.' He came to a stop right in front of the man, invading his personal space in a menacing fashion. 'I distinctly remember you calling me something else.'

'I, I . . . Never! And I wouldn't stick a knife into anyone, I swear.'

'Oh, so you admit that's what you did? Knifed me in the gut? In my own home, which you wrecked?'

'No! I mean, yes. I mean . . . it wasn't me! We were only meant to scare you a little, make you leave, but *he*,' he pointed to Asmund, 'had to go too far. I told him no killing, but he wasn't listening. I just . . .' Knud stopped blabbing and fell silent, swallowing hard as he seemingly realised what he'd just admitted. 'But you are well. All is well. Is it n-not?'

'No. And I'll make sure the entire town hears what you have

done so that no one wants to buy your wares in future. Whether I am well or not isn't the point.'

Knud went almost grey with apprehension, and in his distress he turned on Asmund. 'This is all your fault! I told you not to go overboard, but you had to have it your way because of a stupid woman and some imagined slight and—'

Asmund, who'd been standing quietly while the smith uttered his tirade, suddenly sprang to life. He pulled his sword out of its scabbard and brandished it. '*Þegi þú*, fool!' he hissed. 'You're condemning yourself with every word.' He shoved Knud so hard the man stumbled and tripped over a nearby tent. By the sound of it, he fell on his broken arm, as he gave a howl of pain. No one paid him any attention.

'We meet again.' Rurik was staring at Asmund with as frosty a glare as he could muster. He pulled his axe out of his belt. Sara could almost feel the fury coming off him in waves, but saw that he held himself in check for the moment. 'Let's settle this once and for all. You're not having my woman and that is final. And I'm sick and tired of you trying to kill me like a coward. Now face me like a man.'

'Your woman? We'll see about that.' A sneering grin lit Asmund's features. 'And this time I'm going to send you to the afterlife for good.'

Sara somehow expected Hálfdan to intervene, as she was fairly sure this wasn't how disputes were normally settled, but the only thing he did was pull out his sword and offer it, handle first, to Rurik. 'Best to fight with equal weapons,' he said quietly. His unnerving gaze was trained on Asmund the whole time, and she could see that it discomfited the man even though he tried to ignore it. He must know that even if he won this fight, Hálfdan would protect her. At least she hoped he would, as he'd done so in the past.

'Thank you.' Rurik must have agreed about the choice of weapon, because he put away his axe and gripped the jarl's sword.

The two men began to circle each other, and her gut clenched in fear. She was so in love with Rurik it was ludicrous, and she didn't want to lose him. Not now, when they'd finally found each other – at least in a way – and he *had* just referred to her as his woman. That must mean he cared for her, surely?

But he'd been badly wounded just a few weeks ago, while Asmund had been out on campaign, presumably honing his fighting skills. How was Rurik to withstand him? As the two men began to spar, she put her fist to her mouth in order not to scream out loud. She'd learned her lesson and wouldn't distract him again.

She hadn't noticed it before, but Asmund's right hand looked red and swollen, and she wondered if that was from the bite Beowulf had given him the night of the attack. A piece of tattered bandage also peeped out from his sleeve, and she remembered that Rurik had cut the man's arm with the *seax* just before he'd been knifed himself. If that wound hadn't healed yet, Asmund would be hurting. As if to confirm this, he grimaced whenever he had to grip the handle of his sword tighter, and she began to hope that this gave Rurik an advantage. That hand certainly didn't look great.

'Good boy, Beowulf,' she whispered, ruffling the top of the dog's head. She was holding on to his collar with both hands and could feel the canine quivering with the urge to run and help his master.

Rurik too must have become aware of Asmund's injuries, because he gripped his sword with both hands and brought it down on his opponent's with an almighty clang. The blow hadn't been aimed at the man's body, but it was clear the reverberation pained him, as he hissed in a breath. Rurik took the opportunity to go on the attack, and the other man was forced to retreat, all the while putting up his sword to defend himself. As neither of them had a shield, the only way to parry a blow was to meet the opponent's blade with your own, and that was hurting Asmund a lot more than it was Rurik.

'Come *on*!' Sara muttered, surprised at herself. She'd never been a violent woman, but the thought of what Asmund had so nearly done to Rurik made her see red. Not to mention the horrors she suspected he'd inflicted on hundreds of Northumbrians and Mercians, men, women and children alike. He was despicable.

The two men fought for a while longer, everyone around them giving them space while still encircling them so that neither could run away. Sara assumed that must have been on Hálfdan's orders – perhaps he didn't trust Asmund any more than she did. When the end came, however, it was swift and relatively merciful. Asmund's grip on the handle of his sword slipped a fraction, making him hesitate, and Rurik took advantage. Faster than a deadly snake, he thrust his sword in under Asmund's ribcage, straight into his heart, and just like that, it was over.

An eye for an eye . . . The Bible firmly cautioned against such an approach, but in this instance, Sara felt it was justified. Asmund had stuck a knife into Rurik without hesitation; now the tables had been turned on him. And she had no doubt that had he escaped with his life today, he would have returned to finish the job, probably by murdering Rurik in his sleep or from behind, like the coward he was. Good riddance.

With blood gurgling out of his mouth and nose, Asmund sank to the ground. The onlookers all stared in silence, until Hálfdan went over to him and kicked him hard, making the man jerk one last time. Then he turned to survey those who were watching. 'Let this be a lesson to you,' he called out. 'Asmund's greed knew no bounds and this was his just fate. This land has plenty to offer all of us, and there is no need to covet that possessed by someone else. There's enough to go round. I consider this matter closed, and anyone who mentions it again will be severely punished, understood?'

There were cautious nods.

'Good. Now you – what's your name?' He pointed at Asmund's second-in-command.

'Fastulfr, Jarl Hálfdan.'

'Asmund's ship is now yours, and you will take over as leader of his group of men. All his possessions are to be divided equally between you. Now get him out of my sight and bury him. Without any grave goods.'

'Yes, Jarl.'

Fastulfr beckoned his comrades forward and Sara thought she saw some of them wearing expressions of relief. Perhaps they preferred not having Asmund as their leader any longer. Her own relief was so strong her legs felt like jelly, and she had an urge to sink to the ground and just sit there for a moment, absorbing the fact that the bastard could no longer hurt her. Or anyone else, for that matter. God only knew how many other poor souls had fallen foul of him over the years.

'As for you, Knud,' Hálfdan continued, 'go back to your workshop. I don't want to see your snivelling face ever again. If you have any sense, you'll leave this town for good.'

Sara had almost forgotten the smith, who'd sat cradling his arm during the fight, watching with big eyes. He managed to get to his feet now and took off much faster than she'd thought him capable of. She sincerely hoped never to see him again either.

Her legs were shaking so much, she gave in to the urge and sat down on the grass. Beowulf lay next to her, as if giving her his support. She was only vaguely aware of Rurik and the others talking. Eventually, however, a hand appeared in front of her. 'Come, Sara, it is over. You're safe now.'

She looked up to find Hálfdan smiling at her. With a nod, she took his hand and he pulled her to her feet. 'Thank you. I am in your debt yet again, it seems.'

He shook his head. 'Not me. Rurik did what was necessary and I hope the two of you will now be left alone. I hear you're returning to Birka, and I wish you a good journey.'

'Thank you. I wish you good luck in your endeavours too.'

Rurik came over and took her hand, leading her away from the camp site. They walked in silence for a while, with Tryggve and his uncles following a few steps behind, and Beowulf sticking to her side. 'How is your stomach?' she whispered, glancing at him. 'You didn't open up the wound again, did you?'

'No, I don't think so. It feels fine.' He smiled and squeezed her hand. 'Asmund was made clumsy by too much ale and that wounded hand. I didn't have to exert myself too much.' He took a deep breath. 'I feel as though I can truly breathe again. I hope the goddess Hel keeps Asmund busy for the rest of time.'

'Me too.' And he was right – the air felt somehow purer again, despite the noxious stench of the Jorvik streets. The evil man was truly gone.

Chapter Twenty-Seven

'Birka at last!' Rurik breathed a sigh of relief as the island town came into view. He was heartily sick of travelling and didn't want to see a ship or the sea for a very long time, if ever.

'It looks a lot smaller than Jorvik,' Tryggve commented. The youth had decided to come with them, as he had an older sister living in Birka. He'd said he enjoyed working with the two of them and would like to continue until he had learned everything he could.

Rurik and Sara were happy to have him, and told him so.

'Oh thank the gods! I can't wait to sleep in a bed that keeps still.' Sara was gazing towards the jetties in the harbour with the same longing he felt himself. 'Or are we going straight to your brother's place? You said that was further inland, did you not?'

'No, we'll stay here for a while.' He wasn't ready to return home quite yet. It would be better if everything was settled between him and Sara first, and he also wanted to set up his workshop. 'I'm planning on having a house built here, and it's best if we take advantage of the summer months for that. Visiting can wait. I'll just send him a message to say I'm here, safe and hale.'

She sighed. 'I suppose we'll be in a tent for a while then.'

He slung an arm round her shoulders and pulled her close. 'Not until the weather is a little warmer. May nights can be cold here. I'm fairly sure my friend and fellow silversmith Leifr will let us sleep in his house, Tryggve as well. He has plenty of room. He was the one who taught me all I know. You'll like him.' He was happy that Sara was here with him. It was just a shame they wouldn't have any privacy for the foreseeable future. They'd managed a few secret encounters during the journey, but not nearly enough for his liking. He'd have to set about building that house as soon as possible so they could be alone.

They had packed up their belongings in Jorvik and he'd managed to find a buyer for the workshop there, a man who'd tired of life in the *here.* Since leaving Norðimbraland, Sara hadn't once mentioned going back to her own time, and Rurik had high hopes of persuading her to stay for good. Naturally she would want to visit her grandfather, but if he asked her to marry him, perhaps she'd be content with only going back to the future occasionally. There was only one way to find out, but first they had to get settled here. And it was only fair to allow her to see what sort of an existence she would be agreeing to. He didn't want her to regret her decision later.

Leifr greeted them with a beaming smile, and his wife and children made them all welcome, even Beowulf, who as usual never left Sara's side. 'Oh, he's adorable!' Leifr's youngest daughter squealed, and the hound submitted to being fussed over and kissed on the head.

'You don't know where he's been,' Rurik muttered, but Sara elbowed him and sent him a mock-serious glare.

'He's very clean and you know it,' she hissed. 'I bathe him frequently.' Too frequently for the dog's liking.

Within a week, Leifr had found some men willing to help build a new house for Rurik and Sara, and they'd chosen a suitable plot.

Birka was made up of rows of houses rising up a slope in semicircles around a bay. They decided to build right at the end of one of these, halfway up the hill.

'That way we will only have neighbours on one side,' Rurik said. He'd prefer not to live quite so close to anyone, but that was the price you paid for being in a town.

The sight of a pouch of silver each was enough to have the men working hard from dawn till dusk. Rurik helped as well, as did Tryggve, and Sara insisted on doing what she could.

'I did carpentry at *school*,' she told him when he commented on her skills with a hammer. 'Hitting a nail on the head is not so hard.'

'Not all women would agree with you there, but then I know you're different, Sara *mín*.'

She blushed at the compliment and didn't protest when he stole a kiss behind a newly built wall. 'I can't wait for this house to be finished,' he whispered.

'Me neither.' Her cheeks turned even rosier and he had to make a huge effort not to kiss her again.

As soon as it was done, and their new forge set up, he was going to make her the most beautiful gold ring and ask her to be his wife.

It all seemed too good to be true. At first Sara woke each day expecting disaster to strike, but nothing happened. She didn't know why she felt so anxious. It was just a deep-seated feeling that her dream of a life with Rurik was only that – a dream. He had seemed different since they returned from her time, and had trouble keeping his hands off her. That was flattering, of course, but he hadn't mentioned anything about love. The words he always used were 'want' and 'need', and there was no doubt he enjoyed sleeping with her. The new house was coming along nicely and she could tell that he was impatient to get her on his own. The feeling was mutual, and eventually she started to relax.

She had wondered if they would come across the woman he'd been in love with when they arrived in Sweden, but although she'd watched him interacting with lots of women since his return, he hadn't seemed different with any of them. Instead, he kept taking Sara's hand whenever he could, and touching her surreptitiously. There were lots of stolen kisses too, stoking the fire already burning inside her. She had a feeling their first night alone was going to be explosive.

She couldn't wait.

Two weeks into the house-building project, they were returning to Leifr's house for their evening meal, arguing good-naturedly about the flooring. The smith's wife, Alvis, had offered to cook for them, as long as they contributed their share of the ingredients, an arrangement that seemed to suit everyone.

'We can't have a wooden floor in the forge,' Rurik protested. 'It could so easily catch fire. But in the living quarters, that would be fine.'

'I suppose that's sensible. But can we make sure the planks are sanded properly? I like to walk barefoot and I don't want splinters.'

He laughed. 'Very well. We can't have that, and I quite like the thought of you barefoot.' He leaned closer and whispered, 'Well, bare anything really.'

She was just about to reply when a voice interrupted them. 'Rurik! By all the gods, am I glad to see you!' Looking up, she saw Linnea's husband, Hrafn, coming towards them. She recognised him immediately, even though she'd only met him the once. He was kind of hard to forget, being tall and handsome in an aloof sort of way. Although nowhere near as handsome as Rurik, of course.

'Brother!' Rurik seemed stunned, but then he rushed forward

to hug Hrafn, a slightly awkward manoeuvre due to the fact that the other man was carrying a baby over one shoulder.

Sara stood stock still, shock waves cascading through her. She had barely caught on to the fact that they were brothers when another voice joined in. 'Rurik, welcome back! We've missed you. Why didn't you come straight home?'

Rurik turned to the newcomer and exclaimed, '*Linnea!* What are you doing here?'

She laughed and threw herself around his neck to give him a hug. 'I wanted to see you, of course. You've been away for nearly a whole year, you *fifl*!'

'Oh, yes, I . . .' He seemed completely dazed, and a bit awkward and lost for words, and looking between him and her best friend, the penny suddenly dropped for Sara.

It was Linnea he was in love with. Her best friend. His brother's wife.

No wonder he'd had to leave.

There was no time to ponder this further, though, as Linnea caught sight of Sara, who'd been hanging back. Her eyes opened wide and she squealed in Swedish, '*Sara! Oh my God!* I can't believe it! What are you doing in Birka? No, what are you even doing in this *time*? And how did you find Rurik and not us?' She abandoned Rurik and instead threw herself at Sara, who was nearly knocked off her feet by her enthusiastic friend.

'Um, it's a long story,' she mumbled.

Linnea linked arms with her and grabbed the wrist of a small girl with her free hand. 'Well, I want to hear it all. Come, Estrid, let's go talk to Auntie Sara.'

As she was led inside Leifr's house, where Linnea seemed at home, greeting everyone like long-lost friends, Sara glanced over her shoulder. Rurik was standing frozen to the spot, staring between the two of them as if he was comparing them. He still seemed thunderstruck, and no wonder. Her heart shrivelled. There was no way she would ever come out on top in a straight comparison with Linnea. Her friend was blonde, blue-eyed and beautiful in a statuesque way. A veritable Valkyrie. Probably exactly the sort of woman any Viking male would want.

And Sara wasn't.

The adventure was over.

Chapter Twenty-Eight

'What were you doing holding hands with Linnea's friend?' Hrafn hissed.

He'd introduced Rurik to his new nephew, Eskil, and reintroduced him to Estrid, who had grown a lot in just one year. She'd been a baby last time he'd seen her. Now she was a little hoyden, fast as lightning, and it was amusing to see his usually unflappable brother trying to keep her out of trouble. Rurik rather thought Hrafn had met his match. But these thoughts were barely registering as he tried to catch Sara's eye. She'd been avoiding him ever since his brother and Linnea arrived, and hadn't spoken a word to him all evening.

An unusual sensation swirled around his gut, and he recognised it as fear. Not something he'd ever felt before in his life, but he could tell that his plans had just gone very awry. In fact, his entire life was disintegrating before his eyes and he had no idea what to do about it.

'I met her in Norðimbraland and we've become . . . close,' he murmured. 'But I didn't know until today that she and Linnea knew each other. Or that she'd met you. I, um, didn't discuss my family with her much.'

'Hmm. Well, I don't know what you've done, but I'd say

she is mighty cross with you.'

'Thank you, I'm perfectly capable of noticing that for myself.' Rurik couldn't keep the sarcasm out of his voice. He wanted to punch his brother, but at the same time he knew this wasn't Hrafn's fault. It was all his own.

The trolls take it!

He'd been shocked to see his sister-in-law. At first he'd frozen completely, waiting to see if the familiar longing for Linnea would hit him the way it always had in the past. He'd dreaded coming face to face with her on his return here, just in case he'd been wrong and his body hadn't forgotten her as he'd thought. That was partly why he'd decided not to go straight to Hrafn's hall, but to put it off for a while.

It was a relief to find he didn't desire Linnea in the slightest and could look at her in a completely detached manner now. But by the time he realised that he felt nothing at all, his tongue had stuck to the roof of his mouth and he'd found it impossible to utter a word. He'd been overjoyed knowing that he'd been right – Sara was the woman for him and his infatuation with Linnea was truly at an end – but somehow things had gone wrong anyway.

Had Sara somehow guessed at his former feelings? But how could she? He'd never told her the name of the woman he'd yearned for. She was certainly very displeased about something, though, and he needed to find out what that was.

'You'll have to use your usual charm to get into her good graces again.' Hrafn elbowed him and chuckled. 'I've never known you to fail with any woman before.'

Except your wife. But of course he didn't say that out loud, because he wasn't proud of the fact that he'd even wanted to try. He loved his brother and that was why he had left. Never would he want to come between him and Linnea, no matter his own feelings.

And now those feelings were gone, thank the gods. The only woman he wanted was Sara.

When they lay down a while later, however, she turned her back on him instead of snuggling up to him the way she'd been doing every night since their sojourn in the future. 'Sara?' He whispered her name and tried to pull her towards his chest, but she shrugged him off.

'Don't, Rurik.'

'What is wrong? Why are you angry with me?' She couldn't possibly read his thoughts and he hadn't said anything to annoy her.

'I don't want to talk about it. Go to sleep.'

'Very well, but we *will* speak tomorrow.'

He had to find out what she was thinking and do something about it, because this was pure torture.

'Come, we're going for a walk.'

Rurik took her hand and practically dragged her out of the house, setting off up the hill with long strides. Sara considered protesting, but they had to have this conversation at some point and it might as well be now.

When they had reached the top of the slope, he sat down on a boulder and she sank down next to him, although keeping as much distance between them as possible. She glanced at him, catching his intense gaze, but she didn't want to look into those amazing eyes so she stared out over the bay instead.

'What is the matter, Sara? Why are you angry with me?'

'You never told me your brother's name.'

'That's what this is about? I'm sorry, I thought I'd mentioned it.'

She shook her head. 'No. If you had, I might have realised Linnea was your sister-in-law.'

'Would it have mattered? I mean, I can see that it's nice for you to know someone here from your own time, but surely it made no difference when we were in Norðimbraland?' He sounded truly puzzled and she wanted to hit him.

She turned to face him, glaring at him with all the pent-up emotion of a sleepless night. 'Well, perhaps then I would have realised sooner that she's the woman you love.'

He blinked and went extremely pale. 'No, I don't! It's you I want, Sara.' A frustrated noise escaped him as the colour returned to his cheeks with a vengeance. 'I admit I used to be in thrall to her, but no longer, I swear.'

She snorted. 'A likely tale. I saw your reaction to her yesterday – you were tongue-tied, like a lovesick youth. Of course you want me now because you can't have her. But I told you once before, I refuse to be second best. I can't lie with you and wonder if you're thinking about her. She's so beautiful, there can be no comparison.' She couldn't bring herself to say 'make love', because it had obviously never been that way for him.

'Sara, that's not true. I—'

She cut him off. 'No! I don't want to hear it. This – whatever it was we had – is over, and I'll be going back to my own time as soon as I've visited Linnea for a while. I'd rather not, to be honest, but she's insisting I come and see their home now that I'm here. She's my best friend, I owe it to her. As for you, I hope you're staying here in Birka, as I never want to see you again.'

She got up, unable to stay another instant. He called her name several times as she began to run down the hill, but tears were pouring down her face and she didn't want to discuss this any longer.

They were finished.

'I can't believe she won't talk to me! Odin's ravens, but she's even avoiding looking at me.' Rurik pushed a hand through his hair and sighed for at least the tenth time. He was pacing around his nearly finished house, but it didn't feel like a home any more. Without Sara, it would just be a place where he worked and slept. An empty shell that would forever remind him of her, of their plans, of the life and family he'd hoped to have with her.

Hrafn sat on a newly constructed bench, his face inscrutable. 'Calm down. There must be something you can do.' He hadn't been best pleased to hear that Rurik had lusted after his wife the previous year, but he was a reasonable man, and everyone fell in love with Linnea. It was just something he had to live with, and he was secure in the knowledge that she never had eyes for anyone but him. 'Thank you for telling me the truth anyway. I must admit I was puzzled when you left so abruptly last year, but now I understand.'

'Yes, well, it seemed the best option at the time. And it worked.' Rurik paced some more. At this rate he'd be wearing a furrow in the stamped-earth floor of his forge. *The* jōtuns *take it!* 'So what do you suggest? How can I make Sara see that I'm madly in love with her and no one else when she doesn't want to be in the same room as me?'

It was Hrafn's turn to sigh. 'Give her time to calm down. We're taking her back to Eskilsnes tomorrow and I'm sure Linnea will try to distract her. Once she's had time to reflect, perhaps she'll hear you out.'

'Doubtful.'

'Not if you can make her see that you are sincere. And I'll enlist Linnea's help too. Sara is her friend; she might be able to come up with some ideas. How about a grand gesture?'

'Like what? She told me that once she's finished visiting you, she's going back to her time. I can't stop her, if that's what she really wants.'

'I'm sure you can. In the meantime, we'll keep an eye on

her. I promise I won't let her leave without warning you first.' Hrafn got up and slapped his brother on the back. 'You'll think of something. Come to visit us in exactly two weeks' time. We're having a midsummer feast. That might present you with an opportunity.' He chuckled. 'You're just going to have to shout it from the rafters for all to hear. Maybe she'll listen then. Sing a love song. You have the best voice in our family.'

'Hmph.' He wasn't convinced, but his entire future was at stake and he had to make a plan. 'I was going to make her a beautiful ring. I suppose I could start with that.'

'Excellent. I'll see you in two weeks.'

Rurik still didn't know what he was going to do, but he wasn't giving up without a fight. And he could be extremely stubborn when he wanted to be.

'Are you pregnant?'

'Um, I guess.' Sara had just been caught throwing up behind the privy and knew the game was up. Linnea had gone through this twice already; she'd know the signs.

'And that doesn't make you reconsider?' Linnea had concern written all over her face, but at the same time there was something stern in her voice and her blue eyes were flashing.

'What's there to reconsider? I'm not marrying a man who's in love with you, no matter how much I happen to like him.'

'I told you, he's not in love with me. We're like brother and sister.'

'Uh-huh. Sure you are.' Sara held up a hand. 'And yes, I know you see it that way, but trust me, he doesn't. You didn't hear him talking about the woman he'd lost. I did.'

'But that was last year. Things change. It's you he wants now, Hrafn says.'

She shook her head. 'I'm sorry, but I don't believe that. How can I? Did you not see the way he acted around you? What are you, blind? He has it bad. Hell, he couldn't even speak when he caught sight of you. He was like a teenager with a huge crush on a movie star.'

'It was just the shock. We meant to surprise him, and it worked.'

'Hmm.'

'Sara, honestly, I could shake you! But I know it won't do any good, so I'll leave you to wallow. Come and find me when you've stopped being sick. We've got things to do.'

Linnea's words made her even more miserable. Her friend wanted everyone to be as happy as she was herself, but she couldn't change the facts of the matter. Whether she wanted to believe it or not, her brother-in-law had a giant crush on her. Sara had been a distraction, but only a temporary one. And although it hurt now, she had to be glad she'd found out in time. She might have agreed to stay here with him otherwise, and then things could have got messy if they had children together.

Well, they *were* having a child, and she'd have to tell him. Not because she wanted to guilt him into asking her to marry him – that would be unbearable – but because he had a right to know.

She would insist on keeping the baby, of course – a small piece of him to remind her of the good times, someone to love and cherish. He might want to visit them in her time, get to know his child, and she would have to allow it. It wouldn't be any worse than a couple who were divorced and shared custody. She would be civilised, for the baby's sake, and hopefully he would too.

They hadn't said goodbye. Rurik didn't even come to the jetty to wave them off when they left, and she'd been grateful for that. It was too painful to see him and know that he was not for her. Anders and his perfidy seemed like nothing in comparison to the way she was feeling now. This time she'd been in love for real. With a man who loved someone else.

God, she really knew how to pick them, didn't she? Her love life was a disaster.

But that wasn't the baby's fault. She took a deep breath. Before going back, she'd return to Birka and inform Rurik he was going to be a father. He'd have to travel back to the future with her briefly so that she could give him the *seax*, then he would be able to come back any time he wanted to. Preferably not too often, but still . . . that was fair.

Decision made, she went in search of Linnea and tried to help with the preparations for the midsummer feast. At least that was something different to concentrate on, and soon this would all be over with.

She couldn't wait.

Rurik had arrived after dark and gone straight to what was normally the weaving hut. Hrafn had told him he could spend the night there and no one else needed to know, except Linnea. His brother was there to greet him, and looked him up and down with concern in his eyes before giving him a fierce hug.

'How are you bearing up? Come up with a good plan?'

'I think so. Well, it may not be the best, but it's all I have.' A shiver went through him at the thought that he might fail, but he couldn't allow himself to think that way. It had to work.

'And?' Hrafn sat down on a bench and waited for him to elaborate.

Rurik sank down on to the pile of furs Linnea had left for him to sleep on and leaned on a stack of blankets and cushions. 'I don't want to tell you, because then your reaction won't be genuine. It should be a surprise to everyone, including you. But please can you ask the *skald* to come and see me here tomorrow morning?

I need to discuss something with him. And you'd better bring Beowulf too, otherwise he might decide to give me a boisterous greeting just at the wrong time.' Sara had taken the big hound with her and Rurik had let her. He'd been hoping the bond between her and the dog might make her think again, as he was sure it would be a wrench for her to leave him.

'Very well. And if you want to use the bath house, I'll come and fetch you when the women are busy elsewhere. I assume you need to look your best.'

'Yes, indeed. I already have the perfect garment to wear.' At Hrafn's raised eyebrow, he shook his head. 'No, I'm not telling you. You'd better go back to the hall now or it will look suspicious.'

'Fine. Linnea has left you some food and drink here. Sleep well, little brother.'

'I doubt it,' Rurik muttered, but then he hadn't slept properly since Sara left Birka. Hopefully tomorrow would change that.

Chapter Twenty-Nine

'I can't believe how much food there is! You've worked so hard, Linnea. I'm impressed.' Sara was looking at the trestle tables set up in the huge hall that was her friend's home. They were almost groaning under the weight of dishes, despite the fact that this was what Linnea had termed a lean time of year. Slaughter and harvest were many months away, but she'd improvised, and instead fish dishes and game of various kinds were much in evidence. Apparently Hrafn and his youngest brother Geir had been hunting for days. And there was milk from both cows and goats with which to make *skyr*, cheese and butter, skills Sara was being taught during her stay here. No one would go hungry, that was for sure.

'Thank you, but I mostly direct operations. I'm not great at cooking myself. And I was taught by a hard taskmaster, or perhaps mistress is the right word.'

'You mean Hrafn's aunt Estrid?' Sara had heard a lot about that formidable lady while she'd been here, although the older woman had recently moved to a property her husband had unexpectedly inherited, so she hadn't met her.

'Yes.' Linnea smiled. 'Oh, we had a few skirmishes, but she's all right really. And there's no doubt she knows how to run a place like this, so I tried to pay attention to everything she said.'

'Well, she can't be all bad, as you named your first child after her,' Sara pointed out.

'No, although that was partly to keep her on side. And it worked: she was chuffed to bits.' Linnea grinned. 'Come, let's go and sit down. It's about to start.'

Sara wasn't hungry, but as it was late afternoon, at least she wasn't feeling nauseous. And she knew she had to keep her strength up for the baby's sake, so she helped herself to whatever dishes were passed her way. Hrafn and Linnea had been to a sacred grove nearby earlier in the day to make some kind of sacrifice to the gods, but Sara had stayed behind. For one thing, she felt sorry for whatever animal had to give its life for the sake of the ritual, and for another, she knew she wouldn't have been able to cope with the sight of blood. The slightest thing set off her morning sickness and she couldn't risk anyone noticing.

'Here, have some more water.' Linnea, like her, always kept a supply of cooled boiled water to hand, although in her case it was because she didn't actually like ale much. 'It's a shame you can't taste the mead. I made it myself.'

'Thank you. I'll have to try it some other time.' Not that she was planning on ever coming back to the past. That would just be too painful.

The feast continued all around her for what seemed like ages, and everything became a bit of a blur. It was noisy and boisterous, with mock-fighting, laughter, dares and music. Lost in her own thoughts, she barely noticed. But all of a sudden, Hrafn stood up and bellowed, '*Silence, everyone!*' A hush fell on the room, and she finally came out of her trance and looked around her. What was going on?

The *skald* came in through the door at one end of the room and walked slowly towards the centre. Following behind him was Rurik with Beowulf at his heels looking adoringly up at his master. When had the big hound disappeared? He'd been at her side for most of the evening but must have slipped away and she hadn't noticed. Sara's heart lodged in her throat as she watched the men and the dog make their way through the throng of people. She'd half expected Rurik to be here, but when he hadn't appeared at the beginning of the feast, she had relaxed, thinking he wasn't coming. Seeing him now was like being doused in ice cold water, and she froze in her seat, mesmerised by the mere sight of him. Halfway down the room, opposite the table where Sara sat with her host and hostess, they stopped and the two men jumped up to stand on the bench. Those who had been seated there made room for them with amused and expectant glances, while Beowulf sat down in front of them with a silly canine grin on his face as if he approved whole-heartedly of whatever was going on.

What on earth was Rurik up to?

She couldn't take her eyes off him. He was so handsome it hurt to look at him, and her throat constricted. There wasn't enough air in here and she was having trouble breathing. *Damn him!* Why did he have to affect her this way? It wasn't fair. She blinked as she noticed he was wearing the tunic with woven bands that she'd made for him. What did that mean? He had others, much nicer ones that he'd bought in Jorvik, and yet he had chosen that particular one today?

Before she could consider the implications further, he raised a hand. 'Greetings, everyone! It's wonderful to be back at Eskilsnes and I hope you all missed me?'

A roar of agreement and welcomes greeted this sally and he smiled, although Sara could tell it didn't really reach his eyes.

When everyone had gone quiet again, waiting for his next words, he continued.

'I have a very special song to sing, and then I'm going to make a confession. Please indulge me, good people, and may the gods be with me.'

Sara frowned. What was he doing?

The *skald* plucked the strings of an instrument he was holding, and Rurik started to sing. At first, she only noticed that he had an amazing voice – loud and clear, melodious and silky smooth. It wrapped itself around the listeners like a feather bolster, and she drew in a sharp breath of awe. She'd never heard him sing before.

The melody was sad and haunting, some sort of ballad. Slowly, the words began to register, seeping into her consciousness, and her mouth fell open. He was singing about a young man who'd thought himself in love with an unattainable lady, only to find that he'd been completely wrong because the woman he truly loved had been right next to him all the time. He praised the second woman's beauty, her kindness, her amazing skills as a silversmith – something that made the audience look at each other with raised eyebrows. But he ignored them and continued to the final verses, where the young man found that his love was not reciprocated, and so he was doomed to forever wander the world alone, his heart broken and all hope lost.

Although she knew it was just a song, Sara felt tears trickling down her cheeks, and swiped at them impatiently, even as she saw that she wasn't the only one crying. There were quite a few sniffles all around her, although these turned to laughter when Beowulf decided to join in and raised his voice in a mournful howl. Rurik didn't miss a beat, just leaned down to pat the hound on his fuzzy head while he carried on. When the last note of the song died away, everyone stayed silent, including the dog.

Rurik looked around and raised his voice to speak again. 'Listen, everyone, I promised you a confession and here it is: that song was about me.' He paused and nodded at his brother. 'I owe Hrafn a public apology, as I was stupid enough to think myself in love with his wife last year.' A gasp whispered through his audience, but he held up his hand again. 'I know, it was ridiculous, because anyone can see how much in love he and Linnea are with each other. And she and I would never have suited – I'm sorry to have to say this, sister dear, but you are just too domineering for me. I have no idea how Hrafn puts up with it.' He grinned, and Linnea smiled back after sending him a mock-glare.

He went on. 'I think perhaps I was just in love with the idea of finding the same happiness, and so I mistook my jealousy of your joy for something else. At the time, I didn't want anyone to feel awkward, and that was why I left.' His gaze moved to Sara, his look intense, as if she was suddenly the only person in the room. 'And then I met Sara.'

Everyone turned to stare at her, and she felt her cheeks burning, but Rurik didn't stop talking.

'Sara is completely different to Linnea. Although they are both beautiful, when I compare them, one is ice and one is fire. If you'll forgive me, sister, your cool beauty is not the kind I crave. No, I wish to be burned by the flames of Sara's love and passion, and no one else's.' His expression turned sad and he took a deep breath, looking around at the audience once more. 'And yet you all heard my song – she has refused me because she doesn't believe my feelings for Linnea have gone. Now I have made a fool of myself in front of you all, so can you help me persuade her, please? You have heard my confession. Do I seem sincere to you?'

A roar of '*Yes!*' rose to the rafters.

'And does Sara not look every bit as beautiful to you as Linnea?'

Another resounding '*Yes!*' echoed round the room.

Rurik began to smile. He jumped off the bench and walked towards the table where Sara sat. 'Then please tell her I love her and wish to marry her and no one else. By Freya and Tyr and the mighty Odin, I swear to love only her until the day I die. You are all witness to my oath and may the gods strike me down if I'm not telling the truth!'

The crowd was getting into the swing of this, obviously enjoying themselves, and again raised their voices. '*Marry him, marry him, marry him!*' rang out, accompanied by stamping of feet and rhythmical banging on the tables. Sara stared in helpless wonder as Rurik came to stand in front of her, holding out his hand, palm up. On it lay a ring.

'Please, Sara, say you will be my wife?' he begged, a hopeful yet wary expression in his turquoise eyes. 'I love you more than I can ever say. Only you.' Beowulf, who had come over to stand next to him, gave a loud bark, as if to add his opinion. 'He agrees,' Rurik added, 'and he loves you too.'

As if in a trance, she took the proffered ring and studied it. Of pure gold and quite heavy, it featured two tiny birds, just like the one in the pin he'd made for her, which she still wore. The pair faced each other and each bird held a little diamond in its beak, as if they were about to exchange them. As a trained jeweller, she was almost a hundred per cent certain they were real diamonds and not just rock crystal. The birds' wings were folded, unlike the one on her pin, but the feathers could still be clearly seen. All in all, it was a work of art and showed the immense skill of the maker.

Rurik. Who had made this for her. And who had laid himself open to ridicule from everyone in his brother's hall to make her believe him. She swallowed hard and nodded at him.

'Yes,' she whispered. The word came out croaky and faint, but he still heard it, and he vaulted the table with a huge grin, sending crockery and food flying in every direction.

'Rurik, you oaf!' his brother protested, but he was laughing at the same time, and everyone else joined in.

Sara was more or less oblivious, however, as Rurik had pulled her off her seat and into his arms, his mouth claiming hers in a kiss that seared her to her very soul. More clapping, cheering and stamping of feet was heard, but he didn't let up until they were both gasping for air. Then he looked down at her and whispered, 'I swear you will not regret this. Can we be wed tomorrow?'

She laughed and stood on tiptoe to give him a fierce kiss. 'Any time you want.'

'Does that mean you love me too, or is it just my amazing body you're after?' he teased, although the look in his eyes was serious.

She smacked him on the arm. 'Of course I love you, you dolt. Have done for ages. Why else would I have been so upset?'

'Well, thank Freya for that!' He drew her close and sat down, pulling her on to his lap to more cheers of approval, then waved at everyone and shouted, 'She said yes! You can go back to your feasting now. Thank you for your assistance!'

Eventually they all simmered down. Things went back to normal and people started talking about other matters. Hrafn leaned over and gripped Rurik's hand. 'Congratulations, brother.' He kissed Sara on the cheek. 'And you, Sara, welcome to the family.'

'Thank you.'

Linnea was next to hug both of them, before punching Rurik on the arm. 'That's for calling me domineering and cold. I am no such thing, am I, my love?' This last was aimed at Hrafn, who just grinned until she punched him as well.

'Of course not, *ást mín*. And you know I like it when you're

. . . ah, forceful.' He winked at her. 'You're definitely not icy, though; he's wrong about that.'

'Hmph!' Linnea shook her head at Sara. 'They're lucky to have us, don't ever forget that.'

'I won't.'

'Let's celebrate.' Hrafn handed Rurik a mug of ale and clinked it with his own. 'Tomorrow we'll feast some more in your honour.' He grinned at his brother. 'Good thing you have your own sleeping quarters, eh?'

'Indeed.' Rurik chuckled.

'What does he mean?' Sara looked at him. 'You're not staying here?'

'Not exactly. Come, I'll show you. And yes, you can come too, Beowulf.' He pulled her up again and took her hand, leading her out into the night and over to one of the other buildings. The dog padded behind them, clearly content to have his master and mistress reunited. 'Here we are, the weaving hut.'

'Er, yes? You want me to learn weaving? Now?'

He laughed. 'No, *unnasta*. My brother has very kindly allowed me to sleep in here. On my own. I was rather hoping you'd like to join me.' He raised an eyebrow at the dog. 'Well, both of you, apparently.'

His hands gripped both of hers now and there was enough moonlight for her to see him watching her intently. 'Just you and me? And Beowulf?'

'No one else.'

She smiled. 'Then what are we waiting for?'

'Hell if I know,' he said in English, making her laugh at one of the phrases he'd picked up when they were in her time. Before she could reply, though, he'd lifted her up and carried her inside, kicking the door shut behind them as soon as the hound was inside.

'You'd better close your eyes, dog,' he joked as he put her down on a glossy wolf-skin pelt, kissing her with the same urgency she felt herself. As she wrapped her arms around him, she knew that this was going to be the best night of her life.

And it was only the beginning.

Chapter Thirty

'So we are really married now?'

They were back in their hut after another day and night of feasting, as well as a lengthy ceremony involving oaths and drinking. Sara had mostly pretended to drink, taking very small sips of anything alcoholic, but no one seemed to have noticed, thank goodness. This time Beowulf had been left with Linnea and Hrafn, and he hadn't seemed to mind.

'Yes. Why? You don't believe it is binding our way? Would you prefer the White Christ's ritual?'

Rurik was holding her close, as if he couldn't get enough of having her in his arms. She snuggled further into his embrace, feeling the same way. 'No, no, it's fine. I just can't believe I am your wife at last. It seems like a dream. A very wonderful one,' she hastened to add.

'I know what you mean. But it is real and I don't think anything could make me feel happier than I am right now.'

'Are you sure?' She looked up at him with raised eyebrows.

'Of course. Why wouldn't I be? You're not still doubting me, are you?' There was confusion in his voice and Sara couldn't help it, she had to laugh.

'No, no, but there is one thing that might increase your

happiness . . .' She trailed off, taking his hand in hers and dragging it slowly down her body.

'What? Please tell me, Sara, you are worrying me now.'

Their hands came to a stop over her stomach, and she looked up at him as she placed his palm against her skin. 'There's someone in there who'll be joining us in about six months or so. Will that make you pleased?'

He drew in a sharp breath and stared at her, then his beautiful mouth widened into a huge grin. 'Really? We're having a child? You're sure? But of course I'm pleased! What did you think? I'm overjoyed!'

He picked her up and whirled her around while she laughed, relieved that he was taking it so well. As he put her down again, though, he stilled and frowned at her. 'But you knew this and you were still going to go back to your own time.' It was a statement, not a question, and his voice was suddenly very serious.

She shook her head. 'No. I was going to tell you before I went, and ask you to take me back there so that you'd have the *seax*, giving you the means to visit us if you wanted to. I'm not completely heartless; I'd never keep your child away from you, even when I thought you didn't want its mother.'

Rurik heaved a sigh of relief and gave her a fierce hug. 'Thank Odin for that! But now it doesn't matter, because he . . .'

'Or she.'

'. . . will grow up with both of us to love him.'

'Or her.'

He kissed her. 'We'll see. Whatever it is, hopefully we'll have many more and we will love them all.'

The thought of a big family and a future with this man was almost more happiness than one person could take, so Sara did the only thing she could do – she clung to him, her rock, her love, her forever man.

And she knew that it would be amazing.

Acknowledgments

I want to start by saying a very heartfelt THANK YOU to all the readers, reviewers and book bloggers who take the time to post reviews, interact on social media and support me and my books in every way – I appreciate it more than I can say!

When I first heard about the 'Great Heathen Army' that invaded the British kingdoms during the Viking age, I knew I had to write about it. And it seemed like serendipity when I just happened to watch a TV programme featuring Dr Cat Jarman, where she talked about an archaeological dig at Repton in Derbyshire, the place where that army had their final *wintersetl* (over-wintering) before it split into smaller parts that went their separate ways. She was able to prove conclusively that the Vikings had indeed been there (and at nearby Foremark) so I decided my fictional Vikings would join them. I later had the great pleasure of discussing Repton with Dr Jarman and would like to thank her very much for taking the time to chat to me, and for her vital insights.

In order to describe the journey my Vikings took to get there, of course I had to follow their trail. I have to say a huge thank you to my husband Richard for driving me and our two dogs during an epic 600-mile, two-day trip to Northumberland and Derbyshire. The weather was abysmal, but the Norse gods seemed to be with us as each time we stopped it cleared up long enough for me to see the sights and take the photos I needed. Special thanks to the man walking his dog in Torksey who helped us find the disused railway bridge from which to see the river (we'd already driven past it three times!). And to the Grand Hotel in Sunderland for being so dog-friendly and letting us stay while researching nearby Marsden Bay.

My thanks go to Cat Mills for help with details about silver-smithing; to author Annie Whitehead for help with an Anglo-Saxon place name; and to Dr Joanne Shortt-Butler for all her help with Old Norse words, phrases and pronunciation – it's been invaluable (and any mistakes are my own!).

As always, special thanks to my wonderful writer friends, especially Sue Moorcroft, Myra Kersner, Henriette Gyland, Gill Stewart and Nicola Cornick – you have all kept me sane during the 2020 pandemic! And last year I had the immense pleasure of joining the Word Wenches – Anne Gracie, Andrea Penrose, Mary Jo Putney, Patricia Rice, Susan Fraser King and Joanna Bourne (plus Nicola) – thank you all so much for being so lovely and welcoming!

A massive thank you to my amazing editor Kate Byrne and her team at Headline, as well as Lina Langlee, my fantastic agent, and her colleague Julie Fergusson – it's an absolute joy to work with you all!

Last but not least, to Richard and my two daughters Josceline and Jessamy – love you loads!

Whispers *of the* Runes

Bonus Material

Facts about the Vikings that might surprise you!

Vikings did not call themselves that – they came from various parts of Scandinavia and identified with whatever region or small independent kingdom they stemmed from. Sweden, Norway and Denmark did not exist as unified countries until later. And 'Viking' was just a term that referred to people who travelled abroad and went to raid, trade or settle.

They did not wear horned helmets EVER! It would have been highly impractical in battle and really get in the way. Horned helmets were invented as part of the costumes designed for Wagner's Ring Cycle opera when it was first staged in the late nineteenth century.

Vikings loved bright colours and used dyes from many sources – no boring homespun wool for them unless necessary. They also decorated themselves and their clothing with anything shiny or colourful they could find. The necklines of men's shirts were high since a garment that revealed the chest was considered effeminate! (So images of bare-chested Vikings are not authentic.)

Norse women had considerable rights, at least in law, much more so than Christian women during the centuries that followed. The mistress of the house was an equal partner in the running of a farm and her keys were the symbols of her power.

The image of Vikings as being very tall is a myth – the average height of a Viking man was 170cm (5'8"), a woman 160cm (5'3"). However, Anglo-Saxon men were on average only 168cm, so perhaps Vikings were perceived as slightly taller. The men were also impressively built as they had a fairly good diet and performed a lot of hard physical labour.

Hel is both the name of the place where most Viking people went when they died (if they merely died of sickness or old age) and its mistress. She is often portrayed as a welcoming hostess and her realm is not the burning pit we are used to from the Christian version, but a nice Viking hall. No one went there as punishment for any sins they'd committed.

Read on for a preview of Christina Courtenay's next stunning and evocative timeslip novel of romance and Viking adventure

Tempted *by the* Runes

Chapter One

Eskilsnes, Svíaríki, Early April AD *875*

'Are you sure this is wise, brother? It could all be a pack of lies.'

'It's not.' Geir Eskilsson glared at his older brother Hrafn while continuing to place every item he possessed in his travel kist. No point leaving anything behind because he wasn't coming back. 'The man I talked to at Kaupang had been to Írland, and he said there is land for the taking – enough for everyone. Others said the same; I made careful enquiries. All you have to do is bring everything needed to start a new life, including cattle, and settle somewhere.'

Hrafn was pacing back and forth, but stopped to frown back at Geir. 'Cattle? On a journey across the ocean? And what if every piece of land has been claimed by the time you arrive? You'll have gone to all that trouble for nothing.'

'I doubt it. It's a huge place, by all accounts. And my mind is made up. I want my own domain, not be beholden to anyone else. Not even you.'

The brothers were close, but as the eldest, Hrafn had inherited their father's property Eskilsnes, and everything that came with it. That made the other two, Geir and their middle brother Rurik, dependent on Hrafn unless they struck out on their own. Rurik had trained as a silversmith and was now independent, living in Birka with his wife Sara and their son, and Geir was determined to break free as well. It was past time – he'd already seen twenty-two winters.

'You're not beholden to me. I'd say it's the other way round – I need you to help me run this place. How else can I go off on trading expeditions?'

Everyone knew that Hrafn much preferred trading to running a farm, but it was a privilege to inherit holdings as vast as those their father had left him, and he'd had no choice but to take on the duties that came with it.

Geir shrugged. 'Just ask Rurik to come and stay here. Or Aunt Estrid – she's more than capable of running this place, despite her age.' When Hrafn opened his mouth as if to argue further, Geir held up a hand. 'No! Nothing you can say will sway me. I'm leaving and I'd rather do so with your good will, but if you cannot wish me well, so be it.'

His brother sighed and rubbed his stubbled chin. 'Of course I wish you well. I just don't want you living so far away. When will we see you again?'

'Come on a trading voyage to Írland. If you can go all the way to Miklagarðr, I don't see why you can't sail west from Hordaland for a week or so across the sea.'

'Hmph.' Hrafn didn't look convinced. 'If it doesn't work out, will you give me your oath you'll come back? I know you're stubborn, but I don't want your pride to stand in the way of admitting when you've taken on too much.'

Rolling his eyes, Geir nodded. 'Fine, you have my word. But I won't fail. Just wait and see. Now come and help me load the rest of the implements I'll need, then we'll have one last feast before I leave.'

'Very well. Perhaps you'll drink so much ale you're incapable of steering tomorrow.'

'*Fifl!*' Geir gave his brother a good-natured shove and hefted the travelling chest. 'I can drink a barrel load more than you and still stand up straight.'

'We'll see about that . . .'

Chapter Two

Dublin, 25th April 2021

'Come to Dublin, they said. It'll be fun, they said. Hah! Where's the fun if I'm not even allowed to leave the hotel? I'm nineteen, not nine. Almost twenty, in fact.'

Madison Berger poked her brother Storm in the chest, making him hold up his hands in a peace gesture. 'Don't shoot the messenger, Mads. I guess Dad is worried you'll get attacked or something.'

'I'm a blackbelt in karate and great at kickboxing, for Christ's sake. And why can't I go with you?'

'I'm going on a pub crawl. Who wants to bring their little sister to something like that? It's a guys-only evening, with friends I haven't seen for ages. Come on, be reasonable. It's only for one night. Tomorrow I promise we'll do something fun, just you and me, OK? Besides, you should be exhausted after a whole day of telling fortunes. Chill.'

'It's not that hard.'

The whole family – Maddie, Storm and their parents Haakon and Mia – were in Dublin, taking part in the Clontarf Viking Festival held in St Anne's Park. Every year over five hundred living history re-enactors descended on the city from around the world. Many of them were there to recreate the Battle of Clontarf, when Irish king Brian Boru defeated a Viking army – although apparently he was killed himself afterwards – and this happened twice a day, near the site where it originally took place. But there were lots of other things going on the rest of the time. As well as the warriors, the festival included a Viking village with displays of weapons, crafts, food and much more, bringing this period of history to life. It was entertainment for the whole family and tens of thousands of visitors came along every year.

For as long as Maddie could remember, her parents had been attending such events, although this was their first time in Ireland. Her dad was great at woodturning, making exquisite wooden bowls and plates on a primitive lathe, while her brother Storm was a weapons enthusiast. If there was a battle anywhere, he wanted to be part of it. Her mum preferred to show off her skills at weaving on an upright loom. Maddie sometimes helped her, but this time she hadn't been needed as one of Mia's friends was with them. Instead she'd been asked to do fortune-telling with runes, which was fine by her. She'd become quite proficient at it in the last couple of years, and even believed she had the second sight as she was sometimes able to predict the future for some people. As part of the fun, she was dressed in a Viking outfit, complete with tortoise brooches of bronze and several strings of beautiful beads. She'd bought the amber ones herself with some of her takings and loved their honey lustre.

'Why don't you have an evening of pampering yourself or something?' Storm suggested now. 'I thought girls loved that kind of thing and the bathrooms here at the hotel are full of those tiny bottles of smelly stuff. I'm sure Mum and Dad won't be back too late.'

Maddie shrugged. She wasn't a bubble bath kind of person and he ought to know that.

As for their parents, there was some serious, academic stuff going on in the background with a special Viking conference at the university. As Haakon was an archaeologist of some renown and Mia a respected conservator, both specialising in that era, they'd made time to attend a couple of lectures too. Because of their academic connections, this evening they had been invited to attend some boring dinner with speeches. Maddie and Storm weren't included, but he had friends in the city and had obviously made plans. It annoyed her no end that none of the others had considered her. So was she just supposed to sit in her room and watch tv or what?

Stuff that.

'Fine. Off you go then.' She practically shoved Storm out the door. The sooner he was gone, the better. She was going to go for a walk and sod the others. They had no right to decide over her life – she was old enough to do what she liked.

'Mads . . .' Storm tried out his serious-big-brother face, eyes narrowed as if he knew she was up to something.

'I'll be fine. But you'd better take me somewhere nice tomorrow or else.' She pouted slightly, as if she'd given in even though she didn't like it. That seemed to do the trick.

'I will, I swear. Now be good, yeah?'

'Aren't I always?' She wasn't going to promise any such thing.

'Yes, I suppose so.' He smiled as she made a shooing motion. 'Right, I'm off then. See you in the morning.'

She waited until she was sure he'd left the hotel, then pulled a shawl around her shoulders and grabbed the key card. It didn't matter that she was still wearing her Viking outfit; there should be plenty of other people around dressed the same way. The reception staff gave her a few funny looks as she passed them, but she ignored that. They could think what they liked.

It was late April and had been an unseasonably warm day with temperatures in the low twenties and plenty of sunshine. She'd caught the sun – she could feel her face burning slightly – but by now it was starting to feel a bit chilly outside as she headed south, down Capel Street. Her woollen over-dress – made in an apron style usually called *hangerok* or *smokkr* – and shawl kept her warm, though, as she hurried along the pavement. Besides, she'd cheated a bit and wore leggings underneath so that her nether regions wouldn't get cold.

She and her family were staying in a hotel on the northern side of the River Liffey, opposite where Christ Church Cathedral and Dublin Castle were situated. As she'd been in the Viking village all day, Maddie felt like going to see the river and she knew it wasn't far. This proved to be the case and she quickly crossed the Grattan Bridge towards Wood Quay. To her right, she could see the so-called Viking Longboat statue – like a sunken ship sticking out of water, with three benches in the middle. Two replica longships were moored nearby on the Liffey as part of the festival, and she'd been told there was a full size one somewhere else with re-enactors on hand to tell people all about it.

But that wasn't what she'd come to see, so instead she turned left and meandered along the river. The Liffey was enclosed with walls either side, possibly part concrete and part stone. She supposed it was to protect the streets from flooding. No chance of that at the moment, as it was low tide and only a small amount of water in the middle of the river bed. Maddie had a sudden urge to get down there and look at it up close, but couldn't see any way of getting down. Surely there had to be stairs somewhere?

She carried on walking, picking up her pace a bit now. Past the Millennium Bridge and a pedestrian bridge, then another two larger double bridges. After Butt Bridge, she passed under a railway bridge that snaked overhead. Then one more bridge and *finally* – some steps leading down to the water.

'Yesss!' She gazed swiftly around her, but no one seemed to be looking her way so she ran down the steep stairs, holding up her dress so she wouldn't trip on the hem.

'Urgh!' It wasn't a pretty sight that spread out before her. A wide band of puddle-speckled mud, that probably wasn't doing her Viking leather shoes much good. The walls towered above her, a tidal mark of mud topped with green reaching more than a third of the way up. And all around her, a whole bunch of rubbish left behind by the receding waters. But she didn't care. As she picked her way carefully along the edge, a strange excitement gripped her, and her heart began to beat faster. She'd heard of mud-larking by the River Thames in London – perhaps she could do the same here? Who knew what might be lurking in the mire?

At first she found nothing but rubbish. 'Honestly, why are people such pigs?' she muttered. 'Haven't they ever heard of litter bins?' But every now and then something caught her eye and she almost whooped out loud when she spotted a tiny silver coin lying right there on the surface. She picked it up and rubbed at it with the edge of her sleeve, then tried to decipher the writing. It looked like it might say 'ÆLFR' and 'AED REX' either side of a man's head.

'King Alfred? As in Alfred the Great? *No way!*' She felt herself grinning from ear to ear. This was an amazing find and she couldn't wait to show her parents. It might be valuable too, although perhaps she wouldn't be allowed to keep it if it was treasure trove. In order to carry it safely, she wrapped it in an old tissue and stowed it in one of the two leather pouches hanging off her belt. The other one contained her fortune-telling rune staves.

The mud-larking bug had well and truly bitten her now, and she carried on walking, almost bent over double so she wouldn't miss anything. She searched for ages, although she was careful not to stray too far away from the stairs in case the water came rushing back, but found nothing else of value. The light was fading and she decided it was probably time to head back to the hotel. Hopefully her parents wouldn't be too late returning as she wanted to show them her coin before they went to bed.

She kept her eyes on the ground while walking slowly towards the steps, but just as she was about to give up, she spotted something. It was sticking out of the edge of a puddle and she hunkered down to see what it could be. Pale in the fading light, it looked like a small piece of bone, but there were markings on it – a design of some sort. Intrigued now, she pulled it out of the mud and found herself holding a small knife.

'Oh, wow, nice!'

She wiped the mud off it by rubbing it against her apron dress, unheeding of the splodges left behind on the material. The ivory was inlaid with a pattern picked out in black – coal mixed with beeswax to make it stay put. Maddie knew how this was done as she'd learned the technique on one of the many craft courses she'd attended. The end of the handle was slightly thicker, tapering towards the blade of the knife, which was fastened with what looked like two small screws. There was a deep crevice in the handle and the blade folded into it, fitting perfectly.

'A folding knife? *Awesome!*' And a fairly old one at that.

Maddie opened and shut it a couple of times. The hinge seemed to work just fine, as if it had been oiled only yesterday, and the blade wasn't very rusty at all. The decoration on the handle was fairly basic, but still attractive. It consisted of a symmetrical pattern at one end, and some tiny runes etched in along one side. *Wait – runes?* That was seriously old then. Over a thousand years. She squinted at the writing in the fading light and tried to decipher the words. Being dyslexic, runes weren't much easier to read than the normal alphabet, but she knew if she went slowly she'd get there.

'"*Með blođ . . . skaltu . . . ferðast?*" Huh?' Oh, hang on . . . 'No! *Shit!*'

She knew exactly what those words meant and what she was holding in her hand. A time-travel device. Yet another one. 'How the hell many of you are there?' she wondered out loud.

They existed. For real. Maddie knew that because first her sister Linnea had found one, then Linnea's best friend Sara. And now they were both living in the ninth century. A short while later her foster-brother Ivar had disappeared too. Although no one had told Maddie outright where he'd gone, she'd heard enough whispered conversations to know that he'd stolen something from the museum where he worked. Probably a magical artefact.

Like this one.

'Whoa, that means . . . I can time travel!'

She hugged the little knife to her chest for a moment, imagining that she could feel the power emanating from it, even though it was such a small and insignificant thing. With this, she'd be able to visit her sister in the Viking era whenever she wanted to. Or go somewhere else entirely. 'I could even have my own adventures,' she muttered, as this idea took root.

Yes, why shouldn't she have some fun by herself? Linnea loved it there, and Sara seemed equally as happy, judging by what her grandfather had said. And it wasn't as though anyone here wanted her around, was it? Not normally, anyway. Her parents were busy with their academic commitments and jobs, which always seemed so much more important than anything she ever did. Even though they never said it out loud, she could feel their disappointment in her. They made allowances because her dyslexia meant she'd always had a hard time keeping up at school, but it was as though they still expected her to try harder. Make something of herself, preferably in the world of academia. As for Storm, he was living his own exciting life, training to become an officer in the Swedish army, travelling, girlfriends . . . Sure, he was always nice to her when he was around, but how often was that? And could she really expect him to want to hang out with his baby sister all the time?

No, it was up to her to strike out on her own. To show them all that she could be independent. Find her own way in life.

She bit her lip, hesitating. What if it was dangerous? Linnea had said the Viking age wasn't exactly a bed of roses. Not at first, anyway. 'Maybe I could just visit briefly? Check it out?' she murmured. What harm could it do? With the folding knife safely in her belt pouch, she could go back any time. And she was already dressed for it . . .

She swallowed hard and stared out across the Liffey. With a small cut to her finger, and the recital of those words, she'd find out what this place looked like back then.

Yes, why not?

Their love was forbidden.
But echoed in eternity.

Don't miss Christina's sweeping, epic tale of forbidden love – read on for a preview.

Available now from

Prologue

On the outermost tip of the peninsula, she waited and watched through the lonely hours of dawn, scanning the water as far as the eye could see for a glimpse of the familiar snake's-head carving at the prow of his ship.

He would come back, she knew it. The runes had told her so, and Old Tyra said they were never wrong. It might not be in this life, but in the next, and although that possibility made her sad, her distress was temporary when she thought of spending eternity with the man she loved.

He would come back.

And she would be waiting.

Chapter One

Sweden, February 2000

One single Viking ring, displayed against a background of blue velvet, shouldn't even have merited a second glance from Mia Maddox. She handled such items on a daily basis as part of her job. And yet, at the sight of this one, she stopped and gasped out loud, barely registering the impressive two-kilo neck torque in the next glass case.

No, it can't be.

The basement of the Historical Museum in Stockholm definitely deserved its name – The Gold Room – as it contained unimaginable amounts of treasure trove. The ring she was staring at, by no means even the largest or finest in the collection, was nothing special. Merely a stylised snake, a common motif for the period in the same type of design as many other items here. It was hand-made and should have been unique, but Mia knew for a fact that it wasn't – because she was wearing an identical ring on her right index finger.

She felt light-headed for a moment, and imagined she heard a susurration echoing around the vault, as if the little serpent itself had just slithered round the perimeter and hissed, its soft scales brushing the stone floor. The fine hairs on her arms and the back of her neck stood up, and she shivered.

'I don't believe it,' she murmured.

Frowning slightly, she looked from one ring to the other, holding up her hand to compare every detail. There was no difference, as far as she could see, other than the size – hers was definitely smaller, in circumference at least. Still, they could have been cast from the same mould, so alike were they. Another shiver went through her.

It was uncanny.

She caught movement out of the corner of her eye and realised someone had been watching her, but whoever it was had ducked out of sight. Probably another tourist, wondering why she was talking to herself. Self-consciously, she stuffed her hand in her pocket while still staring at the exhibits. She blinked several times, as if that would change things, but the rings remained the same. If she hadn't known better, she would have said that their little snake faces had looked pleased to see one another, but that thought was just too bizarre for words. Shaking her head, she tore herself away and headed for the exit. She would have to make enquiries at the information desk to solve this mystery.

The Gold Room was underneath the museum, in a specially excavated vault. Shallow stairs, dark and dimly lit, led back up to the entrance hall. The walls here were painted with Viking motifs in rusty red and ochre, and several enormous rune stones guarded the top and bottom of the staircase. Mia had studied them with interest earlier, but now she was lost in thought and hardly spared her surroundings a glance. As she reached the halfway landing, a man appeared out of nowhere and blocked her way, making her jump.

'Excuse me, but could you come with me for a moment,

please?' he said in Swedish, staring straight at her, his blue eyes intense under a deep frown.

Mia came to an abrupt halt. 'Sorry? Are you talking to me?' She understood him perfectly, being half Swedish herself, but didn't know why he'd be addressing her. She glanced around, but she was the only person on the stairs at that moment and his gaze was firmly fixed on her.

'Yes, I'd like to ask you a few questions, if you don't mind. It concerns your ring.' He glanced at the golden serpent that encircled her finger and she fancied she could feel its coils gripping her more firmly, defiantly hanging on for dear life, as if this man posed a threat to it. But that was just ridiculous. What the hell was the matter with her? She wasn't normally this fanciful.

'M-my ring?' Unconsciously she made a fist to conceal it, but that was futile, as he'd obviously seen it already. And once seen, it wasn't easily forgotten. The reptile had a head at either end of its body, which was curious to say the least. Beautifully shaped, it was covered in tiny decorations consisting of lines and swirls all along its back. Whenever she moved her hand, the pure gold glinted. Eighteen carat? Maybe even twenty-four. For a brief moment now she thought the snake's eyes glittered with . . . what? Excitement? Anger?

She shook her head again. The snake was an inanimate object; it had no expression whatsoever.

'That's right, your ring,' the man said, bringing her back from her strange thoughts. Mia noticed that his accent was Norwegian and wondered what he was doing in Sweden's capital. More to the point, what authority did he have here, challenging her like this?

'And who are you?' she asked. She knew she sounded curt, perhaps even rude, but he had disconcerted her with his sudden appearance.

He pointed to an identity card that hung round his neck. 'Haakon Berger, one of the archaeologists based here.'

'Oh, right.' How stupid not to have noticed the ID, which was right in front of her nose. He must think her a complete idiot. 'Well, I . . .' Panic assailed her, as if she had been caught doing something illegal, but she quashed it. This was ridiculous. She had a right to visit the museum just like anyone else, and the fact that her ring happened to look exactly like one of the exhibits she'd just seen was mere coincidence. Wasn't it?

She'd been going in search of some answers herself. Perhaps this man could provide them. 'OK, fine,' she conceded. 'Lead on then, but I don't have much time, so you'll have to make it quick.'

He nodded and began to mount the remaining steps up to ground-floor level, taking them two at a time. Mia followed at a slower pace, belatedly registering his appearance properly. About her own age – late twenties, early thirties – tall and athletic-looking, with a shock of white-blond hair that stood up as if gelled in place, he could have been an advertisement for pure Viking genes. She had noted that his blue eyes were set in a sharply angled face with a very straight nose and high cheekbones, and with that uncompromising mouth he resembled nothing so much as a Norse god bent on vengeance. She shivered yet again. His anger had seemed directed at her. Why would that be?

The reception area was quiet when they reached it. Two guards stood next to the information desk, talking in hushed voices. Berger nodded to them, as if he knew them well, but didn't pause. He strode across the hall, Mia trailing behind. The huge space was lofty and modern, with enormous windows overlooking a courtyard quadrangle. In front of her was the obligatory gift shop, and in one corner was a door leading to an exhibition about Vikings, which she had wanted to visit. She resented the fact that because of this man there might not be enough time for that now.

'This way,' Berger said, and entered a door marked *Private* set in the far wall. Inside was another staircase, this one much steeper, and they climbed it in silence. As before, he was much faster than her and had to wait at the top, holding open a door that led into a corridor. Mia could hear the hum of voices from somewhere nearby, but there was no time to listen as the archaeologist ushered her into one of the first rooms on the right. It was nothing more than an untidy alcove really, with bits of paper strewn everywhere and old artefacts in boxes and bubble wrap. She wondered how he could work in such a mess.

He removed some items from a chair. 'Please, sit down.'

Mia did as she was asked, then waited as he took the room's only other chair, behind a cluttered desk. He crossed his arms over his chest and regarded her thoughtfully.

'May I ask your name? And do you have any ID with you?'

'Myfanwy Maddox, but I'm usually known as Mia.' Her name was none of his business, but she had no reason to conceal it either. She took out her wallet and handed him her English driver's licence. He gave it a cursory glance before passing it back.

'You're not Swedish, then?' He looked surprised, but she was used to this, since most people took her for a native.

'Half. I'm British, but I have a Swedish mother. I'm visiting her at the moment.' That wasn't quite true, but he didn't need to know that.

'I see. I take it you come here a lot?'

'Yes, but I don't see what that has to do with anything.' Mia frowned at him, but he ignored this and ploughed on.

'Miss Maddox, are you aware that any ancient finds have to be reported to the relevant authorities here in Sweden?' His Norwegian accent was more pronounced now, and she wondered briefly why he was working here in Stockholm instead of in his home country.

'Yes, of course I am. As a matter of fact, I—'

He didn't allow her to finish. 'When you dig up an ancient artefact, you have to take it to the nearest museum or council, where someone will tell you whether you have found anything of interest or not. If you have, they will add the item to the register of antiquities, and then possibly they'll make an appointment to view the site where it was found. In certain cases, you may be allowed to keep your find, but mostly you'll be recompensed and the item placed in a museum.'

'Yes, yes, I know all that, but—'

He interrupted once more. 'Under *no* circumstances are you allowed to keep the item for yourself if it's valuable. That is a crime.' He emphasised the last word while he glanced at her ring, and Mia followed his gaze, again suppressing the urge to hide the snake.

'Is that what you're accusing me of, Mr Berger?' she demanded, tired of being harangued. 'You think I've dug up this ring and kept it without telling anyone?'

He nodded. 'Judging by the length of time you stood in front of the display case downstairs, it can't have escaped your notice that there is a ring exactly like it in the museum's collection. As far as I'm aware, no permission has been granted to any jewellery company to make replicas of it, although I know a few of the others have been copied. That must mean that yours is as old as the one kept here. May I see it, please?'

He held out an imperious hand and Mia felt obliged to remove the gold snake and pass it across to him. It was an almost physical wrench. That ring was her last link to her beloved grandmother, who had died only a week ago. She couldn't bear to part with it now, and she could have sworn the serpent was just as unwilling to leave her, since it took her a moment to wriggle it off her finger.

He received it reverently, turning it this way and that so the gold glimmered in the light from the small window. After a while, he hunted in his desk drawers until he came up with a magnifying glass, then studied the ring some more. At length, he looked up again and regarded her with a solemn expression.

'Viking. Ninth century, probably the middle to later part. An exact replica of the one downstairs, or as near as makes no difference. I happened to be looking at it only the other day. Now, I should very much like to know where you found it. Wherever it was, I'm afraid you can't keep it. It belongs to the state.'

Mia took a deep breath to contain the anger swirling inside her. How dare he treat her like a thief? She was nothing of the sort, and she knew as much about the subject as he did. Staring him straight in the eyes, she prepared herself for a fight.

'Now that's where you're wrong. And I can prove it.'